DRAGON EQUINOX

IMMORTAL DRAGONS BOOK SIX

OPHELIA BELL

Whoever yields properly to Fate, is deemed Wise among men, and knows the laws of heaven.

— EURIPEDES

I have a confession to make. Maybe not the worst confession for a dragon like me, but not exactly something I'm proud of, either…

I've been faking it. For centuries I've been leading on the ones who mean the most to me, making them believe I share in their pleasure equally, but really, I'm just one big, fat liar.

No, no… I'm not faking *that*. Orgasms are my bread and butter. I give as good as I get in terms of fertile magic. Better, in fact. The power bestowed on my lovers through the release of my own Nirvana is transcendent, and not exactly the kind of thing an immortal dragon like me could fake, even if I wanted to.

What I'm faking are my dreams.

But why in the world should mere *dreams* matter? Because these dreams… the ones I am *not* having, but all five of my siblings have been blessed with … are messages from Fate. Beacons on the path to finding our true mates, our destined partners who will be with us until the end of time. Or so I am told by my brothers and sisters.

I have not had these dreams they go on about. Somehow

they've come to the consensus that the dreams are messages from Fate, that mixing our blood with the other higher races' is the key to defeating our oldest enemy. Don't get me wrong, I *adore* the idea. I've been ready to leave the Glade for ages, but the time was never right.

I still doubt the time is right for me, or that it will ever *be* right. But after witnessing each one of my siblings seek and find precisely the image of their mates who visited them in dreams, I can't help but feel a little forlorn. What makes them so special to be granted these amazing gifts—love and happiness and the prospect of new families? I feel I have lost each of them one by one, and now I am left to stand alone.

The worst part is that I doubt my own desires because I don't know if the love that's already blossomed between me and any of these five men I adore has any merit. Has Fate abandoned me? Do I have no destiny of my own? How can I ever be sure if this love is meant to be if I don't have Fate's messages to guide me?

Is this even love?

In the ancient past, I would never have worried. I'm a dragon, after all, a goddess among the humans who serve me. Love was never an option. It was a human construct. But the more we live among humans, the more my kind breeds with them, the more their desires seep into our blood as if it isn't *our* power influencing *them*, but the other way around. What use do immortals have for love, after all? All I needed was a willing collection of human males to mark who could provide me with their seed. I never wanted more.

Not until my siblings were granted the promise of immortal love through their dreams. I watched each one fall as if their wings were clipped. First Belah, who bravely ventured forth in search of the pair of turul males she'd dreamed of. She still bore the scars of grief, yet agreed to be the first of us. We knew the enemy would be drawn to her, and her presence in the world again would distract them from their constant search for a way into our sacred home in the Glade. But she was still damaged from the loss of her old lover who had become our enemy.

Nikhil's defection to our side was perhaps the most astonishing occurrence to come of any of my siblings' matings, but welcome nonetheless. It meant my sister could be whole once more, with three worthy mates to love her.

When Ked finally found his love with a turul female and yet another defected Ultiori soldier, we realized Fate must indeed have plans for us, and that these dreams must be taken seriously. Yet my nights remained dreamless.

I could fool my siblings, but I couldn't fool myself. My Red brother, Gavra, was the last person I expected to tie himself permanently to a partner who was likely to live as long as he, yet tie himself he did. Or rather, he *let* himself be tied, so I hear.

Aodh was less of a surprise, as the brother most given to sentimental moods. The artists are always like that, aren't they?

And Aurum was simply born to love without restraint.

So where does that leave me? I am the boring one. I have no scandals in my past. My desires for another immortal remained unrequited, and so I diverted my attention to the humans who served me as their goddess. I followed all the rules and did my duty to our Mother and to Fate. Do I not deserve a message too? Does this mean I am destined to be alone?

Is there some rule I can break to get Fate to notice me?

CHAPTER 1

BEKIM

The world could have ended and Bekim Rainsong wouldn't have cared. If there was such a thing as ursa heaven, he'd found it. His entire body buzzed with the immense power that flowed through him, his ears ringing with the sonorous cry of the woman—the dragon—whose glorious orgasm had just shattered his entire concept of what it meant to be *alive*.

"Gaia fucking save me, I can't hold back." Theron's brown eyes were wide with the same wonder, staring at him over the pale shoulder of the woman who was swiftly beginning to mean more to them than their own goddess.

Numa let out a breathy moan between them, her hips still pivoting just enough to drive Bekim mad. "I'm not done yet. If you two hold out a bit longer..." Her green eyes flashed wickedly at Bekim before she kissed him, leaving him even more breathless from the way she owned his mouth just long enough to make him want more. Then she pulled away and twisted, grasping behind her for a very willing Theron, who leaned in and surrendered his own lips to hers as her fingers raked through his short beard.

"How much longer?" Bekim asked, squeezing her hip with one hand while the other cupped the back of her head, urging her back to his mouth.

She laughed into the kiss, her breasts brushing against his chest. "I want to see how much power you two can hold and give back to me. The longer you hold off, the more it builds and builds and, *oh* …" Her eyes rolled back and her lashes fluttered as her mouth fell open. Inside the tight channel of her pussy Bekim currently shared with his partner, Theron's rhythm had changed, his angle shifting in a way that made Bekim's hold on reality even shakier than it already was.

"Fuck, I can't… Theron, what the fuck?"

His friend grinned down at him as Numa moaned again and pressed her chest flat against Bekim's, burying her face against his neck.

"Going for broke, man. I aim to take her with us when we come. I want another taste of her power, because I fucking swear I felt roots ready to grow under me that time."

"Bullshit," Bekim said, but grabbed both Numa's hips and picked up his tempo to match Theron's.

Numa bit into his shoulder, her fingers sliding up his scalp and pulling at his hair as she let out a sweet little mewl. His partner's cock was a hot, hard piston sliding against his as they rammed into her in tandem.

He and Theron had serviced dozens of ursa females through their estrous since they'd become an official bachelor pair more than a decade ago. Never had the experience been as transformative as this. Numa's skin heated beneath his hands and her entire body seemed to vibrate with a strange subliminal hum that he didn't feel so much as experience from the inside out. It was as though their very souls were vibrating at the same frequency. Theron bent lower over her back, sliding his hands up her sides and clamping them around her shoulders. Bekim recognized the wild abandon in his lover's eyes, the heavy breaths and lowered lids and flushed cheeks above his dark beard that signaled his imminent demise.

"Gaia save me, I fucking love you," Theron blurted just as the hard length of him surged alongside Bekim's cock, signaling his end. Bekim's eyes widened at the outburst, but he didn't have time to dwell on it. Numa's core tightened around their cocks, her teeth released his shoulder, and she arched her back as she cried out her pleasure. The vibrating magic that had danced beneath her skin flooded into him, lighting his entire body up as though he'd been asleep and was only now waking. His orgasm tore through him like wildfire, drawn out with the squeezing pull of her tight sheathe and Theron's cock still pulsing as he released his pent-up climax.

Theron leaned back, looking dazed, his big hands resting lightly on either side of Numa's full, round ass. Numa's face was buried in Bekim's shoulder again and he raised his eyebrows at his partner, mouthing the word "Love?" and pointing his thumb at Numa's back.

Theron gave him a helpless look and a half-shrug. He moved to pull away and Numa's muscles clamped down on them both, eliciting from them a pair of startled gasps.

"Don't go," she said, turning her head to reveal her beautiful flushed face and wet eyes.

Theron patted her gently on the rump. "Not going anywhere but that bed right there beside you, honey. I need to be horizontal for about the next year after that."

Bekim frowned at Numa's green eyes looking up at him. Her eyelids fluttered, her gaze darting away. He hadn't known her long, but in the two months since he and Theron had met her, she'd always seemed every bit the self-possessed immortal, just like all the ursa Shamans. More so, in fact. He'd even go so far as to describe her as *regal*, owing to her color. Gaia's color was green, after all, and he knew that dragon queens were also green. Numa might only be one of the six dragons who ruled the ursa's sister race, but something about her had always elevated her above her five siblings in his eyes.

Not even her red brother had stirred up his need so acutely, and he and Theron both agreed that Gavra had to but say the word and they'd have both happily bowed to his will. Even though their greatest desire was to be chosen by a strong and fertile ursa female, dragons like these weren't likely to cross their paths again.

Numa's sweet kisses, soft curves, and delicious magic put her brother to shame.

She remained flat atop Bekim's chest, his cock still half-hard inside her. Theron flopped down onto the pillows beside them and turned onto his side, sliding his hand down her back, then up in a deliberate caress. It was as though he meant to comfort her, despite the fact that he couldn't have seen the haunted look and the wet lashes Bekim had caught a glimpse of before she pressed her face back against his neck.

He closed his eyes, simply enjoying her warm weight atop him, idly stroking his fingertips up and down her spine with one hand while he sought out Theron with his other. His partner's fingers twined with his amid the bedsheets and squeezed, the touch a signal that they were of one mind when it came to this woman.

"We can't keep meeting like this," Numa said, hoisting herself off Bekim as though her limbs weighed heavy and she'd love nothing more than to stay where she was. Bekim resisted the urge to wrap his arms around her and pull her back down, but his training made him resist. Ursa males took their lead from their females. If she didn't articulate explicit desire for contact, they didn't act, but Gaia help him, she looked like she needed to be held a lot longer than that.

"I have no complaints," Theron said.

"No…" Numa shook her head and slid off of Bekim, retreating to the end of the bed. "It wasn't fair of me to barge into your room like some entitled princess demanding you fuck me."

"We've all had a shitty day," Bekim said. "I think we earned an epic screw after pulling off the impossible."

Numa exhaled a cloud of green smoke that gathered around her as she slipped off the bed and stood, looking down at them. "But we didn't pull it off yet. All we did is confirm *what* we need to do and how to do it. We still have to actually get it done. We still have to find enough power to open a sky portal in the barrier so Nikhil's army can join the war."

"We're ready and willing to do our part. Just say the word," Bekim said. He sat up all the way and scooted to the end of the bed, looking up at her. The green smoke became a solid, sheer wrap that covered her from her breasts to her ankles. The gown was still translucent enough to reveal the lush curves beneath, and the dark pink of her erect nipples showed through. He itched to touch her again, but wouldn't unless she asked.

She gave him a pained look while the smoke tendrils filtered through the messy strands of chestnut hair that fell around her shoulders, untangling and rearranging them into a tidy bun at the back of her head. "It's more complicated than that. You two have been more than accommodating of my needs. But I can't ask you to commit to this with me."

"Why the hell not? We're here, and I don't see that you have a whole hell of a lot of options," Theron said, hopping off the bed and standing beside it with his arms crossed.

"No, but you *do*. Or you will, once this is over and things are back to normal. You two don't need me getting between you and your chance at a normal life with a normal ursa female."

Bekim glanced at Theron, who just gaped at her, speechless. Had she even heard what he'd said?

"I heard your declaration," she said to Theron as if she'd read their minds. "Bekim's a very lucky man. I'd only get in the way of that. I'm already getting in the way of that. Please don't feel obligated to join this ritual with me."

"We're not the ones, are we?" Bekim asked.

Numa stared at him for a beat, her expression guarded as though she was trying to decide how much to say.

Theron picked up the thread of Bekim's question. "Gavra said you all had dreams of your mates. That's why he never shared our bed … he only tagged along on our assignations to take advantage of the excess fertile magic. I take it you didn't dream of us, and you don't want to commit us to the ritual if we're not supposed to be yours. How close am I to the truth?"

Her haunted look returned, and she shook her head and turned away. "Close enough," she said, striding to the door.

"Let us help anyway," Bekim called after her. "We can help you find him, or them, or whoever it is, if you give us a clue."

Her shoulders stiffened when she reached the door, and she stood with clenched fists for a second before turning, a stricken look on her face.

"That's the problem. I don't *have* a damn clue myself. I wasn't blessed with dreams the way my brothers and sisters were. It could be anyone. Or no one."

"But it has to be someone … doesn't it?" Theron asked. "Fate's got to have some idea. You wouldn't be fucking stuck in this situation without some way out."

"I wouldn't be surprised if Fate just doesn't care. I'm the unremarkable daughter … the one who follows the rules, who keeps a level head. I've never sought out attention—

never wanted it, really. I did my duty as a goddess from afar for the humans who worshiped me before we were forced to protect ourselves with barriers, portals, and hibernation temples. Maybe I did something wrong and Fate just … forgot."

"Maybe that means you get to choose," Bekim offered.

Numa gave him a sad look. "If that's true … if the decision really is mine to make, then I have to consider what's required of the ritual. Love has nothing to do with it. I need a mate with enough power to open a sky portal in the Sanctuary's barrier. I've spent several wonderful afternoons with the two of you. You have more than enough to keep any dragon satisfied for ages. But nothing short of divine power will be enough for me, I'm afraid … or at least something close." She speared them both with looks that drove straight to Bekim's heart. "I love you too, but that just isn't enough."

The door shut soundly behind her and Bekim let his head drop forward. He inhaled sharply, gritting his teeth against the agonized yell threatening to burst from him. Theron closed the distance and squeezed his shoulder.

"Her hands are tied. If we want her to open that portal, we have to trust her to know how it needs to be done."

Bekim just shook his head and stared blindly at his lover's feet. After a moment, he narrowed his eyes, finally focusing and for the first time seeing something that made no logical sense.

"Theron … since when did you start sprouting leaves from your ankles?" He bent down, worried he might be hallucinating, perhaps still high on green dragon magic. His fingertip came into contact with the edge of a pale green leaf that gave slightly under his touch, the little limb it sprouted from solidly attached to Theron's left ankle.

The foot in front of him tilted and turned.

"Holy shit." Theron dropped to the floor, propping his

foot up on his knee. He stared at the little sprout that gradually faded and sank back into his foot.

Bekim gave him a sad look. "I guess this means you might have a chance with her after all. If you have Gaia's blessing, you might have enough power to satisfy her requirements for the ritual."

"Dude, you'd better lose that fucking grim expression. *We* have a chance with her now. I might have had a dinky little leaf, but you've got a little more going on than that."

He gestured to the floor at Bekim's feet. Bekim looked down, and it took a moment before the image before him finally registered. It was as though the veins beneath his skin were filled with sunlight, and each one flowed up as far as his ankles, feeding a ring of blossoms that opened up before his eyes. The centers of the blossoms all glowed a vivid green and the aroma of jasmine filled the air.

"Gaia's gift," Bekim whispered. "But we know there's a price … there always is. You remember what happened to Silas."

"And Vrishti helped him find a way around that. But Sathmika unlocked that gift for him. How the hell did *we* get it?"

The early morning light warmed and grew dense with humidity. Both men tensed at the abrupt change and met each other's eyes. Brilliant green light flashed beside them and they both stood, but Bekim found himself immobilized. When he glanced down at his feet, he saw they were rooted to the floor—quite literally—with dark, woody tendrils twisting into the planks.

The light in front of them coalesced into a blindingly beautiful female shape. She was naked, but seemed to be clothed in the long, curling tendrils of her own hair that flowed around her curvaceous body like thick vines. Flowers sprouted from the locks, beginning with a crown of them encircling her head.

Bekim's eyes bulged and he nearly choked on his surprise.

"G-Gaia?" Theron stuttered.

The woman gave him a warm, maternal smile. "Yes, my child. You are correct that there is a price for my gift, but I imagine this is one you would not hesitate to pay."

"What is it?" Bekim asked, finally finding his voice.

"There is to be a contest. A sort of wager between the gods. I have chosen the pair of you as my proxies. Win this wager for me, and you can keep your gift."

He narrowed his eyes. Neither he nor Theron had ever been gambling men, but perhaps that was why they had yet to find a female willing to mate them. "What are the stakes of this wager?"

"The stakes are the same as the prize. Win the dragon Numa's love. Secure yourselves as her mates, and my gift is yours to keep as well."

With that, she disappeared in a cloud of green-gold mist, leaving behind the scent of fresh summer blooms.

Bekim swallowed. "Well, all right then. I don't suppose we have a choice in this, do we?"

"Why would we *ever* say no to this?" Theron asked. "We have a chance now. A really fucking stellar chance, considering we already know how she feels about us and there aren't exactly any other blokes beating down her door. Tell me you feel the same way I do."

"Yeah… you know I do. I love her too, but I can't help but feel like there's a catch."

"Mates, man. We'll be her mates if we do this. Does anything else even fucking matter?"

Theron had a point, and if this was a chance for them to drive away Numa's sad looks, whatever catch would no doubt be worth it.

CHAPTER 2

OZZIE

Assorted tomes were scattered across three big tables in the library of the Rainsong Clan Lodge, the dusty scent of ancient paper mingling with the aromas of the midday meal that wafted in from the kitchen. The fragrant reminder that it was lunchtime already was at odds with the dawn light that shone in from outside, but the light had barely changed in the last six hours.

A new scent filtered in, putting Ozzie on edge at the same time his immortal passenger perked up. He'd been reading a book on balancing elemental forces and reluctantly sat up in his seat, placing the big book back onto the table. He cursed the tightness in his trousers and took a deep breath to get his libido under control before she came in. Dragons could *see* if you were turned on, even if you managed to hide any physical effects of it, and the last thing he wanted to do was encourage this particular dragon.

"You want her as much as I do," Zephyrus taunted from inside his mind. *"Just let it happen and we'll be all the happier for it."*

"I want no such thing. Just because the idea of a little afternoon

delight turns me on doesn't mean I'm in love. The entire fucking lodge is probably horny after hearing her get off with those two. They're a better match for her than I am. In fact, you and I both know I'm the last man who belongs with her. She isn't mine."

He hated the ongoing argument, and it didn't help that the voice inside his head belonged to one of the four Winds who ruled his race, the very same Zephyrus who he was descended from many generations past. He'd only agreed to the arrangement at his grandmother's insistence. To enter the Sanctuary, they had needed another immortal to balance the power fluctuation they'd cause by breaching the barrier uninvited.

He'd happily be rid of the man if he could come up with a good argument, because his fallback clearly wasn't working.

"Who cares if she's yours? She's the last of Fate's and the Mother Dragon's offspring who isn't mated. And now that the higher races are mingling, I have my chance, but I need you on board to make it happen. Besides, she likes you. I can see it in her eyes."

The eyes in question latched onto Ozzie the second Numa walked in, and a brilliant smile spread across her face. He smiled back out of reflex, because a dragon that dazzling was simply impossible *not* to smile at.

"Did you feel that?" Ozzie asked his passenger.

"Feel what? Your completely irrational lack of interest in such an exquisite creature?"

"Precisely. No spark. If I had a choice, you bet your airy ass I'd be on board with the idea of wooing her, but I'm not immune to Fate any more than you are. I don't have a choice. My One mate isn't in the picture yet. I'd know if they were."

Which was what made it so damn difficult to deal with that look she was giving him now: expectant and affectionate. She pulled the chair out beside him and sat, leaning in to peer down at the book that lay open on the table in front of him. Her fresh green scent filled his lungs, and he had to admit her presence was calming, but it didn't abolish the dread he felt over the inevitable rejection he'd have to give her when she made yet another pass at him. As if the wild sex he'd just heard from somewhere above wasn't enough, now she was making the rounds to sate her voracious appetite.

"You don't have to be so damn precious about your power. Let her have a taste of us," Zephyrus said. *"She'll need as much power as she can absorb to complete this ritual."*

"Any new discoveries?" Numa asked. Her warm breast brushed his arm as she leaned in, and hell if his entire body didn't respond, thanks to the effect Zephyrus had on his reactions to this woman.

"Not fair," he griped, but the West Wind just silently basked in her lovely scent and nearness.

"Ah … nothing good, I'm afraid." He shifted away a tiny bit and was gratified that she leaned back and looked at him rather than lean closer.

"Oh. Do I want to know? You know what … I can probably guess." She looked defeated then, giving him a plaintive look. "I need a mate to produce enough power to open the portal, don't I?"

"You knew already," he said.

She gave him a little shrug and looked away. "I guessed. And I'm guessing it needs to be someone at least a match in power to me."

"If not greater."

"Such as yours truly," Zephyrus interjected.

"Shut it, windbag."

"Is that any way to speak to your elders?"

He ignored the immortal spirit as she sat back and sighed, her gaze drifting to the ceiling. In that moment, he felt a perfect kinship with her and impulsively reached for her hand.

"Wanting someone who isn't Fate's choice for you complicates things, I know. I've been burned enough that it's hard to even know who to open up to."

"You can be honest with me, Ozzie. I know it's my sister you're talking about. But I'm not her. If you feel something, at least admit it. Fate listens to you. The turul have always been Fate's favorites."

Zephyrus let out a derisive snort in his mind. *"Fate's favorites, my ass."*

"It isn't that I don't want us to win. If I knew you were the one, we wouldn't be having this discussion—we'd be opening the goddamn portal now. How can you not know that it isn't me?"

Her brows descended and her eyes flashed with irritation. "How the hell can *you* be so sure it isn't *me*? Evie found her mates by unconventional means. It could work for you too. You've earned some happiness. If nothing else, we could enjoy each other long enough for Fate to get the fucking hint that I need to know who he is. Or who *they* are. Who my mates are supposed to be! Maybe you'd get a hint of who yours is too."

The bitterness in her tone hit him like a slap to the face. She blamed Fate for this? He set his lips in a grim line. Why shouldn't she? He'd looked for more than two centuries for his One and hadn't had any luck. Fate had made a fool of him too. He and his cousins had even named their band for their futile situation where finding their mates was concerned, but Iszak and Lukas had found theirs, so Ozzie was the only "Fool" left of their trio.

"It won't work," he said. "If there's one thing I've learned, it's that the turul can't escape our fates. And I don't want to tempt Fate into putting me through the kind of shit Evie and Marcus had to go through for their love. Sure, it worked out for them in the end. Ked found them both. But at what cost? You and I *both* deserve better."

"How can you be so sure?"

Ozzie picked up a pencil and began gently tapping a rhythm onto the cover of one of the big tomes. With another pencil, he added a counterpoint, his foot tapping on the floor with the beat that had been stuck in his head for ages. "It's in my head like a song that worms its way in and gets stuck." The rhythm became more intricate and Numa's gaze fixed on his hands, her brow creased. "I hear this constantly. My cousins had a song that was *their* song. They never taught it to me until they were desperate to win Belah back when they thought they'd lost her. Only Evie knew the last part."

"Is that their song?"

"No. *This* is my song." He stopped abruptly and Numa looked up at him.

"Why didn't you finish it? That couldn't have been the end."

"Because I don't know how it ends. But what I do know is that when I meet her, the rest will come to me."

"I can help you write a new song with her," Zephyrus offered. *"Forget Fate."*

Numa picked up one of the pencils and twisted it between her hands. "I wish I shared your certainty that I'll find my mate. But even if I did, I don't have time to wait. There aren't exactly that many options here."

Ozzie tilted his chin to the ceiling. "What about them? We're not oblivious to the bond you three have."

"They aren't strong enough. Every time I'm with them, I hope they'll have gained more power somehow, but they haven't yet. You have an immortal inside you. Surely his power would be more than enough."

Zephyrus preened. *"See? She doesn't just want you. She wants me too."*

"And he'd have you, if he could, but it isn't his choice to make and he knows it. I won't risk mating someone who isn't meant to be mine."

"Spoilsport."

Despite the immortal's pouting, Ozzie couldn't help but sense genuine disappointment, and no small amount of helpless longing. It gave him the urge to write a ballad.

"Then I need your help. You have Fate's favor. Help me find my mate."

She squeezed his hand, her touch emphasizing the desperation in her tone. Ozzie gazed into her eyes a moment longer before nodding.

"I'll talk to my grandmother. We'll figure this out."

BEING in such close proximity to a dragon as beautiful and powerful as Numa gave Ozzie serious doubts about his willpower. Zephyrus' constant longing didn't help.

"Why does it have to be *her* anyway? Can't you just wait until I find my own mate?"

"That will take too long. One of the reasons I agreed to this ride-along was because I knew she'd be here. Fate as much as promised her to me. If I'd known you would be so damned resistant, I'd have found another way to get to her."

Ozzie stood and paced to the high bookshelves at the edge of the room, raking his fingers through his hair. What the hell had he done to deserve this? It was worse than an addiction, of which he'd endured many over the years. Whenever the failure to find his mate brought him down enough, he'd wallow for a decade or so in whatever the latest drug happened to be. Alcohol was his near constant companion, and whenever he'd get so sick of himself he couldn't stand it, the climb out of those pits was the hardest. It was like having a voice in his head trying to convince him he should do the exact opposite of what he *knew* was right.

Now he had an *actual* voice in his head telling him to mate a woman he knew deep in his soul was the wrong woman for him. But if she was the one for Zephyrus, how could he reconcile that?

"We can petition Gaia for another body. A permanent vessel for me." For the first time since their partnership, Zephyrus sounded subdued and genuinely concerned.

"You would do that?" Ozzie dropped his hands and raised his face to the dawn light streaming through the floor-to-ceiling window nestled between two tall bookcases. It had been several hours since the temporal bubble went up around them, but the light still lingered low like they were frozen in time at early morning, which he supposed they were.

"As much as I enjoy this partnership, I fear my usefulness is going to waste. I don't blame you, but I also can't just passively observe while she struggles. She would have you despite her uncertainty. I can give her certainty, if granted autonomy."

"Tell me what to do."

"Is Sophia near? We need her help."

Ozzie whispered the need to his grandmother, trusting the wind to carry the message, then waited, staring at the door to the big room. Moments later, she entered.

"We need to speak to Gaia. Can you help us summon her?"

"In the garden," Sophia said with a nod, then turned and walked back out the door.

When they reached the garden, he joined his grandmother on the moss-covered island in the center of the pond.

"We must join our power to call to her. What is the message?"

"Zephyrus needs a body so he can woo Numa. It's in all our interest for him to succeed."

Sophia narrowed her eyes and let out a soft snort of a laugh. "More immortals mating. How did I not see this coming?"

Ozzie frowned down at his grandmother. "Nanyo, that is an excellent question. How come you didn't know? You always seem to know exactly who to pair up when humans come to you for matchmaking. Every single couple you've matched still sends you Christmas cards."

"Humans are easy. Fate doesn't meddle in their lives to the degree it does in ours. Reading their desires is simple. The higher races are much more complicated. We are all part of the games Fate plays, in one way or another. Some of us have our paths predetermined by design. But just because a path is unclear doesn't mean Fate hasn't decided on your destination."

"We're just a little casual entertainment for the bastard, then, is that it? And you're fine just playing along?"

How do you think I know she's mine? He said as much. But I can't have her without a body willing to try to win her.

Sophia raised her eyebrows at his frown. "What is Zephyrus telling you?"

"That he believes Numa belongs to him, but I don't think she knows *who* she's meant to be with. Can we get on with this so I can be spared his constant reminders of my own lack of clear direction?"

His grandmother nodded and pulled him closer, threading her fingers through his and raising their hands up to the sky, palms flat together. Within his mind, Zephyrus surged forward, pushing his power through Ozzie's limbs to merge with Sophia's, and Ozzie let the West Wind take over.

His voice rose in a low chant, the rhythm matched by the pulsing glyphs that appeared on their arms and around

Sophia's neck and collarbone above the edge of her dress. His body tingled with the appearance of similar glyphs that represented the call on their elemental power reaching for the goddess of earth and life.

Sophia slowly released his hands and moved backward a step at a time. Ozzie followed suit, the space between them filling with a swirling funnel of power that grew and grew, wind whipping around between them and tossing their hair across their faces. At first the whirlwind was simply white with electricity, but as they widened the space between them, it spun into the green earth and changed, as though the moss beneath their feet was being sucked into the vortex. Even the sparking bolts of electricity turned green.

A figure began to take shape between them, a nude female clad only in tendrils of her own hair and cascades of summer flowers. She resembled a female ursa with her voluptuous, almost pregnant looking figure and maternal features. Her raw, fertile beauty was fully on display, and Ozzie's cock stiffened at the earthy, very *female* scent that filled the air. He'd been immersed within that scent countless times between a woman's thighs, and had always loved the way it betrayed her arousal moments before he buried his tongue within the wet velvet of her core. It was yet another drug to him, though, no more than an escape from the reality of life without the true mate who waited for him somewhere.

"Immortal Winds, you have summoned me. I won't pretend to think you wish to simply honor me. What do you want?"

Ozzie remained in the shadows of his mind, allowing Zephyrus to have the spotlight to say his piece.

"Your divine grace, I wish to honor the aspect of you that lives within the green dragon Numa. By Fate's decree, she is unfettered by a pre-determined mate, and by that token, I wish to woo her to choose me as her partner. But to do that, I need a body of my own that is not already fated for someone else."

She fixed her brilliant green gaze on Ozzie, his body reacting with a shiver so close to an orgasm he was surprised his cock didn't erupt inside his pants. She tilted her head from side to side, as though shifting her perspective of him, then smiled and nodded. He'd barely started rejoicing when she answered, shattering his excitement.

"No."

"What?" both he and Zephyrus blurted, their voices reverberating in the wind.

"I am aware of the dragon's status as an unattached daughter of Fate. She is far more desirable than you realize for that fact alone. You will not be her only suitor. In fact, I have staked my own claim on her and intend to see that my proxies are given their fair shot. If I were to grant your request, you would have an unfair advantage, and we simply can't have that. Good luck!"

She sang the last two words, and the notes lingered on the air for several moments after she'd disappeared back into the earth, leaving Ozzie gaping at her in astonishment.

"Fuck!"

Sophia merely shook her head at him. "It's as I feared. I could not get a sense of who her match should be when we arrived. I believe Fate is leaving the choice to her."

"What the hell does this mean?" he asked. Within his mind, Zephyrus seemed too stunned to react.

"It means you and I have our work cut out for us, grandson. We need to help Zephyrus secure a body so he can pursue her properly, and hope there aren't any other suitors available besides the ones we are aware of."

"Her proxies," Ozzie said with a slow nod. "Gaia must have meant the ursa pair Numa is already attached to. Numa would only choose them if they were powerful enough to complete the ritual to open the portal. If they have Gaia's help, this will be tricky."

"Find me a body and I will give them a run for their money."

"Easier said than done. Nanyo, are there *any* eligible hosts within this temporal bubble?"

"All the residents I am acquainted with are either female or children, but there must be others. Let's see who we might have missed."

She walked to the edge of the pond and squatted down, waving her hand over the surface of the water. Ozzie dropped to his knees beside her as she recited the brief spell to turn the water's surface into a reflection of the world around them. The vision swiftly traveled through the Rainsong Lodge, fixing briefly upon face after face. He saw exactly what his grandmother had said—there were few residents left in the Sanctuary, much less in the lodge itself. Vrishti and her mates were here, as well as Numa, the pair of ursa males she'd been spending most of her time with, the lodge's staff, and their children. Almost every ursa who could fight was already in the Haven doing just that. Their options were slim, and the longer they looked, the more Zephyrus twisted uneasily inside Ozzie's consciousness.

"Wait, what was that?" Ozzie asked when his grandmother's waving hand passed the image over the outer edge of the lodge's perimeter where the forest began. She pushed the image back and then paused. An unfamiliar ursa male trudged along the outer edge, right inside the temporal barrier, stopping every so often to tap at the shimmering membrane that blocked them from the outside world.

"Who is he?" Ozzie asked.

"My new host," Zephyrus said.

The man was one of the biggest ursa Ozzie had ever seen, with cascade of blond hair secured in a half-bun at the back of his head and a beard in a darker gold covering his face. He was stark naked, which suggested he'd recently shifted. On both big biceps were dark spiral tattoos with tails stretching down his forearms.

"Windchaser," Sophia said, pointing at the tattoos. "He's at the west side of the lodge's boundaries. Why don't we go and say hello?"

CHAPTER 3

CADE

ade Windchaser squinted at the shimmering wall that blocked his passage to the outside world. Not that he *wanted* to go that way—he'd only just arrived at the Rainsong Lodge at dawn—but the moment he'd stepped foot beyond the gate, the light had changed and he felt like he'd plunged into cool water. He'd stopped and shifted just to try to figure out what the hell was going on. Some strange magical barrier blocked his way back out, not unlike the portal barrier leading into the Sanctuary itself.

He poked at it again and tiny ripples formed, expanding outward like he'd tossed a pebble into a pond.

"Gaia's tears, what the hell is going on here?" he muttered.

"She isn't crying, I guarantee you that."

Cade spun around. A well-built man with shoulder-length blond hair stood on the path, an older woman beside him. A cool breeze had arrived along with them that set Cade's skin tingling and reminded him of home. It was the spark of electricity in their eyes that gave them away.

"Turul … How did you two get in here?" He frowned and

glanced in the direction of the portal on the mountain in the distance.

"We came with Vrishti's mates. They needed our help to enter the Sanctuary without damaging the barrier," the man said. "I'm sorry we didn't have time to make a tour and announce our presence. There wasn't time, what with the Haven under attack."

"Vrishti's mates? Did she and the old satyr find their dragon? Are they all right?" He took a step closer, eager for news. The only reason he'd come here instead of heading straight to the Haven to fight was to make sure the girl had made it home safe.

"They are well," the woman said. She gave him a warm smile and her eyes twinkled in a way that reminded him of his old Windchaser grandmother who had died centuries ago. "But there isn't time to get acquainted. We need your help."

"Anything."

The pair looked relieved, but the man shook his head. "You don't have to agree until you hear what it is we're asking. My name's Ozzie West, and this is my grandmother, Sophia North."

"Pleasure," Cade said, nodding and smiling at them both, but internally bracing himself. He had little enough to live for, and if a pair of turul that had the look of immortals asked for his help, he'd give it. "It's to help win this war, I hope."

"It is. Come, let's get back to the lodge and we'll talk on the way," Ozzie said.

By the time they'd escorted him up into the Rainsong Shaman's chambers, his head was spinning, but he'd take time to process their request after he'd done what he came here to do.

The door swung open and an all too familiar face

appeared. "Dion's balls, man, do you *ever* wear clothes?" Neph asked.

Cade broke into a wide grin. "I seem to recall the tables being turned once, and I didn't give you shit about showing up skyclad at my door."

Neph opened his arms and they embraced, laughing. Cade held on for a moment longer and murmured into the other man's ear, "I need to know what you saw that day, friend. The day we met, when you showed up naked at the cabin. You told me you'd seen my life. Does it end with me mated to a dragon?"

Neph stilled and pulled back, studying Cade's face with a frown. His aqua eyes swirled with that strange pull that Cade had to work to resist being bowled over by.

"Huh," Neph said, blinking at him. "That day, no. There were no dragons in your future. I saw a clear path for you that ended with your death. But that isn't what I see now."

"What do you see?" he asked, desperate to know whether this offer he'd been given was what he was meant to do.

Neph's brows went up and he let out a soft laugh. "I see a blank slate. Consider this a blessing, man. It means Fate's got plans for you that I'm not privy to, but whatever it is, I promise you it's better than the future you had."

Cade wasn't sure whether he liked that answer or not, but his friend wasn't any more forthcoming. He nodded and shifted his attention to the room beyond.

Over Neph's shoulder, he caught sight of a big, white-haired man standing protectively at the side of an over-stuffed armchair. In the armchair sat Vrishti, beaming at him in excitement.

He stepped into the room and his eyes widened at the sight of her big, round belly. "My lord, you two sure didn't waste any time."

"It's a long story. Here, put something on before you put an eye out with that tree trunk."

Neph tossed a pile of clothing at him and he obliged.

When he finished dressing, he turned just in time to have a curvy, feminine body pressed against him as Vrishti gave him a tight hug.

"Not sure this is appropriate, you being the Summer Shaman now and all," he murmured into her hair, enjoying the fresh, fertile smell of her. Gaia's tears, he missed this kind of female attention. Hell, he missed *any* kind of affection, really.

"I don't really care, Cade. It's so good to see you." She lingered and sighed, and Cade warily glanced up at her two mates. Neph and the dragon merely gazed back with a level of adoration Cade had hoped this lovely ursa would receive from her mates. He gave her one more squeeze and stepped back.

"These turul tell me there's a ritual I can help with. I want to hear it from you."

"It isn't really for me to tell," Vrishti said. "I'm not actually part of it. Aodh's sister is in charge." She glanced past Cade's shoulder. "Numa, will you share the details with Cade? He's here to help."

Cade's skin prickled with acute awareness. He hadn't heard anyone else arrive, but could sense the immense fertile power in the room, strong enough to rival the power Vrishti held inside her.

Before he could turn, she slipped up beside him, and he understood instantly why the West Wind was willing to share a body with another man in order to have her.

"Welcome," the dragon said, smiling and giving him a once-over that made him straighten his spine.

"Numa, this is Cade Windchaser," Vrishti said, her brows

lifting as though she expected something to happen. Cade frowned at the girl, then looked at Numa again.

"Is there something you want to share?" he asked.

Numa let out a long breath and shook her head. "I think Vrishti is just hoping I'll look at you and it'll *click*. I'm sorry to say it hasn't, and I don't think it ever will. You seem like a lovely man, but Vrishti knows I need more power in a mate than a single ursa male can provide."

"Ah … these two said something about that." He jabbed his thumb over his shoulder to where Ozzie and Sophia waited near the fireplace. "I may not be blessed with all of Gaia's power, but one thing I have is the determination to do what's right. It won't be the first time a Windchaser has partnered with the Winds. But I pray you'll give me a chance once I *have* more power."

Numa's brows furrowed and she darted a look at Ozzie. For a second, Cade thought she looked hurt, but her expression softened to curiosity when she looked back at him. Tilting her head, she said, "So Zephyrus has enlisted you as his new chauffeur? He is more persistent than I thought. And you would have no reservations about being mated to a dragon if I choose you once he's … on board? This would be a permanent arrangement."

Cade chuckled. "I'd like to think it'd be more than just an *arrangement*, sweet pea."

"You aren't bonded to another ursa male? No mate at all?" Her gaze traveled down his body in a more leisurely fashion this time. Cade's blood heated when she darted her tongue out and licked her lips. It wasn't just any tongue, either, but her true dragon tongue, pink with iridescent green at its forked tips.

"I'm all yours, if you'll have me," Cade said. Gaia save him, had his luck finally turned? Was this dragon seriously contemplating taking him as her mate? Even conditionally, he couldn't complain about that.

She could just as easily be sizing him up for a snack with that hungry look of hers, but his cock was more optimistic, bless the little bugger.

"Can I watch?" she asked in a husky voice. Her gaze darted back to Ozzie again. Cade tore his eyes away from Numa to look at the turul who'd offered the proposition of his life.

Ozzie looked like he was about to implode from the offer —aroused, but for some reason not the least bit happy about it. Having a horny immortal for a ride-along must not have suited the man all that well. But far be it from him to disappoint the lovely lady. He shrugged. "I'm game, if you are."

Ozzie clenched his jaw. "There won't be anything to watch. All Zephyrus needs is your consent. Do you consent?" He closed the distance to stand in front of Cade, blocking his view of Numa. His trippy turul eyes sparked with his impatience.

Cade gave him a lazy smile. "As long as she's all right with it, I am."

"Good," Ozzie said, and reached up to clasp the back of Cade's neck. An instant later, the other man claimed his mouth, and Cade opened more out of startlement than willingness. He shifted closer, resting his hands on Ozzie's hips, but making no more overt moves to carry the kiss further. He had no clue what was expected of him, only that this turul was a damn good kisser and he'd happily let this be the start of an orgy, if that was how things worked. Hell, there were two dragons and a satyr in the room, and while orgies weren't really a turul *or* an ursa thing, so much had changed in the last year.

Ozzie didn't react to the press of Cade's groin against his, despite the fact that Cade could feel the other man's erection hot and hard through his pants. But when cool air tickled his tongue and pushed farther down his throat, he had no choice but to inhale.

With that first breath, his mind went white with the rush of pure power flooding in from the other man's lungs. The presence made itself known by increments, the way the scent of ozone in the air portends a storm. The hair on Cade's arms stood on end, and his entire body prickled with the energy.

"This is ... different. But good," a voice said. *"Like you're a perfect fit. Why do you think that is?"*

Cade barely noticed that Ozzie had pulled away. He remained standing with his eyes closed, simply soaking in the experience of this new presence inside him. A presence he'd had no idea would feel so damned familiar.

"You feel like ..." *Lennox*. Even thinking the name pained him after all this time.

"They can hear you if you speak aloud. You need not speak for me to hear you, Arcadius Windchaser. I hear you clearly. He was your partner, your bachelor mate. Lennox Sundance. You loved him."

"Until his last breath at the hands of a Hunter. Why does your voice ... your magic ... feel so much like his?"

"You are not the first ursa I've had a partnership with. Ages ago, I helped another ... a Sundance ... win the favor of the ursa maiden he loved. She would not have accepted a solitary male without my help. Some of my power infused the child they made before I moved on. I believe Lennox was the name of that child."

Cade let out a sigh—of relief or disappointment, he couldn't be sure. When he opened his eyes, the rest of the room was staring at him expectantly. Ozzie stood a few feet in front of him with his arms crossed, as though he were standing his ground in case Cade changed his mind.

Sophia North stepped in front of her grandson and

peered up into Cade's eyes. Finally, she gave him a nod and patted his cheek with a cool, smooth hand. "They make a good pair."

The statement left Cade feeling as if he'd walked into some kind of trap.

"You and me both, friend. She's the one turul I've yet to figure out."

His gaze shifted to Numa again, and his heart did a somersault that was wholly at odds with the simple attraction he'd experienced when he'd first met her. *"Gaia's tears, man,"* he said to the new resident that shared his mind. *"You are just a little more than smitten. How did your boy there not fall for her too?"*

"It seems Fate's curse can't even be broken by my desire. He knew she wasn't meant for him and refused to give in to my urges. The best part about partnering with you is that ursa males don't get to choose ... you get chosen. So now it's my job to make sure she chooses us, because that pretty piece of dragon tail has been all I could think about for centuries."

The pretty dragon in question was giving Cade that hungry look again. "Shall we see what kind of power you have now?" she asked. "We are quite literally on borrowed time."

Cade smiled at Numa and reached for her hand. As their palms touched, the light in the room flickered, brightening to a blinding flash before returning to normal. Vrishti let out a sharp gasp and clutched her belly.

"Something's wrong! Oh, god. Why can't my mother be here?"

Numa rushed to her side, casting a quick glance back at Cade. Her look seemed to hold a promise, a message that they would pick up where they left off, once she'd seen to Vrishti.

"It's all right, honey," Numa said, crouching beside Vrishti's chair. "Can you show me your belly?"

Neph looked stricken, his face as pale as the dragon by his side. Cade gripped his friend's shoulder. "Want to explain to me how she got this way so fast? I have the sense that this is a story I'll want to hear, especially now that it's thrown a wrench into this ritual we need to get done yesterday."

The big satyr grimaced. "The child isn't ours. Vrishti was captured by the Ultiori long enough for Meri to implant a fetus inside her womb. Meri needed Vrishti's link to the Source to keep the child alive. Her plan, we believe, was to transport the child to the Haven, remove it by killing Vrishti, then use direct contact with the Source to complete its transformation into whatever creature she intended it to be."

Cade let out a low whistle and looked at Vrishti, whose pregnant belly was exposed now with Numa's hands resting gently against it. Her hands glowed with subtle power and a green ring of smoke slowly encircled Vrishti's head, tiny tendrils of it seeping into her mouth and nose.

"What is the creature?" he asked in a low voice.

"It's a baby," Aodh hissed. "Innocent. But something's not right about the pregnancy, beyond the obvious. She wasn't that big when we brought her here."

"Aodh!" Numa called. The white dragon jumped to action, crossing the room in two strides to reach Vrishti and his sister. "Carry her to the bed. She's going into labor. Sophia, help me calm the baby, my magic isn't reaching it."

Cade stood by, feeling like a useless lump. *How's your singing voice?* Zephyrus asked.

"Fine, I guess? Why?"

Because I need your vocal cords to help. My magic will do far more good this way.

Cade had no idea what he meant until Ozzie and Sophia took a spot on either side of the bed and began to sing. Ozzie beat out a slow rhythm like a heartbeat on his thighs with his palms while his grandmother swayed. Their voices merged, a deep tenor and a sweet soprano, and Cade knew exactly what he had to do. He opened his mouth and sang, letting Zephyrus provide the words.

35

CHAPTER 4

NUMA

The music filled the room with a lulling rhythm that soon banished the sense of urgency Numa had been feeling all day. Even with Vrishti's impending delivery, she became calmer and more centered than she'd felt in ages. She rested on her knees between Vrishti's spread thighs, one hand on the other woman's belly, urging Vrishti to breathe.

Ozzie and Sophia perched at the edges of the bed on either side, Ozzie still beating out that comforting rhythm on his thigh while the others sang. But while the song itself was beautiful and had succeeded in calming Vrishti's distress and easing the baby's delivery, it was the deep bass at her back that had captured Numa's attention.

Cade was a striking man to begin with. Compared to the pair of Rainsong ursa she spent most of her time with, he had a much easier manner. Bekim and Theron had each other, and they fed off each other's mutual need to please her. There was no such urgency in Cade. He seemed to simply accept what came his way, to take it all in stride.

She didn't have time to feel guilty about her need to find a mate powerful enough for the ritual. Bekim and Theron were dear to her, but simply lacked the magic required.

Now that Zephyrus had a willing host who was free to agree to a mating, she hoped his power would prove to be enough. He was the immortal West Wind, after all, and she'd seen the way his aura flared with that power when Ozzie had transferred Zephyrus to the ursa. Perhaps she'd been a little disappointed that the transfer had been so simple. She'd have enjoyed an excuse to sample Ozzie's Nirvana once, but none of that mattered now that Vrishti's mysterious baby was about to arrive.

"Push, honey," she said in a soothing voice. Vrishti nodded and obeyed, bearing down enough that the smooth crown of the baby's head appeared. "Good girl."

Vrishti let out a long groan. "Neph … Aodh … I need you!" she cried, tears streaming down her face.

The two big men pushed close, and the two turul didn't miss a beat, continuing their song while they made room for Vrishti's mates to take up the spots on either side of her. Numa's brother lent his breath to his mate, expelling a cloud of white smoke that encompassed her.

"Not too much, brother," Numa said. "She needs to be conscious for this."

Aodh nodded and settled on the big bed beside Vrishti, gently kissing her sweat-soaked temple and smoothing her dark hair from her face. Neph rested on the other side, accepting Vrishti's hand and squeezing tight.

The trio's strong affection touched Numa, and she darted a glance over her shoulder. Cade was there, still carrying on the same harmony with his deep voice. His blue eyes twinkled at her, making her heart flutter. She'd have loved nothing more than to close her eyes and let his song lull her, but Vrishti and the baby were too important.

At Numa's urging, Vrishti pushed again and the baby

surged free in a torrent of power-rich fluid. Sophia was ready with a blanket, never once faltering in her singing.

Numa tended to the baby with practiced efficiency, cleaning it and severing the umbilical cord with a swipe of a talon, then searing the end with a quick, flaming breath.

"She's a perfect little girl," she said, setting the tiny bundle into Vrishti's outstretched arms. When she stepped backward off the bed, Cade rested a hand on her shoulder and squeezed.

She gave him a grateful look and covered his hand with hers. He would be an easy man to mate, of that she was certain, but she couldn't shake the feeling that she was betraying Bekim and Theron somehow. They all knew the stakes, and that the mate she chose had to be equal to the challenge the ritual dictated. She just wished making the choice didn't have to be so complicated.

The turuls' singing had softened. Cade no longer added his voice. Only Ozzie and Sophia still hummed quietly, Ozzie's steady, rhythmic beats continuing while Vrishti bared a nipple to the baby who greedily latched on. When she began to suckle, it was as though a collective breath was released. Cheers rang out, and Numa realized they had a much bigger audience than she'd been aware of during the ordeal.

She glanced around to the people spilling in the doorway and her gaze landed on the two pairs of eyes not fixed on the new mother. Theron's bearded face concealed his expression, but Bekim's frown left no mystery. Their eyes fixed pointedly on Cade's hand where it still rested on Numa's shoulder, hers clasped around it. She dropped her hand and pulled away, ready to go after the pair as they slipped back out the door.

"By the Winds, something isn't right," Sophia said. Her strident tone drew Numa back.

"What is it?" she asked, forcing her attention back to the tableau on the bed.

"This child has no soul."

Numa stared in disbelief at the idyllic scene of the mother ursa with her newborn and her two doting mates. Nothing could have been more perfect. But Vrishti's adoring look registered no alarm at the declaration, nor did Numa's brother or the Dionarch, both of whom had happily claimed the child as their own despite her uncertain parentage.

That was when she realized how right Sophia was. The baby's aura was a strange, shimmering cloud with no clear identity. While a new child was often a blank slate as far as personality traits went, their auras always held some hint of their destiny. Numa wasn't adept at reading them the way her sisters were, but she did feel an odd kinship with the uncertainty that surrounded this baby.

"Is that a bad thing?" Cade asked.

"It is troubling, but not dangerous for the child," Sophia explained. "Somewhere in this child's creation, Fate failed to note her existence. It will make for a lonely life for her … without a soul, it will be impossible for her to find a soul mate. The more pressing concern is how quickly she grows. She's already opened her eyes and recognized her mother. Look."

The baby had released Vrishti's nipple and kicked her blanket away. She lay cradled in her mother's arms, her fat little hand reaching toward Vrishti's face as soft cooing sounds emanated from her chest.

Vrishti cooed back and beamed. "Perhaps if we find out her true nature, we can find a way to give her a soul. Can you tell what she is? When I first saw her, she had wings and talons, but she looks like a normal human baby now. Except for her aura …" Vrishti directed her gaze to Numa, pinning her with a stare that reminded her of the Summer Spirit who resided inside the young ursa now. "Her aura looks like yours."

Numa stiffened. "My aura?" She lifted her hands and looked down at them, shifting her sight so she could be aware of her energy. It was tricky to see one's own aura, but not impossible. Nothing seemed off to her, beyond the flickering of uncertainty about her choice of mates. "My aura's just fine."

"No. I see something different from the others," Vrishti said. "I don't know why only I can see it. It's fading now, though... When you came to us this morning, it was a bright, flickering rainbow, like hers." She looked down at the baby. "But now it's only... green." Vrishti frowned. "So strange."

Sophia hummed softly and moved to the side of the bed closer to Vrishti, forcing Aodh to lean back to give her access. The ancient turul seer rested her hand on the child's head and whistled a low, melodic tune that tickled Numa's ears. She rubbed her ears slightly, trying to decide where she'd heard the song before. The baby's eyes widened and she punched her fists into the air, gurgling and laughing.

Sophia looked up at Numa with a brow lifted. "You heard the song too?"

"Yes. What was that?"

"It was a test. Confirmation that the child has been overlooked by Fate. In her case, accidentally."

Numa's stomach dropped. "But in my case by design... is that what you're saying? But I know I have a soul."

Sophia stepped back and let out a long sigh. "You are Fate's daughter. There is no way he'd have overlooked you by accident. Unlike this child, you do possess a soul. But without Fate's mark to guide you, it will make your quest to find a mate a bit more complicated."

Numa laughed. "As if it isn't already complicated enough?

I'd like to just get on with it. With Zephyrus's power, there's no reason Cade isn't perfect. I'd rather not wait."

"We're happy to get things moving too," Cade said. He dipped his head when the others looked at him. "If I'm not out of line in saying so, it was mentioned we're on borrowed time. And my new partner seems like he's itching to get a move on. He seems to think what you say next is going to slow things down even more."

Sophia's lips pressed into a thin line. "Zephyrus isn't above Fate's rules. And I fear your lack of clear direction was indeed part of a bigger plan, Numa."

An unexpected breeze blew in through the open window, smelling of spring flowers. Numa couldn't bring herself to enjoy the scent, not when she was sure what came next would very likely ruin her life. It was bad enough that she'd been neglected by her own father while all her siblings were given clear foreknowledge of the mates they were meant to be with.

She set her teeth, grimly waiting for the other shoe to drop. "What is it to be, then?"

"A contest for your favor," Sophia said. "When you and your siblings were born, Fate decreed that one of you would be free to choose, and that when the identity of that one became clear, any of the immortals who wished for a dragon mate would have the opportunity to win your love."

Numa opened her mouth to protest. They didn't have time for such nonsense. But Ozzie was the first to speak.

"This is bullshit, Nanyo. You've had all day to warn her that this was happening. She didn't have to be left wondering." He turned a piercing stare to Cade. "And *you* ... Zephyrus, I mean ... You knew too, didn't you?"

Cade's brows drew together and he raked a hand through his hair. His gaze turned inward, and a second later, he nodded. "He says he knew about the promise, but not who it would be. He only hoped Numa would be the one." Turning those laughing blue eyes to her, he said, "He's been in love with you since time began."

Numa felt weak. "I don't believe him. I know all the bets he made with my brother Gavra over who would bed Nyx first. None of the other immortals ever showed an interest in me."

The truth was, she'd been relieved when she and her siblings had ultimately decided to cloister themselves in the Glade. She'd grown weary of life as a goddess with only weak humans for company. A few of her siblings had developed deeper attachments that had ended tragically, so none of them were particularly keen on remaining in the human world by then. But Numa had always secretly envied her siblings for the love they'd found in those early days, and had seen herself as undesirable for the lack of interest she'd received from their sister races.

Cade pressed his lips together as the contemplative look crossed his face again—Zephyrus making his case, no doubt. Then he began to speak, but in a voice very different than the one she'd heard when she first met the big ursa.

"Do you remember how you were in the beginning? The dutiful daughter who sought only to do what was right. You followed all the rules, never once showed any interest in testing boundaries. It was intimidating, but the most beautiful thing about you. Not to mention the sheer power ... You are the reason dragon queens are always Greens..." Cade paused, his brows lifting with interest. "No shit, you're the reason? I always wondered..."

"Tell Zephyrus if he's trying to gain some advantage in this damn contest, he's wasting your breath," Numa snapped.

Cade's mouth quirked and he scratched his beard. "He can hear you just fine." He gave her a grin. "And he says the reason he made those bets about Nyx was because she was safe. He knew she'd wind up with Nereus … I guess Fate told him. You, he feared … If you were the one who would be allowed to choose, he risked getting in too deep and winding up out in the cold if you rejected him. He says he tried getting Fate to promise you to him, but was told no every time."

She moved to the empty chair by the window and sat, barely conscious of the warm spring breeze blowing across her face. She was numb amid the revelations. The West Wind had wanted her all this time. But within the last two months, she'd become so attached to a certain pair of ursa, her heart broke at the idea of hurting them by choosing someone else. And now to be told she'd have to choose between all the *immortals* who might have secretly been waiting all this time just to mate a daughter of Fate?

Taking a deep breath, she gathered herself. "Sophia, who are the suitors to be, then? I know Zephyrus is one … with Cade as his proxy…" She gave the big ursa a formal nod, but refused to show more of the churning confusion that plagued her now. "Who else?"

"That, I can't say," Sophia said. "We should gather in the throne room, if the Summer Shaman allows, and I will make the formal call. We shall see who arrives and set the terms of the contest then."

Numa glanced at Vrishti, and her demeanor softened at the sight once again. "What of the baby? Will she be all right?"

"Her fate is undetermined, but she is perfectly healthy," Sophia said. "We will keep a close eye on her, regardless. I'm more concerned about how quickly she's growing. This temporal bubble may not be the ideal environment for a newborn."

"Then we should waste no more time," Numa said. "The sooner we get this contest over with, the sooner we can take down the bubble and win this war. I need to take care of one thing, and then I will meet you in the throne room."

She stood and brushed her hands down the skirt of her dress, bracing herself for the conversation she knew was imminent.

THE OTHERS HAD CLEARED out of the room by the time Numa finished ensuring that Vrishti and her baby were doing fine. Sophia was right about the baby's growth, however. It had barely been an hour, and she was already half again as big as she'd been when Numa had caught her tiny body slipping out of Vrishti's womb.

"Come and get me if anything worries you," she said, giving both of Vrishti's mates hard stares. The men both dipped their heads obediently.

She left the room feeling out of sorts. All her life, she'd been the wise one—the one her siblings came to with their worries, the rational voice who kept order when it was needed. They listened to her. And it wasn't just them, either. It was a product of the power she held as a Green Dragon, partially tied to the Earth and Gaia herself. That protective maternal magic could give life, but was capable of great destruction if needed to *protect* life instead.

Perhaps this was why Fate had decided to let her be the one to choose. Had her father understood something about Numa that even she wasn't aware of?

After watching each of her siblings seek out the mates from their dreams, she had asked herself if she could have even accepted being told who to be with. She couldn't deny that her siblings had all found love and happiness with their fated mates, but had also marveled at how *easy* it had seemed that they accepted the ones chosen for them.

She would get to choose. Even though the idea should have pleased her, she was terrified. What if she chose wrong?

She paused outside the door, taken aback by the sight of Cade in his golden-maned glory leaning against the wall in the corridor. High roof lanterns allowed morning light to stream into the space, and it caught the silver highlights in his hair, his beard, and his eyes, making him seem less like the summer sun worshiper she'd first thought him and more like a winter god.

His knowing smile reminded her of the spirit inside him and left her flustered. She'd once fantasized about being the West Wind's lover. While flying, she liked to pretend that the air currents carried secret caresses from one of those four brothers. Now she couldn't help but wonder whether those old instincts had been the truth. Had her secret moments alone on the windy peaks of the mountains she'd flown to been witnessed by this immortal? Her entire body heated at the very idea that Zephyrus might have observed her solitary indulgences, too afraid of rejection to join her.

She clenched her teeth and shot an irritated look at Cade. "Was he there all those times I … I worshiped the wind with my naked body? Were my fantasies closer to reality than I knew?"

Cade's brows shot up and his smile widened. "He's shown me a memory or two. Trust me, I'm on your side, sweet pea. I'd have joined you. His excuses don't hold water."

"Oh? And what are his excuses? If he'd come to me, we might not be in this situation."

"Seems the Winds are harder to pin down than the Seasons. He didn't have a body and couldn't find one he felt worthy of you then. I will take that as a compliment."

"He had a body at Belah's wedding. I was there, yet he said nothing to me." Though the truth was she'd been in no mood to stay for the festivities that day. And after the disaster that happened later, she and her siblings barely left the Glade before ultimately locking themselves in indefinitely.

Cade nodded and stepped toward her. "If there's one thing I've learned, it's that dwelling on the past gets you nowhere. I've heard his piece, and I can't say I agree with everything he did or didn't do, but there's one thing he *didn't* have back then that I think will make all the difference now."

"Oh? And what is that?"

Cade grinned at her again. "He's got me. And you can have us both, if you want."

Numa deflated. Something about the big ursa made it impossible to stay angry at Zephyrus. "I have a feeling you'll be good for him, but you heard what Sophia said in there. Any immortal who might have been secretly interested in me before will get to have their crack now. For all I know, you two might be the only ones, which would make my decision easy. But if you're not, I can't make any promises now. I'll see you down in the throne room soon."

"Just one more thing, sweet pea," Cade said, shifting closer to her. "You don't know me yet, and I know Zeph's the reason I have a shot with you, but if you do choose us, you need to know you won't regret it."

Cade's voice had lowered in pitch, the deep timbre vibrating down to her core and paralyzing her as he closed the distance between them. Her body flushed and her pulse raced at his proximity, but she stood her ground, lifting her gaze to his and holding it. His hand came up to her face, callused fingertips tracing the line of her jaw. There was something about that rough touch that appealed to her. Something different from any other lover she'd had in a long time.

His beard brushed her chin a second before his mouth found hers, and the softness of his lips startled her. All the sensations were so at odds with one another, but that kiss was more than enough for her to grasp that this man was experienced at pleasing women.

He started slow, with just the gentlest brush, his beard tickling her skin and sending a rush of desire for more. He would be a tease in bed, of that she was sure. Then he took her mouth fully, and Numa wasn't quite sure how they'd gone from something chaste and barely there to his mouth claiming hers, owning it like she'd offered herself to him and she was his to take. *That* was nothing like the way Bekim or Theron kissed her. They were attentive, yet deferential lovers, like most ursa males were known to be. This one was different in a very, *very* good way.

When he finally pulled away, he left her breathless, and she stared up at him at a loss for words. She swallowed and pressed her hand to her throat, hoping the heat would subside.

"Was that all you, or…?"

His straight white teeth appeared amid his beard again, the smile as cocky as before. She couldn't help but smile back. "All me, sweet pea. Zeph talks a good game, so if he's not lying, you will be well and thoroughly loved."

Numa forced herself to take a breath, the cleansing inhalation helping to steady her racing pulse. "You two are making this difficult for me, you know. But thank you."

"See you down there," he said with a final nod before turning and walking away.

Numa watched him go, enjoying the way his muscular frame moved with casual grace. She had no idea how old he was, but everything she'd seen so far suggested a level of experience that rivaled most immortals, and if Zephyrus hadn't influenced that kiss, she *really* didn't relish the choice she'd have to make later.

No more than she relished the news she had to deliver

now. Taking a deep sigh, she turned and headed in her intended direction. She paused a moment later outside the door to Bekim and Theron's room, bracing herself before knocking.

Theron opened the door, and for a second, she was sure excitement flickered across his features before his expression stilled and turned more serious.

"Come in," he said, stepping back and pulling the door wide for her to enter. Bekim stood by the window, leaning against the frame and peering out as though looking for something. He turned and stood up straighter when she entered.

"I have bad news. You guys left too soon to hear, but things just got a little more complicated for me."

Her gut churned, her apprehension made worse by the way they both seemed so nonchalant.

"Has your life ever not been complicated?" Bekim asked.

"It was less so a long time ago. Today's events kind of blow everything else out of the water. I've been informed that there's to be a contest for my favor. That Fate has promised any immortal who wants me can compete to be my mate. I … I'm sorry, but I will have to choose from whoever arrives to enter this contest."

She left out the part where she knew it wouldn't be them. If there were multiple immortals like Zephyrus involved, there was no way these two ursa she held so dear could compete.

"Has your criteria changed?" Theron asked.

"My criteria?"

Bekim nodded. "Yeah, you're still after the best source of power for the ritual, right?"

"I have to be. I can't let my other desires get in the way of finishing this. You understand that our whole world depends on it, right?"

"We understand perfectly," Theron said. Then he surprised her by pulling her into a tight hug and kissing her on the cheek. "Good luck."

She was stunned when he released her, but gratified even further when Bekim followed suit.

"Um … I'm glad you're being so understanding. I don't know what happens after this, but I want you both to know how much I care about you. Please know I want you both to be happy."

"Don't worry about us, Numa," Bekim said with a smile that made his sweet dimples deepen in his cheeks. "We aren't about to sit around moping. We'll get what we want, one way or the other."

She let out a sigh of relief. "I'm glad to hear that. Take care."

They walked her back to the door then, and as she departed, she couldn't help but wonder about the odd look the pair exchanged after giving her their farewell kisses.

Ozzie and Sophia were both waiting in the throne room when Numa entered. All the other residents of the Rainsong Clan Lodge were in attendance as well, no doubt having heard Sophia's proclamation at Vrishti's bedside and itching for some kind of entertainment. They'd all been informed of the temporal bubble that surrounded the place, and that it would enable them all to help turn the tide of the war waging in the Haven today, but without access to the rest of the Sanctuary, they had no access to any real action.

As much as she understood their desire for a spectacle, Numa hoped this contest would be over before it started. Surely there couldn't be other immortals with any interest in her? There were Zephyrus's brothers, Boreas, Eurus, and Notus, but they would respect their brother's desires and not throw their hats in the ring. All of the ursa shamans except for Vrishti were fighting in the Haven, but they were happily mated already, and the nymphaea Dionarchs were also both taken, one of them upstairs with his mates and a newborn baby right now.

That left the immortals who existed beyond the realm of the Earth, the contemporaries of Fate, Gaia, and the Mother Dragon, but she couldn't imagine any of them had an interest in sullying themselves with the crisis at hand. They had to be aware that whomever she chose would be tied up in the war the very second they completed the ritual. There would be no going back once the portal was open and Nikhil came in with his army.

The throne sat empty with Sophia and Ozzie standing to either side. As Numa walked down the center of the grand hall with its dark, polished wood, the weight of all the stares dragged at her like an undertow. Cade stood near the front, looking as casually confident as the first time she'd seen him. Would he be the one after all?

She couldn't bring herself to sit on the throne of the Summer Shaman, so she remained standing between the two turul. Sophia had a knack for matchmaking. Perhaps if Numa had trouble deciding even after testing each contestant, the ancient seer could provide some insight. Yet again, she silently cursed Fate for forcing her to make a choice when all her siblings had been given their answer ages ago.

Sophia glanced at her and Numa nodded, indicating she was ready. Her skin prickled with anticipation as Sophia stepped forward.

"Fate decreed five thousand years ago that one among his offspring with the Mother Dragon would be granted the gift of choice. The time has come for her to make that choice. The hand of Numa, daughter of Fate, is the prize in this contest. This is the formal call to any who wish to enter and test their worth. Who here will enter? Step forth now and announce your intentions."

Cade wasted no time stepping forward, his lazy smile in place. Numa suppressed her own smile at his confidence.

"Cade Windchaser, at your service," he said with an exaggerated bow. "With the immortal West Wind as my partner. Zephyrus and I together will compete."

Sophia nodded, then cast her sharp gaze around the room. A commotion came from the back and a pair of figures emerged into the aisle. Numa inhaled sharply when Theron and Bekim jogged forward, grinning from ear to ear.

"How ...?" she whispered, shaking her head in astonishment when they stopped at the bottom of the dais.

"We are Bekim and Theron Rainsong, a bonded bachelor pair, and we wish to compete," Bekim said. "And before you object, my lady, we have the blessing of Gaia to ensure the contest is balanced." He glanced at Theron and nodded. They turned to face each other and joined hands, then lifted their arms to the sky.

Numa's eyes widened as their auras brightened to a shimmering green and leafy shoots erupted from their joined hands. Beneath their bare feet roots emerged, tangling together across the stone floor. The display of power was immense, suggesting the goddess herself had infused the pair directly.

But as she watched, she realized how much more difficult this made things. Now that she was bound by the rules of the contest, she would have to give the contestants a true challenge to test their power and show no favor over one or the other.

Cade crossed his arms and narrowed his eyes at the other ursa pair. She couldn't read his mind, but sensed an internal debate going on with Zephyrus over how to win.

Sophia leaned in and whispered, "Have you your own tests in mind for them, or shall I set them for you?"

As much as Numa would have liked a longer courtship with either of these contestants to truly test her own desires, there was only one simple criteria she cared about: They had to possess enough power to join her in the ritual. "I know what I need, Sophia. Thank you. Shall we start, then?" She cast an apprehensive look at the three men in front of her and the rest of the crowd beyond.

Sophia gave her a solemn nod and addressed the room once more. "If there are no others who wish to vie for the hand of a daughter of Fate, we shall begin …"

Before Sophia could complete the sentence, the big double doors at the end of the hall flew open with a crash. Collective gasps erupted from the onlookers, followed by a wave of more curious exclamations. Numa picked up dozens of whispered exchanges, all asking the same question: "Is that who I think it is?"

Astounded by this new arrival, she shot a quick question to her brother. *"How the fuck did he get in?"*

"He is a god, sister. Neph's a little surprised he's here, but if anyone could pass through the barriers, it'd be him."

Even from her vantage on the dais at the far end of the hall, Numa could sense the raw power surging through the air in waves. Women and men alike in the audience fanned themselves and scents of pure arousal filled the air. If Numa didn't know better, she might have thought her brother Gavra had arrived to cause trouble, but he was past those old diversions, and too busy fighting the enemy in the Haven.

Besides, the figure who strode into the room then was more enticing than any Red had ever been. Numa's heart pounded, a flush of desire rising unbidden at the mere sight. He was truly glorious, as large as a fully shifted satyr. But while he sported majestic horns atop his head, rising up from the mass of shining black curls that spilled around his thick, broad shoulders, his long, muscular legs remained the shape of a man's.

He said nothing as he strode toward her. His rich, wine-dark eyes remained fixed on her face, the desire in them more potent than any spirit. His leather sandals made almost no sound against the floor, but Numa's pulse thundered in her ears with each step closer. The straps of his sandals bound his strong calves, but from his knees up, he was completely naked, and what creature as divinely beautiful as him would ever find a garment befitting him? All that adorned his skin were a pair of golden rings wrapped snugly around the thick girth of the cock swinging between his thighs.

Sophia let out a soft curse beside her and whispered, "Stand your ground, my dear. Don't let him bully you into breaking the rules."

Numa barely heard her. The answer to her prayers had just entered the room. Why in the world did they need to continue the contest now? She could already *taste* the pure, raw, magic that this man—this *god*—was filled with.

She took an involuntary step down when he drew close, pulled by his gaze like he'd caught her in some spell. Within the bounds of his expansive aura, her skin tingled and her core grew engorged and wet. Closer now, she could not only smell but see the dew that coated his skin and knew it would taste like wine. One taste of him would be akin to one hundred Nirvanas from a normal human lover.

They met at the base of the dais, not one word spoken, yet he took her hand and bent to kiss it. She forced herself to suppress the moan of pleasure when his breath and lips caressed the back of her hand, his mere touch almost enough to send her to instant climax. Sweet Mother, she needed to get hold of herself. She blinked swiftly to clear the haze of lust and snatched her hand away.

He stood straight again, a sardonic smile on his achingly beautiful face. "Do you know who I am, little one?"

Numa's chest heated. She thought Cade's rich baritone was sexy, but this … She'd go mad if he said one more word.

She took a deep breath, bracing herself for a request she knew she had to make, but hating it all the same.

"You are Dionysus. And I really need you to dial your power back so I can fucking think."

"Is this not a contest of power? I have more than you need, daughter of Fate. You need look no further. I will give it all to you here, with one touch, if you agree to be my mate."

Numa's entire being told her to say yes. Here he was, a god, filled with more than enough divine power to create a sky portal ten times over. She should have said yes, but something stopped her.

She glanced to one side, absorbing the very worried expressions on Theron's and Bekim's faces. They had a goddess on their side—not simply an immortal posing as a deity among humans like she and her siblings had been for the first part of their lives. No, her pair of beloved ursa actually had Gaia's blessing, and no doubt her full use of that power as well.

She turned to the other side to see Cade as cool and collected as ever, sizing up the competition. His gaze flitted to the gold-adorned beast of a cock between the god's thighs, and Numa was certain she caught a smug smile playing at the corners of his lips.

She hadn't yet announced the exact terms of the contest, but one of them would involve rousing her own power to its very peak, and that involved skill as a lover more than it did power, something she doubted even a god like Dionysus could fake.

"I will agree under one condition," she said, pleased that she maintained the upper hand.

Dionysus lowered his brows and blinked, the only sign that she'd surprised him. "Anything you wish, daughter of Fate."

"Make that two conditions," she said, gritting her teeth

and shooting him an irritated look. "You will compete with the other contestants according to the rules I dictate."

He nodded, his horned head bowing only slightly and not a single curl shifting out of place in the process. "And your other condition?"

"You will learn my fucking name, because I am *not* some trophy for you to hold over my father's head when it suits you."

His head jerked back as though he'd been struck and his eyes widened. A second later, he smiled. "My sincerest apologies, Numa. I look forward to proving myself to you, though I must say you are nothing like your father … and far more spirited than any of us were led to believe."

Numa's nostrils flared in her effort to hold back her ire. Fuck her father and whatever the hell he'd led his cronies to believe. This infernal god had probably had his eye on her from the start. She hoped that either of the others would prove themselves strong enough, because she hated the idea of this one having the satisfaction of winning.

She turned around, facing the throne again just to catch her breath and calm herself. Ozzie and Sophia both watched in silence, but they both had equally satisfied smiles on their faces, and Ozzie surreptitiously gave her a thumbs-up behind one hand. If nothing else, he'd been a loyal friend in all this, and her heart went out to him. He deserved love, and if anyone knew how rough it was to be jerked around by Fate, it was him.

Turning, she strode across in front of the dais, past Bekim and Theron, then spun and made her way back. "There are only two tests I expect the four of you to complete," she began. "Each test will span six hours, with each of you proving yourselves within that time." She paused and turned at the other end of the dais and met Cade's blue eyes. "The first test is to determine how much power *you* are capable of producing and sustaining at my hands. Your stamina is the key in this test."

She paused and gave Dionysus a once-over. The cocky bastard was the only one fully on display, and certainly *looked* like he could go for days. But she had spent long nights with Theron and Bekim and was well aware of how long they could last, even without the aid of divine power. Striding on, she gave the pair of ursa what she hoped was an encouraging smile, and they both smiled back.

This might actually turn out to be fun. She smiled to herself when she turned again and paused, scanning the men from which she would soon choose her mate.

"The second test will show me how well you can drive my power to its peak. No man in existence has found that peak." She narrowed her eyes at Dionysus' knowing smile and shook her head. "I am a dragon. Don't ever forget that. I've had plenty of orgasms, but my capacity to absorb power until the need grows beyond my control is far greater than my own small indulgences have been.

"I like orgasms, but I can hold out longer than most of my lovers are comfortable waiting. You will each only have a few hours and no longer, but that is all we need for the ritual. Your willpower pushed beyond its limit and my own at least halfway met. The longer we each go, the more the power is drawn to us, the more power we have to contribute to the creation of the portal. And with enough power, we will be able to target its placement on either side with precision that will give us the advantage we need to win this war."

She'd stopped pacing and moved to stand at the top of the dais before the throne once more, yet the room seemed small now compared to the vast chamber she'd walked into a little while ago. Her skin tingled and her head felt heavy. All gazes were fixed to her, eyes wide. Even the cocky Dionysus had his brows raised, his gaze quietly assessing as though he were sizing up an opponent. She glanced down at her hands. Sharp talons jutted from where her fingernails had been, and emerald scales plated her hands and lower arms.

Far from embarrassed at the inadvertent loss of control over her power, she settled her shoulders and gazed back at the room, daring anyone to challenge the rules she'd created for the contest. A contest in which *she* was the ultimate prize.

Dionysus was the first to bow, this time even going so far as to fall to one knee and lower his head. "I accept your terms, Numa."

Cade, Bekim, and Theron all followed almost as a unit, stating their own acceptance.

Silently, she sent a message to her brother, who was still upstairs with the newborn and his mates. *"Exactly how much time have I got for this contest?"*

"We had hoped to hold the temporal bubble for a week, but there have been some troubling fluctuations in the shield that we can't figure out. It's affecting the baby, so we need to speed things along. Will two days be enough?"

"I can make it work."

Numa took a long breath and exhaled, returning her gaze to the contestants. "We will begin the first phase in one hour. Dionysus, you are to come to me first. Six hours after, Cade will join me, and then six hours after that, Bekim and Theron. Once the first phase is finished, we'll take a short break before phase two begins. You are all free to go prepare or rest. The staff will furnish you with rooms, if required."

She waited while the four men departed and the rest of the residents of the lodge followed after. When the door closed behind the last ursa, the dawn light flickered, casting a strange shadow like a cloud had passed across the sun in an instant.

"That can't be good," Numa said. "We're trapped in a time bubble. The light should remain static."

Aodh's worried voice echoed through her head. *"Sister, something has happened."*

She hurried out the door and up the stairs, jogging straight to Vrishti's room. *"What is it? Is the baby all right? Is Vrishti?"*

"It's hard to explain. Just come."

When she entered, she stopped in her tracks. She'd left barely an hour earlier, mother and child comfortably dozing on the bed. Now, Vrishti was still reclining against the pillows, but where there'd been an infant before, there was now a bright-eyed toddler with deep, burnished skin and curly black hair.

She stared open-mouthed at the little girl who sat in the center of the bed, happily playing with a stuffed toy someone had found for her. As Numa approached, the baby looked up at her. She smiled a huge smile with two little teeth already visible and dropped the toy. Her chubby brown hands reached for Numa and she let out an excited squeal. The child's eyes were more vividly blue than any normal newborn's. A blue Numa would know anywhere.

"How is this possible? This child is dragon-blessed. By my sister."

"It isn't possible," Neph said. "But what *is* possible is that she's the blood of a dragon-blessed. This baby was one of Meri's experiments. We've released most of her captives from the higher races, including the four Elites who used to serve her as Nikhil's lieutenants. As you know, one of those Elites was Belah's goddaughter, Neela. I believe Deva is Neela's daughter."

"Then who is her father?" she asked, darting a look to Neph.

The Dionarch just gave her a helpless look and opened his hands. "He could be any one of the male captives. Calder is the only one who saw the notes she kept on her experiments, but the grimoire was nowhere to be seen when we stormed Meri's lab. Her parentage is less important now than these growth spurts."

Numa went to the bed and sat down near the little girl. She smiled and reached out, pleased when the child's tiny hand clasped around her finger. "Hi there, Deva. I wish you could tell me how you got so big." She looked up at the others. "It happened when the light changed, didn't it? Is this the fluctuation you were worried about?"

"Yes. It occurred at almost the same instant," Neph said. "The fluctuations in the temporal barrier even out as quickly as they occur. We are not concerned about it failing. The three of us have more than enough power to maintain it until you've completed the ritual, but if the fluctuation happens again, we should investigate. I don't want any surprises."

"Me neither." She brushed a hand over the top of Deva's head, her heart warming at the softness of her curls and the way she reached again for her toy. "We don't want you to grow up too fast, little Deva. Give us enough time to understand who you really are first."

Deva grabbed the toy in both hands and clutched it to her, laughing. Numa watched her in silence for another moment. The little girl's aura still gave no hint that a destiny awaited her, but there were new signs Numa hadn't seen before.

"Aodh, do you see what I see?" She glanced up at her brother, who nodded.

"She has dragon in her," he said.

"The power is there, yes, but not just that. There's something more, but I can't make it out."

Aodh leaned against the big post at the far corner of the bed, lips pressed together as though he didn't want to say what was on his mind.

It was Vrishti who broke the silence. "She is a chimera. I

remembered a passage in one of the books in the library that describes her aura exactly. Not the strange rainbow I first saw when she was born. Sophia explained what that was. This is a hint of her origins. Thanks to the bond I share with Neph and Aodh, and the fact that Deva and I shared blood for a short time, I can sense the essences of what made her. She has the power of all four of the higher races, and the blood of humans in her as well. She is the first of her kind to exist on Earth, and every bit as immortal as any of us in this room."

Numa's blood chilled. The strange changes in light tied to the child's growth spurts…

Meri had created this child in her lab. Was it possible she had a way to find her too?

CHAPTER 6

MERI

eri's mind spread out, tethered to her body by only the finest thread. As long as her broken shell of a vessel still breathed, she would be chained to it, but that didn't matter now. The very air inside her home held magic enough for her purposes, and while they carefully kept her separated from the Source itself, she had another source to draw from.

There were humans within the Haven now, and while the life's blood of the higher races was still just beyond Meri's reach, the life's blood of humanity was not. She had begun this trap at the start and built it little by little over the centuries. Her first choice had been accidental, but oh so fortuitous. Choosing to assume the identity of a physician's daughter in the court of a pharaoh had given her access to more than enough humans to test her blood on while she still carried enough of her original power to affect them.

She doubted she could have grown so powerful without those small exchanges, and she'd never expected them to pay off to such a degree. She'd been too wrapped up in her research and maintaining control over Nikhil and the Elites to test how far those links went. Her Ultiori weren't an isolated system, however. The men and women she recruited —mostly men—had all been blood melded to her, but she'd never restricted their breeding. She'd had no interest in how they spread their seed around after learning that the lower-ranking Hunters were useless to her, save for as pawns in her ongoing scheme.

The strangest thing happened after the first generation of her Ultiori Hunters began to die … She didn't lose the connection. She'd fully expected the link to be snuffed along with the Hunter's life, but it remained strong, though distant. At first, it was just one child of the Hunter's blood that was still bound to Meri through that link. And then another Hunter died and left behind not one, but *five* offspring. More and more were added as the first generation expired, leaving behind a network of blood-bonded offspring among the human world.

Meri only occasionally tested that network, reaching out with her mind to see how far it spread. The effort it took was too great to maintain for long, but she credited those succeeding generations of growing links for her growing power. Humanity itself was linked to her by blood, whether it knew it or not, and now that she had no real body of her own worth controlling, she could finally let her power ride free using those thousands of flowing tributaries of blood to serve as her own River, her own *Source*. It wasn't quite as strong as the *true* Source, but it was enough to keep her link to her Hunters strong and her enemies guessing.

It was also enough to allow her to focus all her energy on the one thing she knew could give her the advantage she needed: the flow of time. The only problem was that she'd lost the last creature that *had* the most pure nymphaea blood under her control. All the satyrs had been taken from her, and she'd mistakenly chosen the most dangerous vessel to carry the precious cargo of her life's work into the Haven.

She'd learned the lesson centuries earlier not to fuck with a mama bear. The day Maia Stonetree had escaped her clutches, Meri had lost an entire squadron of Ultiori mercenaries to get that baby back. Vrishti had lashed out exactly as fiercely as Maia had to protect a baby that wasn't even hers. In a way, Meri supposed she had to thank the ursa; she'd never have discovered the extent of the blood link she had with the human race otherwise. But she'd lost the child in the process and had to find her, if she were to succeed.

She stretched the very limits of her consciousness, drawing on the power at her disposal to find that flow of time within the blood of humanity. All living creatures had a miniature River within them; all she needed to do was tap into it to manipulate the flow for her own purposes.

Once within the flow, it took only a moment of practiced observation to find the anomaly, a bubble at the very edge that glowed with the power of the Source that sustained it. When she used her sight to peer inside, a wild rage consumed her. Neph and Aodh had escaped with the pregnant Vrishti and were now blood melded. The bubble they were inside now wasn't just powered by Neph alone—it was reinforced by immortal dragon power and the magic of the Summer Spirit. She railed at it with all her own considerable power, beating as hard as she could, but barely causing more than a flicker in its strength.

Something happened inside with that flicker, though. Vrishti's pregnant belly grew bigger until the baby insisted on being born.

Meri stilled and watched, focusing sharply on the child, reaching out with her mind for the link she had lost. That child meant everything. If she could just get her away from diligent parents who had claimed her…

She pressed at the barrier once more, with slow, deliberate care this time. With an effort of will that could have torn down mountains, she exerted herself. It took all she had, but the barrier finally flickered again, if only for a moment. In that time, the child grew. That feedback Meri caused in the temporal bubble had flowed straight into the child, making her age.

If she could just break through, the child would be hers, but aging her would serve a purpose too. It would do her no good if she could reach her own link with the child and finally transfer her soul to the baby's vessel if the baby was too small to care for herself. This would take time, and if this bubble was any indication, time was exactly what it was designed to provide.

CHAPTER 7

ZORION

It felt strange for Zorion to walk the halls of the temple his own race had once slept within, and to sense the power of the creatures he called kin, but who he had never known. Somewhere within these halls, his own parents waited. Would they greet him with fear and revulsion, or something else? Would they be as accepting of both his aspects as his beloved Neela was?

He caught Zil's glance and met his darker half's ebony gaze. Zil's brow was creased, his lips pressed tight with the same dread Zorion felt.

Ahead of them, Asha practically dragged Naaz along by the hand, bouncing with eager enthusiasm. She glanced back and gave Zorion and exasperated look. "Come *on*, you two!" she called before running ahead. Naaz gave them an apologetic shrug before tearing off after her down the spiral staircase that seemed to have no end.

Neela pulled up short, tugging on his and Zil's hands. She looked up at them both with eyes of glowing embers. She still radiated heat, but with practice, had learned to keep her raw phoenix power tamped down to a comfortable temperature, though they'd learned that only clothing conjured from Zorion or Asha's breath could withstand being against her skin for any length of time. They'd arrived dressed like soldiers, because Neela and Naaz both insisted that was what would be expected of them.

"They will love you both," she said with certainty. "I promise."

He shared a dubious look with his darker half. "If you say so. We'll believe it when it happens," Zorion said, and reluctantly followed when Neela began walking down the stairs again.

He could feel them as he drew closer. There were thousands of dragons in residence, and he was acutely aware of them all around him, but even more aware of the pair of powerful minds that had joined eons ago to create him. He didn't dare reach out; they seemed just as reserved as he was. He almost wished for Zil's relative isolation—without the power of fire running through his veins, Zil lacked the same mental link to their origins and could remain comfortably oblivious.

They finally reached the bottom and found themselves in a huge foyer in front of a pair of double doors. Smaller doors branched off to either side, the presence of all the resident creatures buzzing beyond, but within the room beyond the bigger doors, Zorion only sensed five heartbeats.

Asha and Naaz waited by the doors expectantly. "We should go in together, brothers. The three of us."

"You ready?" Naaz asked. Neela moved to her brother's side, each of them grabbing hold of one of the big door handles.

Asha took Neela's place between Zorion and his darker half and reached for each of their hands. She gave Zorion an excited look, then bestowed a matching one upon his other half.

"Reunion time," Asha said, the subdued tone the only thing betraying her own nerves.

Neela shot him an encouraging smile before she and her brother pushed the big doors open.

Five sets of eyes shot to the door, and the instant Zorion stepped past the threshold, he was aware of the hopeful mood within. Not just hope, though… *desperation* greeted him as palpably as if he'd walked into cold water.

Relief quickly followed, and before he knew it, a strikingly beautiful, dark-haired woman rushed toward their group. She shot her blue gaze to each of their faces, her brows only twitching once when she darted her glance back and forth between him and Zil.

"You're here! Oh, Sweet Mother, finally. My children are here, and safe. Come, my babies, let me hold you!"

Asha didn't hesitate, and instantly released his hand and flew into her mother's arms. Belah held her daughter with one arm, waving at Zorion and Zil with the other. He closed the distance to her and embraced both mother and sister in his big, glowing arms while Zil mirrored him on the other side. He didn't care where this damned temple was, he was home.

After a few moments, Belah slowly extracted herself, though she kept reaching up and touching his face, her eyes wide as she marveled at his appearance. She did the same to Zil and Asha in turn, somehow unable to avoid touching them. She clutched Asha's hand in hers on one side and gripped Zorion's tightly on the other, then turned to face the room.

"My babies have come home," she announced to the four men who waited solemnly by the big table that occupied the center of the huge space.

With only a glance, Zorion knew their souls and that each of them held a measure of uncertainty about him. However, it was most difficult to look at the one man who he knew he would be answering to as a soldier soon enough.

One thing at a time. He faced the big dragon whose dark power was barely held in check. Zil moved up to his side and for the first time, his darker half's presence gave him comfort as they stood facing their father for the first time in their entire lives.

Ked … the Void … was true to his name, and Zorion sensed the depths of a darkness that even he had trouble comprehending. Ked looked between them both, his expression a solemn mask. He was taking their measure, not just as dragons, but also as his own blood.

Zorion and Zil waited, and Zorion sensed the same dark dread in his other half that he felt roiling inside his own gut. Would their father accept them? Zorion couldn't see beyond the emotionless void to know his thoughts. He only knew they shared a darkness that would bind them as closely as their blood.

Just when he was nearly certain Ked was going to curse his existence, two new figures joined the group, slipping up behind the big black dragon to flank him. A petite waif of a woman whose belly was swollen with the first signs of a healthy pregnancy touched Ked's arm gently. "Are you going to introduce us?" she asked in a soft, melodic voice.

On Ked's other side, a russet-haired man as solid and sturdy as Naaz came up and lifted an eyebrow at the big dragon.

The change was minute, but powerful. Ked's gaze softened and he swallowed. Then his mouth spread into a subdued smile.

"Evie. Marcus. I'd like you to meet my … my sons?" He glanced between Zorion and Zil. "I must truly be the luckiest dragon alive."

Before Zorion could react, he found himself hooked

behind the neck by Ked's huge arm and drawn into a half-embrace, with Zil suffering a similar fate beneath Ked's other arm. His father made no sound, but his big chest vibrated with satisfaction. When Ked finally released Zorion and Zil, his eyes were glassy with emotion.

Reunions and introductions continued. The red-haired man Ked had introduced as Marcus eyed both Zorion and Zil carefully. This was the man Neela had said was one of her brother's closest friends—one of the three other Elites who had once served under Nikhil as the commanders of the Ultiori army.

"She's special to us. You take good care of her. Or else."

"Marcus," Neela admonished. "There are two of them *because* they were taking care of me. I'm fine. Better now, thanks to Z." She grinned and lifted a hand, her fingers outstretched. Flames flared from each of her fingertips. "I can fly now too."

Marcus relaxed and gave in to the smile that Zorion had sensed under the stern mask he'd displayed since arriving. "I'm glad you guys are here. More firepower ... literal fire power ..." He glanced at Neela with a smile. "... will go a long way. On that note, I think the boss needs us."

Zorion's veins chilled, the steady glow from beneath his skin dimming at the thought of facing the one man he hadn't yet been introduced to after meeting Evie, Marcus, and Evie's two brothers, Iszak and Lukas. Nikhil and Belah had been preoccupied talking to Naaz and Asha, but now they'd moved to encircle the big table and glanced up when Marcus led the way over.

He supposed he owed his sister's father more respect than he felt capable of offering. In his mind, this was the only other man his mate had ever made love to, and part of him despised Nikhil for that. He met the man's gaze across the table. For a second, Nikhil darted a quick glance to Neela, and then to Zil on her other side before looking at Zorion again and giving him a slight nod.

"We found the child," Nikhil said, holding Zorion's gaze for another second before looking at Neela. "Our child."

Neela let out a gasp, her skin heating to nearly searing. "The baby Meri took? You found her?"

Nikhil nodded. "Calder found her in a tank inside a secret lab within the depths of Meri's base. Unfortunately, we weren't able to get her out before Meri took her, but we know she is now safe, thanks to Neph and his mates."

"Where? Can I go to her?"

"That's the tricky part. Belah's sister is inside the Sanctuary now, and is on the verge of being able to open a portal for us to join them and to finally end this war."

"What can we do?" Zorion asked.

Nikhil waved his hand over the surface of the map, and a quartet of colorful, glowing orbs appeared. He tapped one and it enlarged. "Unfortunately, nothing but wait until we get word from Numa. The Sanctuary and the Haven are on lockdown. No one is getting in or out. And even if we could get into the Sanctuary, the time it would take to reach Numa to help would make no difference.

"Neph and his mates have created a temporal bubble around the entire Rainsong Lodge. Time is moving swifter there, but we still have no idea how great the time displacement is between us and them. It's only been an hour since Aodh let us know they were about to create the bubble. It could be hours longer, or only minutes. We essentially have to be ready at any moment."

"But what about the baby?" Neela asked. The edge of the table blackened and began to glow with molten heat beneath her grip.

Nikhil directed his attention back to her with no hint of

impatience or condescension. He was direct and honest, qualities Zorion found he could admire.

"Meri made the mistake of using a fertile ursa female as an incubator for our daughter. Vrishti is the Summer Spirit's daughter—now the host of the summer spirit herself. She attacked Meri after they made it into the Haven. This is the first good news we've had. Meri's body has been neutralized within the Haven. All we need to do is *get there* and destroy the rest of her army."

Neela tensed, and her temperature rose about a hundred degrees, forcing the human members of their party to flinch and step backward. "She is not neutralized," Neela said in a brittle voice. "She had the power to get to me halfway around the world."

"When was this?" Nikhil asked, leaning against his closed fists on the map. "She entered the Haven at midnight, taking Vrishti and her army with her. The attack happened shortly after. Calder's mother confirmed her body's a broken shell, though her heart still beats. They're keeping her alive to keep her soul tethered. If she dies, they fear it'll release her spirit to head either into another blood-melded host, or straight to the Source, now that she's in the Haven."

"Eight hours ago, I was dead," Neela said. "Meri tried to recapture me and nearly succeeded. You're telling me she lost that child because Vrishti escaped, right? She must have needed me back because she believed I was the only one capable of giving her a viable baby. There is no fucking way she's out of commission and locked inside the Haven. Some-how, she still has Hunters out in the world, controlling them."

"This is bad," Nikhil said. "It means her power is greater than we feared. There's no telling where her spirit will land when we finally kill her, if her armies aren't completely contained. Belah, ask your sister and her mates to come. We need Calder's help."

Within moments, three more figures appeared, and somehow the mood of the entire room lightened. It was as though a ray of sunlight had broken through the clouds when Zorion's golden aunt swept in, two large men on her heels. Nikhil explained the dilemma to them, and the lankier of the two men let out a filthy curse.

"That bad, is it, Calder?" Nikhil said.

"Worse, I'm afraid. If she can reach beyond the Haven to the outside world with her mind, that means she has another power source. It shouldn't be possible without a proper blood meld, but we all know she's not above breaking our laws. We can't discount the possibility that she has another way into the Sanctuary without passing through the Source. We have to warn my uncle."

"The problem is that *we* don't have a way into the Sanctuary. Not the way Aodh and Neph got in. We're a bit light on immortals who could risk the toll the barrier takes."

"What if I told you I have a way to get a message to them within a blink of an eye?" Zorion asked. "Would I be able to lend aid inside?"

Neela squeezed his hand, acknowledging his unspoken ulterior motive. If he could get her to her child first, he would.

Nikhil regarded him for a second before nodding. "Every second matters. If you can get into the Sanctuary without a portal, can you get others in?"

Zorion cast a glance around the room, mentally tallying the multitude of auras within the temple beyond. "Not that many. I can take Neela, her brother, and my sister without issue. If we can help speed things along once inside, we will. We have power of our own to offer."

"Should I waste time asking how you can do this?" Nikhil asked.

"I can't promise it will actually work," Zorion said, "But it got us through the barrier to this place."

Nikhil chuckled and shook his head. "I was afraid to ask, but Belah was too happy to see you all. The barrier is still intact?"

"Like we were never there."

"Then go now. Hopefully we will see you in there soon."

CHAPTER 8

NUMA

uma's rooms at the Rainsong Clan Lodge were not the most luxurious by dragon standards, but they were comfortable. Most ursa preferred to bathe in the numerous swimming holes scattered around the Sanctuary, and while there was running water in the lodge itself, it wasn't heated.

She didn't need hot water, but it would be nice to indulge in a bath while she waited for her first contestant to arrive, so she filled the big tub and heated the water the dragon way … with magic.

She studiously avoided allowing her mind to wander to thoughts of the man who would be arriving soon. He would be her toy for the next twenty-four hours, and it was crucial that she maintain the upper hand for the entire time. Not that she had ever been prone to *swooning*, but if ever there was cause for it, it was in the presence of the very god of ecstasy himself.

She'd been tempted to call Bekim and Theron first, to see how strong their new magic really was. But it had been painfully apparent just from their auras that their earlier display of magic had sapped much of their power. She'd heard of Miteradoros—ursa males who were chosen by the goddess Gaia to be conduits for her power—and she knew that tapping into and controlling that power required practice. Hopefully the next several hours would give them the opportunity to hone their skills so they could prove themselves worthy when their time came to be tested.

Cade and Zephyrus were the mystery. She doubted Zephyrus could match Dionysus' power, but as a Wind immortal, what power he had would perfectly complement Numa's own. How that manifested, she couldn't be sure, but of all the prospects, she admitted to herself they might surprise her the most.

She took her time washing, and when she was finished, she refilled the tub with fresh water and swiftly heated it again with a breath of pure dragon fire, then sank back into it to wait. Putting a lusty god in his place would not be easy, but a part of her knew she would enjoy it.

The warmth in her core broadcast his proximity before he even knocked on her door. It was one sign of the lack of discipline she suspected would be the reason he failed. She didn't need a mate who threw their power around with wild abandon. Focus and control were required for the ritual. Determination and a true understanding of the need for it were a close second. Being able to demonstrate a wealth of raw power was far less important than this god realized.

She waited several beats after the knock sounded before calling out, "Come in!" He would need every reminder that she was the one calling the shots today.

The door opened, then closed, and she imagined him looking around, trying to find her before his footsteps approached. Numa took a deep breath, readying herself for the start, but deliberately remaining as relaxed as possible while she slowly sponged warm water over her naked body.

He paused in the arched opening that separated the bath from the rest of the rooms, his big horns obscured by the lintel. Burgundy eyes regarded her, his dark-fringed lids blinking slowly as he took her in.

"I am ready, but it seems you are not. Shall I return later when you are?"

"Ready is relative, don't you think?" She lowered herself beneath the water and came up again, standing and letting the water sluice off her, surreptitiously watching his aura as she bent to the side of the tub to reach for the cloth and soap. "Come," she said. "And watch your head."

His aura brightened, but there was no other reaction from him. In fact, he looked distinctly displeased by her command, but he glanced up and carefully ducked his head to enter the room. He paused by the tub and crossed his arms, staring at her.

"We are wasting time," he rumbled. "We should do your little ritual and be done with it. Get on with our mating."

Numa narrowed her eyes at the god, realizing he would be a bigger challenge than she expected. "This isn't just some game to me. There's a full-on war taking place in the Haven. The race of creatures *you* are responsible for creating is in danger of extinction at the hands of a mad nymph. Oh, but wait, you are a *god*. Maybe you have a better solution?"

Dionysus' brows dipped and he bared his teeth at her. "Why do you think I'm here, little one? Until you found this ritual, I was doomed to watch while my children were torn apart by mind-controlled madmen. I am a fucking *god*, yet my power is useless without the right vehicle to deliver it. Your sweet cunt is that delivery mechanism."

Numa snorted. "So you don't *actually* want a daughter of Fate, do you? Well, lucky for you, I'm not in this for love, either."

"Does that mean you agree?" His tension hadn't eased a

bit, and it still came through in his words.

"No."

Dionysus scowled, his irritation overwhelming the waves of lust he'd emanated when he came in. He wasn't a difficult man to read—if his face hadn't clearly betrayed his displeasure, his aura would have.

"I have enough power to take down the entire fucking barrier."

"Yet the only tool you have is between your thighs, and there are only two things a cock is good for." She let out a sigh and held the soap and wash cloth out toward him. "Wash me, and I'll explain."

"You look clean," he said, pouting at her.

Numa sighed again. Mother preserve her from petulant gods. "Humor me. You may learn something."

He dropped his hands and strode toward her, stopping at the edge of the tub to prop one foot on it and unfasten the leather thongs that wound around his calves, securing his sandals to his feet. The thick golden rings around his cock shimmered in the sunlight and Numa's core heated at the mere sight. Her palms itched to touch this glorious specimen of a male, even though he'd gotten on her last nerve already. With any luck, after six hours with her, he'd sing a different tune.

Once he'd shed his sandals, he gracefully stepped into the tub, his immense size completely dwarfing it. Numa's pulse raced as she peered up his thick chest, craning her neck to meet his eyes again. The irritation in his gaze had disappeared, replaced by amusement.

"You seem rather intent on having my hands on you. Shall I?" He gently removed the soap and cloth from her grasp and proceeded to lather her up while still holding her gaze.

Almost twice her size, his big hands completely encompassed her shoulders as he slid his soapy palms over her skin.

Every nerve lit up under his touch, and Numa had to force herself to focus on his face. Somehow it had become more of a game than she'd intended, with the pair of them staring each other down, almost daring the other to falter.

"You had something important to explain to me, did you not?" he asked, the deep rumble of his voice causing her to inadvertently heat the water they stood in. The discharge of her power helped a bit, but the ache between her thighs didn't subside.

"Yes … the ritual. We will only have one shot at it. If we fail, the barrier really *will* be destroyed. It isn't just a matter of throwing *enough* power at it, but ensuring that power is focused. I need a mate who is disciplined…"

She paused. His gaze had dropped to her breasts, which he was slowly encircling with each hand, coating the round globes in thick suds. It felt amazing, especially when his fingertips brushed over her hard nipples. He hefted both and squeezed, his head tilting to one side. A half-smile played at his lips.

"Dionysus!"

"Hmm?"

Numa sighed. "Are you listening to me?"

"Mm …" He nodded. "Something about you needing to be disciplined. I'm not above a good spanking, if that's what gets you going. Just bend over, little one, and I'll take care of that backside for you." He easily slipped one hand down and grabbed her ass.

Gritting her teeth, Numa reached back and forcefully extracted his hand from her ass. She was normally a patient woman, but he was testing her limits. Not to mention the limits of her desire, because he'd grown fully hard while soaping her up, and his erection was every bit as long and thick as a full-sized dragon. The golden rings adorning his shaft just made it all the more beautiful to behold.

Good girl that she'd been her entire life, she'd yet to experience sex with one of her own kind, much less any of the other races capable of sporting cocks that big. Human men could be well-endowed—and she'd entertained herself with many who were—but they all paled in comparison to Dionysus' impressive shaft.

She snatched the soap from his hand. "I think it's your turn now. Hands down. No touching."

He gave her a playful frown. "Aw, maybe the rumors were true after all. I didn't believe there could be such a thing as a prudish dragon, yet here you are."

Numa huffed and lathed up her hands. "You've entirely missed the point. If you'd listen to me, you'd understand. Focus. Look into my eyes, Dionysus."

She pressed soapy hands to his chest and slid them around in circles, marveling at the hard solidity of him. Looking was out of the question, though. She *had* to keep him on task, and that meant she couldn't let her own impulses get the better of her.

To his credit, he held still and remained focused on her while she worked her soapy hands up and down his big torso. "As I was saying, discipline is required. And by that, I mean a disciplined *mind* capable of controlling all that power so we can use it how we need to. I also need someone capable of building up enough power to supplement mine. A full day's worth of energy from each of us."

"I merely have what I have," he said, frowning at her. "It's all yours, however you choose to use it."

"The ritual is not a solo endeavor. You *need* to know how to direct your power. It's easy for you, isn't it? To just walk through a room and draw playmates to you with your aura like a magnet. It's effortless. It's like this for Red dragons, but they do at least understand how to use their breath for other things. Have you ever used your power for something other than seduction?"

She slid her hands lower, the sides of her wrists grazing his rigid cock. He blinked, but otherwise didn't react to the accidental touch. At least he'd grasped her need to remain focused and was making a concerted effort now.

"Never needed to," he said, his jaw clenching when she slipped one hand between his thighs and cupped his balls. They filled her palm and then some, two heavy, warm globes contained in a sack of velvet.

"The first test is finding out how long you can hold out. These…" She slid fingertips around the golden ring at the base of his cock. "Will get in the way."

With soapy hands, she gripped the first ring and tugged. It came free and she slowly slid it along his shaft, enjoying the way his shoulders tensed as she took her time removing it. When she reached his tip, she caught the second ring along with the first and they clinked together. It took one more tug and they were both free. Dionysus let out an involuntary grunt when she released him.

"I'll hold onto these for you," she said, pushing each hand through one of the rings. They fit snugly around her forearms and remained.

His aura had flared wildly and was now a vibrant, pulsing red on the verge of bursting. She could almost taste the raw power that it held, but needed to push his limits as far as possible for this day to be a success.

"Sit and relax," she said, gesturing to the contoured seat beneath the water behind him.

"What demented, useless test are you giving me now?" he asked, but he obeyed, turning and sloshing down into the bath. He rested his forearms on his knees and slid a little farther into the tub until the water covered his navel. The thick head of his cock still peeked out from the surface.

"Now, we talk," Numa said, crouching down into the water and crawling toward him. The bath covered her almost entirely, but she knew her shoulders and backside were visible, if not from the air filtering across, then from the way his gaze flicked over her with interest. He moved his legs apart and shifted his hands to grant her passage between his thighs. His lips parted, and heat flared in his gaze when her face came within an inch of his cock.

His musky scent was intoxicating, and she indulged herself with a slight brush of her lips across the crown, darting her tongue out for the tiniest taste of the divine precum that had leaked from the tip. The droplet left her tongue awash in tingles, and her vision blurred for a second. She shook her head and blinked to clear it. She had best take care for the rest of her time with him, if she wanted to last the full six hours.

"Do you hate me?" he growled.

"I barely know you," she said, turning between his thighs. She settled back against his chest, carefully positioning so that his erection was aligned with the very center of her back. It wasn't the most comfortable position, but her comfort wasn't as important as ensuring he was reminded of his arousal while they talked.

"You definitely don't like me very much. If you liked me even a little, I'd be inside you now."

"Is that how it usually works with women? You show up, and if she has even a passing interest, you fuck?"

"Pretty much that, yes."

"There are better ways to get to know a girl. Have you ever loved one?"

He swallowed audibly, the sound causing her to inspect his aura once more. His arousal hadn't ebbed, but there was a darker halo to it now that spoke of old wounds. Was there indeed more to this arrogant god than his libido? She'd heard of a few of his lovers, but had never gotten the impression they meant much to him.

Her hands were resting lightly on his knees and he covered one with his own, threading his fingers between hers. He squeezed slightly and then let out a breath.

Numa twisted her torso to look up at him, frowning at the strange display of affection. "You did, didn't you?"

"Yes."

He said nothing more, but from the look in his eyes, she could tell there were endless emotions buried back there that he'd likely never once shared.

"Tell me," she said softly.

He gave her a wary look. "Part of the test?"

"If it needs to be. Buried emotions can block your energy, Dionysus. If you want to be my mate, you need to let go of these things. I need you at full power."

"Call me Dion, please, Numa."

"As you wish." She smiled and lifted her brows expectantly.

Dion's shoulders fell, and he gently urged her to turn and face away again. She complied, settling against his chest once more. His cock had gone flaccid between them, which wasn't a bad thing. Rousing his lust and letting it fade several times in succession would stretch his limits.

He didn't speak immediately, but began tracing small whorls along her forearm with a wet finger, ending at the golden band that encircled below her elbow and trailing back down again. Finally, he took another breath and began his story.

I AM YOUNG, by god standards. Older than dragons, but not by much, really. Pleasure wasn't recognized as a power until

Fate realized it needed a mechanism to control the rest of us. Whether I was born to fill that need or not, I don't know— only that I instantly had a use once I existed. It was my power that aided the creation of the four higher races, one of which was spawned from my very own seed.

You already know that Fate had a hand in the creation of all the higher races. The day Fate came to me with the offer of creating a race of my own, I was lost. I had no purpose beyond fornicating with whatever beasts walked the earth. The humans were the most interesting, but so easily influenced they lost their allure if I spent too long with them.

I was … entranced. Beautiful doesn't begin to describe the aspect of Fate who came to me that day. She appeared as a naked and luscious woman emanating fertile power, much like you do now. She spoke to me of a world filled with creatures who would be my playthings, if I would only share her bed but once.

The night lasted a hundred human years, and by the end of it, I knew I would never want any of these so-called playthings that my power contributed to creating. I only wanted her.

My desire for her stayed strong until she birthed the twins, Nyx and Neph. And even after they were born, I still wanted no one but her. I couldn't find desire for the offspring, of course … they were my blood. She told me they weren't the only ones, only the first … the Dionarchs. And if I would just be patient, there would be others worth my attention.

But I didn't *want* any other. I told her this, but she was done with me. She left, and all I had were my children, who I taught the only thing I knew once they were grown … pleasure. And I warned them never to mate with those such as me because gods weren't to be trusted. They understood and made it their law to only mate with their own kind or with humans, since humanity was plentiful, easy to seduce, and wasn't tainted by Fate.

Then I learned Fate had done the same with the Mother Dragon, appearing to her as a virile male dragon, impregnating her and giving her not two, but *six* children. Still, she was no luckier than I was. Fate never stayed.

Gaia was the third victim, but desired her own race to worship her despite knowing she would be used and thrown away by Fate the same as the rest of us. The nymphaea and the dragons were thriving when the ursa's four seasons were born.

We weren't happy with Fate's treatment of us. The three of us got together and conspired to get even. There was one element Fate hadn't seduced. We found Ouranos before Fate got to him and warned him in advance. He was ready when Fate arrived, once again in the aspect of a beautiful woman. Ouranos overpowered her, took his pleasure, and laughed about it afterward. Even though Fate got what she wanted, she cursed the turul race to be lost and lonely until they found their true mates, which she predetermined for them at their birth.

But we had had our revenge, and during our victory celebration, the Mother Dragon, Gaia, and I became lovers, producing a daughter who would be immune to the hand of Fate. You know her as the Diviner, who is the only creature in existence truly outside of Fate's grasp, but who can see Fate's plan for those creatures brave enough to ask her. Not even the other gods can make that claim.

Fate doesn't always have a plan, as it turns out. You are evidence of that, otherwise you'd have never been given this choice. My hope is that mating you will allow me to exert my power within the Haven, to preserve our creations in spite of Fate's influence. And that maybe a bit of the choice you were granted will rub off on me.

CHAPTER 9

NUMA

Numa remained silent for several moments after Dion finished his story, unsure what it all meant. She knew of the origins of the higher races, but it had never occurred to her how manipulative Fate had been in their creation.

She took a deep breath and carefully chose her words. "Am I a way for you to get even with Fate?"

"The thought did cross my mind when word came that you were available. But our desires are too well aligned for me to discount the offer of an alliance. We've all been made fools of in some way … either by Fate's meddling or by its neglect. We have to do something. Winning this war is only one step."

She turned to look at him. "What makes you so sure you're not being manipulated now? Sophia North has a direct line to Fate. She knew this contest had to happen."

"She had no choice. The turul are cursed to be Fate's puppets. But the dragons have the power to subvert that control. Sophia's been scheming to break the curse, and getting her own grandchildren bound to mates Fate *didn't* choose is part of it."

"My sister dreamed of Lukas and Iszak … Fate sent my siblings all their dreams. What makes you so sure…?"

"Because I'm a god, little one, and as long as you stick close, I can protect you and those you love."

"I don't know if my brothers and sisters would agree that it's a bad thing. They'd probably never have left the Glade, if they weren't compelled to go searching for their mates."

He cupped her face and gave her a serious stare. "Numa, if not for Fate, you'd have never had a reason to *be* there in the first place. Your brother would have never fallen in love with my son. The creature we are preparing to fight would have never had a taste of immortality. She'd have been a happy consort of a Dionarch, bearing his babies and living the hedonistic life of a nymph in the Haven."

"We'd have never been forced to protect our children at all costs …" Numa added.

"Unfortunately, there is no way to break free from Fate's grasp. The best we can do is subvert that hold in whatever way we can. My presence here is my best attempt at that."

"Whether this is Fate's plan or not, it doesn't change what we need to do here. The ritual has to happen if we're going to have a chance to beat Meri's army."

"And I will do whatever you wish to help make that happen. If it isn't me, so be it, but there are other ways I can contribute, even if it's just to spur things on." He leaned forward and cupped her cheek again, and Numa gravitated toward him, leaning sideways between his thighs. She tilted her head back as he lowered his mouth to hers, the steam from the bath gathering like dew on his upper lip. She opened for him, savoring his lips and the liquid coating, realizing too late that it wasn't water that coated him, but whatever honey-flavored magic he exuded from his pores. One taste of his mouth, and her desire soared.

She pulled away with a start. "Sweet Mother, that's not what I expected."

He grinned at her. "What isn't?"

"Your kisses are literally intoxicating. Whatever that is, I need you to save it for next time. The next few hours are about testing *your* limits, not mine."

Dion leaned back and sighed. "Ah, spoil my fun. Fine, then. What do you need me to do? My offer still stands for the spanking."

"Next time," she said. "But perhaps *you* wouldn't mind bending over for me?"

"I don't *bend over* for anyone."

"In the interest of teaching Fate a lesson, maybe you will?"

He studied her solemnly for a moment before surging up out of the water and climbing out of the tub. He was halfway back to the bedroom before she heard him call out. "You win! But whatever you do to me, I get to do twice as hard to you *next time*."

Grinning, she hopped out of the bath and followed him, quickly wrapping a robe around herself on the way. Dion didn't bother drying off, and his big, muscular body glistened in the sunlight that streamed through her big windows. He climbed onto the wooden bed and reclined against the pile of pillows. The white of the linens stood out starkly in contrast to his deep bronze skin, and the dampness that bled out from his body made it appear as though he floated above the sheets.

His cock was fully hard again, and Numa nearly stopped just to admire it. There would be enough time for that later.

"Turn over," she said, hating the fact that what she intended to do would obscure that majestic appendage from her view for a little while.

"Nothing that happens in this room makes it out of here, you got it?" he said, narrowing his eyes at her before slowly rolling onto his belly.

Numa took a deep breath as though admiring the most glorious vista she'd ever seen from the sky. Yes, he was most certainly a god. And he was most certainly submitting to her whims for the next several hours.

She removed her robe and ensured her hair was secured tightly with the pair of sticks she used to bind it. Then she climbed up onto the bed beside him and gently patted his backside with one hand.

Dion turned his head and gave her a quizzical look. "Is that what you call a spanking?"

She shrugged and dropped her hand back down to his ass again, rubbing in a slow circle. "It's not the pain I'm after. Would it arouse you if I smacked you harder?"

She pulled back her hand and gave him a hard smack that made him jump and flinch.

"Fuck! Ah, no … that doesn't really do it for me. Whatever you were thinking when you came over here … it made your scent stronger. Do that. Smelling you get turned on turns me on."

"Are you sure? You might not like what I was actually thinking."

"You're the good girl, Numa. You don't even like spanking, so how shocking can it be?"

She pressed her lips together to hold back her smile. Zephyrus likely had a better idea of what she secretly enjoyed after spying on her moments of solitude when they were younger. She also doubted any of the ursa had any compunctions against it, either.

An overly masculine god like Dionysus, however, probably was not nearly as open-minded as he liked to think he was.

She straddled his lower back and bent down, brushing her lips over the top of his ear. "I'll give you one more chance to take that back, Dion, my dear. Because taking you to the edge is the goal here, don't forget that. Pushing that limit until it almost breaks is my intention. Have you tested *all* your limits?"

"I got fucked by Fate. Whatever you do can't be as humiliating."

"Perhaps, but a figurative reaming by a manipulative female aspect isn't the same as literally being fucked by a woman." She extended her dragon tongue and traced the outer edge of his ear with it, then teased the line of his jaw before sliding down his back, her hard nipples rubbing as she went. As she made her way down, her entire body lifted and fell with the force of his heavy breaths. His aura was tinged with fear along with desire now, and while she couldn't see his cock, she was absolutely certain he was still as hard as a rock.

She tickled his spine with her tongue all the way down, deliberately slowing as her breasts grazed the mounds of his ass. She paused when her knees slipped between his and gripped both cheeks in her hands, spreading him open.

"You can breathe, Dion," she purred. "This isn't going to hurt."

His tight anus clenched even tighter, his cheeks marble beneath her hands. "It's my pride I'm concerned about, not my ass so much."

Numa laughed and released her hold. "We'll work up to that, then. Spread your legs a bit more for me." She pressed her palms to both his inner thighs and pushed. He spread his legs wide—much wider than she needed him to—and tilted his hips as though adjusting his position.

"You can't be enjoying that view," he commented over his shoulder.

Numa quirked her mouth and tilted her head, raking her gaze up his backside to his shoulders and back down. "You are every bit the god from any angle. When you're tormenting *me* later, maybe you'll indulge me by doing it from your knees."

Dion groaned and looked over his shoulder again. "You are enjoying this way too much for my comfort."

"Shhh... I know what I'm doing, and I'd really rather not tie you up. If you tried to break free, you'd just damage the bed, and I need the bed to last for the next two days."

She patted his backside again and slipped her hand down between his spread thighs to caress the underside of his balls with the backs of her fingers. He let out another harsh groan into the pillows and kept his face buried, but reached up to grab hold of the carved wooden rods that lined the head-board like a row of sturdy tree trunks, branching out to carved leaves at the top.

His aura flared bright red, as intense as it had been earlier when she'd removed his rings, but this time he had more endurance to spare, so she pushed a little further. Reaching beneath him from behind, she found the base of his cock and stroked upward. He accommodated her by lifting his hips until he was up on elbows and knees, his heavy sack hanging in front of her face. Numa darted her tongue out and tickled both orbs until slick fluid seeped from the head of his cock. She stroked him again, teasing his balls over and over, until her hand was coated in his pre-cum and the scent of honeyed wine filled the air. She craved a taste of him, but would have to avoid it—she had a feeling if she swallowed his seed, she'd be left drunk and under his spell, and she didn't have time for that kind of a diversion.

Fingers slick with his essence, she teased along his perineum, sliding her thumb up and down. How long would he last this time before his aura warned her of his limits?

Dion instantly clenched, and Numa didn't force her thumb past his opening. She only rubbed in a slow circle while she bent her head and opened her mouth to suck one of his heavy balls in and lave it with her tongue. He let out a long groan when she continued for several seconds, continuously swirling her thumb around his anus while sucking on one testicle. She paused long enough to take in his aura. He could stand a little more of a push.

With her free hand, she reached between his thighs and grasped his cock, gently stroking it with no more pressure than a caress and gathering more fluid on her fingers from his tip.

She transferred the fresh collection of slick fluid to his anus, giving the tightly clenched pucker a little push. "You will open up for me before the day is done."

"I'm happy holding onto my pride for as long as I can," he said. "I just have one question…"

"What is it?" she asked, brushing her lips over the soft skin of his ass and resting her cheek on the warm mound while she idly observed her thumb still moving in tight circles around his stubborn opening.

"Will I be allowed to come today?"

"I want you functional if I choose you, so yes. But not for several hours yet."

"Will I get to come inside you?" he asked, his voice even gruffer than before.

Her core clenched and a rush of heat flooded her body at the very suggestion. Dion turned his head and lifted an eyebrow at her.

"I…"

"You want it so much you're driven to distraction. It's all right, Numa. It *will* be as glorious as you think."

"It isn't a good idea. Not today. I need to remain coherent

for the other tests. Having your essence inside me will make that impossible."

He gave her a heated look filled with promise. "It is heaven to become delirious from my gifts, little one."

"It is also deadly to be chosen by you. I have heard the stories of what befalls your mates."

"None of my former mates were daughters of Fate," he growled and faced the head of the bed again. "Just get on with your torture, then."

Numa's mouth watered at the thought of what she'd like to do most, but after their first kiss, knew she had to tread carefully when it came to tasting him. Every pore exuded power as heady as a drug, stronger than even her brother Gavra's red dragon breath. Whether she liked it or not, she'd inadvertently put herself to the test today by inviting him in.

His cock kicked in her hand and Dion let out a low, rumbling moan. His panting breaths quickened and he turned to her with fevered eyes. "Please," he said, and his agonized look betrayed how difficult it was for him to beg.

Numa released his cock and shifted back between his thighs, placing her hands on either cheek and grazing thumbs up and down between them. She pursed her lips into an "O" and blew. Green smoke billowed out into a dense cloud and with her mind she commanded a measure of it to coil around Dion's head.

"Breathe," she said.

He inhaled a long breath, and bit by bit began to relax. His aura flared with renewed energy, the sedating effect of her breath having melted away some of the few inhibitions this god of the rut possessed. With the rest of her smoke, she mentally crafted a long, slender shape that solidified and fell heavy into her palm. It was about the length of her hand and half the thickness of her wrist at its widest point, tapering into a rounded tip. She slid it between her thighs and into her slickness, coating the cool, smooth object generously with her own juices.

Dion's ass had relaxed along with the rest of his body, but he dutifully kept it poised in the air. She grazed her thumb over his opening once more, letting her touch trail down until she cupped his balls again. He was truly a joy to molest this way. If she *did* choose him, she hoped he would allow her to play with him again after the war was won. She'd happily indulge in his every whim and let herself get drunk on all the considerable intoxicants that ran in his blood, but for now, he had to pass her test, and this was only one small part.

"Relax, Dion," she said, delicately caressing along the underside of his shaft and back down to his balls until he dropped his hands from their stranglehold on the headboard and simply clutched a pillow under his cheek.

She pressed the tip of her conjured toy to his opening and eased it in, her own lubricating fluid letting the very end slip past his barrier without much effort. Dion panted, his aura fluttering wildly between desire and fear.

"You surprise me," she said, pausing with only the tip barely breaching his opening.

"What surprises you?" he growled.

"That this is not an avenue you've tested. You spawned an entire race of creatures who will do *anything* if it gives them pleasure. This will give you pleasure, if you let it."

"What makes you think I haven't?" he asked, his voice half-muffled by the pillow.

"Your aura tells me this terrifies you."

He let out a low chuckle. "Oh, Numa, this is nothing new to me. It's only the first time a female as lovely as you has been party to the adventure. The last time I had a dildo in my ass, I was the one who put it there, and there was no one to witness but a silent grave. It's different submitting to someone else. Like I said..."

"I know. Your pride. Would it help if I let you do it yourself?"

"Mmm, I find I am rather enjoying the fact that it is you, but I do wish you would speed things up. Fuck my ass with your toy, Numa. Stop equivocating to try to preserve my precious pride."

He affected a domineering tone when he spoke the words and a shiver coursed through his body at the same time. Numa's own body warmed in response.

"Yes. Again."

He looked over his shoulder, his dark eyes flashing with lust. "Do it. Fuck me. I command it."

"Yes, sir," she said, shooting him a delighted smile. She slowly pushed the toy into him and began to plunge it in and out, keeping her gaze fixed on his face and the steadily brightening glow of his powerful aura.

Dion's spine arched and his head flew back, shining black curls splaying over his golden shoulders. A deep, thunderous groan erupted from his throat. "Fuck, that is *good*."

"It will get better," she said, sliding it in one last time until the flared base was the only part visible. She stopped and moved around to his side. "On your back now."

He gave her a confused look, reaching back with one hand. She grabbed his wrist. "Leave it. It's conjured so will fade on my command, but until it does, consider it a part of you."

Dion slowly turned over, delicately resting his rump on the covers and stretching out as she'd asked. He winced and shifted.

"Does it hurt?" she asked.

"No... I just feel *full* and it rubs in a way that makes me need to come. I didn't leave the thing in when I fucked myself. I just took care of business and went on with my life."

"You will be able to come soon enough." She moved to

straddle his waist and settled with her backside on his hips, his heavy erection brushing hot against her back.

"What next, more torture?" he asked.

"No. Now we give you a breather. We rest."

She lowered herself to his chest, carefully positioning her backside so that his cock lay along the cleft of her ass and her slick, hot core pressed against his pelvis. The slight friction of the movement sent a brief thrill through her body she knew he'd notice.

"If I could see your aura, would it show me the same thing you see in mine?" he asked, his warm breath brushing the crown of her head. He lowered both big hands to her back and rubbed slow caresses all the way down until he held both her ass cheeks in his hands. He spread her wider and tilted his hips up, deliberately pressing his cock tighter to her channel.

"Not quite," she said. "Your limits are lower than mine."

"I could overpower you now. Fill you with my cock until your sweet little cunt overflowed with my seed. I've always wondered what kind of immortal god-child you and I would make."

"You mean you and a dragon," she said, certain he didn't mean her specifically

He stilled and then shook his head. Numa turned her head to face him, resting her chin on his sternum.

"You, little one. There's always something about the good girls that makes men like me hunger for a taste of you. Neither of your sisters had the same allure."

"I'm not a 'good girl.' I'm a dragon," she said with a glare.

Dion's chest rumbled with a deep laugh. "I know this now. You are as wicked as they come."

His laugh faded and his expression sobered. The luscious bow of his mouth parted slightly as his gaze heated. He lifted a hand to cup her cheek and craned his neck to capture her mouth with his.

Numa's breath stopped with that kiss, more hungry and desperate than the first one they'd shared, and ten times as intoxicating. His tongue delved deep, demanding her reciprocation, and she gave it, shifting up to hover over him and kiss him even harder while he pressed back into the pillows.

Dion groaned into her mouth and pushed back against her, clutching at her hips. With an easy, graceful twist, he had her on her back with his hips pressing hard against hers. He pulled back from the kiss and gazed down at her.

"It would be so easy to take you now, little one. Once I was inside you, you wouldn't even object to it."

Numa forced herself to inhale. "You know what's at stake, Dion."

He shifted his hips back, dragging his erection along her soaked core. His gaze grew heavy-lidded as he teased her like that, and Numa's control wavered. Sweet Mother, she did want that glorious beast of a cock inside her. If he took her, could she stop him soon enough? Was her self-control as strong as she believed?

"Yes. I know. That's why I'm not going to fuck you … not yet." He gave her one more lingering kiss before moving lower, trailing a very talented tongue down the center of her chest and pausing to tease and suck her nipples until they ached.

"What are you doing?" she asked when he continued lower.

"Driving myself mad," he rumbled. "But there's no sense in both of us suffering today, is there? I'll have time to torture you in return before you choose."

"True…" she said, then gasped when his mouth covered her swollen pussy and he sank his thick tongue deep into her channel.

Numa moaned at the tortuous way he devoured her, suckling at her clit for several moments before returning to fuck his tongue into her. He pushed her thighs up and spread them wide, then trailed down lower to tease at her rear opening.

She shoved her fingers into his thick black curls and cried out, "Yes!" when he penetrated her backside with his tongue.

Dion laughed. "How did I guess you would love that? I had you all wrong. Numa. You are even more perfectly filthy than I imagined."

"Please," she said when he paused to give her a long, adoring look, still idly teasing her pussy and ass with his fingertips.

"How much time do we still have?" he asked. "I can't gauge by the light."

Shaking her head to try to focus she said, "The temporal bubble was put into place at dawn. The clock beside the fireplace is still synchronized to the outside world, so it will mark about ten minutes for every hour that passes in here. We have roughly five hours left."

He followed her gaze to the clock in question, which at the moment read ten past eight in the morning, though her internal clock insisted it was well past noon.

"Good. Then I plan to spend at least four of those testing another limit of yours."

"No … it isn't time for that."

"Little one, you misunderstand. I'm not interested in torture the way you are. Pleasure is my game. I aim to learn how many times I can make you come in the next four hours. After that, you can finish what you need to do with me. And if you're worried that your own test is being derailed, you tell me … How much power is trapped in my aura now compared to when I arrived?"

She nearly lost her focus on him when he pushed two

fingers deep into her pussy and began to fuck her with them. When her vision cleared, she saw his point. Every time he touched her, his aura flared bright, seemingly on the cusp of a true climax, yet he didn't lose control.

"You do this to me, Numa. Never has it been so worth it to hold back, but I want you, and if this is what it takes to have you, I will restrain my need. That doesn't mean I can't indulge in your pleasure until you beg me to stop."

He buried his face between her thighs again, and she writhed under the sweeping strokes of his tongue. True to his word, he had her at the edge and hurtling over within moments. She went, crying out his name at the same time as she despaired that the others never had a chance.

THE SCENT of food roused Numa some time later and she opened her eyes, acutely aware of the warmth of the big body wrapped around her. Dion's hand rested on her hip, his fingers tracing little circles on her skin. She groggily twisted in his arms and looked up at him.

"I must have fallen asleep," she said.

"You did. For about an hour, in fact."

"I'm sorry."

He chuckled. "No, you aren't. Perhaps it wasn't part of your plan, but you most certainly intended to leave me in this state for as long as possible. I think if I were a human man, I'd have died from lust by now."

"Are you hungry?" she asked, darting a glance to the huge tray of food that must have been delivered only moments ago. Aromatic steam drifted up from a platter of roasted meat surrounded by a cornucopia of fruits, vegetables, and treats, as well as a giant jug of wine. It was a feast fit for a god.

"I've already eaten, in case you forgot. I hope having *your* essence all over me doesn't skew the other tests. I had no idea dragons were capable of so many consecutive orgasms."

She inspected his aura, and was more than pleased to see it had deepened in color and grown even more potent. The very sight made her crave a taste the way she might crave a piece of ripe fruit.

Dion narrowed his eyes. "I'm not sure if I like that look. I'm afraid holding you while you slept was the pinnacle of sexual torture for a man like me. If I have to endure more, I probably *will* go as mad as a virgin nymph coming of age."

She pulled away and slipped off the bed, trotting over to the food. "Then it's a good thing your time is nearly up." She peeled a drumstick off the big roasted bird and pointed it at the clock before taking a bite. According to the clock, it was only about ten minutes before nine in the morning, which the light in the room validated, but he'd been true to his word and spent several hours pleasuring her to exhaustion. This meal she devoured was supper for her.

Dion stared at the clock, frowning, then looked back at her. "This is it, then," he said. "What do I do?"

"Nothing. How's your ass feeling?"

He rolled his eyes and collapsed back against the pillows. "My ass is still being tortured. Why do you think I'm not getting up to share that with you? I'm afraid just moving too much will set me off, and the last thing I want to do is disappoint you."

Numa stuffed a couple more bites of food into her mouth and filled a large goblet with the wine. She took a long swallow, refilled it, and sauntered back to the bed.

"Thirsty?" she asked, holding the goblet out to him.

Dion sat up and took it from her, stuck his nose in the goblet, and inhaled. His brows rose and he made an appreciative sound before tilting the glass up and drinking.

While he drank, Numa settled herself between his thighs again and took his cock in both hands. Unable to resist a small indulgence, she bent and swirled her tongue around his tip and sucked it between her lips. He was far too big to do more with, and it took both hands wrapped around him to encompass his girth. He lowered the wineglass to watch while she continued kissing the head of his cock and slowly stroking the full length of his shaft.

His gaze grew molten and he reached down to halt her movements with one hand.

"This should help," he said, and tilted the wineglass over the tip of his cock, letting a small stream trickle out and run down over her hands. "Lick it off, little one."

The sweet, pungent aroma of the wine filled her senses. Numa bent and extended her dragon tongue, flicking it lightly at the underside of his cock, beginning at the trickles of wine that had covered his balls and lapping it up before encircling his shaft and sliding up. She licked him clean, only to have him tip the glass again, spilling more wine over his hot erection.

Once again, she carefully sucked every inch of him clean, and he repeated the process, this time upending the glass and flooding his crotch with what remained.

Numa descended on him, sucking at his balls and stroking his cock with one hand. Dion watched, enraptured as she made full use of her agile tongue to clean his entire length. His chest heaved with pent-up desire, and she bent to take as much of his throbbing tip into her mouth as she could fit, sucking and swirling her tongue along the underside. She reached between his thighs where his ass met the mattress and found the flared end of the toy still buried in his backside. She twisted it once, pulled it partway out, and pushed it back in.

Dion's head flew back and he let out a deafening roar that

shook the entire room. His hands tangled into the blankets and his hips jerked up. Numa gripped him tight with both hands, stroking swiftly as his cock erupted in thick, shining streams of semen. At the same moment, the overwhelming potent power that had built in his aura came bursting forth, flooding Numa with more magic than she'd ever tasted before. Her body shuddered at the intensity of it, nearly sending her into another climax of her own.

Dion's orgasm lasted for several minutes, until finally, his aura dimmed and shrank, and his cock softened in her hands. His eyes fell closed and his entire body went lax.

Numa released him gently, and with a thought, dissolved the conjured toy in his ass.

Leaving him barely conscious on the bed, she wandered into the bathroom for a towel.

"I don't think it should be me," Dion said.

Numa froze and turned back to look at him. "It isn't your decision."

"Perhaps not, but my motives weren't pure when I came. You deserve better. If either of the others can give you enough power, please choose one of them."

She returned to the bed and carefully wiped his belly clean, growing lightheaded from the mere scent of his potent seed.

She kept her lips clenched tight and slipped off the bed again, tossing the towel into a hamper nearby. In a tight voice, she said, "I will choose who is best suited for the task. Your remorse or my desires are not factors. Now, if you don't mind, I need time to get ready for Cade and Zephyrus."

Grabbing the golden bands around each of her arms, she slipped them off one at a time and set them on a table by the door, then opened the door and held it. She avoided looking at him, furious at his sudden change of heart. After all his posturing, had she done something wrong to earn his rejection?

"You are a good girl, Numa. Too good. I will still help, but I don't deserve you as a mate. Today made that crystal clear. Please choose wisely. Whoever he is had better be good enough for you."

He left the bed and strode across the room, pausing at the door beside the table that held his matched pair of golden cock rings glinting in the sunlight. Reaching out, he traced the beveled edge of one. "Keep these. They suit you. And they are more than mere ornaments. They will enhance the stamina of your chosen mate—or mates—if you use them as they are intended. You *will* win this."

Numa swallowed, avoiding his gaze when he fixed it on her once more. "Just go. Tell Cade to come when he is ready." Her heart ached when he nodded and departed. Within an afternoon, he'd turned her entire plan on its head.

Sweet Mother, why couldn't Fate have made this decision for her?

CHAPTER 10

CADE

Waiting was an exercise in endurance for Cade, if there'd ever been one. He'd spent a little time catching up with his friends and falling head over heels for the tiny girl Vrishti had given birth to. Deva was already a precocious toddler, testing her legs and her parents' patience and parroting their every word as they held conversations around her. To think that when he'd arrived, she was only on the verge of even being born.

Once he left the new family to some private time, he wandered the lodge feeling anxious and out of sorts, a mood that wasn't aided one bit by the impatient wind spirit who shared his body. He tormented the kitchen staff, rummaging for snacks, then wandered into the interior gardens seeking whatever peace could be found. He paused at the water's edge and stood looking at his reflection, frowning. It didn't look like him…

"We need a plan," Zephyrus said, startling Cade. Not only was the face looking back not his, but its lips had moved, and Cade knew he hadn't spoken.

"Zeph … That you?" he asked, tilting his head this way

and that, then winking each eye. The face in the pool reflected his movements, but was a very different-looking fellow, one with close-cropped, dark gray hair and a neatly trimmed salt and pepper beard. Handsome fuck. Almost as handsome as Cade himself.

The face smirked. *"You're as cocky as Dion in more ways than one. Yes, it's me."*

Cade settled onto his knees and tapped the pool with his finger. The reflection rippled, but the features only looked wobbly for a moment before returning to the clear, calm reflection of the smiling, mischievous Zephyrus.

"Don't suppose you have a plan, do you? I can match the man in stature, but who knows what he's got up his ass where power's concerned?"

"We may not be able to outmatch his power, but Numa is a dragon ... With my wind, we can drive her fire magic hotter, which feeds more to us. You're no Miteradoro like those two Rainsong boys who have Gaia's power in their pocket. Can you hang onto some dragon juice without feeding it straight to the goddess?"

Cade slipped a hand between his legs, hefting his balls through the fabric of his trousers. "Can give it a shot. These boys haven't had much action in ages. I stayed away from the human women back in Black Mountain. Didn't want to risk one getting attached. It ain't easy for the girls to have a taste without wanting more, if you catch my drift. And the ursa females don't want a sad old single bear like me."

The Wind's voice grew suggestive. *"Are you game for a little ... experimentation? It won't be quite the same as fire magic, but I can pull some of my power into you and see how you manage."* His eyes sparked with the subtle challenge and his lips tugged to one side.

Cade narrowed his eyes, but smiled back. "I'm game for whatever you care to throw at me."

"Good, then strip."

Cade grunted in amusement. "Is that how it is? How 'bout I show you mine and you show me yours?"

A low chuckle sounded inside his head. *"You want to see mine, you pretty much have no choice but to show me yours. Until this is over and Gaia's willing to grant me living flesh of my own again, this reflection's one of the only ways we get to see each other."*

"About that … Why don't you have a body of your own? Not that I mind sharing the wealth Gaia gave me, but all the ursa shamans have a system that's been passed down since the dawn of time to make sure they have a body ready for them. Seems like the turul might have overlooked something."

For the first time, Zephyrus failed to meet Cade's gaze. His cheek twitched and he lifted his hand to rub at his beard. *"It's our choice. My brothers and I like the freedom of the open sky, and wingless bodies only weigh us down to the Earth."*

"I can get on board with that," Cade said with a grin as he tore his shirt over his head and untied the string of his borrowed trousers, letting them drop to his ankles. "Free as the wind is my personal motto, in case you were wondering." He gave Zephyrus a wink and stood close to the water, looking down at the now naked reflection.

It was strange not seeing his own thick thighs and bulky, muscular torso. But despite the distortion of perspective from the angle of the water, the man he saw was impressive. Zephyrus was as tall as Cade, with arms and shoulders easily as wide and thick, but from the waist down he was more slender, with a slim torso made of angular planes of muscles hardened over centuries and long, toned legs.

"You ain't a runner like me, are you?" he commented.

Zephyrus glanced down and laughed. *"No, but I do fly."* He stretched out his arms, flexing his shoulders. *"Birds of prey are usually happy to let the spirit of a Wind possess them. I spend much of my free time soaring inside the body of a falcon."*

"That'd be the life."

"I can make you feel like you're flying," Zephyrus said, his expression growing more serious, his voice gruff. The tone wasn't lost on Cade, and it struck an odd chord inside him … one he hadn't felt in a long, long time.

He cleared his throat, his heart pounding. "Somehow I didn't think we'd have that kind of partnership. Didn't think I'd ever have that kind of partnership again. I don't do halfway, you should know. This … chance we have with Numa is likely the last chance I'll ever have for a mate."

"Even if we fail—which we won't, by the way—it doesn't need to be the end for you. Don't forget I'm inside your head, Cade. I can see what you lost, what it meant to you. What he meant to you. If we can be that to each other, I think it can give us the advantage we need."

Cade tamped down the tightening burn of that old pain. A lover lost, one of countless who had fallen victim to the very enemy his kind were in the final throes of battle with at this very moment. But they'd only been portal guardians, not high-ranking enough for any widespread mourning among the ursa. He had borne the grief in his solitary fashion for so long he'd simply grown used to not having someone to help shoulder that burden.

Through clenched teeth, Cade said, "It ain't that fucking easy."

"Then don't decide now. But do consider the offer and at least let me show you what I can do to improve our odds. The more your desires sync with mine, the better off we'll be."

Forcing himself to take a breath, Cade nodded. His gaze drifted down to the hardening cock between the other man's thighs, the sight causing his own groin to heat and tighten.

"Let's just get one thing straight: I'll bottom for you this once, but if we stay together, your ass is mine."

Zephyrus laughed and rubbed the back of his neck. His gaze slid away, then back, and he eyed Cade's erection. *"We might have to work up to* that," he said, pointing between Cade's thighs. *"If I get a new body, it'll be a virgin."*

"Well, ain't that half the fun? The working up to it? Tell me what to do."

"Get into the water and float on your back."

Cade waded in until the cool water covered his hot erection, then dipped beneath the surface to wet himself thoroughly. When he came back up, he stretched out, spreading his arms wide and staring up into the shimmering blue sky above where the barrier of the temporal bubble blocked them from the outside world.

"Close your eyes," Zephyrus said, his voice a near whisper rasping inside Cade's head. It tickled erotically at the base of his skull, once again reminding him of the intimacy he'd shared with only one other man. He closed his eyes, wishing his heartbeat would slow down.

Wind rustled the trees and plants around him, warm air rushing across his exposed skin. He remained floating, his hair drifting out around his head, waiting for whatever it was Zephyrus had in mind.

"Relax and open your mind to me, Arcadius."

Cade inhaled slowly, letting his mind drift the way it did when he ran, his strong legs carrying his huge bear form to whatever destination he chose. During those runs, he was wild and free, much the way he was on the motorcycle he rode in the human town he had lived in outside the Sanctuary portal.

A cool gust washed over his skin, making his hard cock tingle and his nipples stiffen. Then a whooshing sound filled his ears and the world spun and tilted. For a second, he expected to find himself face down in the water, but breathing was still easy and he relaxed.

"Open your eyes," Zephyrus said.

Cade did as he was told. When his lids fluttered open, he was greeted with a view of the Earth such as he had never seen before. Instead of a blue sky high above the Rainsong gardens half-blocked by tall trees, he saw nothing but open sky with the horizon far ahead. Wind ripped through his hair and across his skin, chilly but crisp and invigorating. He turned his head and spotted mountain ranges in beautiful shades of dark blue-green, softened by the moisture-dense haze he'd grown accustomed to in the Blue Ridge Mountains he'd come to think of as home.

"We ain't really flying, are we?"

"Yes and no. This is in your head. Your body is still floating in the pool, but you can experience it as though it were real. Look at me."

The voice that had previously only reverberated inside his skull seemed to come from a distinct direction now. He turned to see a huge bald eagle, its golden eyes sharply focused on him. The big bird blinked and let out an ear-splitting screech, then banked and dove toward a mountaintop. Cade laughed and followed, his body twisting instinctively as though he'd always known how to fly. He didn't have wings, though, which helped remind him this was only a waking dream of a sort, though it definitely felt real enough.

He followed the eagle down through the valley, skimming across the tops of the trees until the forest opened up to a huge, sun-drenched rock face that overlooked more of the mountainous vistas. The eagle landed, and by the time Cade caught up to him, Zephyrus stood naked on the rock in the bird's place.

Simply knowing what they were about to do had him aroused beyond rational thought. It didn't matter that this was all in his head; when Zephyrus stepped close and looked into his eyes, his entire body ached to close the distance. It had been decades since he'd felt the touch of a lover, and this man may only be a spirit, but if he could camp out inside Cade's mind and still want him, that counted for something.

"I need you as much as you need me," Zephyrus said. "And I don't intend to abuse this partnership. Do you understand how important this is to me?"

"You love her," Cade said. "That part was crystal clear when she walked into the room. I can't say I feel the same yet, but I see why you do."

"By offering us both to her, we will by necessity become hers. When it's done, what we have doesn't need to continue. We can be her mates without a relationship of our own, but I don't want to discount the potential for more. If we can be true partners to start with, we'll be better off for it. I'm sure you understand that as well as anyone could. I just want to make it clear that I am *not* using you."

Cade shrugged. "Even if you were, I'd intended to enjoy it and see where it takes me. I've been alone too long to pass up a chance like this."

"I'm serious," Zephyrus said, closing the distance so their faces were barely an inch apart. He gripped the back of Cade's head with one hand and squeezed. "This partnership was a surprising opportunity for both of us, not just to win Numa, but to find each other. I need you to be sure it is what you want, not only because it happens to be the thing offered and you have nothing to lose by taking, but because you actually want it. You want her. And me."

Cade swallowed, his eyes burning from an unexpected surge of emotion he couldn't quite place. He remembered the wistful sense of longing he'd had after seeing Numa's sister, Aurum, and her mates together. He'd wondered what it would be like to be marked by a dragon, claimed as the mate of a creature so beautiful.

Numa was every bit as beautiful as her golden sister, though she had darker hair and fairer skin. She was somehow both more delicate and stronger at the same time, with a kind of quiet grace that reminded him of trees swaying in the breeze, or ripples across the surface of a lake. She fascinated him in a way no ursa female ever had, and he couldn't deny a draw to her unlike any he'd felt for a woman before.

As for Zephyrus, the wind spirit's desire was already in his head, and that alone made Cade's blood hot to know the other man. Whether something deeper came of it, he wouldn't know unless he tested their connection. He feared wanting more if that wasn't meant to be, but Zeph's speech managed to shatter that illusion. If Cade was indeed the risk-taker he claimed to be, he could let himself want more and not be afraid to own that desire.

Cade let out a soft chuckle and reached up to cup the back of Zephyrus's head in return. "Call me a greedy bastard, but I fucking want it all. Every last bit." He spoke the last syllable with lips brushing against Zeph's, the other man tensing against him. But when Cade closed his mouth over his, the spirit groaned into the kiss and sank into Cade's embrace.

He hadn't realized how much he missed this feeling until he was wrapped inside it once again—to be held by a lover, with the promise of something even more lasting than he could have ever imagined. If they did this right, they could have *her* too, but they would have each other regardless.

Zeph tangled his fingers in Cade's hair, his warm body flush against Cade's chest, their hips pressed together and erections hotly resting side by side. He hated for it to end after so long without, but they had little enough time as it was. Cade finally pulled away, breathing heavily and resting his forehead against Zeph's.

"Tell me what to do."

Zephyrus nodded. He reluctantly stepped back, then slid around Cade to stand at his back, hands resting on his shoulders.

"Keep your eyes on the mountains," Zephyrus said. "Listen to the wind and follow my lead. When I give you my power, focus on holding onto it, and if you must release it, try to give it back to me, though the earth will try to take it from you. Numa will need us to prove we can build enough power without spending it too soon. I don't have the capacity to see what a dragon sees, but you…" He slipped his hand down Cade's belly and between his thighs to cup his balls. "You have your own built-in meter, if you know how to sense it."

Cade relished the sensation of the warm hand gently hefting his testicles. His cock pulsed in response, but he wasn't confident in his ability to hang onto that power for long.

"You said yourself, I'm no Miteradoro. Gaia didn't choose me."

"The sky chooses you, Cade. Just … humor me."

Zeph pressed a kiss to Cade's shoulder and gave his balls a gentle squeeze, then released him. "On your hands and knees," he said, pressing down lightly on his shoulders.

Cade lowered himself to the warm stone and glanced over his shoulder to see the other man follow. "Just getting right down to business, are we?"

Zeph chuckled, his blue eyes flashing with mirth. "You are a magnificent creature, I hope you realize. You honor me by allowing this. Just remember, when I release my magic, you hold onto it. Don't let Gaia have a fucking drop."

"And I take it you're planning to release said magic in my ass?"

Zeph's gaze darkened and he gave Cade's ass a playful squeeze. "My spend is only part of it. You know this. The power will flow through your veins and will want to flow into the earth, but you won't let it. You'll hold it here."

Again, he cupped Cade's balls, but this time he stroked gently, brushing his knuckles along the underside of Cade's cock, then sliding his fingertips back down his length, past his sack, and farther along the root to his perineum.

Cade's body heated with each successive touch, his cock growing harder until he worried he didn't have the staying power he once had in his youth. *Hold on, you can do this.*

Turning back to face the horizon as instructed, he listened to the wind whispering an incoherent rhythm into his ears. Somehow it helped him focus, kept him centered while Zephyrus continued to erotically torture him from behind.

The other man had a thumb pressed to Cade's ass and was rubbing in tight circles. Cade instinctively relaxed—he was no stranger to the pleasure of being well-fucked by another man; it'd just been a really long time. Then the warmth of a breath gusted over that spot and a hot tongue tickled around his opening. He groaned and dug his nails into the stone.

"You don't need to be gentle," he said. "I can take you."

"I wasn't …" Zephyrus paused and laughed. "I have no doubt you can take me. I was just enjoying myself, but you're right, we shouldn't waste time. Hold on."

Zephyrus gripped both of Cade's ass cheeks, spreading him apart. When the hot tip of his cock brushed Cade's opening, Cade took a deep breath and let himself relax, his body and mind both giving in to the surrender required to make the experience as good as he knew it could be.

Zephyrus pushed into him so slowly Cade thought he'd go crazy with the need for more.

"Fuck, you might have to coach me on how to take a cock so easily," Zeph said. "I intend to repay the favor when this is done, but you make it look effortless."

Cade shot an irritated glance over his shoulder. "Just fuck me, will you?"

"Your wish is my command." Zephyrus plunged in hard enough that they both uttered curses from the pleasure. Then he began thrusting in a relentless, even rhythm, each stroke sending pleasure coursing through Cade's entire body, to the top of his head, the tips of his toes, and the throbbing, swollen head of his cock.

Cade's body thrummed with his quickly rising need. He lowered his head and pushed back into Zephyrus's hips, aching to be filled deep every time the other man slid out. The pleasure became almost too great to contain and he grunted, worried he would lose it.

"Eyes open, hear the wind," Zephyrus said, pressing a cool hand at the base of Cade's spine.

The trees rustled around them, and Cade forced himself to focus on the sounds and the sight of these mountains he loved until the pleasure became part of the background. His ecstasy merged with the scenery, and his growing affection for his new partner became part of his love for his home. Gaia, but he wanted to come, and knew that if he did it would be the most mind-blowing orgasm he'd had in ages. But that wasn't what this was about, so he held onto the feeling the way he held onto his memories of spring and cold winter nights and reached between his thighs, past his own aching cock, and cupped Zephyrus's balls in his big hand, cradling them while the other man rammed his cock into him.

Within a few moments, Zephyrus began to grunt louder,

his thrusts growing harder and more violent, his hips smacking against Cade's ass with each plunge into him. Cade reveled in the sensations he had missed for so long—the fingers digging into his hips and the feeling of his lover's orgasm building by increments.

Then Zephyrus rocked into him hard one last time and held him tight, letting out a melodious cry to the heavens as his cock pulsed and hot semen shot into Cade's ass.

This was it. Cade bowed his head and braced himself for the magic that tore through him like a hurricane so hard he nearly came himself. The power raced through his veins just as Zeph had said, reaching for his extremities and seeking a way out and into the earth beneath him. Cade tensed, using all his focus to redirect that power. It was an offense to Gaia to deprive her of it, but under the circumstances, he thought it only fair.

The energy burned inside him at his palms at the soles of his feet, but soon it changed direction and followed his whims. When Zephyrus pulled out of him, he was left empty in one sense, but so much fuller in another. His balls felt like hot lead weights between his thighs, and he sat back on his haunches and looked down.

"You did well," Zephyrus said, moving to kneel in front of Cade. "How do you feel?"

He reached down and gently held his tender sack. They felt no bigger, despite the sensation of being filled to bursting.

"Like I'm about to explode."

"But you kept hold of the power. It gets easier each time. Let's ease some of that pressure and then try again. Next time, I'll give you more."

Cade's eyes widened. "You've got more to give? How?"

"Believe it or not, I held back. That was only about half what I'm capable of. Numa is going to have far more, if we do this right. I want us to be able to take as much as she can give us without spending our own. The fact that you didn't come is good."

"Yeah, well, I can manage that for only so long. It's been a while for me, so this ain't exactly easy."

"It'll be easy by the time we're in her chamber. Now lie back and let me take care of you, then we'll go again."

Cade let out a sigh as he reclined against the smooth, warm rock. He kept his gaze fixed into the cloudless blue sky, but when Zeph wrapped his warm mouth around his cock, he let himself get lost in the pleasure.

CHAPTER 11

CADE

Cade had no idea how much time had passed while he was lost in that floating dream-state with Zephyrus. When he opened his eyes in the Rainsong garden again, the light hadn't changed, but both his cock and ass felt well-used. If nothing else, he'd been given the endurance to last the full six hours with Numa, even if they failed to impress her with their gift of power at the end.

Just as he was about to swim back to the shore and go asking for the time, Dionysus slipped into the garden, looking broody and preoccupied. Cade treaded water, warily eyeing the other man.

"That bad, eh?" he asked.

Dionysus shook his head. "The torture isn't to the body with her. She'll leave you satisfied eventually, but hating yourself for wanting to draw it out. To give her pleasure until she begs you to stop. To *be* with her forever." He crossed the bridge to the center island and flopped down onto the cushiony moss with a defeated sigh.

Cade frowned as the big, horned god stretched out and clenched his eyes shut like he was trying to banish some memory. He appeared otherwise intact and still radiated the same overtly sexual power he'd possessed when he'd arrived. Then he noticed that Dionysus was no longer clad in his sandals and cock rings.

Choosing to take this as a sign that the god hadn't performed as well as he'd hoped, he said, "Cheer up, man. If it isn't meant to be, no doubt you've got the skills to capture the heart of any number of other lovely dragons."

Dionysus rolled over and propped himself on his elbow. He regarded Cade thoughtfully. "Ouranos' little demigod's inside you, isn't he? Hello, nephew. How does it feel to be the reason for your race's curse?"

"Ignore him," Zephyrus said.

"To hell I will. What's he mean about a curse?"

"He's just bitter she rejected him, obviously."

"He's denying it, isn't he?" Dionysus said. "Not that it's his fault directly. But his father's desire to have the upper hand on Fate when he and his brothers were conceived is why the turul are cursed to have no free will where love is concerned. Zephyrus and his brothers were only given the freedom to choose their lovers because they couldn't very well sow their wild oats without it. Their only curse was having to beg for physical bodies to do the sowing in."

Cade's passenger was conspicuously silent, which made his gears turn. Zephyrus hadn't called Dionysus a liar. Their choice as falcons as their hosts made more sense now.

Zephyrus eventually spoke, reminding Cade that no errant pondering was beyond his new partner's hearing. *"It's true, falcons were the most willing hosts, their natures pliable enough to let us transform into men when we found our chosen lovers, and then back again to escape into the night. Though my brothers sometimes chose other birds as well, the falcons were always our favorite. It's an inconvenient curse, especially when we lack a body to properly mate another immortal with. A human or a falcon body wouldn't be strong enough to mate an immortal."*

Cade shot a quick mental nod to Zephyrus, then said out loud half to himself, half to the reclining god, "That's all well and good, but it doesn't change the fact that Mr. I'm-Too-Sexy is deflecting. Did she send you packing for not bringing the power to the party, Dion?"

Dionysus sighed and flopped back down onto the mossy bank, scrubbing a hand over his face. Every movement made his glistening, golden body flex, displaying muscles Cade didn't think normal men possessed. Cade's cock stiffened at the errant thought of having a body that fine beneath his own.

"Am I to be pushed aside so easily, then?" Zephyrus asked at that glimmer of arousal.

"You owe me after today, breezy boy, but I'm only fantasizing about taking the payment out of his ass, don't worry. Besides, he just called you nephew, *so I'd just as soon not force you into screwing your own uncle."*

Zephyrus made a sound that was half-laugh, half-choking cough inside Cade's head. *"It's a figure of speech. He fucked an aspect of Fate to spawn the Dionarchs and father the nymphaea. My father, Ouranos, also fucked an aspect of Fate and spawned me and my brothers, who fathered the turul. Haven't you studied ursa history? You should know the rest. It's... complicated, but not precisely incestuous... really. Don't overthink it."*

"So where does this curse come in?"

"Fate may or may not have been exactly willing when Ouranos got to her."

"He raped her?" Cade blurted in alarm before he could censor himself.

Dionysus turned a startled gaze his way and Cade cursed under his breath.

The god's lips twisted into a smirk. Then his mouth

opened, and a full-blown laugh erupted from his chest and reverberated around the garden. "If you could call it that. Fate never does something she doesn't wish to do. No, Ouranos pissed Fate off by giving her what she wanted before she could bully him into it.

"Let it be a lesson to you, ursa: Never presume to take the upper hand away from Fate. She'll punish you for it, likely the way she punished Ouranos. She didn't just curse the sons she bore him and their entire lineage; she came back later in her male aspect and took it out of Ouranos' ass much the way you were just contemplating having a piece of mine. But if it would make you feel better …" He stood up and wiggled his golden backside at Cade, then smacked himself hard on one round cheek before diving into the deeper water with a grace that barely disturbed the surface.

Cade shook his head and turned to wade out of the pool. "I always suspected that the gods were a bunch of sex-crazed lunatics, what with the way they created us. I shouldn't be surprised, especially seeing how Gaia left you in a lurch without a body of your own."

Zephyrus let out a slow mental sigh. *"Gaia's just as eager to win a round against Fate as Dion is, but the only way to breed a dragon is with a cock, else she'd have come herself. I count myself lucky that she didn't agree to grant me flesh. Had I known about this contest from the start, I'd have avoided petitioning her at all. I'd rather not owe her any favors. You, on the other hand, are in my debt, friend."*

"Just 'friend'? After all I've done for you?" Cade said with a sly smirk as he wandered naked toward the entrance to the lodge.

Comfortable heat filled his chest, and a warm breeze gusted around his body even after the door closed behind him. The wind trailed like a silken touch, drying the droplets of water from his skin and brushing lightly across his lips and cheeks like a caress.

"You are more than a friend, but how much more we will have to wait to learn. Whether we win or lose Numa, I hold out hope that we have won each other. With luck, Gaia will be willing to grant me flesh after the contest is done and we will be free to explore further."

"I do love to explore," Cade said, giving Zephyrus a detailed mental image of exactly the extent of exploration he hoped to embark upon when they got a chance.

DESPITE THE AFTERNOON spent testing both the mental and physical limits of his libido, Cade found he was already half-hard by the time he made it to Numa's door at the designated hour. He stopped in the hallway outside her room and brushed his hands down the loose silk tunic and drawstring pants he'd been loaned from the closet of communal garments kept in every lodge in the Sanctuary. Ursa often arrived at the lodge in bear from and required clothing before seeking an audience with any of the shamans.

He felt oddly anxious, which was unlike him, but his spirit passenger had a history with the dragon that he'd only begun to understand. Under his breath, he murmured, "She's really got you flustered, huh?"

"I've wanted her for ages, but she's been out of my reach. I never believed I'd have this chance."

Cade chuckled. "Settle down, man, I've got this. But my body's yours, if you want to take the wheel once you get comfortable."

"Thank you," Zephyrus said with a clear note of relief.

He held up his fist and was just about to knock when the door swung open and he was yanked inside with a force strong enough to give him whiplash. The door slammed shut and he found himself pushed hard against it. A pair of hands gripped him by the shoulders as a mouth crashed against his.

He registered her scent first, the familiar fresh pine underscored by a more earthy, fertile aroma. So the test was to begin right away. He could handle that. Fuck, with the way her curves felt pressed against him, he would happily handle just about anything, particularly if she made sounds like those needy moans when he slid his big hands down her back to cup her round, utterly squeezable ass through the thin fabric of whatever she was wearing.

He pulled her tight against his hips and she let out a little gasp into his mouth in response, then moaned and ground her pelvis against the achingly hard length of his cock. Her fingers hooked into the split collar of his tunic and ripped, tearing the silk easily from neck to navel.

"I need you naked," she growled, fumbling at the ties to his pants. She was a wild thing, her thick brown waves cascading around her shoulders in disarray and a green silk robe hanging halfway off one shoulder. Her green eyes flashed with hunger.

Cade leaned back against the door and looked down at her with a wry smile. "You can have whatever you like, sweet pea. Just say the word."

She cursed when the drawstring managed to get tangled into a knot and a razor sharp talon shot from her fingertip. Cade jerked his hips back as she aimed the deadly claw at his groin and grabbed her wrist before she could do damage.

"Whoa, there. Just chill for a sec, baby. You don't need to rush this."

"There's no time. Don't you see?" she said, giving him a desperate, almost anguished look. "I need either you or Theron and Bekim to prove you can outlast Dionysus. Which means we need to start *now*."

She dropped her free hand to the waistband of his pants and tugged hard, the ties straining and cutting into his skin.

"We've each got the same amount of time, right? We'll play by the rules, and trust me, with that greeting, I'm already worked up pretty damn good."

Abandoning the tie, she slid her hand down the outside of the silk, tracing the outline of his shaft. Her gaze grew feverish and her lips parted as she explored his length. Cade's skin broke out into a sheen of sweat just from the heat she exuded as her arousal increased. He was used to cold, reveled in it, so being this close to a creature so hot was a little outside his level of tolerance. That and she made his fucking blood turn to lava with the way she stroked him. It was as though she'd never seen a cock before.

"Help me get these off you," she said, tugging once again.

Cade grabbed the front of his waistband in both hands and wrenched the ties apart. The offending length of cord snapped, the fabric ripping easily once the barrier was broken. His cock emerged as his pants fell to the floor, and immediately, she clasped his length in both hands, shuddering as though simply holding him gave her pleasure.

"Sweet Mother, you *are* bigger than him." She gazed in overt amazement down at his cock as she ran her hands up and down his length.

Cade struggled to keep his voice even, the steady slide of both her hands up and down his raging erection making it difficult to focus. He reached out and stilled her eager stroking just so he could form a coherent thought. "You've got me at your mercy now, sweet pea. What's the plan?"

"No plan, except for the next six hours, I want you to fuck me like our lives depend on it. There's only one rule…"

Cade didn't wait for her to finish. The second she said "fuck me," he hooked his arm around her waist and spun her, pressing her flat against the door hard enough that her breath left her lungs. He shoved the silken fabric of her robe up her thigh and hiked her leg over his hip. His cock slid along the soaked crease of her pussy until his tip felt the welcoming give of her opening, and he shoved home hard. Numa dug her fingertips into his neck and her head flew back.

"Oh, Sweet Mother, yes!" she cried, wrapping both legs tight around him as he began to pump into her with reckless abandon.

Sweet Mother, was right. Gaia's tears, he'd never felt a snatch so fucking perfect. Inside his mind, Zephyrus hummed a rhythmic tune that matched the rhythm of Cade's thrusts, the wind spirit's ecstasy nearly as close to the surface as Cade's own.

"Rules, ursa…" Numa said in between her own moans of pleasure.

"Don't worry, sweet pea. I'll hold out until you say so. I'm happy enough just feeling you wrapped around my cock like this."

She sighed and her eyes fluttered shut, her hips moving to meet his steady thrusts. The force of his fucking had slid her robe off both her shoulders, and he lowered his lips to her collar bone, then bent to tease his tongue around her exposed nipple. Her core heated and tightened around him, testing his limits. Gaia's tears, he needed her to come soon or he'd lose his fucking mind—and lose the damn contest in the process.

He hooked his hands under her ass and hoisted her a little higher, angling his hips to spear her deeper. She let out a resonant yell that echoed through the room and held on as he grabbed her around both hips and began to slam her down on his cock over and over. The new angle seemed to do the trick. Within seconds, she trembled and a gasping, hitching moan escaped her throat as her pussy tightened around his shaft in the most delicious squeeze. That glorious sensation made him regret so hard that he wasn't shooting the contents of his balls deep into her.

The power of her climax that flooded into his body soon after was like nothing he'd felt before, and it was all he could do to channel it into that empty well Zephyrus had helped him prepare. Her entire body went slack except for her arms and legs still wrapped tight around him as she nuzzled his neck.

"Thank you," she said.

Cade gritted his teeth in his effort to hold his shit together. His balls felt like molten lead again. Zephyrus was no fucking help, either, the wind spirit apparently struck dumb by the experience. Cade was only halfway coherent as it was.

"I'm here. What a fucking beautiful thing that was. You are a master."

Cade ignored him, instead focusing on controlling his need to start fucking her again. She let out a soft sigh, but offered no other directions. Cade turned and surveyed the room, then headed toward the big bed against the wall on one side.

"I'm gonna just lay you down here, all right?" He climbed onto the bed, then slipped out of her as he gently lowered her to the mattress.

When he glanced at her face, he paused and frowned. Wet streaks marred the clear, pale skin of her cheeks, and her eyes and the tip of her nose were red.

"Honey, please tell me I didn't hurt you," he said, reaching up to brush one knuckle lightly over the tracks of her tears.

Numa let out a soft laugh and cupped his bearded cheek. "Oh, no. You'd have a hard time hurting me, even if you wanted to. I just really, *really* needed that." She sighed heavily and turned onto her side, tugging him by the hand. He followed her, still uncertain, but not wishing to disappoint her at any point during his trials.

"You feel like talking about it?" he asked.

She studied him in silence, then tilted her head. "That song you were singing … was that you, or Zephyrus?"

"Song? Ah …" He shook his head and chuckled. "That wasn't me. I didn't even realize you could hear that. I thought it was just some gibberish syllables he was chanting. Do Re Mi shit."

"It wasn't gibberish," she said. "Tell him I heard him and … me too."

A gust of wind blew across them both, catching tendrils of Numa's hair and toying with it. The wind spirit hummed once again in pleasure inside Cade's head.

Cade's brows lowered. "He's here … You talk to me, you talk to both of us. And whatever you meant by that, he's pretty damn happy about. Do you two mind cluing me in?"

Numa's eyes twinkled. "He keeps secrets from you? That really isn't fair."

"I'd say not," he agreed, shooting a quick impression of his irritation at his smug passenger.

"Zephyrus and I have history, though I never realized how much history until today. His song was just a reminder that he's wished for this day for a long time. I used to wish for it a lot when I was young … to be the object of his affection. If I'd only known…"

"Can I take the wheel?"

"Be my guest," Cade said, then lifted his gaze to Numa. "He's yours now, sweet pea. Just don't abuse this body too much while he's got control. It's the only one I've got."

Numa sat up excitedly, and Cade almost regretted the fact that her eager look wasn't for *him*. Zephyrus slipped past his consciousness with practiced ease, and Cade barely even noticed he'd lost control over his own body. The only sign was the strangely distorted view of the world now, as though he were watching from behind thick glass. Every sensation was slightly dulled, but every emotion his new master felt hit him as hard as if it was his own.

Gaia's tears, but the man hadn't been lying. Cade's heart broke all over again at the reminder of what it felt like to love so strongly. He'd never expected to have his own loss haunt him with such acute potency, and at the same time be counterbalanced with such optimistic hope.

The wind spirit took Numa into his arms and proceeded to make slow, deliberate love to her as though it were their first time together. Cade could only watch and hope that somehow the two of them succeeded in winning this contest, because he didn't think he could survive having to deal with *two* broken hearts inside one body.

Meri wished she'd discovered the breadth of her power in this incorporeal form before. Having the bloodline of a million human souls as her personal tributary of the River gave her a range of abilities she had only dreamed of before. The lack of a physical form to experience the world firsthand meant little when she had access to so many at once. She couldn't wholly inhabit any of the bodies, however—only share them with their native spirits. And only her army of Hunters fighting in the Haven seemed to respond to her mental commands. Those men had tasted her blood directly.

She found she could split her focus more easily without the distraction of a single body's consciousness to keep track of. The broken shell that was held captive in the Haven was merely her anchor now, but her true power resided outside that body, in the minds of her Hunters and the millions of humans who carried traces of her bloodline after centuries of breeding.

The temporal bubble she struggled to break through still held strong, though the barrier fluctuated with each surge of power she sent through it. It took immense effort to force those ripples, but she had the sense if she persisted long enough, it would soon deteriorate to the point she could break through and access the mind of the creature she had created to be her immortal vessel. The child she had implanted inside Vrishti's womb was free from a soul, making her the perfect host for Meri's own itinerant spirit to make a permanent home within.

But the fight inside the Haven could not be forgotten. She still needed to reach the Source if she intended to have all the power she required once she did reclaim the child. While the baby's genetic makeup was ideal, she was too young for Meri to inhabit yet and remain in control. The Source would help speed her growth along.

With other fragments of her mind, she continued flitting through the bodies of her Hunters, keeping a keen eye on the fight unfolding in her home. The ursa and nymphaea had banded together and were defending the Source to the death. Their numbers were greatly outmatched by her Hunters, thanks to Nyx's excellent job locking down every access point and guaranteeing no reinforcements would come, but neither would any more Hunters be able to aid Meri's fight if she needed them. All Meri needed was for her Hunters to maintain the upper hand. It was just a matter of time before they broke through to the Source, and she wanted to have control of the child when that happened.

On her sojourn through the minds of her troops, one Hunter's vision triggered an old memory and she paused to observe his surroundings. He was with a small squad that had split off from the others, chasing down one of the Thiasoi she had once called sister. The wounded female had run, leaving a trail of blood behind her the four men were intent on tracking with intentions of both blood and carnal lust. She reveled in the strength of those urges she had fostered in them. They would not cease their fight until they'd sated those desires. All the nymphs who had spurned her so long ago would be crushed.

The bloody trail stopped at the edge of a waterfall, but the path the men stood on was one she remembered well. When they wavered at the edge of the water, perplexed by the nymph's disappearance, she took over. She filled the leader's mind with her own will, shoving his spirit aside.

The power of the Source itself infused the waterfall, but there was no way to harness it without controlling the origin pool. Yet there was something within the cave beyond the falls that could give her an advantage, if she were brave enough to venture inside.

"The nymph we followed has passed through the waterfall," she said, her voice sounding strange coming from an unfamiliar mouth, heard by someone else's ears. The other three men snapped to attention, having been conditioned to understand when she spoke through one of their number. They knew who their true master was.

She settled into the big soldier's body, giving him a mental stroke as positive reinforcement for allowing her control as well as the continued eagerness to find and subdue their prey. The adrenaline that lingered in his bloodstream felt good, his arousal a potent influence making her revel in her possession of this man.

She looked down and found the gap in the vegetation that flanked the edge of the falling water. Cool spray soaked through the tight cotton t-shirt the man wore, cooling his hot skin. She pushed through the bushes to the ledge that led past the curtain of the falls and carefully stepped onto it, turning back to beckon to the other three to follow. They obediently stepped through the bushes and trailed her as she made her way into the darkness of the secret cave beyond.

The scent of blood was stronger there, and she crouched

down, waiting for her vessel's human vision to adjust to the dimness within. The dawn light only filtered through a small amount, but the dank interior of the cave that served as the antechamber to one of the oldest creatures in existence was as familiar to her as her own mind.

The nymph may be out of their reach if she ventured farther in, but Meri no longer cared about chasing a broken, terrified enemy. Not when she could take advantage of a greater power she had all but forgotten about over the centuries.

She rose again and sought out the entrance to the deeper caves, a void in the far wall. Walking forward, the power grew, the hairs on her vessel's arms standing on end. The three men behind her hesitated.

"We aren't going in there, are we?" one asked.

"That is precisely where we are going. Either you follow on your own, or I make you follow," she said, giving them a dark look with one eyebrow raised.

Another soldier's Adam's apple bobbed as he swallowed. He nodded toward the corridor. "After you," he said. "Just tell us what to expect. Whatever's in there has my hackles up."

Meri let out a low chuckle. "The answer to our prayers."

The three men gave each other resolute looks, but fell in behind her as she stepped into the darkened passage.

The ancient, primal power that filled this place grew more potent the farther in she went. Soon the walls and ceiling closed in, forcing the four of them to crouch, and then crawl on all fours for several meters before it opened again and they were able to stand and stretch. When the ethereal light of the Diviner's chamber bled in, the magic that filled the passage made it feel like Meri was pushing through a dense barrier to move forward.

She gritted her teeth, the big soldier's body sweating from the exertion of simply walking the last few feet only to reach an invisible, yet seemingly impenetrable wall that refused to give, no matter how hard she pushed at it.

Scales slithering against wet stone sent a chill running down her spine, and the ancient, all but forgotten memory of her last visit to this place bloomed in the forefront of her mind. All Thiasoi soldiers, male and female alike, were required to visit the Diviner's lair as part of their initiation, to arrive in their true primal form and undergo a test of wills against the ancient creature before being allowed access to the River. That network of water magic was what allowed the Thiasoi their link to each other and to access the infinite, endless flow of time through the universe.

Meri had been stripped of her link when she was banished from the Haven, but if she could win over the Diviner now, she could gain access to that flow of time once more and gain greater power to affect the bubble that barred her access to the child. It would also allow her a clearer view of events as they unfolded, giving her the ability to react more swiftly if anything went awry.

"I sssee you inssside that human man, little nymph. You know the price of entry to my chamber." The Diviner's voice slipped inside her skull and drifted over her skin in a cool caress.

The price of entry. Of course. It hadn't occurred to her because she had no ability to take a primal form in the bodies of these human men. But she could take them as close as possible.

"Strip," she commanded over her shoulder and began to tear off the clothes of her vessel. From within the Diviner's chamber came the soft, terrified pleas of the injured nymph they had chased, begging the Diviner not to let them in. But Meri no longer had any interest in that nymph, not when there was a greater prize to be had. Still, she could use the promise of that smaller conquest to encourage the other men to action.

Once she was naked, she gripped the large cock between her thighs and stroked it to full hardness. At the same time, she crafted a vision of the thing that had provoked these men into chasing the nymph to begin with and sent it to the three of them through their blood meld.

Before her eyes all three's fearful expressions turned hungry, and they all hurriedly removed their clothes and stepped closer to the barrier that blocked their entry to the Diviner's lair. Their basest, most primal urges at the surface now, she turned and smiled into the mist-filled room.

"We are ready," she said, and reached out to test the barrier once more. The slithering sound from within grew louder, accompanied by the wet, rhythmic tempo of waves lapping at stone.

Beneath her hand, the barrier dissipated, and she stepped into the room. Her entire body immediately flushed with hot arousal, the erect cock between her thighs aching painfully. It was a distraction she didn't need, but would have to endure in order to see this scheme of hers through to the end.

"Why are you here, little nymph?" the Diviner said, her voice ricocheting off the walls.

"To offer you a bargain. I will soon control the Haven and the Source itself. I propose an alliance. Grant me a fresh link to the River. Open the Haven to those who share my blood, and I will set you free."

The mists shifted and thinned, the slithering sounds reaching a crescendo around them as the old, familiar shape coalesced before her. An immense female figure loomed from the center of the pool, a woman who was part-nymph, part-dragon, with hair like tiny snakes and hands tipped in claws. The water churned and bubbled around her, a writhing mass of huge tentacle-like tails with iridescent blue-green scales twisting in and out, as thick as the torso of a man where they emerged from her hips, all tapering to fine tips that slipped over the edge of the pool. Several of those creeping tails made their way beyond, reaching for Meri's vessel and the men who stood behind him.

"Freedom. That isss a novel offer, one I have never had before. What makes you think you have the power to grant me thisss *freedom?*"

"I have forged a bond of blood with humanity that grants me power in the outside world. I can release you from the Haven, give you free rein among the humans, allow you to see for yourself what wonders there are to find out there that you never got to see trapped in this cave."

The Diviner tilted her head, her hypnotic eyes swirling with interest. The tiny snakes framing her face coiled around each other.

"Ssshow me this power. What can humanity do for me that your kind doesss not already? That I cannot do for myssself?"

The mass of tentacles before her rose up from the water. The shape of a naked female body emerged, a nymph in full primal shift, her head lolling back from the weight of her antlers. Red gashes slashed across her torso, welling blood that dripped down her flesh. The Diviner cradled the nymph with several of her tails while the tips of others caressed the unconscious woman. Water flowed over her, cleansing the blood from the cuts the Hunters had given her and uncovering a deeper wound that had pierced the nymph's side. More blood seeped from that gash, and as Meri watched, the wound closed, and the anguished expression on the unconscious nymph's face eased as she fell into serene slumber.

"You are a creature of certain needs," Meri said. "The nymphs will be defeated soon. Any who stand against me will die. I am merely offering an infinitely abundant substitute if you grant me my request. Taste for yourself."

With only the barest exertion of her will, the three men beside her stepped into the water and swam toward the Diviner. Halfway there, one man let out a harsh yell and disappeared beneath the surface, only to reappear a moment later, gasping for breath, his body wrapped in one of the Diviner's tentacles. Within seconds, the Diviner had bound the other two in her tentacles. They struggled in her grip.

Meri knew well how inescapable those tentacles were if the Diviner didn't wish to let go, but she also knew the one driving need the ancient creature possessed.

The three men looked terrified for only a moment before their eyelids fluttered or widened and they all began to moan in pleasure. With only their shoulders above the surface of the water, Meri couldn't see what the Diviner was doing, but she had no doubt they were enjoying it.

The power this creature possessed surpassed even the Dionarchs, and yet the Diviner had been trapped inside this cave for as long as Meri had been alive. Her only sustenance came from the nymphs and satyrs who visited to request blessings of their matings or seek the wisdom of this immortal creature who served as an oracle to their race.

The Diviner's attention to the three Hunters continued, and all the while her gentle caresses of the nymph held close to her body persisted. The nymph's eyes opened and widened at first in fear, then in fascination when she caught sight of the men the Diviner held in her grip, pleasuring to greater heights than they had ever experienced, Meri was certain.

The nymph twisted her body and turned to gain a better view, the tentacles that supported her adjusting to continue cradling her. The need that swirled in her eyes was something Meri knew well. That ache to be filled and fucked into oblivion was something not even a human body had dulled in all her eons walking among that lesser race and wearing their skins.

As if sensing the nymph's requirements, the Diviner adjusted her hold on the woman until the nymph's back was pressed flush against the Diviner's torso, her legs spread and her glistening core visible. The nymph's potent scent reached Meri from across the room, and her human vessel's libido raged in response. This was one acute drawback of taking a male human's body in a place like this. Their urges could be overwhelming, but with effort, she channeled their carnal desires into blood rage to urge them to kill rather than fuck. The killing could be every bit as satisfying and conditioned them to want it more, the more she encouraged it. But a willing nymph opening herself like that to a roomful of naked men could override any other urge they possessed.

The Diviner turned the three captive Hunters to face the nymph, and they all struggled and clawed at their bindings in the effort to reach the prize.

"She is yoursss if you wisssh," the Diviner crooned. "Come and ssshow me how much esssence that human body can feed me."

The cravings of Meri's vessel grew too strong to deny, but this could be the opportunity she needed to prove her point. She walked into the water, intent on showing the Diviner how much delicious energy the humans possessed. It would be at her disposal, were she to leave this place.

Meri reached the center and found tentacles arranged in short steps that gave her access to the nymph, whose pussy was spread wide and slick with readiness to be filled. The mere scent of the nymph had her virile male vessel's blood heated to the point she had no doubt he'd have long since lost control of his reactions and buried his cock into the nymph, had she not been in control of him. Meri took her time, however, knowing that due to the Diviner's part-dragon nature, she reveled in the delay of gratification. The longer she drew out the pleasure, the greater her reward at the end.

This would be a first for Meri, however. She had inhabited her hunters when they coupled with each other while under her control, but had never bothered riding along or even taking the wheel when they fucked a female. Still, she knew how to use the body she was in, and as she sank the man's thick cock into the nymph's eager, molten depths, she made use of that knowledge to her advantage.

The nymph wrapped her legs around the Hunter's hips as he fucked her, her hands tangling into his short hair and pulling him down into a deep, hungry kiss.

It wasn't until the Hunter's orgasm hit that Meri realized her mistake. The flood of orgasmic bliss dulled her senses, and she was sluggish as the nymph's grip tightened. Her kiss grew fierce and brutal as she bit down and drew blood from the Hunter's lip. The nymph was at full power now, having been healed by the Diviner's magic, and despite being strong and healthy, the Hunter Meri possessed was no match for a nymph in full primal shift with just as strong a hunger for blood and sex.

The other three hunters yelled out in pleasure behind her, but a second later came the sickening snaps of breaking bones as the Diviner crushed them in her python-like grip.

The immense creature's eyes were a disorienting maelstrom of power as she peered down at Meri, trapped within the embrace of the nymph, her vessel's cock still pulsing inside her snatch. The Diviner's voice was chilling in its power, and her fingertips just as icy when they reached down and ran a caress over Meri's cheek.

"You pressume to know what will pleassse me, little nymph? Freedom is not my greatessst dessire, nor even is ssseeeing you perish for your betrayals of the higher racesss. But you have a purpose to ssserve yet, and one I will happily bear witnesss to. Do your worssst, but know you will never be able to influence the godsss."

The mist closed in around her, and the nymph who held her captive tightened her grip and writhed her hips, clenching her muscles tighter around the Hunter's cock.

Enraged by the Diviner's taunts, Meri split herself from the mind of the man she'd taken over, and realized it was none too soon. Without Meri's spirit to maintain control, the nymph who held him forced another climax from his captive body, and at the very peak, gripped his head in both her hands and twisted.

With the snap of the Hunter's neck it was as though an elastic tether had yanked Meri back into her own broken body. She howled furiously into the emptiness she now inhabited, her impulsive plan an utter failure. Once she won this war, she would find a way to make the Diviner pay. But for now, she had to make sure no others could reach her lair, friend or foe.

Still hot with anger, she sent a command to the Hunters nearest the Diviner's lair. They responded instantly, heading to the waterfall and venturing inside, but only to set the charges that would collapse the opening of the cave, blocking off both entry and escape.

Once that task was complete, she flew back to the temporal bubble in the Sanctuary. With fresh fervor, she attacked the barrier again, more determined than ever to break through.

CHAPTER 13

ZORION

Zorion rematerialized in the middle of a forest, his skin tingling from the released grips of all his companions' hands. It was just the five of them, with Neela's barely contained fire glowing just beneath the surface of her skin, hot enough to tickle his craving for her, but not enough to set him ablaze. He moved into the circle of stones and tested the center. An invisible barrier bounced back against his hand when he pushed.

"This is the portal," he said. "But we can't enter the Sanctuary as we are. Zil, are you ready? The other three of you, hold onto me once more so you're with us when we stop time."

Neela moved to stand at his left, clutching his hand while Naaz and Asha both clung to his other hand. Zil faced him, his dark eyes filled with the half of their shared power that would create the frozen interlude once they joined again. He and his darker half had practiced this several times while in Nikhil and their mother's presence, demonstrating the uses of the power and trying to determine how best to take advantage of it. Their hope was that with time halted, they could pass through the Sanctuary's magical barrier without harming the security of it, similar to how they'd breached the shield surrounding the army's dragon temple base. Once inside the Sanctuary, they would be able to reach the Haven to lend their aid. They'd barely discovered how to stretch their time in the stillness, but hopefully, they would only need the few seconds it would take to pass through the barrier.

All Zil had to do was step into the field of Zorion's shape and the pair merged instantly. The merging sent an icy chill through Zorion's body as though the flow of his fiery power had been snuffed. He still couldn't get used to the coldness of it, and beside him, Asha's teeth began to chatter. Stillness was freezing, but the temperature shift was a good gauge for how long they had.

"Hurry," he said, and the five of them stepped forward as a unit, aiming for the barrier that had taken on the appearance of frozen molasses struck through with ripples.

Leading the way, he stepped forward, and the portal flowed around them like fog, leaving him feeling sticky on the other side. He kept a tight hold on the hands that held his and they all passed through behind him, faces scrunched like they were passing through a barrier of spider webs.

"We'll try to stretch this as long as possible, but let's make use of the stillness quickly," he said, holding onto them all and ignoring the beginning of Zil's protest. He pushed his power to the south, in the direction they knew his aunt and uncle would be. If they couldn't lend their power to the opening of a sky portal, they would go straight into the battle itself and do what they could there.

They landed outside yet another barrier that looked similar to the first, only this time, it seemed to flow in a direction that was disconcerting to view.

"Once more, brace yourselves," he said, and they passed

through, once again succumbing to the urge to wipe the sticky residue off their faces upon passing.

The frigid sensation began to warm, and he readied himself for the surge of motion that would grasp them all when time started again.

"Something's up there," Asha said, frowning at the way they'd come. "What is that?"

They all turned to look, and Zorion had to tilt his head to make sense of what seemed to be a trick of light playing across the barrier of the temporal bubble they'd passed through, but then it moved ever so slightly.

'Ugh, what is that?" Neela asked. "Looks like a snake stuck to the dome.

"Zil, try to hold onto the moment with me," Zorion said, and the dark presence in his mind agreed. What they had caught sight of certainly didn't belong.

He manifested Zil's wings and rose, flying up to get a better look at the huge, twisting shape that clung to the membrane of the bubble like a lamprey. The chill grew inside him once more and the creature slowed, then stopped moving.

"I can't push my power much harder," Zil said.

"No need..." Zorion shot his hand into the barrier and grabbed the slithering creature, but he couldn't yank it through. Its fangs were buried deep into the membrane itself, and it was fixed there as though a part of it. But though he couldn't budge the creature, he could read it as easily as his own mother had read his shame, and understood.

This abhorrent creature was none other than the spirit of the beast that had imprisoned and tortured his love. He squeezed as hard as he could, but it did no good.

"Fuck! I can't kill it while we're frozen. It has to fucking *breathe* in order to suffocate."

"What is it?" Neela called.

"The enemy," he growled. "Meri herself is leeching the power from this barrier somehow. She is after …" He could only read the frozen moment of thought in the creature's mind. "The child…" he whispered.

Rage gripped him then, and Zil let out a mental curse inside his head. *"Hold on to that filthy thing,"* he bit. *"It's going to get hot."*

With the flood of heat coursing through their body again, time surged into motion once more. A piercing screech echoed through the air, bouncing off the barrier. The creature wriggled and thrashed in Zorion's hand, and he pushed fire through his palm in as much force as he could, his teeth clenched hard as he tried to hold on. But the barrier snapped tight and his reflexes simply obeyed the constricting force. His hand flew open and the creature hurtled away in the other direction.

"Fuck!" he bellowed, pulling his hand back through the barrier. "I had her!"

Neela looked stricken when he landed again. "It was her, wasn't it? What was she doing?"

"Sucking power from the barrier, from the looks of things. We need to warn the others, but more importantly, we need to get to your daughter. Protect her."

Neela's blue eyes flashed wide. "My … my daughter?" she said in a weak voice filled with cautious hope.

"That creature had one thought in its mind when I grabbed it … to get to the child. Nikhil confirmed that the child existed and was saved by the ursa who mated my uncle. That must be the child Meri wants. Come, we don't have time to waste."

He didn't bother splitting from Zil again this time, and his shadow made an unholy sound in his head when he let the fire burn to transport them into the lodge itself. Once they landed, Zil forcefully pushed him out, sputtering loud curses, his dark eyes blazing hot enough to make Zorion think he'd kept some of the fire for himself.

"Don't you ever fucking do that again! I can handle fire from the outside, not the inside!"

"You'll live," Zorion snapped and headed for the nearest staircase, aiming for the familiar white aura of his uncle on the second floor.

They'd only made it up to the first landing when a voice called from below. "Hey! Who the fuck are you, and how did you get in?"

Zorion's first instinct was to subdue the intruder with a mental shackle, but he remembered that he and the others were the actual intruders. They were among friends here, or should be, and he needed to keep it that way. He turned and stepped back down, giving Neela's hand a comforting squeeze on the way past.

"I am Zorion, and I come at Nikhil's command to aid the fight. But first, my mate wishes to see her child."

The blond-haired man who stared him down had an aura of wind about him and his eyes were the color of summer storms. His gaze lifted to the group on the staircase behind Zorion and he studied each face in turn, his brows gradually easing.

Still looking past Zorion at Neela and Naaz, the newcomer said, "Oh, thank the Winds, you two finished your mission. I take it these are the so-called Wildcards Nikhil sent you after?"

"That was a secret," Naaz said, his eyes narrowing.

The man shrugged. "Not much gets past a turul. Whispers carry. What I'm not privy to is how the fuck you five got past the barrier."

"We have ways," Zorion said. "Zil and I can stop time. None of the boundaries hold us back when they are only so much frozen mist. But you should know your temporal bubble is doomed. Meri has discovered it. We caught her leeching power from it when we came through, I tried to strangle the ... *thing* that held her essence, but it fled. She will no doubt return once she recovers from the burn I gave her. If you are the guardian of this place, you would do well to increase your patrols. Watch the barrier for signs of her."

The man winced and rubbed the back of his neck. "We are a little light on security, but I will see what I can do. I'm Ozzie West, by the way. You, I know by reputation ... Zorion, is it? Or..." He shot an uncertain look at Zil.

"I am Zorion. Zil is my brother, you could say. And my sister, Asha." He gestured between the other two dragons. "I presume you are acquainted with Naaz and my mate, Neela?"

Ozzie nodded. "You guys have quite a history."

Neela slipped her hand into Zorion's and said, "I'm more concerned about our future, which is somewhere in this lodge. Do you know Vrishti? Nikhil said she was the one Meri implanted our baby into. Is she here?"

Ozzie's eyebrows rose and his mouth opened, then closed again. "Yeah, it's been an interesting day for us all, especially for her. She's upstairs. Come, I'm sure she'd like to meet you, but there's something you ought to know first."

Zorion and the others stood aside to allow Ozzie to climb the stairs and lead the way.

"What is it?" Neela asked. "Are she and the baby all right?"

"She is fine, and so is Deva ... the baby ... who she gave birth to this morning. Actually it's been almost twenty-four hours since she was born. It's tricky to keep track of time inside this damn bubble."

"That ... can't be. It's barely been five months since she was conceived," Neela said, her fingers tightening in Zorion's hand. "Are you sure she's all right?"

Ozzie refused to say more as he led them around the wide arc of a corridor that circumscribed the lodge. Up above were roof lanterns that gave a clear view of the sky outside, which shimmered oddly, distorting the morning sun. There was other potent energy infusing this place, the scents of fertile power everywhere.

They passed by one big door that barely contained the sounds of a female's pleasure beyond. With a glance, Zorion identified a powerful green dragon's aura inside, along with two other creatures who shared a body, their potent male auras superimposed atop each other as they pleasured the female.

He paused and frowned at the door, trying to place the familiar green of the aura.

"Ah, she isn't in there," Ozzie said. "That's Numa, completing round two of her contest to find a mate. We need to avoid interrupting—she's going as fast as she can."

Zorion's lips twitched in understanding. "My aunt has made a great sacrifice today. Are you a contestant? I can see from your aura that you have affection for her."

Ozzie shook his head sharply. "No. I'm fated for someone else. All turul know their mate on sight, and she isn't mine, or you can bet the contest never would have been necessary."

"Why a contest?" Asha asked. "She's a dragon. Mama had a whole harem before I was born. Can't Aunt Numa have one too?"

"The ritual to open the portal calls for a level of power that exists only between fully bonded mates. The harems the immortal dragons like your aunt used to keep were humans who were never fully marked. There is no reversing an immortal dragon mark, so she needs to be sure the mate she chooses is both powerful enough to help her complete the ritual, and is compatible with her for an eternal bond."

"You fear her," Zorion said, sensing a deeper secret under Ozzie's words. "I suspect you are relieved she is not your Fated mate."

Ozzie's shoulders dropped when he stopped outside another door. "I would do anything to help destroy the enemy, but the truth is I don't think I'm cut out to be an immortal's mate. Though I admit I am weary of waiting. Whatever Fate has planned, I wish I could just get on with it."

Zorion let out a soft snort of understanding and patted Ozzie on the shoulder. "The wait sometimes makes it all worthwhile. You will appreciate your mate all the more for it, trust me." He bent and gave Neela a soft kiss on the temple, but his mate was too agitated and impatient to register the gesture.

Ozzie looked at Neela, his expression softening. "Deva is an amazing child. She is well-loved here, for all that she is barely a day old. I think the entire lodge witnessed her birth, which Numa midwifed. She particularly adores Numa, perhaps because hers is the first face she saw when she opened her eyes."

Neela's skin flared hot beside him. "Better let her in soon," Zorion said. "Everything in this lodge is made of wood —wouldn't want her to catch the place on fire making her wait."

Ozzie eyed the subtle crackling glow beneath Neela's skin and pushed the door open. Beyond was a big, comfortable sitting room with an immense fireplace against the inner wall. The room was empty, its picture windows overlooking the gardens below. Zorion caught sight of a huge horned man lounging on the bank of a pool, his skin glistening. His aura was like nothing Zorion had ever seen—a pure, watery aqua with deeper green veins threading through it. That creature, whatever he was, was beyond simply immortal.

A knocking drew his attention back to the room where Ozzie gently rapped at another closed door. Neela was practically climbing the man in her eagerness to get to her daughter.

A moment later, the door opened, revealing a big man with jet-black hair and swirling eyes. His entire frame blocked the view into the room. He scowled out at them, but when his gaze found Neela, he froze and stared in incomprehension.

"Neph, please let me see my baby," Neela said.

The man's brows twitched and he darted a glance over his shoulder, then shoved through the door, closing it behind him.

"I apologize. I seem to have lost track of time. My link to the River is distorted due to the bubble we're in. I wasn't sure when you would arrive … I had hoped we would have more time with her."

Neela's heat flared, betraying her agitation at being made to wait. "Why are you keeping me from her?!"

Neph rested big hands on Neela's shoulders for a split-second, but let out a hiss and jerked away. "I will let you see her in a moment, but I don't want you to be alarmed. She is a very special child."

"So you keep saying," Zorion said, pushing forward to confront the satyr. "Why not tell us exactly how special so we know what to expect?" He tilted his chin to the door. "I can already see through the walls that her aura is unusual. She is not human, despite being conceived by two human parents, but after witnessing Meri's experiments, that does not surprise me. I suspect there is far more to her than that."

Neph took a deep breath. "She is a hybrid of all the creatures Meri held captive. Born of two Blessed human parents, and then mutated with the genetic material of all four of the higher races. This is what Aodh, Vrishti, and I have been able to discern from observing her since her birth. The time surges are accelerating her growth, and with each surge, she displays evidence of potential power."

"Is she healthy?" Neela asked. "Please tell me she isn't hurting after what Meri did to her."

Neph gazed deep into Neela's eyes, and her barely contained fire slowly dimmed. After a second, he gently gripped her upper arm and steered her to a chair near the window. To Zorion's amazement, she willingly sat, looking eagerly up into Neph's face.

The big satyr pulled up a footstool and sat facing her. "Your daughter is a chimera, which we are far from equipped to understand. The higher races have never inter-bred before, so we have no idea how *two* would mix, much less all five. To add insult to injury ..." He paused and in a gentler tone continued. "Deva was born without a soul. We believe this was by design, that Meri intended to use her as a vessel. Her permanent vessel, owing to Deva's exposure to the power of the Source inside Vrishti's womb. Deva is immortal."

Neela's brows crinkled with worry. "But if she doesn't have a soul, how is she even alive?"

"Souls are bestowed by Fate. Thanks to her origins, she was likely overlooked—or Meri found a way to hide her. She is a perfectly well-adjusted child. Or she was, until the latest power fluctuation of the temporal bubble." He frowned and glanced back at Zorion and the others. "It was Meri, wasn't it?"

Zorion nodded and moved to stand at Neela's shoulder, Zil slipping silently up to lean his big, dark frame against the windowsill beside her. "What we saw was a leech, but it was most definitely powered by Meri's essence."

"That's what we feared," Neph said. "We believed we had neutralized her in the Haven, but there were signs that she still maintained her power over her puppets. That she is here suggests she has far more power than we believed."

In a shaky voice, Neela said, "You keep referring to Deva

as a child. Don't you mean baby? She can't be more than a few hours old."

"That's the other thing," Neph said. "Every time there is a surge in the power of the barrier, Deva ages. The last one was more pronounced than before. Not only is her physical growth accelerated, so is her mental development. She has already learned to talk, quite eloquently, and has mastered basic motor skills almost the instant her body is capable. But the acceleration isn't without side effects."

A fierce, child-like wail interrupted their conversation, and Neela jumped.

"I'm going in," Ozzie said, and before the others could react, he shoved the door open and was gone.

The pitiful cries of a child continued for a moment longer, Zorion's heart aching with each sound. But as he and Neela passed through the doorway, another sound hit his ears. A rich, deep voice rose in song, quiet, yet powerful enough to cause a hush to fall over all the others.

Neela slipped her hand into his and held on tight, her palm a searing brand, her emotion barely contained, but even her agitation settled when they drew close to the big turul where he crouched on the floor beside the crying child. Zorion's uncle, who he recognized from the bright glow of his aura, was holding Deva in his arms.

Far from the infant they had expected, Deva was the size of a child of about six. She was clad in a dress of white silk that contrasted with the rich brown of her skin. His heart-beat raced when Neela fell to her knees on the other side of the chair opposite the singing Turul. Deva looked like a younger version of his mate in almost every way, from the smooth, flawless richness of her skin to the dark, shining curls on her head.

She seemed entranced by Ozzie. Her hitching sobs slowed and her breathing calmed bit by bit.

Neela reached out, but paused when she came close to touching Deva's small hand where it clung to Aodh's shirt.

"You won't harm her," Aodh said gently. "She is part-dragon."

Neela nodded. "Deva, honey, it's all right. You will be all right. I'm here now. Mama's here."

She touched Deva's hand gently and the little girl's brows twitched. Her gaze tore away from Ozzie to look at Neela's hand, her head tilting in wonder before her teary eyes lifted.

That was where the resemblance to Neela stopped. While Neela had the most vibrant blue eyes that were a reflection of the dragon who had blessed her and infused her blood for most of her life, only the very center of Deva's irises were blue. The outer edges were an oddly variegated gold with veins of other colors. In the right light, Zorion saw the power beneath.

Neph was right, though. While evidence of her origins was clear in her aura, as was her potential power, something was missing that all the other creatures in the room possessed. Their auras all had a more tangible quality that Zorion recognized as tied to their purpose—to their fates. Neph, Aodh, and Vrishti's auras were all linked by threads of power that made them almost identical. His own mate's aura was bound to his and Zil's in a similar fashion, as were Naaz and Asha's.

The Turul male who had greeted them did not have such threads reaching outside his aura to twine with someone else's, but he possessed a layer of power that cocooned him like silvery summer fog with the same quality of the power around the others. As he sang, however, his aura's power enveloped Deva, giving hers the briefest illusion of that layer of a soul the others already had.

Deva's gaze fell on Neela and she frowned in confusion.

"Mama?" she asked, darting a look to Vrishti where she stood beside Neph at Aodh's shoulder.

Vrishti's worried expression eased into a soft smile. "She is your mama too."

The little girl's tear-streaked face split into a wide smile, and she lurched off Aodh's lap and into Neela's arms with a squeal of delight. "Mama! I missed you!"

Almost bowled over by Deva's enthusiasm, Neela barely kept her balance. Her heat flared once again as she wrapped her arms around her daughter, but Deva barely seemed to notice.

"Oh, baby, I missed you so, so much. But I'm here now."

She settled onto the floor with Deva on her lap. After a long embrace that she didn't seem keen on ever ending, she finally let Deva ease out of her arms. The little girl sat back on Neela's thighs and stared up at her in childish wonder, taking in not only Neela's face, but more, as though tracing the outer edges of her mother's shape.

"She can see auras?" Zorion asked, looking at the trio who had become Deva's surrogate parents.

"That is new, if it's true," Aodh said. "It's a skill dragons develop in their early years, so she is coming into it on schedule. We've seen evidence of other powers manifesting. Rudimentary ones. She has the powers of all four of the higher races, yet still possesses qualities that are uniquely human."

"Such as?" Zorion asked.

"This is her true form," Aodh said. "While she can manifest features of the other races, she seems disinclined to shift fully into any other shape. Any child of the higher races whose nature isn't magically bound will learn to fully shift not long after they are born, if they are even born in a human form to start with, as most dragons are."

Deva's intense gaze moved from Neela up to Zorion and

Zil. "Are you my papas too? You belong to her, I can see it." She moved off Neela's lap and stood, peering up at the pair of them with a fearless look.

Zil crouched down to eye-level with the girl and smiled. "You are right. We belong to her, so I guess that does make us your papas, too. You have another father who is not here yet. You'll meet him soon. His name is Nikhil."

She gave them a serious look and nodded. "He is *your* mama's mate."

Zil blinked at her and glanced up at Zorion. "She's perceptive." He pointed at Asha, who had entered the room, but stood back from the group with Naaz's arm wrapped protectively around her waist. "Do you know who she is?"

Deva's strangely shimmering eyes brightened and she ran across the room. Naaz responded just in time for her to launch herself into his arms, catching her easily. The pair of them gazed in pleased bewilderment at the little girl.

"My family," Deva said with a firm nod. "And she is my sister." She leaned over and gave Asha a brief peck on the cheek then proceeded to tangle her fingers in Asha's gleaming iridescent locks.

But then she stiffened and pushed away from Naaz, sliding back down to the floor. Neela's big warrior of a brother looked abashed, then crouched when Deva collapsed and huddled in on herself.

"Make it go away!" she cried, casting a terrified look at the ceiling and covering her head as she continued to whimper and whine. Neela rushed to her side and rested a hand on Deva's back.

"We won't let her get you, baby. I promise."

"No! It's too strong. It pulls, it hurts. Make it stop!"

She let out a wail, half-surprise and half-pain, clutching at her head. At the same second, the morning light that filled the room dimmed and flickered in an unearthly rippling rhythm.

"Give her space," Aodh said, coming to Neela's side and gently squeezing her shoulder to urge her back. "We have no way to stop this, but we *will* protect her at all costs. I can only ease the pain for her when it happens." He shot a look over his shoulder. "Ozzie, will you sing again? Your song calmed her more than anything else has. It must call to her turul blood."

Neela stumbled back, and Zorion caught her and held her tight, her body hot with apprehension. Zil moved in close, the pair of them cocooning her in their arms.

Aodh bent down, exhaling a white cloud that swirled around Deva's hunched body. She let out an agonized cry as her skin rippled, her bones lengthening and realigning beneath the surface.

Zorion clung to his mate and his shadow, tormented by helplessness as he watched the little girl's transformation. She didn't magically shimmer and shift, but grew physically, her skin thinning until it was near transparent and taut over her expanding shape. Aodh's magic helped, healing her swiftly, but Zorion's own perception made it clear that it wasn't just her body expanding as she grew. Her aura's power reflected the maturation as well, as though she hadn't simply gotten bigger, but had aged as well. The darkening tinge to her aura reflected an inner change that only occurred with age and experience.

"Can you do something?" Neela asked, her gaze beseeching as she peered up at him.

"They've been through this before," he said. "My powers likely could do no more than delay the inevitable. Let it pass."

Along with Aodh's healing smoke, Ozzie had begun to sing, his soulful rhythm visibly easing Deva's transformation. Her cries stopped, and even though the fluctuations of her physiology still rippled, she seemed to give into it. As the change gradually ceased, she stretched out a hand to Ozzie, who took it and squeezed, never slowing the tempo of his song. A moment later, Deva took a breath where she lay, and when she opened her mouth again, the sweetest melody arose in harmony with the turul's song. It was not the song of a child's voice, however, but a young woman on the verge of maturity.

"I hate to do this," Neph said, coming toward them with arms outstretched, "But we need to let her rest. Meet us in the outer room so we can talk in a few moments."

It was all Zorion could do to urge Neela out of the room. As they departed, Aodh was lifting Deva in his arms and setting her down on the big bed before coming to join them.

Only Ozzie remained behind, his voice still mingling with Deva's for several moments until hers gradually faded and her aura calmed in sleep.

He closed the door softly behind him and faced the room with a worried frown. "If this keeps up for the full extent of Numa's contest, it could kill her. We need to find an alternative."

"Why is it happening at all?" Neela asked.

"She was in Vrishti's womb when we created the temporal bubble," Neph said. "I think somehow the magic of the bubble became entwined with hers. So whenever the power fluctuates and the timeline of the outside world floods in, her own timeline is magnified. I can sense the surges when it happens—it's like a dam breaking. The barrier repairs itself, but it becomes weaker each time."

"We can't let it fail," Zorion said. "If it does, Meri will be able to reach her."

"Can we go on the offensive? Find her wherever she's attacking the thing and kill her?" Naaz asked.

Neph gave them all a grim look and shook his head.

"Meri is pure spirit now. What you saw out there was likely only a small fragment of her power. When we rescued Vrishti from the Haven, her entire army behaved like it was possessed. If she has the power to inhabit their minds at the same time as attacking our shield, neutralizing that creature out there likely would only slow her down for a time."

"Then we need to get Deva out, before it's too late."

"I can get her through the barrier, perhaps out of the Sanctuary as well," Zorion said.

"The barrier needs to come down to stop these surges. If we leave it up, she'll remain linked to it," Neph said.

Aodh nodded. "And we don't dare take it down until we're sure my sister is prepared to begin the ritual with whichever mate she chooses as the strongest."

"There's still the trouble of Meri to address," Ozzie said. "If we send Deva out into the world, there is nothing stopping Meri from reaching her. She is *safest* right here, as long as the barrier remains strong."

Neela paced, her skin glowing with inner fire. The others in the room exchanged looks of concern and warily edged backward. "There has to be someplace we can take her that's just as secure." Turning to Zorion, she asked, "What about the Glade? It's protected, isn't it?"

"You've seen the Glade?" Aodh asked, a touch of alarm in his voice. "That's impossible. Humans shouldn't be able to access it."

"I'm a little more than human. So is my brother," Neela said in a brittle tone. She lifted a hand, and flames sprouted from her fingertips.

Aodh crossed his arms." What *are* you, anyway? You were an Elite once, and I know what kinds of mutations Elites undergo to gain their powers, but you are something different now. Something unlike anything I have seen—your aura is pure fire."

"Pure dragon fire," Zorion said. "Neela died at Meri's hands only yesterday. She was resurrected by my fire—I had no idea that would happen, but I am grateful for it nonetheless."

"A phoenix," Aodh said in a subdued tone. "Do you have wings as well?"

Neela nodded, and her back shimmered with golden fire. Zorion hastily stepped close and pressed a palm between her shoulder blades. "Not here, *adara*. It's too ... flammable." To Aodh, he said, "Yes, it seems this is what being resurrected by dragon fire does."

"The Sun spoke to me when I died," Neela said. "She gave me a new life so I could protect my daughter. I intend to do that. Can we take her to the Glade or not?"

Aodh's shoulders dropped. "Sadly, I doubt it would be any safer than the Sanctuary. Deva is like a beacon to Meri. If she could find her here, we have to assume she'd be able to find her at the Glade or the turul Enclaves as well. Nothing short of a higher plane would be secure enough."

"Did I not see a god in the gardens earlier?" Zorion said. "Would he help?"

Ozzie was already headed for the door. "There's one way to find out," he shot over his shoulder as he departed.

CHAPTER 14

CADE

Just when Cade was becoming comfortable wallowing in his own memories and studiously avoiding eavesdropping on the actions of the two lovers, he was abruptly pushed back into his conscious body.

He found himself lying on his back, blinking up into a beautiful, green-eyed gaze.

"Cade, there you are," Numa said with a warm smile.

He blinked as he took in her disheveled appearance and flushed cheeks. She had a hesitant look as she reached up to stroke his beard, her touch inciting a pleasant flutter of longing inside him. He turned into her touch, pressing his lips to her palm and holding it there while he took a deep breath to gather himself.

"Yeah, I'm back. I take it breezy boy took good care of you?"

"Mmm, yes. He did have excellent tools to work with." She slid off him and settled against his side, the warm press of her body fanning the flames of his longing. With Zephyrus' presence back in his mind, practically glowing with gratitude and affection, he was immersed in more love than he had been in ages. "How are you holding up?"

Cade glanced down at his stiff cock, still glistening with her sweetly scented essence, and still aching with all the pent-up desire he'd held back for … how long?

"How long was I out for?" he asked, glancing around the room. His gaze landed on the big clock that stood against the wall in the sitting area across the room. Could that be right?

"It's nearly Midnight," Numa said. "You've been here for several hours already. I know the light can be deceiving. The outside light only moves about ten minutes for every hour that passes inside."

"No, I got that part. I just usually don't lose time so easily."

"It's a side-effect of being a passenger. Thank you for allowing me the time to be with her in a body. You are a true friend."

Cade turned to face Numa, leaning on one elbow and looking down into her flushed, yet lovely face. He let his gaze drift down her body, drinking her in and trying to ignore the pang of regret at not experiencing the lovemaking firsthand —to feel her come apart beneath him with that look of utter adoration in her eyes.

The look she was giving him now.

His brows twitched. "You could have had him for the rest of the test. I'd have been happy just riding along."

"I know. That's why I needed to spend more time with you. If I do choose you and Zephyrus, I'm choosing you *both*. Not just him. It's your body doing all the work—and very well, I might add—but I want to know more about what's up here." She tapped him gently on the temple. "Or here…" She lowered her hand to the center of his chest and curled her fingers into the thick blond hair that tufted up across his pecs.

Cade's heartbeat sped up at her expectant look. He let out

a shaky sigh. He knew what she was asking, and he wasn't even close to ready to go there.

"What was his name?" she asked softly.

Cade had spent the last several hours lost and able to do nothing but spend that time in the company of the ghosts inside his head. In the midst of the wind spirit making love to the woman in his arms, he had restricted his perusal of those old memories to the happy ones, but feared saying the name out loud would call forth all of his old demons.

But as he looked at her, he deflated. He couldn't disappoint her, not when she seemed so desperate to give him a fair shot at her love.

"Lennox Sundance. We paired up young and had a good long life as bachelors guarding the Sundance portal. I didn't care for life in the desert, but it suited him. He loved that life, and I loved him. Maybe a bit too much."

"Why would you say that?"

"Because I wound up alone after he was taken. Had we not been so wrapped up with each other, we may have tried harder to catch the eye of a female. Maybe the enemy never would have gotten him, but even if he had still been killed, I'd have had a family to focus on instead of spending the last century or so feeling sorry for myself."

"You couldn't have known ..." Numa began, then frowned, her words trailing off. "I ... am sorry."

"What the hell do you have to be sorry for? You're the best shot I've had in ages to be happy again, win or lose."

She shook her head and pulled away from him, sitting up and hugging her knees. "No, I can't discount the possibility that Fate still had a hand in all this." She swept her hand around in an arc that Cade knew encompassed their entire situation, even beyond the temporal bubble they were in. "If it was *my* path you were meant to cross, even if I ultimately would have to choose, then my father would have known the outcome. No doubt he already knows, but is still forcing us to play these games."

"Well, then let's play," he said, gripping her arm and forcing her to look at him. "What do I need to do to win this?"

Numa dropped her gaze and a pained look crossed her face. When she met his eyes again, she was resolute. "Your aura suggests you have power to rival a god built up within you. If it is as potent when I release it as it seems to be now, you will be a true contender. But there is another pair remaining who I have to give a fair shot." Her voice broke and her gaze filled with something that resembled agony. Whatever she'd been about to say seemed to lodge in her throat and her eyes welled with tears.

"Sweet pea," Cade said gruffly, pulling her into his arms. He held her close, his throbbing erection an unwelcome distraction when she pressed against him, her entire body shaking with soft sobs. "What's got you so upset?"

"Oh, Cade. Please forgive me if it isn't you I choose. I don't know that it won't be, but I *have* to keep this fair. If I don't ... if I make any of the gods—or my father—angry, it could go badly for us all. I can't give you an answer. If I show favoritism, they will know."

Cade chuckled. "You do what you have to do. My life was going nowhere before I signed up for this. It would break my heart for the second time if we lost, but I promise you if Zephyrus is willing, he will have me no matter what."

"I wish things were different," she said with a long sigh. "If only Fate had sent me the dreams my siblings received, I would know one way or the other. Making this choice will be the hardest thing I've ever done."

Despite the clear, razor-sharp apprehension tightening his gut, Cade understood the emotion was not his own. He mentally comforted Zephyrus and cupped Numa's cheek at the same time, hoping to comfort her as well.

"You have a dragon's heart, sweet pea, and yours is bigger than most. Simply being loved by you is an honor I won't forget, even though I know it's directed at the man who's borrowed my body. I don't think any of the others could ever regret this chance, even if we lose to a god. Because as much as we can't help but love you, we know what's at stake. You can't choose us all, but whoever is best will be a very, very lucky man."

She let out a soft sniffle against his shoulder and nodded. "Or men … If I did choose you, my mark would affect both you and Zephyrus. And Theron and Bekim are a bonded bachelor pair—they're a unit. Dion's the only solo male."

"Then I suppose I got lucky meeting Ozzie out there when I arrived. I'd never have stood a chance without a partner."

Numa twisted in his arms, her lower body pressing tighter to his as she arched her back so she could look into his eyes again. With her full breasts flush against his chest, he became acutely aware of her hard nipples like little pebbles between them.

"I don't know, I think you could hold your own, but I do love the idea of having you both in separate bodies. Would he be as well-endowed as you are, do you think?" She slid a hand down his stomach in a languid stroke, then wrapped it around his thick shaft. The previous dull ache had become a background annoyance, but with her touch, a jolt of arousal shot straight up his spine.

He wrapped his hand around hers and held her still, pinning her with a determined gaze. "You needed something when I got here that I was more than happy to deliver, but if we're as close to finishing this day as I think we are, I'd like a chance to give you what I think will prove we're the ones you need, and not just because we can bring the power."

Numa glanced over her shoulder at the clock. He knew there wasn't much time left, but he was also damn sure there was enough for him to prove himself worthy. Zephyrus didn't have anything to worry about, but Numa had only known Cade for a day. All he'd been able to show her was how skilled he was at delivering a good, hard fuck on demand.

If it came down to the wire, he would need her to know without a doubt that she'd be the center of his world in every way. Even with another man in the mix, they couldn't let themselves forget that detail, which was the one thing he and Lennox had lost sight of. They'd been too wrapped up in each other to remember what their purpose was as male ursa. They'd been selfish, and if nothing else, he owed it to his lost lover's memory to honor this dragon and prove to Gaia or Fate, or whomever, that he hadn't forgotten what it meant to be one of Gaia's children.

He hooked his hand behind her head, turning her attention back to him. His fingers tangled in her thick, silken strands as he pulled her close, his heart beating so hard it nearly drowned out the aching pulse in his cock. His gaze met hers and he regarded her for a second, wanting to be sure she understood that it was him now. That this was how he would prove to her that *he* was as worthy a mate as the wind spirit who had spent the last few hours making love to her.

Numa swallowed, and that desperate look of yearning returned to her eyes. "Cade, please …"

His grip tightened in her hair and he gritted his teeth. Gaia's tears, did he love hearing her say his name.

"I will love you every bit as hard as he does, if you give me the chance. At least promise that you will remember this when the time comes to choose."

She took a shaky breath, one hand braced on his arm, her fingers digging in as though she was halfway between pushing him away and pulling him closer. "I will never forget this, no matter what happens," she said. "Please … your aura is so *perfect* right now. Don't make me wait."

His entire body ached to take her hard again like he had at the start, but all that would prove was how much he needed to empty his balls of all the power he had built up over the last several hours.

"Sweet pea, I'm gonna give you what you want, but you might have to be patient and let it happen at my pace, got it?" He bent and brushed his lips across hers, teasing his tongue along the full lower lip and inhaling deeply of the fragrant, fertile scent enveloping her.

Numa shivered as he captured her mouth and eased his tongue between her lips. He tasted her slowly, enjoying the way her entire body seemed to mold itself to his, her pelvis grinding into his cock as she slipped one leg over his hip. Wet heat brushed against his shaft, and it was all he could do to keep from shifting positions and shoving his cock deep inside her again.

This wasn't meant to be a quick, hard fuck. He had no idea whether the tide of longing she'd summoned to the surface was a side-effect of Zephyrus' love, or something of his own that grew whenever he was in her presence, but he wanted her to know he was just as capable of making love to her as his partner was.

"This is all you, friend. She is easy to love and too long overdue for it."

Cade's skin tingled with the caress of a soft breeze that seemed to urge him on. He and Lennox had always had an almost unconscious connection that enhanced their ability to satisfy the female ursa they were tasked to service, but they'd only spent a short time in that role before being transferred out of the Sanctuary to serve as portal guardians. They'd rarely shared lovers after that. Having a partner who was equally invested in the woman's pleasure was a long missed experience, but even better now for the simple fact that he was also invested in winning her love, not just driving her desire to its peak.

Numa broke away from their kiss with a gasp and a breathy cry of his name. Her core rubbed hot and wet against his shaft, and he took a deep breath to tamp down that need once again. Soon they'd be joined, but not until he was sure she understood what this meant to him.

He pushed her gently onto her back and shifted partway over her, propping himself on one hand while he cupped her cheek with the other. He raked his gaze down her body again, taking in the smooth curves and the shimmering green pattern that seemed to ghost across her skin with each quick breath. It reminded him what she was, and that every second he held back would be more of a gift to her when he let go.

He drifted his hand down her side and around the swell of her breast, palming the luscious, pink-tipped orb and squeezing before lowering his head to take her nipple into his mouth. Every caress, every taste he took extra care to draw out, despite the rising need for release that had become an ever-present ache in his lower body. The soles of his feet itched and he ventured a glance down, worried that he'd lost his hold on the energy and Gaia was somehow forcing him to let it loose, but nothing seemed amiss.

He moved to kneel between her thighs, still hovering over her and alternating between both delicious nipples, reveling in the roughness of her voice. She tangled her fingers in his long hair, hanging on for dear life. Her harsh moans of his name mixed with affirmations he never in a million years imagined he'd hear a woman speak followed him as he slipped lower. He gripped her inner thighs with both hands and spread her open, palms slickening from the arousal coating her inner thighs. She parted for him eagerly, but even as he began to tongue her hot, wet snatch, she called his name again.

"Cade, please fuck me. I need to taste that power. Have to know if it's enough. Please!"

He closed his eyes as he wrapped his lips around her throbbing little clit and sucked, determined to taste the flood of her juices on his tongue just once before he sank his cock into her again. Her panting grew and he teased her clit with swift flicks, spreading her wider so he could access more of the sensitive silken flesh between her thighs.

Pushing her leg up to spread her wider, he exposed her backside to his view. Her sweet, tight rosebud seemed to beckon to him, reminding him how much his old lover had loved when he tongued him there. Experimentally, he lowered his head again and swept his tongue in concentric spirals while he rubbed at her clit with his thumb. Within moments, Numa's orgasmic cries rang out, nearly loud enough to hurt his ears, but the sweet rush of her energy counteracted any discomfort.

It was almost too much. His cock screamed for relief, his balls hot and achy to the point he worried he'd done true damage by waiting so long, but if this all worked out, it would be worth it. He kept his mouth between her legs, teasing her spasming flesh with gentle licks until she finally relaxed, but he didn't let her put her leg down. He held it high and hooked it over his shoulder as he raised up and aligned his cock with her cleft.

Both her holes were on display now, and he had the sense she'd welcome him fucking either one. He tentatively rubbed his tip along the crease of her ass, teasing across her rear opening before pressing between the swollen lips of her pussy.

She'd reached above her and now gripped the thick, carved wooden posts of the headboard, staring down at him with a fevered gaze.

"Please, Cade …" she begged again as he teased her entrance.

He slid his hand down her thigh to cup her ass, and just as he began to slide his cock into the confines of her pussy, he pushed two fingers past the tight opening of her ass. He forced himself to take his time, though his mind was nearly gone from pleasure by the time his cock sank all the way into her and both fingers were in her ass to the last knuckle. She shuddered and moaned, her hips bucking of their own accord.

"I want you to feel ever single inch of me, sweet pea. When I'm done fucking this tight pussy of yours, my cock is going in your ass. I've got enough power saved up to come about ten times before we're done, so I hope you're ready, but I want you to know I'm taking this slow so there's no question what it means to me. What *you* mean to me. Zeph already proved his love. It's my turn to prove mine."

All she could do was beg, but when he slid out and slammed back in, she gave him a look that proved he'd made his point. Now all he had to do was give her all the power he'd saved up, and he was more than ready to do just that.

CHAPTER 15

NUMA

There was no question in Numa's mind that the man making love to her now wasn't the same one she'd spent the last several hours entangled with. He may have had the same body, but the look in his eyes was different, a little uncertain, but no less determined to prove himself to her. He had the look of one who had very little to lose, but everything to gain by winning her over.

He moved differently too, his body adjusting effortlessly to accommodate her pleasure in a way that spoke of long practice and innate understanding, allowing mind and body to be united in a single purpose.

Zephyrus had used Cade's body well, much to her delight, but he'd had an air of fascination with the form he'd borrowed that had almost distracted him. He'd acclimated quickly and made love to her with a desperation that betrayed the ages of pent-up longing he'd had for her. It was everything she had hoped, despite knowing he wasn't quite at home in the borrowed body.

Cade was very much at home, his hips twisting as he slid his cock slowly into her, his shoulder bunching with the slightest pressure of his fingers into her backside. It was all she could do to keep from losing focus to her own pleasure, but she found herself enraptured by the utter ease with which he moved, even as his aura brightened to a nearly blinding cloud around him, the power growing with each long, determined stroke.

Her own energy swelled yet again, and while he'd been determined to make her come under his mouth a moment ago, this time she caught a glimpse of the effort he put into drawing her pleasure out for as long as possible.

"Hold on for me, sweet pea," he growled. "I want to make this good … show you what you mean to me." Her ankle rested against his shoulder as he plunged deep, and he turned his head to press a reverent kiss to the side of her foot. In that moment, she was disarmed by the utter lack of self-consciousness this man possessed. His expression was completely bare and open, his adoration of her so complete a warm fluttering filled her chest.

That she could have two such different, yet completely focused men as these two for her mates had never occurred to her. Theron and Bekim she adored, but they felt like two halves of a whole. Zephyrus and Cade, however, were only together for one purpose—her—and they'd both worship her in their own way.

She held on tighter to the bars above her head, arching up as he cupped one breast and squeezed, then lightly pinched her nipple. He slid that hand down her torso and pressed his thumb between her legs, applying pressure to the hardened flesh of her clit. She let out a sharp gasp at the spike of pleasure that shot through her and realized at the same time that he'd pushed a third finger into her ass.

Sweet Mother, his cock was so big he'd rivaled the god who'd come before him. He rivaled full-sized dragons in their true forms. That he promised to use it in other ways was more thrilling to her than she could have expected. But the care he took to prepare her for it spoke of his determination to ensure her pleasure more than his own.

"You can come inside me," she said. "I want you to."

His eyes flashed, and she thought she saw a spark of the other being that resided within his body, as though Zephyrus might regret not being the one in control while they shared their final climax. But he'd had his turn and had used it well, proving how true his love was and had always been.

A low growl built inside the big ursa's chest, the vibration rippling through him until she felt it deep in her core and at the base of her skull. "You're damn right I'm going to come inside you. I hope you're ready, because I've got a lot to give, sweet pea. I've saved every last drop for you."

"Yes!" She pushed her hips up, meeting his quickening thrusts, the rising pleasure of her own climax swiftly surging to the surface.

Cade's body glistened with sweat from his hours of exertion, yet he showed no signs of flagging. She should have guessed a Windchaser would possess such stamina. Though she adored her Rainsong lovers, she was often grateful there were two of them because she doubted one would be enough. How this Windchaser had been left behind as a lone bachelor made no sense. He had the skill and power to satisfy a dragon, not to mention any number of ursa females.

His jaw clenched and his torso arched, the hard lines of his abs standing out in the perpetual morning light. He shoved deep into her with a harsh grunt and threw his head back. The fingers inside her ass stilled even as his thick, hard shaft pulsed his hot seed into her.

Cade groaned long and loud, continuing to fuck her hard with each spasm until his thrusts made lewd squelching sounds from the copious essence that filled her. Numa's entire body lit up from the surge of energy, but it was only a fraction of what she'd been sure he held back. Her heart fell when the waves of power subsided and he pulled out.

"I ain't finished yet," he said and gripped her by the hips, flipping her over in one swift movement. He hauled her close and shoved his cock back into her dripping snatch once more, but eased it out again and slid the shaft up along the cleft of her ass instead, coating her opening with their shared juices. He repeated the process, his cock still stone-hard and searing with the heat of his arousal as he stretched her well-used pussy, once again reminding her of his generous girth.

Three fingers slipped into her ass again, pushing the gathered lubricant past her barrier to coat it from the inside. Then his tip was at her rear opening and she braced herself, clinging to the bars of the headboard and mindlessly staring out the window behind the bed into the shimmering distortion of the temporal barrier.

"Tell me to stop if it hurts, sweet pea. But if you trust me, this will blow your mind."

"I trust you."

Just as his thick tip breached her barrier and she gasped in pleasure, his hand slipped around her hip and between her thighs. He hooked two fingers into her pussy, pushing them deep and fucking her with them as he eased his enormous cock into her ass. She clung to the pillows, digging her nails in until sharp talons erupted from the tips and downy feathers floated into the air from the rents in the pillowcases.

Every part of her told her to shift, that she couldn't accommodate a cock that large where he wanted to put it, not in the shape she was in now. Her dragon form could take him easily, but she desperately wanted to feel what he promised her and knew that wouldn't happen if she cheated. It didn't hurt; it was just a mind-crushingly full sensation coupled with the stretch of the most sensitive part of her body.

Then his fingers found her clit and began to lightly tease, swirling more of the already overflowing fluids from her pussy until her entire lower body was awash in conflicting sensations.

"Come here, baby," he growled behind her, sliding his hands up her sides and around her chest, pulling her up and tight against him. The shift in position forced her back and down onto his cock, and she cried out at the sudden and complete invasion of his entire shaft into her backside.

"Cade, please!" she yelled, too lost in pleasure to do more than beg.

He began thrusting deep, arms wrapped tight around her. Numa let her head fall back against his shoulder, surrendering fully to his hold. Cade pressed his lips to the side of her jaw, brushing them along her ear.

"This isn't the end, sweet pea," he murmured. "I'm going to fill you up more after this."

"Yes," she gasped, reveling in the sensation of his steady thrusts and the warm clasp of his palm at her throat, fingers sliding up her jaw to tilt her head to the side. He grazed his teeth along her neck and bit down lightly on her shoulder, sending a shiver of anticipation through her. He could mark her like this, and she didn't think she would even object. It was rare for a male ursa to mark his mate, rather than the other way around, but it was done. Sweet Mother, she wished he would do it … take the decision away from her. Force her hand. Because she would love him as much as she loved any of them; she was as sure of that fact as she was of anything.

"Please … bite me, Cade. Mark me …"

He let out a rough groan and his teeth tightened on her shoulder, the pressure painful, but despite her plea, she knew it wouldn't work. He didn't have the magic to break her impervious skin.

Rather than try harder, he released her from his bite and shoved another finger deep into her pussy, finger-fucking her in tempo with the fiercer thrusts of his cock. His fingertips hit the inner wall of her pussy, the heel of his palm rubbing perfectly at the swollen bud of her clit.

Her disappointment of her unfulfilled wish dissolved amid the pure, bright pleasure of her orgasm as it rushed through her in a torrent. In her ear, he rumbled words of encouragement and promises of more power to come if she could take what he gave her now.

And give he did. His cock pulsed into her, the heat of the power flooding her body with even more potent energy than before, like he was saving up and doling out increasingly delicious servings to her with each round.

Numa shuddered in his arms as her pleasure abated. He held tight, his embrace warm and protective as he nuzzled at the tender flesh of her shoulder where he'd bit her. With one gentle kiss, he began to pull away, easing out of her with the care of someone well-acquainted with the sensitive nature of the part of her he'd been buried inside.

Before she could process the change in position, he'd scooped her up into his arms and stepped off the bed.

"What are you doing?" she asked, eyes widening.

"I saw a big-ass bath in the other room. Thought we'd finish off our date in there. I mean to feed you the last of what I've got, but after being buried in your sweet little ass, I figured we ought to get clean first."

She couldn't argue with his logic, and the promise of more of his increasingly potent power made her mouth water, particularly since she realized that was precisely where he intended to deliver it. She bit her lip at the thought, remembering how desperately she'd wanted to taste Dionysus' essence, but didn't dare risk allowing herself to become drugged by that immensely powerful magic. She had no such compunctions against tasting Cade, and was suddenly giddy with the prospect of drawing the last of his pent-up power from him with her mouth on his beautiful cock.

He stepped into the cooling water with easy grace and lowered them both until he rested on one of the wide benches with her on his lap. Numa dropped her hands into the water, and it warmed at her command until steam rose up around them, clinging to their skin.

Cade sank lower and sighed as he drifted a wet hand up her naked back and back down. "Wish we'd had dragons in the Sanctuary a long time ago."

"It wouldn't take much effort to add hot running water, you know."

"Oh, we have it at the Windchaser Lodge. Gets too damn cold up there to go without. Rainsong ursa mostly bathe outdoors, so it never seemed necessary. But this is heaven."

He pulled her against him, and the two of them luxuriated until Cade's breathing grew slow and even. Numa glanced up to see his head tilted back against the edge of the bath, his eyes closed. Yet despite his relaxed state, his cock was still a hard, thick presence sandwiched between his belly and her hip.

Numa leaned over to the edge to grab the soap and a cloth and began to slowly wash his shoulders, taking care to maintain gentle strokes to avoid waking him yet. Their time together was to end soon, but she didn't want to rush the final moments. The power he'd granted her so far was not quite enough for what she would need for the ritual, but if his aura was any indication, he still had quite an impressive supply to let go.

She eased off his lap and crouched in the water between his knees. Soaping up both hands, she smoothed the suds across his chest, enjoying the coarseness of his hair beneath her palms and the way his nipples hardened when she passed her fingers across them. Cade let out a soft murmur of pleasure and his aura flared under her touch.

"Zephyrus, you chose your partner well. Thank you for him."

Cade laughed softly and a warm breeze blew through the room, dissipating the steam and cooling it on her skin. He lifted his head, but the eyes that regarded her were not the ursa's. Numa's heartbeat quickened and a smile stretched her lips in recognition of her other lover.

"I had little choice in the matter, but such is the way of Fate," Zephyrus said. "I don't doubt your father put the man in my path just to toy with us both."

Numa gave him a stricken look. "I don't know what I did to deserve this. I followed the rules. Kept my siblings in line when we were governing the dragons. I was *good*."

His expression grew somber and he lifted a wet hand to cup her cheek. His touch eased her agitation. "Sophia would have a better answer for you than I have. She has Fate's ear and Fate's trust, but I doubt she can influence Fate any more than we can. Were I to hazard a guess, it is because the dire nature of your mission requires a clear head uninfluenced by outside elements. There are greater powers at work in the universe than the gods who spawned us. Whatever it was that corrupted the creature we are fighting may have Fate backed into a corner."

Numa frowned up at him and narrowed her eyes. "That explanation is a little too specific for me to believe you don't have *some* information. What do you think we are up against? Dionysus wasn't very forthcoming."

"Dionysus is too close to the offending party to know. It's one of his spawn who succumbed to the corruption. My brothers and I only know that an older evil once existed, but was believed dormant: an elemental force that abhors light. We hoped that Meri's corruption was merely a superficial desire for immortality, but can't discount the possibility of something more sinister at work. Something cursed since the beginning of time."

Numa's skin prickled as an ancient memory shifted beneath the surface of her waking thoughts: The curse her kind had long dreaded coming to fruition, but which had taken a backseat to more pressing perils over the past year since the most recent Ascension.

There was one creature she trusted to tell her the truth, but at the moment, that individual was out of reach. Once she completed the ritual and opened the portal, she may have the chance.

"The Diviner may be able to tell us the answer. She is more attuned to primordial forces than the rest of us."

The air cooled around her as another, more agitated breeze rippled the surface of the bath. "Would she offer more than riddles in answer to your queries?" Zephyrus asked. "I have never liked that creature. She is too close to those old forces for my taste."

"She's my sister. I would trust all my siblings with my life." There was more to her optimism about getting answers from the Diviner. The ancient creature was also the offspring of a secret union between Dionysus, Gaia, and the Mother Dragon. She possessed immense primal power and was immune to Fate's influence. If anyone had a clear view of the truth, it would be her. But they had to reach her first.

Cade pressed his lips into a line and his brow twitched. The muscles in his face rippled and shifted, then stilled. He let out a sigh.

"Zephyrus? Or Cade?"

"Cade is insisting I allow him to finish what he started. But before I give him control again, please know that my brothers and I have more resources to help if we find the fight more dire than expected. They will come when the portal opens, regardless of who you choose as your mate."

"Thank you," Numa said, reaching up to stroke his cheek. He leaned down and kissed her, the press of his lips a soft, sensual farewell. Within seconds, the kiss deepened and his hands tightened at her hips, then slid up to cup her breasts.

A low, rumbling growl rose from Cade's chest, signaling that the bear was back, and he was hungry. His cock surged against her hip, and she reached between them to wrap her hand around him.

He gripped her thigh with one big hand and she parted for him. He slid his fingers along the inside up to her tender folds and stroked. Pulling away from their kiss, he gave her a wicked look.

"I'm half-tempted to leave you filled with my spunk for those Rainsong boys to have a taste of when they get to you. Think it would give me an advantage?"

Numa shuddered under his deliberate strokes already sending her close to another climax. "That would be rude and mean," she said, forcing an admonishing tone, yet lacking conviction under his expert touch.

"Mmm." He nodded. "Then we'd better make sure you're good and clean."

He twisted, gripping her by the hips and lifting her out of the water. Her eyes flew open as he set her down on the edge of the tub and pushed her knees wide.

Gazing down at her wet pussy, he shook his head and made a tutting sound. "A real shame to wash that scent off you, but you're right. Want to keep things fair, after all."

He shot a grin at her, then reached to the side of the tub for the cloth. His aura flared bright when he dropped to his knees on the bench beneath the water and dipped the cloth in to soak it. First he squeezed the cloth over the top of her cleft, the warm water trickling down into her folds. With his other hand, he gently parted her and held her open while he pressed the cloth between her lips and stroked. He was businesslike in his movements, focusing intently on his task, despite the clear arousal flaring his aura to a bright red-gold that betrayed the generous amount of power he had left to give.

Numa was enthralled watching him carry out what he'd convinced her was a task of utmost importance. It would be unfair to make Bekim and Theron taste the other man on her when their turn came, though the idea made her blood heat. She was well-acquainted with the taste of both ursa males after sharing her bed with them for the past several weeks. They both enjoyed tasting each other on her as well.

"How well do you know them?" she asked, breathless from the slow, steady strokes Cade gave her clit with the soft cloth. He still made a pretense of washing her, periodically dipping the cloth back into the water before squeezing it over her pelvis and then returning to rub it in tight little circles over her clit.

He lifted his blue gaze to her face and raised his eyebrows. "The Rainsong boys? We've crossed paths. I used to think they had the right idea, opting to commit to serving the females in the Sanctuary rather than seeking out a permanent arrangement with one, but now I wish they hadn't. Less competition would be nice, even if I still had to go up against a god to win you."

"We have a bond already, I should warn you," she said, the words slipping out amid a haze of pleasure that made her far too comfortable and eager to open up to this man.

He lowered his gaze and seemed to contemplate his steady stroking, then tossed the cloth aside. Before she could react, he'd pushed her knees up, yanked her hips to the edge, and pushed the massive length of his cock deep into her once more.

Numa let out a gasp of surprise that degenerated into a moan as her back arched, and she pushed her hips up into his urgent, pumping thrusts. Cade hovered over her, his blue eyes blazing.

"How much of a bond do you think we'll have, after I give you all I've got?"

She whimpered as he slowed, aching for him to give her the release his touch had promised only moments earlier, but that he seemed intent to withhold from her now.

"One that would last forever, if I chose you," she said. "But it doesn't matter, does it?" Her core screamed for release, even as the ache of acute longing took up residence in her chest. She wanted this. Wanted Cade and Zephyrus every bit as much as she ached for a more lasting bond with Bekim and Theron. But she was right; none of it mattered when they were up against a god who she was almost positive had held back his true power. Despite Dion's lapse and display of a level of honor she didn't think the gods possessed, she had a sinking feeling that the rest of these tests may be an exercise in futility.

"Then it won't matter if I leave your sweet little cunt filled with me, will it? Maybe it'll give them something to fight for if they think they're in danger of losing, because I sure as shit hope it's clear how much I want you. And that isn't breezy boy talking, it's *me*. Cade Windchaser."

He slammed into her harder, each thrust of his cock stretching her and branding her from the inside out. The brutal honesty in his gaze destroyed her, because she was sure she would encounter the same thing from her other lovers. It wasn't enough that she had to choose between these men who all were skilled and potent lovers, but she had to weigh their potential as true mates as well.

It might have been easier if she'd been able to keep emotional ties out of the equation. Numa had expected her close involvement with the other two ursa males would be the hardest part of her decision, if she wound up having to choose another. But after today, she wasn't so sure. Dionysus had made a confession that floored her, suggesting that his interest in her was personal and had less to do with having an upper hand on Fate than on his desire for her alone.

Now the ferocity of Cade's lovemaking drove home how much she meant to him, not just the wind spirit who was ostensibly along for the ride. Both of these men would be bound by her choice as much as the others.

It was all too much. She let out an anguished yell and surrendered to the pleasure, to the desire for a kind of gratification she rarely allowed herself.

"Give it to me!" she called to him. "Show me what you've got, if you want to keep me, Cade. Give it all to me. Show me you can own my body with yours and maybe you'll win. Do you have it in you, ursa? Or are you too beholden to Gaia's laws?"

He let out a harsh laugh. "Those laws only apply to ursa females, sweet pea. You're a dragon. You want all of me, you got me."

His entire body tensed and he grabbed her knees, pushing them wide as he slammed deep and let out a rumbling groan. A torrent of magic rushed into her as his seed filled her once more, but the flood didn't cease. His aura brightened and shimmered as he pulled out of her, the fluctuation in his energy betraying his next move.

Numa pushed herself up on her hands in time for the next wave of his orgasm to hit, the energy still flooding into her where their bodies touched. He gripped his cock and stroked, more streams of hot, sticky semen shooting onto her torso.

His gaze was bright with fevered intention and he gripped the back of her neck with his free hand. He pulled her forward, holding her head held tight as he pushed her down.

"Not leaving without seeing your lips wrapped around me, baby. I've got more, and it's all going in that sweet mouth of yours."

She didn't resist, leaning forward to grip his hips for support at first, then wrapping both hands around his shaft as his fingers tangled in her damp hair. She slipped her lips over his tip, but could go no farther. Still, she eagerly sucked the head of his cock, his seemingly endless orgasm continuing with surprising power.

Sliding one hand between his thighs, she cupped his balls and squeezed, reveling in the way his hands tightened on her head and he let out a roar. Then she urged him on by slipping her tongue out in all its full draconic glory, wrapping it around and around his length and sliding it up until her lips popped off the tip.

Semen still shot from it, hitting her cheeks and chin with hot, tangy wetness that she gathered onto her tongue and swallowed. She savored his flavor and the musky scent that was distinctly him, though it held a note of summer sage that only the West Wind had ever smelled like.

"More still?" she asked, gazing up at him with bright eyes as she kept stroking him with both hands. Hot, sticky fluid dripped off her nipples as the energy finally started to ebb, the spurts of his semen spilling over her fists and slick beneath her palms where she gripped him. Her body buzzed from the inundation of his final dose of magic, her well overflowing.

Cade's eyelids fluttered, his gaze lazily drifting down over the mess he'd made of her. He grazed a knuckle down her semen-covered breast, swirling the slick fluid around her nipple until she gasped.

"I want one more taste of you, sweet pea. A taste of you

covered in me so breezy boy can have a farewell gift before we go."

He teased a sticky finger down her belly and swirled it around the still flooded channel between her thighs. As he dipped down, she caught the shift in expressions—Cade giving way to Zephyrus, whose hungry eyes flashed with stormy silver light a second before they slid closed and his mouth covered her cream-soaked pussy.

She let out an involuntary cry and gripped at his head, only abstractly conscious of the fact that her hands were still coated in him, and now his silken golden waves would be sticky with his own essence.

Soon nothing mattered but the expert tongue lapping at Numa's core. When a deft fingertip probed at her backside and fingers sank into both her slick openings, she was no longer sure which of the two men who shared that body were driving her to orgasm. When she looked down her torso at him, his lashes fluttered, and she caught glimpses of multicolored eyes that hinted of summer storms and winter revels all rolled into one.

She surrendered again to the pleasure, arching into his attention and bucking her hips against his mouth as he tormented her to one last mind-shattering climax.

When the echoes of her resonant cries faded, the chiming of the clock in the other room filled her ears. Cade pulled back with a frown, still gently stroking her inner thighs despite the sticky residue he'd left on her skin.

"You have to go," she said. "We went too long already. They're due to arrive now."

"No time to let me finish washing you?" he asked, eyeing the mess he'd made of her.

"Do you really want me clean after that show?" she asked.

His lips twisted in a wry smirk. "Sweet pea, I love how put together you usually are, but seeing you a mess like this because of me has got to be the sexiest fucking thing I've ever seen. If you choose me and breezy boy gets a body, we'll take turns making sure you stay filled with us."

Numa shivered at the promise, knowing that he meant it despite the reverence both he and Zephyrus had displayed while making love to her today.

"Hurry and go. I need time to clean up before they get here," she said, climbing up and offering him her hand.

Cade clasped it, though he easily stepped out of the bath without trouble. He seemed utterly at ease, even though his wet hair still dripped over his shoulders, half the liquid likely carrying traces of his own essence as well as hers. Numa didn't bother with a robe, intending to sink back into the bath and rinse as much of him from her skin as she could before the others arrived.

She saw him to the door, but before she could open it for him, she found herself pressed up against it once more and his mouth clasped over hers in a hungry kiss.

When he pulled away and she caught her breath, he said, "I hope that was enough. If it wasn't, we'll have to work extra hard in round two. I aim to test your limits."

She laughed, enjoying his cocksure attitude. He and Zephyrus had given more than necessary, but the day wasn't over yet.

She opened the door, ready to give him a smack on the ass and send him on his way, but her heart skidded to a stop when she looked into the hallway.

Bekim and Theron stood leaning by the window opposite her door, arms crossed and worried frowns adorning both their handsome faces. Cade let out a soft curse as they took him in, completely naked and no doubt covered in her scent.

Without missing a beat, Cade stepped into the hallway and reached out a hand.

"Good luck, you two. Give her all you've got, and then

some. I won't lie and say I wish you luck. I want to win this so bad I can taste it, but hopefully the little taste I left behind for you will give you some incentive, because we *need* her to win no matter which of us she chooses, and that's what you guys need to remember before you walk through that door."

He gave them a nod when they neglected to accept a handshake. Then he turned and winked at Numa before ambling off, a pleasant breeze toying with her hair several moments after he was gone.

CHAPTER 16

BEKIM

Bekim only realized the big ursa had been offering him his hand after the man had turned to go. He should have taken it and shook in the spirit of sportsmanship. Even if they were rivals, Cade had a point. The outcome of this contest would affect more than just their mating prospects. It would determine the course of the war, and their entire lives after the fact.

But he had been too stunned by the image that greeted him when Numa's door opened to do anything but stare. Naked skin wasn't unusual in the Sanctuary—none of the residents had any compunctions about wandering around bare. It was easier to shift, after all. But the big, virile ursa male who had preceded him and Theron in Numa's chamber was a bit of a legend, and even more intimidating when he was practically glowing from the residue of Numa's essence that seemed to seep from his very pores. She'd been all over him, which was no surprise considering the nature of the contest, but he'd given them a look as though her essence was a badge of honor he wore.

Theron made a low, chuffing sound beside him as Cade

passed by and headed down the hall. The sound was one Bekim's partner only made when his interest was piqued by a potential lover. Bekim glanced at him with an eyebrow raised, and his bearded partner simply gave him a teasing half-smile. Yeah, he'd happily have invited the man to be their third, under other circumstances. Perhaps if all three of them lost this contest to the god, they could pool their resources and join forces. What ursa female would turn down a trio like them?

Or what dragon, for that matter? He turned back to Numa, who stood in the open doorway, eyes wide and clearly unprepared to be greeted by the two of them so soon.

"We aren't early, I know that much," Bekim said, giving her naked, glistening body a once over and crossing his arms. The dressy tunic he wore bunched under his arms and around his biceps, reminding him why he preferred to go naked too. His cock stirred in his pants at the scent that wafted out. Pure sex. And no wonder Cade had walked with such swagger when he left. Not only was he coated in Numa's fragrant, earthy scent, but *she* was quite literally coated in Cade's.

"I'm so sorry," she said, her hand fluttering at her throat as she gazed down at her sticky breasts. "I hoped I'd have time to clean up before you got here. I'll go do that now. I promise I will be quick. Come in and wait?" She gave them both beseeching looks and stepped aside.

Bekim entered and Theron stepped in after, catching the edge of the door and shutting it behind them. Numa gave them another hesitant, worried look before turning away. Theron's hand shot out and grabbed her shoulder.

"Hang on, honey, don't go wasting that ambrosia and letting it wash down the drain."

Bekim's partner's gaze turned brazen and hungry as the startled dragon peered up at him. Bekim himself was just as surprised by Theron's interest, but there was no mistaking his arousal as he bent to press his face into Numa's neck and inhaled deeply.

"Gaia, what is that scent? It's more than male ursa. You smell like … summer wind. You couldn't have gone flying with that bubble around us, though, and it isn't even summer yet. I fucking love that smell."

Curious what it was Theron scented on her, Bekim dipped his head and inhaled. He was met with a wash of ursa musk reminiscent of chilly mountain air, but underneath was a warm, coastal smell like verbena and sage. It reminded him of his pilgrimage as a young ursa, when he and Theron had first agreed to pair up while touring the southeastern coast. They'd become lovers during that trip, and had been insepa-rable ever since.

Impulsively, he lowered his head and swiped his tongue over her glistening nipple, needing to taste that essence to find out if the impression went deeper than the aroma. Rich flavor exploded on his tongue and his cock hardened, straining at the satiny fabric of his pants. Gaia's tears, what-ever Cade had wasn't just ursa male essence. There was something far stronger infusing the fluid he'd anointed their dragon with.

Numa let out a soft whimper and combed her fingers into Bekim's hair, her nails digging at his scalp. "Sweet Mother, you two should let me bathe first. It wasn't fair of him to leave me like this. I think he wanted to intimidate you into making a mistake."

"You'll do no such thing," Bekim said, straightening up and bending to kiss her full, swollen lips. She looked a little shell-shocked, but otherwise energetic and sated. The others had satisfied her well, which might make his and Theron's job harder, but if Cade had hoped to frighten them by marking her with his seed, that plan had backfired.

Theron glanced at him, the look in his eyes telling Bekim they were of one mind on this. In easy synchronicity, they bent and hooked a hand under each of her knees, supporting her back with their other arms. With only a few swift strides, they had her on her bed, holding her down with hands pressed against her shoulders.

She let out a throaty laugh and arched into their mouths when they both bent once more to lap at her breasts, as much in an effort to arouse her as to devour that delicious flavor that coated her skin. "I'm supposed to be teasing you two until you're cross-eyed, not the other way around."

"Don't worry," Bekim said, clasping her hand and pulling it down to his groin. "You naked is enough to drive me wild, baby. But showing up naked and glazed in sweet icing is going to make it so hard not to shoot my load all over you too."

"Six hours," she rasped, gliding her hand along the length of his erection through his pants. She spread her thighs as Theron drifted a hand between them and dipped his fingers into her fragrant depths.

Bekim leaned back to untie his drawstring to give her access to his skin. He watched with a heated gaze as his partner's digits disappeared inside Numa's core and emerged, covered in fresh essence even more potent than the stuff they'd already licked off her.

"Did you like the way he tasted?" Theron asked, waving his fingers beneath his nose and inhaling deeply as if he couldn't get enough of her scent. Bekim impulsively gripped his lover's wrist and yanked it to him, then wrapped his lips around Theron's fingers. Theron let out a surprised grunt as Bekim swirled his tongue around both fingers, sucking the sweet, tangy juices off. His eyelids fluttered shut in ecstasy and he almost didn't hear her response.

"*They* tasted delicious," she corrected, sitting up and

tugging at the tie to Theron's trousers. "And I don't quite understand why you two are so enthralled by the mess they made of me. I had a feeling Zephyrus was present at the end. I had no idea you could taste him too."

Bekim released Theron's hand and licked his lips. "Them *and* you. Sweet fuck, you don't need to touch us when you're coated in an aphrodisiac that strong. Did Dionysus come inside you too?"

She gave him a baffled look as he tore off his shirt and kicked out of his pants, then slipped down between her thighs to have another taste of that mixture he'd sampled from Theron's fingers.

"Ah … no." Numa leaned back on her elbows, her head tilting backward as he descended on her fragrant folds. "Zephyrus *is* a demigod. It didn't occur to me that he'd be so … ohh …"

"Move over," Theron said, pushing Numa's leg up and slipping down beside Bekim on the bed. Bekim scooted over to make room, more than happy to give his lover a taste of what had to be the most delicious snatch he'd ever had. He kept her parted for Theron to lean down and slick his tongue through her channel. Theron made a low, satisfied growl and extended his tongue deeper into her.

She quivered beneath them as they took turns lapping at her slick flesh and sucking her swollen clit until she writhed and cried out their names. When her orgasmic spasms eased, Bekim's cock was rock-hard and aching and wildflowers were growing between his toes.

He left a wet kiss against Numa's hip and eased down beside her with a sigh. Theron remained between her legs for a moment longer, then rose up on both hands to hover over her, his thick erection poised at her entrance.

"I would fucking love for us both to come inside you right now and find out how we taste all together. I bet it'd be even more addictive than just him and you." Theron gave her a languid kiss, his hips dropping and tilting into hers.

Bekim's pulse sped as he watched Theron's length disappear into Numa's depths. He knew the tight squeeze of her so well, loved the familiar sound of her breathy gasps when Theron's cockhead rubbed just right inside her, and reveled in the disappointed whimper when Theron pulled out fully and rested back on his haunches.

"He knows better than to test his limits," Bekim told her. "But I plan on testing them myself." He gave his partner a wicked smile and surged up, grabbed Theron by the hips, and wrapped his mouth around his cock. Theron let out a groan and seized Bekim by the shoulders, but didn't push him away.

"How fucking good is that?" Theron breathed. "Oh, fuck, dude. I'm halfway tempted to get him back in here so we can have a firsthand taste."

Bekim savored his lover's shaft until Theron's fingers tightened on his shoulders, his cock twitching dangerously in his mouth. He slipped off Theron's cock with a soft pop. "My turn," he said with a grin and moved between Numa's thighs again.

She gazed up at him with a bewildered look. "Why are you two so enthralled by him? He's your competition."

"He's one of us *and* he's single, which means he's a free agent. If you choose the god, he's our best chance at landing a mate of our own, as long as he's willing to share."

"And what if I choose you two?" she asked, spreading her thighs and moaning as Bekim sank into her. Her muscles tightened around him and his entire body flushed with fresh need to climax, but he moved carefully, sliding out and back in only once before sitting back again and enjoying Theron's lips and tongue eagerly sucking him clean.

Bekim's mind was abuzz with too much pleasure to

answer, but Theron responded. "Would you be willing to take all three of us?"

"Four …" Bekim said, his mind finally clearing as the throbbing in his cock eased a little. "It'd be four, with the West Wind."

"Four of us. Even better," Theron said with a grin. "Gaia's sweet amrita never tasted so good. If we can have you tasting like that for the rest of our lives, I'm all for it. Not that you didn't taste divine already…"

Numa only stared up at them both, speechless.

Bekim wasn't sure what had stunned her. "Is it against the rules? Would Fate be pissed if you did that?"

Theron jumped in then. "Seriously, you're a dragon. Don't dragons traditionally keep entire harems? I was all about hoarding you to ourselves, but after seeing him and knowing how fucking delicious your juices are mixed with his, I want more of it. Why fucking choose?"

"I …" Numa began, then stopped, her gaze darting to the clock, and then the window behind the bed. "I don't know."

CHAPTER 17

NUMA

There wasn't enough time for her to make this decision. Testing their limits had to be done so she would know one way or the other whether they could provide enough power for the ritual. But if an ursa pair were an option, and Cade and Zephyrus would certainly be a package deal if she chose them ... why in the world *wouldn't* she take them all, if they were all willing?

"Something's got your gears turning, honey," Theron said. "Are we on for our test or not?" He dropped his hand to his cock and gave it a slow stroke, leaving his fist wrapped around it with his thumb aligned with the head.

Numa swallowed at the sight of the droplet that glistened on his tip. She knew very well how much power the pair could bring together, and with Gaia's magic infusing them, their auras were stronger by tenfold now. The goddess must truly be invested in seeing them win.

Then wouldn't it be a coup if she broke all the rules? She surged up into Theron's arms and kissed him soundly on the cheek.

"I knew there was a reason I loved you so much."

"Hey!" Bekim said, waving at her. "Aren't you forgetting me?"

"Never," she said, reaching for him and tangling her fingers in the thick hair at the back of his head. She pulled him into a kiss that he hungrily accepted, sliding his hand down over her hip to grip her ass and squeeze.

Theron's mouth drifted down her neck as he slid his fingers between her thighs again and teased along her folds. Sweet Mother, she couldn't let herself get distracted. Not now.

"No," she said, pushing them both away. "I need to go talk to Sophia before it's too late."

She hopped off the bed and exhaled as she went, commanding her magic to tidy her up and clothe her. By the time she reached the door and looked back at them, she was dressed with her hair neatly done up in a braid coiled at her nape. Her heart fluttered at the sight of the two ursas. Perfect. They were perfect, with their big ursa brawn and deep, earthy complexions. Like most Rainsong males, they had very little body hair, aside from Theron's jet-black beard and Bekim's decadent mop of umber waves.

And they were both supremely confused, probably owing in part to how unbearably horny they were right now.

"Hold that thought, guys. If Sophia says no, we'll need to pick up where we left off. But if she says yes …" She beamed at them both.

"We'll get our wish?" Bekim said.

"If the others are willing, yes."

Excitement flared their auras and Numa's heart thudded hard. Two more generous mates she had never imagined she'd find. That they would willingly share her with others should not have surprised her. They were ursa males, after all, who were conditioned to cater to their female's needs.

Perhaps they had subconsciously sensed the answer to her dilemma.

Either way, she left the room in a rush, too excited to waste more of the precious time Vrishti and her mates had given them.

The Rainsong Lodge was arranged in a wide arc that surrounded the lush interior courtyard. Through the windows, she had a clear view of the trees and the sky above as she ran, hoping she would find Sophia and Ozzie in the library or the throne room on the first floor. The temporal barrier shimmered with iridescent light overhead, but beyond it she could see the distorted orb of the sun, now higher in the sky. It was late morning on Spring Equinox already, and she hoped the forces in the Haven were holding out, but if Sophia confirmed her hopes, they wouldn't have to wait much longer for reinforcements.

Halfway down the wide staircase the light changed, another disturbing flicker in the energy field that surrounded them. Beneath her feet, the world shook, and the big carved-wood chandelier above her swung from side to side. Numa grabbed the banister for balance, staring up through the high windows in alarm.

For a moment, she swore she saw a shimmer of blackness slide across the dome of the barrier. A chill ran down her spine. Something was wrong. Doors opening and closing and quick footsteps sounded in the halls. Before she reached the bottom step, she saw Sophia rushing in from the gardens with Ozzie, Cade, and Dionysus right behind. Both her potential mates were stark naked and dripping wet, but sporting expressions that were distinctly unaroused.

They paused for only a second on the way up the stairs. "The child is in danger," Dionysus said, giving her arm a squeeze before continuing his climb.

"Tell me what's happening," she said, falling into step beside Sophia.

"Your nephew had a run-in with Meri outside," Sophia said. "She is attacking the barrier, draining it. Somehow it's affecting the child."

"Meri is here?" Numa said. "And Zorion? How did he get here?" She supposed his arrival was none too soon, regardless of his methods, if their enemy was powerful enough to be in two places at once. There was no way in hell Meri would have left the Haven before securing the Source, and Gavra would have alerted her if she were anywhere close to winning.

Back on the floor above, they rounded the bend, heading toward Vrishti's room, and she caught a glimpse of Bekim and Theron striding toward them, clothed in just their silken dress trousers now and too worried to still be turned on.

"What's going on? We felt the tremor and saw the light shift. The place never shook before."

The door swung open before they reached it and Neph stepped through, giving them a nod.

"How is she?" Numa asked.

"Older than the last time you saw her," the big satyr said with a grim set to his jaw. He stepped aside to let her enter, and the others filed in behind Numa. Inside, she was greeted by seven worried faces, all belonging to individuals she realized would have called Deva their daughter. Her sister's two godchildren had returned from their mission, it seemed, and there was no mistaking the auras of the trio who accompanied them. They were her sister's lost children, and her heart swelled to see them.

"Oh, Sweet Mother, you made it," she gushed, reaching them where they stood near the fireplace. Somehow Zorion's soul had split in two, but that mattered little when she could plainly see the love both halves had for the luminous woman between them—and the very reason they likely had her positioned on the hearth to start with. Neela had somehow become the embodiment of pure dragon fire—a phoenix, the likes of which Numa had only heard of in tales her mother told when Numa was a child.

She pulled the woman into a fierce embrace, heedless of the immense heat Neela threw off. "Thank you for finding them," she said, squeezing Neela and casting a grateful look to Naaz. "Has Belah seen you yet?"

"We went there first," Naaz said. "Z and Zil can do a little trick that gets us past magic barriers, so we thought we'd come in and offer our help. And I'm glad we did."

"Me too," she said, hugging each of them before turning to face the room.

The outer chamber of Vrishti's rooms barely accommodated all of them, and Numa saw no sign of the little girl.

"Is she all right?" Numa asked the Sanctuary's newest Summer Spirit.

"We aren't sure," Vrishti said shakily, her shoulders sagging. "The last surge accelerated her growth again and she's still recovering. Aodh cocooned her in a healing cloud and she is resting now."

"Can I see her?" Numa asked.

"Hear what Zorion saw outside first," Vrishti said.

Numa looked at her nephew again, her brows raised.

"A leech," Zorion said. "We could only see it when time was frozen to allow us through the barrier. It was the essence of her power, latched onto the bubble's membrane, sucking the power from it."

Dionysus cursed, and all eyes turned to him. "The creature you described is not the essence of a nymphaea. Whatever Meri has become is something far darker and more corrupt than I feared."

"The battle in the Haven persists," Neph said. "My niece

and her mates are keeping the Ultiori at bay with the help of the ursa, who fight alongside the nymphs. We'd hoped to buy time to allow Numa to accumulate power for the portal, but if the temporal barrier fails sooner, we will be out of choices. If there's another surge, Deva may not survive it. Father, we need your help."

Dion returned Neph's stare with equal intensity. "There is one option," he finally offered, then lowered his gaze to Numa's. "But it would mean forfeiting this contest. I will only go if you have made your choice and it isn't me."

"What option?" she asked, her gut a roiling at the very idea of Dion leaving when she'd just made her choice.

"What my father means is the realm of the gods," Neph said. "If he takes her there, she will be safe. Once she is gone, we can take down the barrier, but we need to be prepared for that. Is there any chance you can begin the ritual soon? Have you had time to make a decision on a mate yet?"

Numa glanced between the four men and then back to Neph. "Is there any way to get her there without Dionysus carrying her himself?"

Sophia's brows rose. "So you have made a choice already, then. Interesting."

"No!" Numa yelled. "I just asked a question. Is Dionysus the only one who can get Deva to a safe place? I haven't made my decision yet ..." She regretted the lie, but wanted a chance to speak privately to all the contestants before she made her choice public.

"It must be a god who carries her there," Sophia said. "The doors will only open for the divine."

"I can return, but if I don't stay with Deva, I would need someone to remain behind as my proxy as the girl's guardian."

"I will go," Ozzie said. The room quieted as everyone turned to stare at him.

"What are you thinking, grandson?" Sophia asked.

He sighed. "I am the only option unless you go yourself, Nanyo. Everyone else is committed to the fight in some fashion. I am no less eager to see Meri get her ass kicked, but the fact is I'm more of a bystander."

Sophia's stare turned hard, her jaw clenching. "I don't see why one of the males Numa doesn't choose can't make the sacrifice."

"Then your eyesight must be failing," Ozzie said. "Look at them. She is definitely not choosing me, even if I *had* entered the damn contest you saw fit to finagle."

He gestured toward Numa, where she stood surrounded by four males, Theron and Bekim on either side of her with Cade and Dion at her back. All four had a hand on her, either at her shoulder or her waist, and Zephyrus was gently whispering in her ear his affirmation of the choice she hadn't even come close to voicing yet.

Sophia's gaze turned icy when she turned to look. "Numa, this was not Fate's intention when the contest was devised. You were to choose between contestants."

"Fuck Fate," Numa spat. "I would happily sacrifice one of them to save Deva, if any of these men wanted to make that choice, but I am not doing it because of the contest. I want them all, and more than that, I *need* them all to ensure the ritual succeeds, especially now that we likely have no choice but to move forward with it sooner than we'd planned. The very second Dionysus gets Deva out of here, I plan to start it. And when he returns to help, you can be damn sure Fate won't get in our way."

She shot a glance at Ozzie, who had crossed his arms and was giving his grandmother a smug look. He winked in Numa's direction.

"This is not your path, Oszkar West. You will displease

Fate by proceeding. It might affect your ability to find your One."

"Let the boy do his duty. The child adores him," Cade said, only the timbre of his voice was all Zephyrus. Sophia visibly flinched as he continued. "He is my namesake. My own blood runs in his veins, niece. If I could get my brother here to put you in your place, I would, but he is locked beyond the barrier."

"Are you telling me Fate actually *has* a mate in mind for me, Nanyo?" Ozzie asked. "Because I've waited two centuries to find her. It's honestly not much to lose, at this stage. I will protect this child with my life. She deserves an existence free from the beast that made her what she is, that forced her into being without a soul of her own. If it pisses Fate off for this to happen, then all the better."

The light around them flickered once more, and a cry sounded from the other room.

"So are we decided?" Numa asked impatiently.

Lips brushed her ear, accompanied by the scent of wine and sex. "I will return the very second she is safe," Dionysus whispered. "That is, if you were telling the truth and you intend to hoard us all for yourself. Tell me the others are in agreement with this plan."

"If it means having her, even if it's only on Tuesdays, I'll take it," Cade said, and Bekim and Theron added their hearty agreement as well.

CHAPTER 18

NUMA

The temperature in the room spiked, and across the room, Neela's aura flared bright with panic.

"No! I won't let you go without me. She's my daughter!"

"I can only take one proxy," Dionysus said. "Whoever comes must stay with her until Meri is destroyed and it's safe for her to return to this plane."

"This is as much your fight as it is mine," Vrishti said, starting to approach Neela, but stopping several feet away, her skin breaking into a sheen of sweat. "I would love nothing more than to stay by her side and protect her. My maternal instincts are so strong, I fear that's the reason Meri has increased in power. If I had not attacked her when she threatened Deva in my womb, she would have never discovered the full range of her powers. But all I wish for now is to go on the offensive. To join the fight. To save my own mother too. Neela, there are so many others whose lives depend on us helping. Deva will be fine with Ozzie as her guardian. Join us in the fight."

Neela turned to look at Ozzie. "I barely know you. Do you promise you will watch over her?"

"I give you my vow," Ozzie said. "I want Meri dead as much as the rest of you, but I have less of a stake in the fight and my skills are better put to use with Deva. She responds to my music. She will be safe with me."

"I want to see her once more," Neela said.

"We should not waste more time, if we're going to do this," Numa said. She looked up at Dionysus. "What do you need me to do?"

It was her brother who answered from the doorway to the room. "Your smoke would not go amiss to start with, sister. Deva is still hurting from the last surge. Help me finish healing her. And Ozzie … she's asked for you to sing."

Numa made her way to the door with Dionysus at her side. She abruptly stopped and blocked the big god's path. "Not like this," she said, expelling a breath that twined around his exquisitely muscled body, covering his bare skin in a sheer length of green fabric that draped over one shoulder and encircled his hips. She finished it off with a shimmering copper belt. "She's just a child."

Dion's lips quirked. "As you wish, little one."

Turning to Cade, she eyed him appraisingly, admiring the ursa's physique once more before letting out a sigh. Her breath flowed around his hips as well, settling on his skin in a pair of loose-fitting trousers. "Wait for me here. As soon as she is seen safe, I want to begin preparing. I want to be ready to start the ritual the very second the barrier comes down. Dionysus can join us when he returns."

She passed by Neela, who was exiting as Numa was on her way into the room, and stopped her with a hand to her arm. Neela gazed at her with eyes like fire. "I have said my farewell. We are ready to enter the Haven to join the fight. Please make sure the ritual works."

"You have my promise," Numa said, hugging Neela tightly. The woman's skin crackled with searing inner heat beneath her touch, the unmistakable essence of immortal dragon fire that had the potential to burn her if she weren't careful. Whatever bond her nephew had forged with Neela spoke of a love stronger than any she had known. When she released Neela, she glanced back at Dionysus and thought she saw the barest glimmer of adoration that was quickly replaced by an inscrutable mask.

They joined the small group who had remained in the bedroom, and Numa let out a gasp when Ozzie and Aodh stood back, revealing Deva between them.

Far from a child now, Deva stood between the two men in a flowing white gown draped over the curves of a young woman in full fertile bloom. The gown itself shimmered with the evidence of Aodh's magic that had conjured it, clothing that would persist and adapt to her growth.

Her face was pinched with pain, her variegated eyes displaying the torment that still gripped her even as her voice rose in harmony with Ozzie's song. Numa immediately exhaled a long breath, directing her smoke to cocoon Deva in another layer of restorative magic that flowed into her white gown as deep green embroidery.

The song she sang grew less agonized as her pain eased and her aura stabilized. Finally, she trailed off and stopped singing, taking a deep, shaky breath.

"Thank you, Numa," she said, sweeping into Numa's arms with a sigh.

"Oh, honey, I'm so sorry you've had to go through so much. We would do anything to keep you safe."

"I'm sorry if it ruined your plans. I didn't mean to complicate things," Deva said, peering into Numa's eyes with her own, so full of strangely potent power that had barely realized its potential.

"Nonsense. You just helped push me to make a hard decision. Everything will be all right now."

"I wish I could fight," Deva said with the most earnest expression.

"You are too weak yet," Aodh said. "If you knew what powers you had, how to use them, it would be a different story."

She gave the big dragon a sad look. "I know. All I can do is sing, but that won't be enough."

"Not to kill the enemy, no," Aodh said. "Leave that to us. I promise you will return to a world safe for you to live in."

She turned and embraced the big dragon, her rich, dark skin and hair a stark contrast to his pale, almost silvery features. Aodh held her tightly, his eyes glassy when they met Numa's gaze over Deva's shoulder. It was clear that he loved the girl like a daughter. She had truly endeared herself to all the residents, even the visitors here on this fateful day.

"Are you ready, child?" Dionysus said.

Deva swallowed and nodded. "Will it hurt?"

"You won't feel a thing."

"I'll be there with you," Ozzie said, clasping her hand in his.

That seemed to ease Deva's apprehension and she nodded, giving Dionysus a hesitant smile. "Then I am ready."

Dionysus turned and faced Numa, the intensity of his gaze making her heart race. "Don't wait to start the ritual. I will come, I promise you that. But I ask that you do me one favor before I go."

Almost breathless with anxiety over how quickly things seemed to be moving now, Numa nodded. "Anything."

"Mark me now. The realm of the gods is easy to lose time in. I need an anchor to pull me back to you."

She blinked at him. "Now? You know you won't be the only mate I mark today, right?"

"I do. And a more worthy set of partners I could not have hoped for. Waste no time marking them, either. While I am home, I will have a talk with Gaia about granting Zephyrus his own body as well. He will bring more power with a corporeal form, and I sense moving up the timeline will require all we can get."

"You would be right," she said. "The contest was as much to build the power as it was to test everyone's abilities." Her stomach fluttered—it was far more than she'd hoped for, being able to be with Zephyrus in the flesh and not just as a passenger inside Cade's big, glorious body.

As an afterthought, she added, "You don't think the other gods will be angry that I didn't choose, do you? I know how much you all like to win."

Dionysus gave her a wicked grin. "When they discover that in the end we *all* put one over on Fate, they'll come around, don't worry. Now I must ask that you follow through ..."

"Right, turn around."

He slowly rotated and gave her a look over his shoulder with one brow raised. "Shall I bend over?"

"Not necessary," she said, sliding her hands over his back and gently moving the draped cloth to the side so his entire back was visible. She could just reach the center of his shoulder blades if she stood on tiptoe and gently planted a kiss there.

"Down," she said, pressing on his shoulders. When he knelt, she pushed his luxurious black waves to the side and placed another kiss against the back of his neck. Then, without further preamble, she summoned her power and darted out her tongue to begin the mark. Her heart pounded, her stomach a tangled, fluttering mess. She was marking a god, one who had taken many mates in his life, but never accepted a partnership so permanent as to be a dragon's mate.

She traced the elaborate pattern in swirls from the base of

his neck down his spine before spreading it out across his wide shoulders. This mark would be her claim on him, leaving no question as to who he belonged to. He barely flinched despite the fact that she knew it was a painful ordeal, and when she leaned back to observe the finished product, he kept his head bowed, though he reached back and squeezed her leg.

"I am yours," he said. "And I will be yours always."

Numa's throat was too tight to reply. She exhaled a deep breath, sending green smoke to ease and heal the glowing marks that adorned his back in a pair of magnificent wings spanning both shoulder blades.

Finally he stood and turned, and before she could react, he had her wrapped in his embrace, his mouth solidly covering hers in a passionate kiss that promised all the power she could ask for when he returned.

"Never doubt your own power to make men love you. This is not a sudden thing, Numa, despite the fact that you are filled with uncertainty. Zephyrus and I needed very little convincing, even when you were young. It's no wonder that the other three who you have chosen are as eager to bind themselves to you as we are. We will not fail you if you accept our love."

"I do," she said, taking a shaky breath as she rested her forehead against his. "I just hope I don't fail you all."

"You know what needs to be done," he said. "I will add my power to the ritual as soon as I return. Now go prepare for the barrier to drop. It will happen soon."

Aodh gave Deva a swift hug before leaving the room and joining Neph and Vrishti in the outer chamber. He gave Numa a comforting squeeze of her arm on the way past. "We will wait until she is clear and then take down the barrier right away. Zorion, have your group stay and be ready in case Meri attacks. Numa may need defenders to keep the ritual from being interrupted."

"Where are we going to do this thing?" Cade asked. "Not in the bedroom, I take it. Doubt your bed is big enough for all of us."

Numa turned to her brother. "Aodh, can you drift us to Gaia's Falls when the time comes? That's where the portal needs to be opened to give Nikhil's army direct access to the Haven."

"Certainly," he said.

"We will join you there," Zorion said. "And as soon as Nikhil and the others arrive, we can all join the fight."

Numa nodded, then turned to cast one final glance at the trio in the other room. Deva stood flanked by both big men, Dionysus dwarfing her and Ozzy both with his magnificent size. His gaze flashed with promise, and the very second Numa nodded her acknowledgment that she was ready, the trio disappeared.

"Now!" Neph said, grabbing his mates by their hands. The lodge shook and the light wavered once again. An unholy screeching permeated the air as the room went bright, then dark, then bright once more.

"Meri isn't happy," Zorion said from his station near the window. "Zil, to me. We can at least try to make it hurt when the barrier goes down."

The quieter, darker twin to Zorion's bright, flame-like form went to him, and within a blink, the pair seemed to merge and disappear all at once. Barely two seconds later, they returned, looking harried as they split apart.

Zil scowled. "She'll feel that for a while."

Zorion nodded. "Yes, she likely won't risk pissing us off again for some time. Let's get you all to the summit and get this party started."

*B*etween Neph and his mates' ability to drift, plus Zorion's powers of teleportation, the entire group was transported to the banks of the lake above Gaia's Falls in only a few seconds. Once Cade regained his equilibrium and the nausea of the drift passed, he looked to Numa for directions, only to see her shell-shocked expression as she realized everyone in their group was expecting her to take charge.

He started toward her with a worried frown. "Sweet pea, tell me what you need."

Her brother stepped close and looked down at her. "What is it? It's not like you to shy away from leading. You were always a natural. It's part of your nature as a green."

"I know. And it's the reason I am the only one who can complete this ritual. It isn't taking charge that has me all wound up. It's the impact it is going to have on all of you," she said, facing Cade and the other two ursa males who Cade knew were every bit as enamored of the green-eyed beauty as he was.

"We'll be yours. I call that a win no matter how things shake out," Cade said.

"Don't forget we're ursa," Theron added. "You do us a great honor by choosing us. No other ursa save the ones mated to your siblings can claim as much."

"And you are all willing to share me with a god?"

Cade lifted his brows and scratched his beard. "Well, we need to make sure things are kept fair, but now is hardly the time to decide on a rotation. If his godliness bogarts you, the other four of us will happily take him to task. But the way I see this going is we all get you at the same time. Unless you don't think you can handle us …" He shot her a playful grin.

Numa inhaled sharply, her green eyes glowing with fresh desire at that suggestion. "Oh, I can handle you. I look forward to Dion's return to prove just how much I can handle."

He closed the distance between them and rested his hands on her shoulders. Inside the depths of his consciousness, Zephyrus stirred, his arousal accompanied by a warm breeze that tugged at the bindings in Numa's hair.

Sliding the edge of his thumb across Numa's jaw, Cade peered down into her eyes. "What do you say, sweet pea? Ready to get this going?"

Bekim and Theron moved up behind her, one pressing a kiss to her shoulder while the other kissed her cheek. "Just tell us where you want us," Bekim said.

Her body warmed beneath his touch, and Cade had to resist bending to kiss her lush lips. He needed to hear her answer first.

"Inside me," she breathed finally, and hell if that didn't send his blood pumping straight into his cock.

Cade was only dimly aware of the rest of their group spreading out around them to guard the perimeter. All he cared about was the feel of Numa's sweet curves against his body and the urgent tug of her fingers at the waistband of his pants.

Deva was safe now, and his entire reason for being was in his arms, struggling for the second time that day to get him naked. He didn't even flinch when her talon came out and swiped through the thin silk at his waist, making quick work of the tie. His cock sprang free, and she went to her knees as though in worship.

"Only hold back until I say so," Numa said, her lips grazing the swollen head of his cock. Behind her, the other two knelt and were working her clothes off her body, sliding the straps off her shoulders and pushing the fabric over her hips.

A cloud of swirling iridescent smoke flowed around them, slipping in a shimmering sheet beneath Cade's feet. He followed the trail with his eyes to where it originated from a very curious, pale-haired Asha, who seemed intent on watching and just as intent on conjuring a luxurious bed of blankets and pillows for their lovemaking. As his attention wavered under Numa's eager tongue sliding up and down his shaft, the others faded from his periphery as a darker veil drifted down around them, lending privacy from prying eyes.

"Come away, sister," Zorion was saying. "Let them work."

Cade didn't give two shits who saw. With any luck, Gaia herself was watching as Bekim and Theron both fell to their knees beside Numa and added their own tongues to the mix.

"Oh, sweet Jesus," Cade muttered and let his head fall back. He struggled to remain standing, but wouldn't have moved for the world as one mouth bent lower and wrapped its wet lips around his balls while the other sucked on the head of his cock. Numa's deft hands and talented tongue worked his shaft for a moment longer, then disappeared, leaving the two men going at it on their own.

Bewildered by the change, Cade opened his eyes and looked down to see Numa rising with her green eyes shining.

"Shall I mark you in the ursa fashion or the dragon? Your preference." She extended her talons and gently raked the edges across his chest. Small tufts of the thick blond curls on his chest fell away from the razor-sharp extensions. Either way, it was going to hurt, but with a pair of the most talented ursa mouths steadily working him into a frenzy, he didn't think he'd care much one way or the other.

"Both, baby. I want everything you can give me."

"We'll start with a dragon mark for each of you," she said. "One to match Dion's."

She slipped around to his backside and he shivered in ecstasy at the feel of her warm breasts pressed against his back. She brushed her lips over his ear, her tongue tracing the outer shell. "I'll give you something else I gave Dion that he seemed to enjoy."

Her feet nudged at his ankles, urging him to widen his stance. He obeyed, the action itself a promise of an experience he had yet to have in her presence. A soft sigh escaped her mouth as she pulled away from him, and with one hand, gripped his left ass cheek to spread him open. Another, firmer grip from one of the men encompassed his other cheek, and he found himself more exposed than he'd ever been in his life.

"Open," she said softly, and he looked down to see Theron's slips part and a thick, oblong, and very recognizable shape slip between them. Cade's cock twitched under Bekim's tongue in anticipation of the thick plug's intrusion.

He groaned when the cool, blunt tip touched his opening and Numa applied gentle pressure to ease it into him.

"*Better than my cock?*" Zephyrus asked.

"Gaia's tears, so much better," he said.

"Hmm?" Numa asked and he realized he'd spoken out

loud. "You like this? Which of the others would you like to replace it later while your cock is inside me?"

A pair of interested grunts sounded from below, both of the others keen on his answer.

"Sweet pea, if I'm inside you, they can all take turns."

"I like that answer," she said, slipping her arms around him and pressing her cheek to his shoulder. "You have no idea how happy that makes me. There is no going back after today. I want all of you to be happy."

He let out a groan as his need built under the ministrations of the pair of mouths on his cock. "Baby, I'm guessing you won't let me come until that mark's done. I'd really love it if you would get on with it. I adore you. Breezy boy fucking loves you. We sure as fuck *hope* there's no going back, because we're in this for the long haul."

Laughing, Numa kissed the side of his neck. "Good," she said huskily. "This will hurt. I'll give you the ursa mark after I've tasted your Nirvana."

Even though he could tell she was quick about it, she'd been right—it hurt like the fucking dickens. It was like the lash of a whip striking in a blur over the span of his shoulders and down his spine. The pleasure of the tongues between his thighs only dulled it so much, but in between lashes, she would pump the plug in and out of his ass until he ached for another strike of pain to go with that unbearable pleasure.

Cade bit his lip with the effort of holding back until Zephyrus rumbled inside his head, *"Open your eyes, look at the sky."* He obeyed, fixing his attention on a puffy white cloud and the nearby Silas tree rustling in the breeze with the roaring rush of the waterfall just beyond. The brief distraction helped and the soles of his feet stopped itching, though his balls felt even heavier, and it didn't help that one of the other boys was eagerly sucking on them one by one.

The pain ceased with a wash of cool air against his back and the scent of pine and wet earth. Then Numa was urging him to the ground. Bekim and Theron fell back, reclining against an enormous pile of cushions. He found himself pushed back against another pile with Numa's flushed face looking down at him.

She moved to straddle him, her warm thighs sliding against his hips, her nipples tinged green as her dragon nature bled through her human form. It was the surest sign of how close to her own limit she was, and he meant to push her even closer.

Cade bent his knees and rested his hands on her thighs, sliding them up until he could glide his thumbs along the juncture that was already glistening with evidence of her arousal. Her breasts rose and fell, and he surged up to grasp one nipple between his lips, his passenger eagerly urging him on.

Numa let out a shuddering sigh when his thumbs parted her and he found her swollen clit with the pad of one. Releasing her nipple, he let out a low growl of need. She was so warm and wet, his thumb easily sliding around and around her slick nub. He slipped his other thumb down between her folds and found her entrance flooded with even more delicious essence.

As he pushed his thumb into her, she arched her back with a rough moan. His cock kicked hard against her backside, more than ready to fill that sweet, hot tightness once more.

"Sweet pea, as much as I'm dying to fill you up again, I want to remind you that the rest of us got shorted our turn to drive you crazy. I think it's our turn for that now, don't you?"

She opened her eyes as she canted her hips into his touch, forcing Cade's thumb to penetrate her deeper. A cute crinkle appeared between her brows and she bit her lip, muffling a little grunt when he pressed harder at her clit. "I can hold back. Do your worst."

With a grin, he shot a look past her to Theron and Bekim who still watched avidly, loosely gripping their erections in their fists. He tilted his chin up and they moved. Theron slipped between Cade's legs and gave Cade's cock another stroke before wrapping his arms around Numa's torso and cupping her breasts. He nuzzled at her neck and she sighed, leaning back into him.

Beside them, Bekim settled on his knees, looking at Cade earnestly. "This is better than a dream come true," he said, and leaned down to press a kiss to Cade's lips.

He groaned into Bekim's kiss. He tasted of Numa and, strangely, of Cade's own sharp essence, but then they had joined her just after he had left. Perhaps they'd had time for a taste before their interruption.

The flavor of Bekim's lips turned his blood molten as he realized how close a bond they would have if they pulled this off. He had gone from nothing to everything in the span of a day. Overcome with the fiercest gratitude for their acceptance, he gripped the other man by the back of the head, tangling his fingers in Bekim's thick hair and plunging his tongue deeper. While they kissed, Theron's cock rubbed against his, but then the sensation shifted.

Hot, wet heat met his cockhead as Numa rose up and pressed him to her core. Theron slipped his mouth around Cade's balls again as Numa slid down his length, the mélange of sensations so exquisitely sensuous he bit down on Bekim's lip hard enough to draw blood.

Bekim only chuckled and deepened their kiss, his sweet blood mixing with the other flavors on Cade's tongue.

Breathless from pleasure, he released Bekim's mouth and inhaled to refill his lungs. He held the other ursa close, their foreheads together as he regained his breath and forced himself to refocus to avoid shooting his load into Numa before it was time.

"Let me taste you," he said, looking up into Bekim's eyes. "You got a taste of me. It's only fair."

Bekim's gaze heated and he nodded. He rose up and shifted positions. As he moved, Cade looked up at Numa, who was riding his cock with tortuously slow undulations of her hip. He narrowed his eyes at her and reached up to tweak her nipple. "You're holding off until we say so, right? If we've gotta wait, so do you, sweet pea."

Soft, rhythmic exhalations puffed out of her with each downstroke, and she nodded. His gaze lingered on her for several seconds, too enthralled by her enjoyment of his cock to tear his attention away. Theron's bearded face appeared over her shoulder and he whispered into her ear something Cade couldn't hear over the sounds of her panting breaths and his own pounding heart.

"He asked if she'd like to feel you both inside her," Zephyrus said.

Intrigued by the question, Cade propped himself up on his elbows. "Can you take us both, sweet pea?"

Beside him, Bekim chuckled. "It's one of her favorite things. Guaranteed to make her scream."

Cade's brows lifted and he reached for her. "Come here and give him room," he said, pulling her down to lay against his chest. She remained poised above him with her hands braced against his pecs. He could feel Theron repositioning and spread his thighs wider to accommodate the other big ursa. Numa hunched lower, and Cade took advantage of the proximity of her lips to capture them in a kiss. She sank into him with a moan, kissing him back and clinging to him with both hands.

She tilted her hips up, sliding partway off his length and

the hot, hard shaft of Theron's cock pressed against the underside of his. Cade let out a muffled moan of pleasure. Gaia's fucking tears, this would be good, and like nothing he'd ever felt before.

"I crave to share her with you this way," Zephyrus said. *"To have my cock slide against yours inside her sweet depths. To feel her between us."*

"This time is mine," Cade growled.

Inside his head, Zephyrus chuckled. *"As it should be. I wouldn't dream of depriving you of the experience."*

Then Numa was sinking back down his shaft and her channel felt even tighter, the hot, throbbing length of Theron's cock creating a fresh and delicious friction that had Cade's head spinning with the need to come.

"Give me that cock," he growled at Bekim, who seemed every bit as distracted by the two cocks filling Numa, despite not being one of them. His attention jerked back to Cade and he grinned, rising up on his knees again to give Cade easier access.

Cade twisted his torso just enough to take the man's cock in one hand and eagerly wrapped his lips around the thick head, lapping at the fluid that had escaped and savoring the delicious remnants of Numa's essence still clinging to him. Bekim twisted his hips in rhythm with Cade's sucking.

"Gaia, yes," Bekim said, tangling his fingers in Cade's hair to guide himself deeper. The tip of his cock nudged at the back of Cade's throat, and he opened wider to take more of him. He'd missed this level of wild abandon with a lover, something he hadn't experienced since since Lennox was taken from him. He didn't think he'd ever find such love again. When Bekim slipped out of his mouth and bent to give him a desperate kiss, he knew he'd found the mates he had longed for.

These two ursa were as perfect for him as they seemed to

be for Numa. Cade craved at taste of them both like he couldn't believe. When he bent again to take Bekim's cock, the other ursa shook his head.

"Fuck no, man. If you start again, I'll come, and I don't want to do that until after she's marked me. I'm happy pushing her to the edge, though." He shot Cade a wink before dipping his head to lavish his attention on Numa's breasts once more.

Cade lay back, forcing himself to focus on the clouds and not on the perfect, tight clench of Numa's pussy around his cock and Theron's. After only a few more strokes, Theron let out a gasp and jerked away.

"Fuck, I've got to cool off before I lose my shit," he said. "Bekim, swim?"

The pair of them stood and dove into the water, leaving Cade staring up at Numa's flushed face.

"I wish I could see your aura … could know how close you are."

"I can help with that," Zephyrus said. *"If you close your eyes and listen, you can hear the music made where her aura resonates with yours."*

Cade did. At first there was only splashing from the pair of swimming ursa. With Zephyrus' coaching, he focused his attention on the sensation of Numa's body as she settled against his chest again, her hips twisting with a delicious little swirl that had his blood pressure spiking.

Beneath it all was the strong, repetitive cadence of her heartbeat pulsing in tandem with his own, and from that rhythm, another sound emerged as subtle and ever present as the wind through the trees of his beloved home, or the roaring persistence of Gaia's Falls. But this sound was much closer, surrounding them and only them, like a constant melody that took up residence in his mind. Once he'd heard it, he couldn't unhear it.

Cade moved his hips, pushing slowly into her again, and the tempo of the song changed with her heartbeat and the cadence of her breaths. His own changed too, the pair of them creating a harmonic field he believed he could touch if he reached out to it. Keeping his eyes closed, he did just that, lifting a hand from Numa's back and holding his arm up. He felt it then, as surely as he felt the ground beneath his back—a field of potent energy that heated his skin when he brushed his fingers along its edge. It felt stretched to the point of nearly breaking. As he pumped his cock into her once more, the sensation stretched farther, and Numa let out a whimper and a sigh.

"So close," she said, lifting up and bracing her hands on his shoulders.

Cade opened his eyes and gazed at her in wonder. "I can hear them … our auras. Like a constant note held by the most beautiful voice. How long will it hold?"

"A little longer," she said, though the tightness in her voice told him she was likely already at her limit as much as he was at his.

"Numa, this isn't our only chance to get it right, is it? You haven't even marked the other two yet."

"This is just the start, but hold on … please hold on."

Her muscles tightened around him and she let out a gasp, her entire body growing still as if any movement would set her off. He wrapped his arms around her and pulled her back to him, nuzzling his lips against her temple. "As long as you need, sweet pea. You say when and I'm there."

Gaia, but he hoped it would be soon.

CHAPTER 20

NUMA

*N*uma hadn't counted on her desire increasing by tenfold with just the three of her lovers sharing her. Or four, she guessed, though Zephyrus seemed to be taking a backseat to the proceedings so far. She could sense him periodically, and when Cade confessed that he could hear their auras, she knew that was Zephyrus' doing.

He was right; she was at her limit and had been for several minutes, but she needed to maintain this level of potency for just a little longer. It might be enough to get the first phase of the portal ritual started, but she needed to be absolutely sure.

More magic floated into Cade's aura, attracted like iron filings to a magnet, but the amount had dwindled and nearly stopped, a sure signal that he was also at his own limit. She didn't dare mark Bekim and Theron yet. She needed them primed and ready for round two.

If only Dion would return. His power added to theirs would be the perfect amount to ensure each phase succeeded, because if there was one thing she was sure of, he had the stamina to last the entire ritual. The others might make grand claims of their prowess, but they would need to take breaks, especially now that she'd adjusted her plan to create an even larger portal and target it more precisely to Nikhil's location—which, thanks to Naaz and Neela's intel, she now knew down to its exact coordinates.

Cade's steel-hard length throbbed inside her, his pulse perfectly in sync with her own. She could close her eyes and believe that the two of them had somehow merged and become one body with one singular desire shared between them.

Softly, he murmured, "You're waiting for Dion, aren't you?"

She opened her eyes and turned to rest her chin on his chest. "Yes. I don't want to risk this not working. Is that all right?"

"Not risking failure? I'm all for that."

"No, I mean sharing me with him."

"Sweet pea, I've got a plug in my ass and just spent the last ten minutes sucking off another man. I think there's nothing I wouldn't do if you asked. Sharing you with a god … well, sounds like that falls into the category of things that would make you happy. But tell me, aside from the need, would you still be doing this?"

She smiled, and his cock made a little twitch inside her that sent a shot of pleasure up her spine, pushing her even closer to the point of no return. "Do you mean mating five of the most amazing men in existence and letting you all have your way with me? How could I resist?"

"I think you mean four men and a god." The deep voice came from behind her, the sound of it making her nipples prickle and her spine tingle. Cade's amused gaze held hers for a moment before looking beyond her to Dion, who she could sense simply by virtue of the immense power he brought.

The power drew nearer, her heartbeat racing at the sound of his footsteps and his shadow looming above, nearly blocking out the sun. Big calves appeared on either side of her where she lay atop Cade's chest, still held gently in his arms.

The sheer size of Dionysus overwhelmed her as she pushed up and arched her neck to look back at him. He stood straddling both her and Cade, his eyes filled with a hunger she hadn't witnessed before. He tilted his horned head to one side and licked his lips.

"I think it's my turn to stretch that tight snatch of yours, little one. I have waited a long time for this."

Cade's fingers tightened at her hips and she looked down to see his eyes narrowed. Sweet Mother, he wasn't about to challenge the god *now*, was he?

"You have something to say, ursa?" Dionysus said. "I don't want to keep her waiting longer. I can see she's ready to break."

Numa's skin warmed as the big god crouched above her and slid his hand down the arch of her back to cup her ass. He kept his hand there, squeezing her as he glided his searing length along the cleft of her ass, making sure to apply just the right pressure to her rear opening to make her whimper with fresh need.

"What do you say we share?" Cade said. Numa's eyes snapped open and she stared at him. He laughed. "What is it, sweet pea? I just learned how much you love having two cocks inside your sweet pussy."

Dion's fingers slipped between her thighs and glided around Cade's cock to find her clit and stroke it.

"She loves the idea, if her dripping cunt is any indication. Are you worried we won't fit?" Dion said.

"I'm worried my sanity won't remain intact," she said, hating the desperate pitch of her voice. Both men laughed, and Dion's cockhead teased closer to where she and Cade were joined. Suddenly she realized she may not have a choice, and the idea thrilled her.

Dion shifted above her as he crouched lower. His horns cast a shadow over Cade, making the big ursa look like he had horns as well, the outlines etched into the pale pillows he reclined against. When Cade began to slip out of her through no action of his own, she knew the god had taken matters into his own hands.

Her pussy suddenly ached at the absence of the enormous cock, but Cade resumed his attention on her nipples to make up for the loss. She wasn't wanting for long, however. Mere moments later, something altogether bigger pushed at her opening, and she looked between her thighs to see a pair of cockheads pressed tight and held in Dion's big fist. He rubbed them both in a circle around her opening once, twice.

She was just about to beg for it when he grabbed her hip with one hand, and he and Cade both shoved hard.

They didn't waste time waiting for her to acclimate, and the sudden stretch of her aching channel made her cry out in both surprise and unbearable pleasure.

She couldn't move, her body paralyzed both by ecstasy and the pair of immense cocks that speared her relentlessly from beneath. They held her easily, positioning her just so to allow their cocks the deepest access possible. She hadn't thought she had much more endurance to hold back her orgasm, but somehow Dion's arrival had given both her and Cade a second wind. The god took no quarter, however, his breath hot against her neck as he slammed into her.

"Best fuck of my life," he murmured into her ear, his teeth grazing her earlobe and biting as he let out a low groan. "You ready for the power, baby?"

Numa couldn't find breath to speak, instead giving her answer in an incoherent cry Cade captured with his mouth.

He shoved his tongue deep, a growl rumbling in his chest until nothing could contain their rapture so long held at bay.

Behind her, Dionysus let out a roar to the heavens, and Cade's voice joined his. Their cocks swelled, erupting deep into her, filling her with their seed as well as a torrential flood of the most powerful combination of magic she'd ever tasted. Numa's endurance broke and she arched back with a roar of her own. Dion caught her with one arm, holding her tight against his chest as her climax tore through her.

With her cry, she released the entire flood of magic smoke held in her lungs, the power infusing her providing a seemingly unending source to draw from. The smoke rose in dense coils, and she forced herself to focus even amid the continued tremors of her body as the two men kept fucking her, Cade's fingers between her thighs pushing her to yet another orgasm and his cock hardened anew.

"Feels like we've both got more to give," he said, flashing a triumphant look behind her at Dion, who hadn't shown any sign of pausing. Numa's pussy ached at the punishing thrusts as they resumed, but her body eagerly accepted them, her ecstasy cresting ever higher until her body seemed like nothing more than a conduit for the power to flood from her mates out into the rising column of vibrant green smoke.

With the ritual's pattern in her mind's eye, she directed the smoke above her, pushing it higher and higher until she met the resistance of the Sanctuary's dome-shaped barrier. The magical shield that hid the ursa home from the human world was one of the most impenetrable forces, and she and her siblings had made great sacrifices to ensure its integrity. She had to create this opening to ensure the place remained protected, though. It would only allow Nikhil and his armies to enter.

This surge of smoke was only the beginning. Cade and Dionysus began to slow, and Numa's body thrummed from the waning magic that flooded her. She didn't have time to shift focus to them yet, instead keeping her gaze fixed above on the pattern the smoke created against the surface of the dome—the beginning of an immense circle of green glyphs that at the moment was still incomplete.

Even as the two men slipped out of her, the divine power left behind boiled her blood and brightened her vision. Living fire danced over her skin and the sensation lit up her senses, making her crave even more than they had offered already.

"More!" she yelled. "I need more!"

She stood and turned, her feet on either side of Cade's hips, his stiff cock wet against his belly below her. Before her, Dionysus fell to his knees and tilted his head back with a glorious laugh. "You are as magnificent as I hoped," he said. "See what my essence does to you, little one? You are no less resplendent than Gaia herself."

"Are you ready to go again? Because I am," she said.

"I believe you have some unfinished business before we proceed," Dionysus said, tilting his chin behind her. She turned her head, and the horned shadow cast against the white pillows beneath her betrayed the fact that she'd let her true form out just a bit in her ecstasy. Bekim and Theron had come out of the water at some point during the proceedings, and now they knelt at Cade's head, their gazes fixed on her in utter awe.

When she met their eyes, their gazes turned hungry, and Theron pulled in a deep breath.

She crouched down and sat astride Cade's hips once more, his thick cock a hard, delicious pressure between her spread folds. She would have him again, but right now, she had a task to complete.

Three tasks, in fact.

"Turn," she said to both Bekim and Theron. The pair of

ursa she adored obeyed instantly, baring their backs to her on either side.

She made quick work of their marks, engraving the same design into their backs as she had in Cade's and Dion's. They turned to face her again and she slid backward to rest her backside on Cade's thighs, beckoning for him to sit up. He rose, storms clouding his normally clear blue irises, and she knew Zephyrus was in there, anticipating the next step with as much eagerness as the others.

Even though this stage wasn't necessary to prove they belonged to her, as ursa males, it would signal to any curious female that they were taken.

Numa extended her talons and gently grazed the index claw from each hand along Bekim's and Theron's handsome jaws. She leaned in and kissed them in turn. "I need your essence mixed with his before I finish. Can you give me that?"

Bekim's eyes fluttered closed and he gave her a silent nod. Theron said, "My pleasure," and with an eager smile, slipped in behind her again.

"How 'bout you take them both?" Cade said, scooting to the side and waving for Bekim to take his place.

Theron wrapped his sturdy, strong arms around her, pulling her backward. She went, allowing him to cradle her against his chest. When they were prone together, she shifted her hips to take his cock and he pumped up into her with slow strokes, pausing when Bekim hovered over her and hooked her knees over both his arms.

"I don't think there's anything better than this," Bekim said, gazing down into her face as he pressed his cock alongside Theron's.

The pair began to fuck her with every ounce of their being, their auras even more potently filled with power than they'd been before they took a dip, but she knew they were nowhere at their limit.

Numa lost herself to Bekim's adoring gaze and Theron's harsh whispers of love. Their power built swiftly, but they reached their limit long before she reached her own and were nowhere close to where they needed to be for the ritual.

"Still need more," she said.

Bekim groaned and shook, his stamina wavering. "Gaia, help us!" he called, a desperate plea aimed at the sky.

Once again, Dionysus stood over her union with them, his cock held in hand. "Gaia sent a messenger to help, and I will lend my aid too." He made a strange gesture and a whirlwind kicked up, pushing the dark veil that gave them privacy aside and flashing a prism of rainbows across their pillow-strewn bed.

To one side, Cade knelt and clutched his head, shaking it vigorously.

"It is time," a familiar female voice said. "Zephyrus has done his penance by my children. He shall have a body of his own."

The two ursa cocks buried deep inside her ceased moving as Theron and Bekim turned to stare at the other ursa. Cade's head flew back, his spine arching as his hair caught in a wild wind that seemed to affect only him. For a split second, he opened his eyes and stared at Numa, an elated smile on his handsome face. Then the air beside him shimmered and another male shape began to coalesce, formed out of light at first, but then the very ground beneath his feet surged and formed flesh from his legs all the way up to his head.

Numa blinked up at the familiar figure she'd seen on only a handful of occasions, but had loved on sight from the first moment. He was just as she remembered, with long, muscular legs, a strong chest, and wide shoulders. He appeared older now, silver strands salted through his dark hair and trim goatee.

"Zephyrus, is it truly you?" she asked.

He dropped to his knees beside her and clutched her head in one hand. "Yes, my love. Gaia has blessed me today, and at the most opportune moment, I see." His lips spread into a slow smile as he looked between her and the pair of men who were presently hilted inside her core. Then he kissed her with a long, slow, sensual pull of lips and push of tongue. Numa exhaled into his mouth and clung to his chest, moaning as Bekim and Theron began to move once more.

A bigger hand than Zephyrus' cupped her cheek and urged her to break the kiss. Through a haze of pleasure, she blinked and turned to see Dion gazing down at her with primal hunger.

"Time for you to taste me, little one. Time for all of you to taste me, if we are to fulfill your promise." He held his enormous shaft in one fist and was slowly stroking it. Without further prompting, Numa leaned close and wrapped her lips around his cockhead and sucked, coiling her long tongue around the length to taste more of him.

His flavor was tangier than she remembered, a pleasant combination of her own essence mixed with his and Cade's, and a small measure of the West Wind as well. She sucked him slowly, savoring the delicious, smooth heat of him and the beginnings of the ambrosia that leaked from his tip. Under her sensitive tongue, his shaft pulsed and surged. He tangled his fingers into her hair, pulling her head tighter against him and forcing her to take more of his immense girth. Numa opened wider, allowing his tip deeper into her mouth, though he could only go so far before she was choking.

A sudden flood of sweet flavor filled her mouth. Dion groaned at the same time and pulled back. He kept stroking himself as she swallowed the first taste, and ribbons of thick, shimmering white fluid coated her neck and breasts and belly. Before Dion's orgasm waned, three mouths descended on her breasts, lapping up the god's gift eagerly.

"I need a taste," Theron said into her ear. He bracketed his fingers along her jaw, and Numa twisted enough to accept his kiss. He groaned into her mouth as the remnants of Dion's essence hit his tongue.

All their auras suddenly burned infinitely brighter. Bekim and Theron both speared her with renewed abandon, their orgasms overtaking them swiftly. Bekim released her nipple and groaned into her shoulder as his cock pulsed inside her. Someone's deft fingers slipped between her thighs and teased her clit, pushing her into another orgasm almost instantly, thanks to the fresh influx of power from Dion's essence.

She came hard, her cries accompanied by another lungful of power-infused green smoke that she pushed high into the sky to join the last cloud. The second glyph of six appeared high above them, shimmering with the power they'd provided.

Bekim exhaled shakily and pulled out of her, sinking back on his haunches. His cock still stood proud and erect and glistening with the mixture of essences that filled her now. She eased off Theron's cock and stood, looking around at the five men who were all now dragon-marked.

"Come here," she said, beckoning to the three ursa. They obediently crawled to kneel at her feet, with Cade in the center and Bekim and Theron on either side. Numa manifested her talons, and with three swift swipes, sliced perfect criss-crossed patterns into each man's left pectoral. They hissed and cursed, but remained still and poised, waiting for the next step that would complete the traditional ursa marking by a mate.

Before she could complete the final step, Zephyrus

pressed his warm body against her back and whispered in her ear, "Allow me."

Numa's breath escaped her as a fresh surge of need flooded her body. He slipped his hand down her torso and dipped his fingers between her thighs, deliberately teasing her as he soaked his digits with the mixture of fluids he found there. She leaned back against him, pushing her hips up into his touch, and had almost lost herself to the pleasure when he stopped.

The three ursa looked up at her, grinning in amusement at how well the West Wind had undone her.

"Should have let him out more often today, huh, sweet pea?" Cade said.

Zephyrus chuckled. "You were right before. We owe her some torture, and this is simply me taking what's owed. You first." He held out his hand, fingers and palm glistening.

Cade stood and leaned in for Zephyrus to spread the mixture of essences that would seal his mark and brand him Numa's for the rest of his life. With a swipe of his hand, Zephyrus had covered the collection of cuts, which almost immediately sealed in a slightly upraised scar.

Cade lingered for a moment longer, his blue eyes brimming with love and adoration for Numa, and, as she realized when he shot a similar gaze behind her, for Zephyrus as well.

Then he leaned in and kissed them each, first Zephyrus, who leaned past Numa's shoulder to meet the big Windchaser's lips with his, then Numa herself. She sighed into Cade's mouth, reveling in the conviction that *this* was right. She would never have been so sure about her choice had she chosen only one of the three options she had been given.

Bekim and Theron each took their turns, this time helping Zephyrus tease her a bit longer before he sealed their marks. The final mating of the ursa concluded with Zephyrus pulling Numa back down into his arms, his cock spearing her from behind as the three ursa took turns lapping the remaining essence from her soaked pussy.

They paused when she was on the verge of another orgasm and moved aside, though she wasn't sure what had given them the cue. She found herself rolled onto her back amidst the pillows with Zephyrus hovering over her, wild storms churning in his gaze.

"I would like you all to myself for one round. Can you give me that?"

"What about them?" she asked.

Dion chuckled from a pile of cushions where he'd reclined after offering his dose of ambrosia to them all. "I will make sure they are well entertained, little one. Then the four of us will join you."

Numa's heartbeat fluttered when she smiled up at Zephyrus. "I am yours, then. But I need to make sure we have enough power between us for another phase."

"Worry not, my love," he said with a sly grin. "Just close your eyes and let me take care of everything."

She did as he asked, though she would have much rather kept staring at him, enthralled by his very existence. When he grazed his lips down her torso and settled himself between her thighs, she cracked one eyelid to peek. Bright green light flared from the mark on his back and she bit her lip, remembering that he would have absorbed it while still inside Cade. He was every bit as much hers as the others were.

"Eyes closed," he admonished once more, peering up at her from between her thighs.

Once she did, the music began, first the subtlest rhythm of the breeze teasing at the leaves on the Silas tree in the center of the lake, then the lapping ripples of the water as the wind surged in rhythmic gusts across the surface. The music lulled her just as Zephyrus began to slowly lap at her sodden folds, sliding between with the most agonizingly pleasurable licks.

Then the breeze kicked up, toying with her hair and tickling over her breasts and belly. He kept it up for several minutes, tormenting her with the lightest touch of his fingers along her inner thighs, then beneath her ass and between her cheeks. But while his touch was not overtly geared toward particular pleasure, the teasing gusts made her skin burn hotter with each pass like a breath of wind might cause a flame to flare brightly. The more he teased with barely there caresses, his warm wind, and low song, the more her need grew.

It seemed as though he'd hardly done a thing when Numa's yearning became so potent it seemed to sear her body from within.

"Sweet Mother, please!" she begged, writhing beneath his touch and gripping at his head with both hands.

Zephyrus only laughed softly against her parted folds, the vibration of his amusement sending a fresh surge of heat through her body. He grabbed her wrists and rose up, pushing her arms above her head.

As he moved, his stiff, solid length brushed along her core, and Numa moaned. She opened her eyes, only to discover they were full of tears … of joy, of need, of whatever overwhelming emotion had pushed her to the brink, she wasn't sure.

His brow twitched and a worried frown appeared. "You don't fear me, do you, Numa?"

She inhaled slowly and shook her head. "How can I? I love you. I have always loved you. Make love to me now, Zephyrus."

His eyelids fell closed and he dipped his head to kiss her. At the same time, he shifted his hips, drawing his length back along her sensitized flesh.

Numa's body ached with the heat that had risen, filling her aura with more magic, this time a different quality than the magic that had flooded her with the others, but no less potent. When his tip pressed at her entrance, she wrapped her legs around his hips, wanting to pull him deep, but knowing she would do better letting him set the pace. His skillful teasing already spoke of a talent for driving her to the edge with little effort, and as much as she would have loved to let go, she wanted to see how much farther he would take her.

He plunged into her with one long, swift stroke and began to fuck her in earnest, maintaining a slow but steady pace as he gazed down into her eyes. He kept her hands pinned above her head for a moment longer, then released her and shifted up, fucking her from a new angle. He grabbed her ankles this time and pulled them to his front, resting them on his shoulders. The change built fresh friction in her core, radiating outward until her own aura became as unmistakable as a wildfire cresting a mountain.

With his thumb pressed tight against her clit, Zephyrus proceeded to bring her to the very edge before pausing and slowing, letting the surge of ecstasy subside only slightly before driving her to the brink once more.

When Numa was sure she could bear no more, he surprised her by scooping her up and flipping them both. She slammed down on his cock, inadvertently sending a nearly mind-blowing surge of pleasure through her body.

"Not yet, my love," he rumbled into her ear. "Save it a moment longer." Then over her shoulder, he called, "Now!"

With one arm, he held her torso tight against his own, and with the other hand he gripped her ass, spreading her open. She knew Cade by his scent of earth and cedar and warm woodsmoke, and knew the pleasure he was about to give when his hard cock brushed along the cleft of her ass, just a tease before the truth hit and he pushed the tip of his thumb past her tight rear opening.

"You're good and ready for me now, aren't you, sweet pea?" he murmured in her ear, the soft fur on his chest tickling her back as he bent over her.

She was beyond the point of arguing, especially because she wanted nothing more than for this pair to use her any way they chose. When Cade's thick cock pushed past her tight barrier, she rejoiced.

"Sweet Mother, yes!" she cried, reaching behind to clutch at his head. He growled into her shoulder as he slowly pushed deeper, stretching her once again as exquisitely as he had earlier that day.

Numa lost herself between them, filled so completely that she had no choice but to give into their will. On Zephyrus's command, she let the pleasure overtake her, her orgasm joining theirs with yet another unbelievably potent surge of power. The pleasure was almost too great for her to focus, but she managed to push the lungful of smoke out once again, directing the third glyph up to the heavens to join the other two.

CHAPTER 21

NUMA

"Halfway there, little one," Dion said. "I am impressed."

He gazed up at her from where he reclined against the pillows. Numa tilted her head, amused by the pure adoration he showed that she was sure hadn't been there before. He was more than impressed, and perhaps even a little in awe of her.

"I want to do the final three in one shot," she said. "Do you think you're up to it, big boy?"

"Just me?" he asked, worried crinkles forming between his brows.

"Once the others are ready, all of you," she said. She glanced toward the lake where Cade and Zephyrus had joined Bekim and Theron in the water to bathe and cool off.

Dionysus stood, his immense size towering over her and making the very mountaintop and lake seem small by comparison. He closed the distance between them and tipped her chin up with a finger. There was no mistaking the worship in his aura as he gazed down at her, his thumb brushing along her lower lip.

"I would give you all I have to offer to help win this war, and even more to win your heart, little one. I sense you are still resistant to the last, however."

She swallowed, struggling to maintain her firm composure. The truth was that she was every bit as undone by his attention as she was by Zephyrus'. The three ursa were somehow less surprising. She had known of Bekim and Theron's feelings for some time, and Cade was easy to love from the start.

"It isn't that I'm resistant," she said, then paused and took a breath. "I just find it difficult to believe that I am the one you want. You have had so many powerful lovers—lovers more beautiful than me."

"You offer so much more than you realize, Numa. That you can capture the heart of a creature as capricious as the West Wind, earn the loyalty of a goddess as set in her ways as Gaia, and still have the Mother Dragon's undying love for a favored child—a firstborn daughter—proves your worth. We are all invested in the outcome of this war. I just chose to participate on a more personal level because you, little one, are far too enticing to stay away from, and the number of mates you will command in this ritual is only evidence of that."

"But you would share me with them, even though I know you have the power to keep me for yourself."

"I don't have the power alone to satisfy your deepest needs. That portal…" He tilted his head to look above them at the half-made design flickering against the barrier. "That is your deepest need. Protecting those you love. If all I wanted was your body, I could take it and you would have no choice. You would love it, certainly. Being my lover has few downsides. But I don't just want you to come undone with pleasure by my hand. I want your love, true and pure, and that can only happen if I let you come to it honestly." He gave her a smirk. "And if that means you riding my cock like a wild nymph in rut, that is just a bonus."

The cock in question kicked against his belly between them. Numa dropped her gaze to the glorious pillar between his thighs. Her aching core heated afresh with the desire to be stretched to its limit by that immense appendage, and before she knew what she was doing, she'd manifested her wings and launched herself a few feet in the air, pushing into his arms with a single beat against the currents of light summer breezes constantly flowing around them today.

He caught her with a hearty laugh and was still grinning as he helped her achieve her desired goal. Within moments, his cock was seated fully inside her again, and her eyes fluttered closed in ecstasy.

"You mean like this?" she asked, smiling up at him as she used his shoulders for leverage and beat her wings to help her slide up and down his length.

Dion let out a satisfied growl. "My cock is yours, little one, as is my heart, if you promise to use them both well."

She grinned at him. "I am a dragon, after all. You will not regret the sacrifice."

He widened his stance and wrapped his arms around her, letting her set the pace as she fucked him. After several deliciously pleasurable strokes, he groaned and dipped his head to her breasts, darting out his tongue to taste each nipple. She raised her hands to his horns, curious about their nature. They were similar to dragon horns in shape, but more like the horns of the satyrs she'd known.

"Do these give you pleasure?" she asked, stroking her hands up both as his cock stroked deep into her tight channel.

"No, little one. They are merely there for you to hold onto while I fuck you. And yours?" He lifted a hand, still easily holding her to him with his other arm, and grazed his fingertips along the coiled length of one of her horns. Pleasure even sharper than the sensation of his cock inside her shot down her spine, and she closed her eyes with a desperate moan.

Dion chuckled. "I see. This is fascinating. Had I known, I would have asked to see your beautiful horns when I began my test."

He stroked them each in turn, the sensation akin to him sucking on her nipples, only multiplied by a factor of ten. Her core flooded with fresh, slick heat that eased the way for him to sink even deeper until she was sure his cock had found her very soul.

The world tilted. Numa's eyes flew open in surprise, but Dion had only lowered them both back down to the silken blankets, settling her on top of him and lying back. He finally ceased the distracting, though pleasurable, teasing of her horns to grip her hips and urge her to ride him harder.

"Can you take care of all of us? Dion asked. "That would be the true test of your worthiness, don't you think?

"Are my marks on your backs not sufficient?" she asked through panting breaths, bracing her hands on his chest to give herself leverage to slide up and down his tremendous shaft.

"Worthy enough to secure our love, but to bind us all to you in perfect synchronicity, I think we need to share you fully."

The calculating look in his eyes made her pause. "You've considered this in depth, haven't you?"

"What kind of god of the rut would I be if I didn't imagine all the debauched things my co-mates and I could do to you? Tell me you don't love that about me."

The tight, involuntary spasm of her core gave him her answer. "You know me so well," she whispered when she regained enough reason to speak amid the push of his cock.

With the barest nod from Dion, she was surrounded, the other four men's skin glistening and the scents of their arousal as potent as the glowing clouds of their auras. The four shimmering cocoons of power that surrounded them seemed to merge into one, mixing with Dion's more potent and ever-growing aura that increased its power with every stroke inside her.

Numa's skin prickled with the power of all that pent-up magic. There was so much unreleased energy, she could taste it. It began to rotate as the men moved, seeking out the place where they would fit and seeming to await her command for where to go.

"They are waiting for you, little one. You are the hub. We are but the spokes."

Cade knelt down by her side, resting a hand on her thigh and stroking up through the sticky evidence of all their love in sharing her. He pressed a kiss to her shoulder, then her cheek, then her lips, each time teasing his fingers closer to her apex until he'd found her clit and gently flicked it. "Where do you want me, sweet pea?"

"Oh …" Numa let out a soft sigh as he bent to take her nipple in his mouth and suck. She reached for his erection and began to stroke. "I want you right there."

To Zephyrus, she tilted her head to beckon him closer. "Let me taste you, unadulterated by ursa power this time."

Zephyurus' stormy eyes darkened and he licked his lips, moving to straddle Dion's waist with his long, curved cock in his hand.

"What of us?" Bekim asked.

"One of you can take my ass, and the other …" She blinked, struggling to maintain her sanity despite the surging swell of their power encompassing her in a delicious bubble. Then a thought occurred to her as she spied Dion's avid attention on the proceedings. "Theron can have my ass. Bekim … Dion will service you."

Dion's eyes widened. She held his gaze with one brow arched, challenging him to object. Then he let out a bellow of a laugh that rippled through his entire body and made his cock surge inside her enough that she gasped.

"Yes, I should have imagined after all the tortures you seem to want to put me through that you would need my help to satisfy all your adoring lovers too."

"It's only fair when I have to tolerate an ego as *enormous* as yours," she retorted, deliberately tightening her vaginal muscles around his cock and delighted when he hissed and clenched his eyes shut.

Her lovers all followed her directions, and she braced herself for Theron's deft penetration of her already well-serviced ass. He slipped in easily, the thickness of his cock still no match for the glorious stretch of Dion's inside her pussy.

As she grabbed Zephyrus' hips and opened her mouth to take him, he stopped her and bent down. "Remember to feel the wind, my love. I am here to stoke your flame. Let me do my duty to you as well as you do yours to me."

Finally, he cupped her by the chin and pressed a long, slow kiss to her lips before straightening up again. The two cocks that impaled her began moving in earnest, and she was forced to hold onto Zephyrus lest she lose her balance entirely. When she wrapped her lips around his cock, he held her shoulders to steady her, eventually taking a small step back to allow her to lean farther forward to accommodate Theron's push deeper into her tight backside.

Numa was eventually steady enough to drop her hand again and blindly hunt for Cade's smooth, hard cock. After groping for a few seconds, he wrapped his big hand around her wrist and guided her to the erection she sought.

"Looking for this, sweet pea? Fuck, your pretty mouth looks like heaven wrapped around him. Mind if we trade places when you finish him off?'

She was too determined to taste the West Wind's crumbling will to answer, but he answered for her. "If she hasn't finished you yet when my seed slides down her throat, I will make sure her mouth finds your cock next."

Numa nearly forgot her purpose, so caught up she was in the pleasure of being surrounded and filled by all her lovers. They remained keen on her needs, however, letting her push them past their limits before giving in and releasing their power to her. First Theron cried out, spilling his Nirvana into her as his semen flooded into her ass. He eased out of her, then with a splash, returned to the lake to clean up once again.

Bekim took advantage of his lover's absence, leaving Dion's teasing mouth to plunge into her opening. He began fucking with slow strokes that matched Dion's almost lazy tempo, a rhythm designed to drive her mad.

They were true to their word where torturing her was concerned. Cade continued to tongue and suck on her nipples while he teased her clit. Zephyrus clutched the back of her head and let out a long groan, followed by his hot spend hitting the back of her throat. His power had barely sunk into her when Cade took the West Wind's place. Before she had a chance to swallow everything Zephyrus had given her, Cade cupped her chin and bent to kiss her, hungrily plunging his tongue into her mouth and tasting the flood of the other man's semen that still lingered.

"How are you doing, sweet pea?" he asked, pulling back and gazing into her eyes. Numa could only pant and whimper from Dion and Bekim's steady penetration, fast enough to push her pleasure ever higher, but still slow and deliberate enough to keep her at the very razor's edge.

Cade chuckled and caressed her cheek, the potent musk of his cock filling her senses and making her mouth water. Hungry for another taste of this beautiful ursa who had been such a gift, she stretched her long tongue out and coiled it around his cock, pulling him to her lips. Cade let out a low growl and gripped the back of her head, the hard flesh of him pulsing with a heavy, rhythmic throb as she began to slide her tongue up and down his length.

She dipped her head lower, grazing wet lips across the tender skin of his balls. Cade graciously held his cock up and tilted his hips forward to allow her easier access to take each orb into her mouth and suck. She savored the tangy flavor of her essence mixed with the others that lingered on his skin. There was essence of Dion clinging to him too, making her wonder what the god had done with her three ursa while she was otherwise occupied with Zephyrus. The taste of the god's powerful ambrosia sent a jolt of ecstasy through her and her core clenched tight around his huge cock. Behind Cade, Dion uttered a rough curse and a groan as he shoved deep and so hard she had to grab at Cade's hips to maintain her balance.

Behind her, Bekim groaned, and a second later, both cocks inside her surged and pulsed, shooting their climax deep. The flood of power from both their orgasms made her skin feel like it was on fire, and her core was so engorged with the need to orgasm she couldn't help but beg.

They'd fed her even more power than she could have imagined she could hold, but still she knew it wouldn't quite be enough to complete the portal's glyphs.

"More," she moaned just before descending on Cade's cock with abandon. He groaned as he rested his hands on the back of her head, guiding her while she swept her lips along the length of his cock. She coiled her tongue around his massive girth, teasing and sucking at his tip with each pass.

"I've got more for you, baby, especially if you keep that up," he said.

The big trunk of a cock between her thighs slipped out, and she was dimly aware of Dion shifting positions. Bekim also disappeared, leaving her empty and the evidence of their orgasms coursing down her thighs.

Dion sat up, his arms sliding around Cade's hips and cupping the other man's balls as Numa sucked on his cock. She leaned back, continuing to stroke Cade's cock with both hands. Behind the big ursa, Dion shot her a wicked smile.

"Shall we see how much he has to offer you when my tongue is in his ass?" he asked.

Her desire peaked with the wild flare of Cade's aura. He gazed down at her in adoration, cupping her head with both hands as she continued to stroke him, then took his cock-head between her lips once more. She kept her eyes upraised, watching him, enjoying the clear signs of his ecstasy as she sucked and stroked. When his head flew back and a rough growl erupted from his chest, she dropped her gaze to Dion's big horns twisting back and forth as the god buried his tongue into Cade's ass and worked him into a frenzy.

Cade's aura crackled with vibrant green power, the energy tickling Numa's skin as it merged with hers. A warm body slipped in behind her, cupping her breasts and teasing her already hard and aching nipples. The coarse brush of a beard rubbed at her shoulder, the scent of sage and verbena flooding her senses as Zephyrus murmured encouragement in her ear.

Numa closed her eyes, all the better to enjoy the wash of sensations surrounding her, encompassing her. Within that pocket of awareness, she sensed Bekim and Theron as plainly as if her eyes were open. They knelt on either side of her, lips brushing shoulders and their fingers delving between her thighs. One of them plunged his fingers deep into her sodden core while the other teased her clit. He drove her to the brink, stopping when she was at the very edge.

"It's like I can feel you about to break," Bekim said with wonder. "How can you hold back?"

She was in no position to answer, and at that moment, Cade's fingers tightened on her head, his fists wrapping around her horns as he thrust his cock deeper into her mouth and a bellowing roar echoed above them. His semen burst onto her tongue, sliding down her throat and filling her mouth. His power flooded into her, adding to the abundant well of energy she sought to accumulate for the final push to finish the ritual.

It was time.

Cade stumbled to the side and dropped to his knees, leaning in past Theron to give her a lingering, grateful kiss.

Dion reclined against the pillows with a self-satisfied smile. He lifted a hand and crooked his finger. "Come to me, little one. I'd like to taste you when you give all that built-up magic to the cause. Let my tongue be the thing that unleashes it."

Her body buzzing with the immense power they'd already fed her, Numa dropped her hands to his belly and proceeded to crawl up the god's big torso. His gaze grew hungry the closer she got, until he impatiently grabbed her by the hips and lifted her bodily, placing her squarely across his chin. He covered her pussy with his mouth, plunging his tongue deep inside her and eliciting a surprised gasp at the sudden assault on her sensitive flesh.

The pleasure was so great, she couldn't help but writhe and moan. She leaned back, propping one hand against his chest to hold herself up while she bucked her hips into his mouth. The others were never far. Though she was too lost to pleasure by then to fully track their movements, she was acutely aware of the fact that they were always touching her.

Mouths were at both her breasts, hands squeezing and pinching and teasing all over her body, fingers buried into her backside, and eventually someone's cock slipped between her lips again and she hungrily began to suck, only dimly conscious of the familiar flavor of Zephyrus on her tongue when he came.

"Let go, love. It's time," he said.

All it took was the command, and finally, a kiss. When the West Wind plunged his tongue into her mouth with a demanding thrust, Numa's entire body spasmed and pleasure shot through from her core all the way to the top of her head. Zephyrus broke the kiss just in time for her sonorous cry and the flood of green smoke that billowed forth from her lungs.

Her orgasm persisted, thanks to Dion's diligent licks. He held tight to her hips, refusing to release her and somehow understanding that she needed his help to draw this out for as long as possible. But her lungs could only hold so much air. When the current of magic smoke dwindled, Zephyrus bent again, taking her mouth, only this time he exhaled, swiftly filling her lungs with more even more magic.

Again she exhaled with a cry to the heavens, her body little more than resonating energy as Dion continued tormenting her to draw out the climax. Zephyrus came to her aid once more, granting her the air she needed in the form of his own breath, and allowing her one final push to complete the circle of glyphs that glowed high in the sky above her.

CHAPTER 22

MERI

White-hot pain bloomed inside Meri's mind for what seemed an eternity, so sharp she knew nothing else. She'd been so close to destroying the temporal bubble and finally reaching her vessel. When the agony subsided enough for her to regain her bearings, everything had changed.

The battle still raged in full force in the Haven, her mercenaries edging ever closer to the Source, pushing the ursa and nymphs back with blood-soaked brutality. But when she sent her spirit back to the Sanctuary, she found no bubble to drain, and worse than that, her vessel was gone.

This could not be. She reached out farther, extending the range of her awareness to its very limits, searching the entire world and all the higher realms she had access to for a sign that the baby, the child-creature she'd created, was within reach.

With each mile, her rage burned hotter. How dare they take her child? Her vessel, her surest chance at immortality, was gone!

She blasted back into the minds of her army, fueling their

battle frenzy to a fresh peak with her own unadulterated fury. If she could not have the child, she would have the Source. Once secured, and with the Haven under her control, perhaps she could find a way to release her soul from her broken vessel, even if she had to send one of her own soldiers to do the deed.

Nyx herself stood guard over Meri's body, still sealed within her private grotto in the Haven. She knelt by the bed as though the task of watching Meri was some kind of penance.

"I know you are there," the ancient Dionarch said, her voice rising above the echoes of battle that carried on outside the comfortable cave. "You will not win this war. There is no reward in betrayal. When Nereus returns, we *will* beat you."

Nereus. The old insult should not have affected Meri as much as it did. The one man she had truly desired for a mate had barely shown a glimmer of interest in her. They would have been perfect, once upon a time. She, the highest ranked female Thiasoi soldier, *belonged* with the Thiasoi's general, her male counterpart. She and Nereus would have been even stronger co-commanders, had they mated. But Nyx had seduced Nereus with her charms so thoroughly he believed *he* was the one seducing *her*.

The very grotto Meri's broken body lay in now had been painstakingly crafted, stone by stone, with the satyr's blood and sweat as an offering to Nyx. The bed she lay upon now was the Dionarch's own marriage bed where she had blood-melded with the satyr and formed a permanent, unbreakable bond of love.

She should have killed the bastard and all the other Thiasoi satyrs the very second she'd captured them. If only she hadn't needed their blood—the closest substance to the power of the Source itself and the one thing that would ensure her vessel was rendered immortal once it came of age.

Now her vessel was lost. Stolen and beyond the reach of her powers. Who knew where they had taken the child? For all she knew, they'd found a way to kill the baby to keep her from reclaiming it.

That mattered little now. She was close to claiming the Source itself and taking control of the Haven. When she did, the Sanctuary wouldn't be far behind.

Nyx kept talking, lecturing her on the error of her ways. The longer the woman spoke, the more enraged Meri became. Wallowing close to her body preserved her power for the mercenaries within the Haven, but she couldn't stand being forced to sit and listen to the one creature she hated most.

Her tie to this broken body gave her little choice, however. Her spirit's bond to it wouldn't disappear until the vessel's heart ceased to beat, otherwise she'd have taken full possession of one of her mercenaries the second the ursa bitch attacked, leaving Meri's vessel nothing more than a mauled piece of meat with just enough life to keep her tethered to it.

Enraged and desperate, she retreated through those other bonds, the tributaries of blood that linked her to the descendants of all her former blood-bound pets. What good was all this power if she could use it for nothing more than increasing her spirit's awareness of the world around her? As a creature distilled down to her magical essence, she could only act on *magic* with this power, not on the physical world. Her army was still the best hope for winning, but none of the soldiers as yet had found a way through the magic shield that the ursa shaman had erected around the Source itself.

The *magic* shield ... How could she be so blind? She had come so close to disrupting the power of the temporal bubble before they'd preempted her by taking it down. The shield the shaman held to protect the Source couldn't be that different, and certainly not as strong if it were only powered by a single ursa and not the blood-melded trio of her former lovers and their newly minted Summer Spirit mate.

With fresh purpose, she left the grotto behind, along with Nyx's constant, droning monologue. Bound by blood to all her soldiers, Meri understood much more now than she had before. They were nothing but animals once that blood frenzy was unleashed, only requiring the slightest mental nudge to push harder with little concern for self-preservation. It made them formidable warriors, nearly as durable as the creatures they fought, having been mutated through the blood of their own enemies.

Almost as a single entity, she commanded them to push toward the central target, and they moved. Armed with blades and outfitted in body armor, they mobbed the squads of nymphs and ursa that blocked the way to the Source. No longer seeking a flanking maneuver, they went straight down the middle, surprising their opponents and forcing them to regroup.

But the defenders lacked the advantage of a shared consciousness and couldn't react quickly enough. Their distraction forced them to move farther from the Source, reinforcing the front line with the squad of nymphs that had remained close, defending the sole ursa shaman whose power sustained the protective field around the collection of pools at the base of the massive tree.

Her consciousness glided across the field of battle, the carnage below a red plain upon which her black-clad forces marched. The men were covered in blood, their eyes wild with lust. One tangled with an ursa, deftly avoided clawed attacks, and ducked its snapping teeth to drive a blade deep into the thick fur of the creature's belly. He thrust and ripped, nearly tearing the beast in two. Meri rejoiced, and with only the slightest praise, the man ripped the heart out of the bear and held it above his upturned mouth, drinking in the creature's life.

With that taste, she knew what she was missing, what could help her gain an even greater advantage. As her soldiers shredded their way through the nymphs and ursa, they began to rip out throats and bend to drink the blood of the fallen. The power from that blood would not sustain them for long, but it was cumulative and would last long enough to overpower their adversaries.

And that power became hers. Through her soldiers, she found the links she needed to the bloodlines of those they killed, and could leech the power for her own purposes. She felt its transience, but also its sharp potency. It would fade, but it would not fade so soon that she could not use it to her advantage.

With the intent of a well-aimed arrow, she pointed her entire being at the barrier that blocked her from her goal. Her spirit hurtled forward with the power of her blood-soaked victims that fell at the hands of her soldiers.

When she met the barrier, the magic shattered as if she were a bullet striking brittle glass. The ursa shaman's eyes went wide, her entire body seizing in agony as if she too had been struck by Meri's desperate final blow. But by the time the dark-skinned woman regained her senses, it was far too late.

Meri plunged into the Source's waters, the power flooding through her into her army. The Haven's defenders still fought, desperately clinging to hope and trying to pull the Ultiori back from certain victory. There was no chance of that now.

All she had left to do was reclaim her body and heal it for long enough to find a new host. She had just the subject in mind.

CHAPTER 23

ZORION

Zorion's gaze was fixed to the sky, awestruck at Numa's display of power. She had done it. The circle of glyphs gleamed in the midday sun, a shimmering pattern of iridescent green against the clear blue heavens. He was so enthralled he nearly didn't hear the cries of alarm and the chorus of roars from the lakeshore.

At first he thought the water had turned to blood. Red was all he saw, surging from beneath the surface and over-taking Numa and her five mates.

"We have to help them!" Asha yelled, then shifted into her gleaming, white-scaled glory with Naaz astride. She flew into the fray before Zorion could object.

Neela stood, frozen in fear. "It's her. She's coming."

"*Adara*, we must fight," Zorion said. He shot a look back to the battle that had broken through from the Haven, and beyond the shores of the lake to the maelstrom of blood-soaked men surging up from the center. The monolithic tree that channeled the Source's power ran red with blood seeping from its bark, its leaves cascading down from its branches like so much crimson carnage.

More waves surged from beneath the water, armored men wielding blades of all sizes. To his horror, many of them wore trophies of their kills: bear pelts draped across their shoulders and nymph antlers strapped to their heads. Their auras were black with more than the lust for death. Some deeper corruption drove them on.

In the midst of the onslaught, Numa shifted, her true form rising bright green from the mass of red. At her side, the horned god swung his fists, tossing the enemy back into the water only for them to rise again, somehow refreshed from the contact with the lake.

Her other mates fought hard, three enormous ursine shapes roaring and swiping, drawing blood and tearing limbs at every turn, while above them a gargantuan falcon dove with talons outstretched, its piercing cries kicking up winds and tossing the falling leaves around the battle in little blood-tinged cyclones.

"Neela, they need our help!" He touched her shoulder, only to find she'd gone cold. Looking at Zil, he saw his worry reflected in his brother's gaze.

Zil cupped Neela's cheek. "She cannot hurt you anymore, love, and your daughter is safe. This is our chance to confront her once and for all. To prove our sacrifices weren't for nothing."

Her glowing eyes flared bright again, her skin heating as she regained her fire. "I'm ready to burn the bitch," she said, her jaw set as her fiery wings flared wide from her shoulders.

"Together?" Zil glanced at Zorion with brows raised.

"Yes. The time stop will allow us to take them by surprise."

Without hesitation, he and Zil merged with Neela's hand held in both of theirs. The air instantly stilled, the falling leaves poised above the water of the lake that appeared as a frozen sheet of red glass. Zorion shifted into the dragon form he could only assume when merged with his brother, and he and Neela flew across the grassy expanse to the lakeshore. His mate cast fiery blasts out of her palms into the mass of bodies that surged from the water, but the flames remained contained within spheres where they landed. She peppered several all along the very edge, careful to keep them out of range of their allies.

Zorion's cold rage pushed him to his aunt, where her green wings were outstretched, several bloodied men clinging to her. He'd swiped several bodies away with his huge talons from the air before their power faded and time surged into motion again in a deafening cacophony.

Roars reverberated in his ears from the ursa below him as he soared past their heads and made a wide arc to return. Explosive blasts rang through the air, Neela's fiery bombs detonating in the middle of the groups where they'd landed, tossing men back into the water, some of them landing in pieces.

Before Zorion could reach the group again and light them up with a blast of his own fire, a desperate voice called into his mind, echoed by Numa's roar.

"The portal! You have to complete the ritual. It must be ignited before it can open! Only immortal dragon fire can activate the glyphs. Zorion, please! Before it's too late!"

Immediately he turned, trumpeting behind him for Neela to follow. They had the immortal dragon fire required. He was the son of two immortal dragons, and Neela had been reborn from his own immortal fire.

Together, the two of them angled up instead of down, beating their wings to climb higher toward the edge of the Sanctuary's dome where the immense circle of glyphs still hung above them. Partway up, a powerful gust of warm wind caught their wings, pushing them even higher. The big falcon fell into formation just in front of them, and with the wind's aid, Zorion felt almost weightless, his wings outstretched as the currents pushed him where he needed to go.

Just before the apex of their climb, Zephyrus veered away, and as he descended, Zorion took a breath, aiming his fire at the outer ring of the glyph. Beside him, Neela cupped her palms together, an orb as brilliant as the sun coalescing in between. On his command, they let loose all their fire.

The green smoke of the glyphs ignited instantly, and in a brilliant blast of power, a shimmering elliptical opening appeared above them. The sky beyond was dark and filled with stars, but moments later, that night sky from some other land was completely obscured by winged creatures cascading in by the hundreds.

Dragons and turul abounded, some with riders, but most without. With triumphant roars and piercing falcon cries, they answered his trumpeting welcome and his mental plea for help.

An immense blue dragon soared around the edge of the portal and came back to hover before him where he and Neela watched, suspended in mid-air.

Nikhil rode astride the big blue dragon, the general who led this army.

"What has happened?" he bellowed, eying the continuing carnage beneath them.

Zorion shot Neela a look and she answered for him, calling back, "Meri must have broken through!"

Zorion's mother let out a roar of displeasure and Nikhil cursed. "This means she's gained access to the Source. We will confront her now, before she becomes too powerful to beat! Finish off this wave and join us when you can!"

Nikhil let out a shrill whistle and waved his arm in the air, directing the throngs of winged creatures toward the

edge of the falls. Multitudes of them plunged over and disappeared from sight, leaving behind enough to help push back
the enemy from the Sanctuary's shores.

CHAPTER 24

MERI

The immense power left Meri drunk with elation over her certain victory. It was only a matter of time before she destroyed the last of the nymphs and ursa who opposed her. She shifted her consciousness upward from the depths of the Source's pools into the immense tree that now grew in its center. This was new, but not surprising. She'd suspected it was the ursa's doing, creating an unbreakable connection between the Haven and the Sanctuary to ensure power from the Source was never lost. It would matter little when she controlled both realms.

But her soldiers were falling back, as though they'd met resistance on the other side. No sooner would a squad plunge into the pool than she would see the same men emerge again, some broken and bloody and some floating up as corpses covered in burns or slashes from giant talons.

The dragons in the Sanctuary were not numerous enough to push back against the throngs of her army to that degree. She'd counted them. The Sanctuary only had a handful of residents, mostly elderly ursa and children not fit to fight.

Two immortal dragons were in residence, but their presence was not enough to account for the number of bodies returning from that fight.

The triumphant chorus of roars and battle cries that reached her from downstream made her reflexively turn all her soldiers' heads to that direction. Those were not the cries of the human mercenaries she controlled. They were the bellows of dragons, the piercing calls of falcons, and one cry she knew better than all the others: the distinctive, ululating battle call of the Thiasoi themselves, ringing out in a chorus of deep, male voices.

This could not be. She had not left an opening for any to follow. Yet somehow, reinforcements had come to defend the Haven nonetheless. Then it came together—the temporal bubble. She'd only thought it a shield to protect the child, and it hadn't occurred to her that it served another purpose —it had bought them time to find a way to allow in reinforcements. She'd been so blind, especially when the ancient immortal dragon she'd recognized as one of Nikhil's special treasures had burned her, sending her back to her body with her tail between her legs. That had given them the distraction they needed, forcing her to seek out the child rather than discover their true purpose.

She shot her consciousness back to the Sanctuary then, soaring above the lake. She might have been gratified by the blood-soaked landscape and the leafless tree running red from the blood of the fallen creatures, but the immense portal that hovered in the barrier above the lake told her the truth of their efforts. Dragons and turul still streamed in by the hundreds, most of them bypassing the battle that waned in the Sanctuary, heading directly over Gaia's Falls into the Haven itself.

She had reached the Source. She could still use it to win, but only if she regained a physical form.

She found a mercenary at the rear of the battle, closest to the grotto where her broken body lay. She would spare no others, but one should be enough. Infusing his mind with her command and enough power to sustain him through the task, she sent him to the grotto where her body lay. The barrier at the opening stopped him, which was no surprise.

Latching onto her link to the Source, she drew the power to him. His blood turned to fire in his veins, the pain something that would be unbearable, though she didn't care enough about his welfare to avoid it. As it was, he was paralyzed by her control, forced to take the brunt of the agony while she pulled more and more of the power into him.

With the man screaming in agony, the magic finally reached the threshold she required. Pressing him against the magic barrier, she forced his eyes open and his voice to work.

"Nyx!" she yelled using the soldier's strained vocal cords. "I have won! You may as well surrender. Your precious Nereus is dead, along with all the others who thought they could beat me today."

The Dionarch's attention shot to the mercenary, who Meri commanded to stretch out, pressing his palms flat against the shimmering field that held him back. When Nyx rose, fierce anger churning in her swirling gaze, Meri pushed all the power she could into the man's body, aiming it against the barrier.

The split-second before the energy became too much, she retracted from his consciousness, back into the broken body that lay inside the grotto. Nyx's attention was focused on the explosion that rocked the entrance, the power erupting from the soldier's body and blasting directly into the barrier. It may have been overkill if all she'd wanted to do was breach that barrier—she could have done that without him—but the distraction itself was key. Nyx was frozen in horror just long enough for Meri to do what she needed.

She pulled more power into her twisted, broken shell, commanding the magic to heal what Nyx herself had refused to. Conscious and in command of her physical form once more, she rose up on the bed as stealthily as possible.

The Dionarch stared at the bloody mess left behind by the soldier's exploding body. Red haze still lingered in the air, slowly settling over her skin. Too bad his blood wasn't enough for Meri to force a blood meld. She summoned the Source's power to her once more, testing the limits of this body. It wouldn't sustain much power for long, but she only needed it to last a few more moments.

She took Nyx down swiftly, with a knee to the back and elbow to the side of her head. Grabbing the woman's wrist, she twisted her arm up and pressed it to the center of her back. The other woman was thankfully not shifted into her primal form. Meri's recently healed body twinged with pain, but she channeled that discomfort into the rage that she needed to fuel this task.

Glancing around for an implement, she caught the glint of familiar steel on a stone ledge by the bed. The dagger she carried with her everywhere—they had kept it. It had once belonged to Nikhil, until Meri had claimed it as her own, treasuring it for just such an occasion as this. She reached out and the blade flew to her through the air, pulled by the force of her own will.

"Nereus is close, Meri," Nyx said. "It is only a matter of time before we execute you as we should have done when you betrayed us."

"Bullshit," Meri said, bending over and pressing the dagger to Nyx's throat. "Nereus will never kill the woman he loves."

"He never loved you," Nyx said. "Have you really been lying to yourself about that all this time? He urged me and Neph to kill you. We chose to show you mercy. We will not make that mistake again."

Meri let out a bitter laugh. How Nereus felt about her didn't matter a bit. Baring her teeth, she bent over Nyx's back, nuzzling her ear seductively.

"He will have me today, just wait." Then made a small slice in Nyx's throat, bent down, and covered the cut with her mouth. Hot, sweet fluid flooded her tongue and she drank deep, reveling in the cry of realization as Nyx struggled beneath her. She felt the Dionarch attempt to shift, her body bucking, but unable to throw Meri off while she was weighed down by her newly acquired power.

With another slice of the blade, she cut into her own wrist and forced the bleeding opening against Nyx's mouth. The second her blood touched the other woman's tongue, her spirit carried along with the flood of red fluid and she claimed the Dionarch's mind, pushing in through the horror and shame.

To Meri's surprise, she discovered that the Dionarch herself believed she deserved this violation.

"Isn't this a treat?" Meri crooned. "You were as mad with power as me, weren't you? I imagine you regret ever giving in to your daughter's tricks to subdue you. Your own love for Nereus is what made you fail. His love for you is what will seal the deal and make the Haven mine for good."

Nyx's memories flashed by in a blur, all her desperate attempts to maintain the security of the Haven destroyed by a single red dragon's tricks. But for the life of her, Meri couldn't provoke Nyx into regretting her return to sanity. The only regret was for the nymphs she had betrayed, and for not having faith in her lover's eventual return. That link with Nereus still remained, and Meri grasped hold of it with the elation of a prospector finding a vein of pure gold.

Nereus was here, his blood bond to Nyx so powerful as to be blinding. Meri grasped at it and tugged, gratified by the sensation of him drawing closer, answering her silent call.

She scented him before he appeared, the potent musk of this man imprinted on Nyx's mind so strongly that Meri could feel her new immortal vessel responding instinctively. Meri stood up straight, giving in to the primal urge to shift into the shape the approaching satyr would respond to best.

The big hooved and horned outline of him appeared in the opening of the grotto, a silhouette against the hazy midday light that filtered in through the forests around them. He smelled of blood and lust, and had likely killed his way through the mob of Ultiori mercenaries just to get to her. Her heartbeat quickened at the realization that she was about to have this male who she had wanted from the start. Not even Neph or his accursed dragon lover had incited such desire in her as Nereus once had, and did again.

"Nyx," he rumbled, glancing around at the cave she stood inside. "They said you locked yourself in with her ..." He took a step down into the cave, the lanterns lighting the inside cast a warm glow on his exposed skin. As he approached, she realized the reddish hue on his skin was actually blood. He was coated in it, and the sight aroused her even further.

A few feet in, he stopped and frowned, his gaze falling on the twisted female body at her feet.

"They said she must not be killed. What have you done?"

"I have her under control. Let the others clean up the rest of her mess. Come to me."

The blood bond between them tugged and Nereus responded instantly, his hooves reverberating with each step closer. His horns nearly grazed the ceiling of the grotto, and when he unbuckled his belt, the blood-soaked tatters of whatever clothing still remained on him slid to the floor. His enormous cock shone in the dim light, one of the few parts of his body not coated in grisly evidence of the battle he'd fought to get to her.

"To me, Meri, not to you. He is mine."

She ignored the voice, pushing more of the Source's power into the consciousness she'd appropriated in an attempt to silence her.

Nereus paused and cocked his head, regarding her uncertainly. "Is everything all right, my love?"

Sensing his wariness, Meri shifted the focus of her power back to him, reaching for that blood bond he had with Nyx and manipulating it again.

"Don't make me wait. You always loved to tease, but I've waited far too long for that to work on me now. I need you."

She'd barely finished speaking before he surged toward her, his goateed face wild with unchecked desire. He wrapped his arms around her, hauling her close to his chest and devouring her mouth with the hunger of a soldier too long away at war. Her heart soared at the desperate way he tore at the flimsy fabric of her gown, pushing her back toward the bed with each yank and rip, his mouth never relenting from the kisses he planted on her heated skin.

Her legs hit the bed, but before she could stumble, he hauled her bodily up against him, hooking his hands beneath her thighs. He tilted them both down to the bed in one smooth motion, ramming his cock inside her and fucking her in deep, brutal thrusts.

Meri lost herself to ecstasy, to the inundation of his potent scent blended with the blood of her own soldiers. She would have sacrificed them all again just to have this moment, to experience one time this man's desperate need to possess her.

"It is my body he owns, and your ruse will not persist for long."

She writhed against him, wrapping her long legs around his hips to pull him deeper, urging him to climax with the tightening of her muscles around his cock. All she needed was to trade a small taste of each other's essence, and he would be hers as surely as if she really *were* the Dionarch herself.

His heavy grunts slowed against her neck, his thrusting easing into more gentle, twisting slides.

"Don't stop!" She jerked her hips up harder, seeking to continue the violent, needful lovemaking he'd begun. Somehow despite his bond with Nyx, she lacked the connection she needed with her own spirit. She needed him to spill his seed, to taste his essence for a proper meld. Then she would be able to worm her way fully into his mind and control him from the inside.

But Nereus ignored her begging, chuckling softly as he rose up on both arms and gazed down at her. The adoration in his gaze was enough to drive a spike into Meri's soul, because she couldn't pretend that his look was truly meant for her.

When his brow creased and he pulled back farther, she knew she'd done something wrong, given something away.

"Do you not love me, Nyx? Have I been away so long that our bond has died? I can feel it still … our souls are one, but your eyes say different. You look … disgusted."

Meri forced herself to school her features into something more pleasant, though the disappointment she felt at the depth of love he still held for Nyx made it difficult.

"Let's see how you fare without my link to him," Nyx taunted.

She felt the Dionarch's spirit slipping deeper into some recess of her mind that Meri lost sight of, despite earlier wishing the woman away. When she searched, the Dionarch's spirit was gone, the body she resided in completely hers now as though no spirit had existed to begin with. Her power spread through its limbs instantly, flooding her with a fresh sensation of control she hadn't had before. Nyx had surrendered completely. Why would she give up?

Confused but excited, she smiled up at Nereus, hoping to renew his desire and get him to give in and release his essence into her.

When their eyes met, his head jerked back in shock and he lurched off the bed, stumbling back and away from her.

"Meri, you fucking monster! What have you done with Nyx?"

Fuck. The bitch had known he'd see the ruse without the spirit of his true mate holding court inside her somewhere. Where the fuck had she gone?

"She's gone, you bastard," she sneered. "And you will never get her back if you don't finish what you fucking started."

His face transformed into a mask of pure loathing and he leapt at her. His hands went to her neck and squeezed.

"I will fucking kill you!"

"Not if you love her, you won't. She's still in here some-where," she choked. "You want her back, you had better give me what I want!"

His eyes narrowed and he eased off. "What do you want? I spent two thousand years waiting to see her again, thanks to you. Now that I have her, you've taken even that from me. Tell me what to do and I will do it."

He sounded sincere enough, but his eyes betrayed the lie. The Haven was everything to Nyx, and he knew she would rather go mad than give it up. He was trying to play her.

Meri rose up above him and with a roar of rage pushed the power of the Source through her palms directly at his chest. The wave of power propelled him backward until he smacked hard against the wall and fell limp, his big horns scraping grooves into the floor where he landed.

She didn't need him. Not as long as she had this body. They would either bow to her, or she would kill them all.

CHAPTER 25

NIKHIL

Nikhil's entry into the Haven at long last was far from ideal. He preferred having clearer fore-knowledge of a battle before diving into the fray, but there had been no opportunity to take stock, and there was no time to waste.

The water of Gaia's Falls sent them rushing forth for several dizzying seconds before they emerged from a river somewhere in the middle of a dense forest. The sounds of fighting were distant, but unmistakable, and the second Lukas and Iszak appeared, he sent them to scout. The dense flora in this realm made it clear dragon flight would be a challenge, but a turul's true form was smaller and more agile.

By the time his lieutenants returned with whispered reports of the status at the Source, more of his army had arrived and were forming up, with Calder and the other Thiasoi satyrs in their full primal shift and ready for blood.

But one of the satyrs was missing.

"Where is your father?!" Nikhil snapped, scanning the army for sight of the satyr who led this particular squad, and whose influence he needed most to rally whatever nymphaea still survived to fight.

Calder's jaw clenched, his lips pressing into a hard line. "He followed the River farther downstream. Mother needs him now more than we do. His presence will restore her to full sanity so she can aid the fight."

"And has he reached her?"

The satyr's eyes narrowed. "If it's all the same to you, I'd rather not eavesdrop on my parents' reunion. Trust that they will join us when they're ready."

Nikhil ground his teeth. Now was not the time for heartfelt reunions. But then he remembered Nereus had been held Meri's prisoner, tortured for nearly as long as Nikhil had been under her spell, taken from the woman he loved and forced to believe she was dead. He didn't begrudge the pair their moment, and if Nyx's recent behavior was any indication, the Dionarch wouldn't waste time with sentimental dawdling while there was a war to be won and a Source to reclaim.

His tension eased and he laughed softly. "Fair enough. We won't need their help until it's time to deal with Meri. Our first task here is to neutralize Meri's army. Kill or capture." He turned to look at Iszak, Lukas, and the other squad leaders and lifted his voice to be heard above the noise.

"Evie has taught you the song she sang that chased the darkness out of my mind. We hope it will have a similar effect on the soldiers Meri controls. If they surrender after hearing the song, take them prisoner. If they still show signs of corruption and control, kill them.

"Her army is concentrated around the Source, and they are ripe for an ambush. Turul squads from the air, dragons from the ground, we will fan out and overtake them. It should not take long with our numbers."

Turning to Calder again, he added, "The very second

we've retaken the Source, find your parents. Meri's body is with them. Once her army is neutralized, I intend to be the one to bury my blade in her heart and end this once and for all."

Calder swallowed, his face contorting in a grimace. "Understood, but we need to be prepared for anything. We don't know how long she's had control of the Source or what she may have done with that power. Numa reported an unusual resilience in the Ultiori soldiers who attacked them in the Sanctuary. Nothing short of dismemberment or being charred to ash by dragon fire will take them down."

Nikhil nodded, Calder's concerns validating his own. The turul song was their hidden weapon, though untested in this battle he recalled with perfect clarity the moment when Evie had used her angelic voice to push the black corruption out of his mind. Meri's hold over him had ended that day for good, but the brutal destruction he'd wrought had still tainted his soul. For that he still must atone, and to complete his redemption that required he finally face the woman who had used him as her puppet for so long.

"Kill them, if we must. Use dragon fire if necessary. The men she commands are as much her puppets as I was once. I would have them freed before harming them, if at all possible. We cannot take the time to discover which are truly loyal to her and which are merely under her control, but the turul song will make it clear enough in the thick of things."

He cast his gaze around at the army filling the forest and the clearing near the shores of the river, extending all the way to a sandy inlet flanked by vine-covered cliffs. The majesty of this place had been corrupted, and even though it was not his home, he recognized Calder's fierce, protective urge to get on with the business of ejecting the enemy once and for all.

Nikhil had once felt the same about Belah's kingdom

along the Nile. He would have given anything to protect that place, but had trouble seeing it now, knowing that he'd contributed to the corruption in the end. He could save the Haven and the Sanctuary, and preserve the two realms from further corruption.

"We are ready," Iszak said. The wind swirled in his eyes and sparks crackled across his skin. Beside him, his brother Lukas stretched his wings, already half-shifted and ready to fight. The pair of brothers embodied the kind of loyalty Nikhil valued most in his soldiers, but his instincts warred with his aptitude for war. They had become as dear to him as Belah, who moved up to Nikhil's side and clasped his hand in hers.

He had just as little inclination to see the two brothers fly into battle as he had for Belah to fight, yet he knew better than to deny them the chance. They were his family, his blood, and so recently discovered that he had the strongest urge to protect them lest he lose them too soon.

After millennia of a blood tie with a creature he now reviled, he cherished the purity of the love he had found— first his reunion with Belah, then discovering that her two new mates were not his adversaries, but viewed Nikhil as merely an extension of the woman they loved. And finally ... perhaps the most potent tie of them all ... discovering that the daughter he had always longed for had been within his reach all along.

"We are with you, my love," Belah said. "Together, we will win."

Taking a deep breath, he turned to face her. "Yes, *Tila-hatan*. Together, we will. And when this place is purged of Meri's evil, I plan to spend some serious time teaching your other mates how best to satisfy you."

"I, for one, am ready to work up an appetite," Lukas said. "There's something in the air here that makes me horny as fuck. Not sure I like mixing that feeling with the need to make some heads roll."

"Channel the lust into the battle," Nikhil said. "If you are as skilled with a blade as you are with your cock, this will be a quick fight."

Lukas frowned, opened his mouth to retort, then closed it again. "I think that was an insult, but I'm not really sure. Watch out, or I might need to prove myself to your ass again."

Iszak bumped his brother's shoulder with a fist. "Don't forget who's boss here, brother."

With a chuckle, Lukas gave Nikhil one last look of wicked promise. "Oh, I know who's in charge of us, Iszak. All three of us belong to *her*, and he'd better not forget it."

Then the pair launched into the air with eager calls to the wind. Thousands of other turul followed, shifting and rising above the rest. They took to the air in a tight formation, leaving scant room between their wings as they soared upriver and into the fight.

"To me!" Nikhil roared to the remaining throngs of dragons and the handful of humans who had joined their mates. They remained only partly shifted, the five huge satyrs dwarfing the smaller human shapes the dragons remained in for now.

At Calder's command, the satyrs broke into a dead run, drawing swords crafted of gleaming translucent material that looked like ice. The turul's song began ahead of them, filling the entire Haven and the satyrs' battle cries rose in haunting harmony.

When his vanguard attacked, Nikhil followed, reaching the line of battle swiftly and diving in, his blood hot with elation over finally being on the right side of a war for the first time in an eternity. The difference this time was that the woman whose honor he fought for stood at his side, resplendent in her conjured armor of deep blue leather, her talons and horns shining with the blood of their enemies. This was a side of his little beast he'd never seen, and was further proof of how much he had underestimated her all along.

One by one, the Ultiori soldiers fell, many simply collapsing to their knees and repenting as the turul song affected them. Others fought on, their bloodthirsty rage unaffected by the purging music that surrounded them. The dragons made quick work of them with talons and fire, until nothing was left but the charred remains and rows upon rows of Ultiori prisoners bound and kneeling to await their final fates.

The battle was coming to an end. With a nod of acknowledgment from Nikhil, Calder met Assana and the pair of them peeled off and left to find their parents. Gavra and Aurum and their other mates followed close behind.

CHAPTER 26

MERI

The bitch had sabotaged her body somehow. Even though Meri's spirit flowed into it like she belonged there, there was a wrongness that kept her from finding complete comfort in this shell. She stared down in detachment at the smears of blood Nereus had left on Nyx's body, then over at where he lay slumped against the grotto wall.

Grief and shame overwhelmed her and she shook her head vigorously to clear it. Those were Nyx's emotions, not hers.

"No. He is not my lover. Fuck him."

But the cold detachment Meri relied on to do her work escaped her. Raw, wild emotion flooded her instead. A desperate need to protect all she held dear. The Haven. Her home. She had to expel the invaders at all costs.

No. *She* was the invader. She and her army of Ultiori soldiers. She had come to conquer, to possess, and she had achieved her goal. All except for the final step of securing an immortal shell she could use to begin the next phase with—

that of producing an entire army of immortals who would bend to her will. With her new power, she needed only the blood of the other immortals here to do what had taken her centuries to complete outside the Haven.

She pushed the power of the Source through her body, becoming dissolute as a fine mist, leaving the grotto and Nereus behind.

Her warriors were scattered, the ones that had survived no longer compliant to her will. Pity that Nereus was no use to her now. He'd have made the ideal stud for her plan. But he was not durable enough, despite his virile beauty and the cock she'd always imagined would pleasure her the way he nearly had before the fucking Dionarch's betrayal.

"The Haven will never *be yours."* The words were an itch inside her mind, taunting her with a lie. The Haven *was* hers. The other realms would be as well, once the day was out.

Her first targets appeared through the trees. Nyx's children and their mates—the perfect place to begin.

With the Haven itself as her servant now, this should be easy. Meri could sense the very limits of her home, every locked portal and link to the outside world. All the tributaries of the River that flowed through this place, connecting it to the waterways on Earth and in the higher realms. And connected to that water was the life of the creatures who were tied to it, not least of which were Nyx's own son and daughter.

For whatever reason, Nereus's bond to Nyx's spirit was too strong for her to break, but she may yet be able to fool the others.

She hovered in the air around them as they approached, the six of them striding hurriedly down the mossy path. Within seconds, Meri encompassed them fully in her cloudy mist, using her newfound power to immobilize them completely. Their faces barely registered shocked realization before the six were frozen in place, completely at her mercy.

Meri reformed her primal shape, coalescing out of the mist to stand before them.

"Mother, what are you doing?" Assana cried. "We have to secure Meri's body. Make sure she's contained." The nymph's eyes darted back and forth in confusion.

"We're too late," the red-haired dragon at her side said, his eyes narrowed. "Where is Nyx, Meri?"

"And what have you done with my father?" Calder growled.

A surge of tenderness for them all nearly destroyed Meri's resolve. She quashed it and pushed more power into the mist that held them. Assana attempted to speak again, but the mist sank into her throat and all she emitted was a strangled squeak. It was not as strong as a blood meld for control, but it would do for now.

Only their eyes moved, tracking her as she produced the blade she'd kept on her for this very purpose.

She approached Gavra first. The Red's potent magic would provide the ideal foundation for the rest. The point of the blade sliced easily through the conjured armor he wore, straight down the center of the chest to reveal his smooth, unblemished muscles beneath. She pushed the leather apart and grazed the metal tip across one tight nipple, circling it around and beneath the bulging pectoral. A muscle ticked in the man's jaw, but he remained frozen, his red eyes blazing.

"If looks could kill, I might be in danger," she drawled, still teasing the blade in a crisscrossing pattern across his chest, enjoying the way it left tiny scratches in skin that was effectively impermeable to any other weapon. But this ancient blade had been tempered by immortal dragon fire and would easily cut the skin of any immortal Meri used it on.

She moved farther into his space, gazing up into his eyes, as though standing even closer to the fire were a test to prove her own power. To prove that she could break him.

The challenge in his eyes grew even fiercer up close, and a spicy aroma suddenly filled the air. Meri's focus shifted, her mouth watering as she gazed down between them, admiring the cut of his muscles and the way is thighs bulged in the leather that covered them. The generous bulge at his groin made her core heat and her vision tunnel with the craving to unleash the wild, sexual beast this red dragon must be.

The blade slipped from her hand, and in a reflexive burst of panic, she grabbed at it to hold on. Sharp pain shot through her palm, obliterating the brief wash of desire that had nearly distracted her from her goal.

"You son of a bitch," she snapped, realizing he'd tried to seduce her with his breath. "No more of that." She commanded the mist to flood into his nostrils until she heard the strangled sound of his throat closing up and his eyes watered. Raising the blade, she aimed it into the center of his chest, started to push, then paused, thinking better of it.

The blood from mortal dragons lost all potency once its owner died. She didn't want to take the chance that shoving this blade into his heart could actually kill him.

His gaze still held hers, calmer now despite the fact that he had lost the ability to breathe. Suffocating couldn't kill an immortal, of that she was sure. But where to cut …

The throbbing pulse in his neck drew her eye, mesmerizing her with its strength.

She raised the blade and aligned it with that arterial pulse, entertained by the fresh look of challenge in the gaze that met hers. The second she applied pressure and made the slice, he blinked and his eyes widened as the blood began to flow.

"Didn't expect that, did you?" she said, holding up the blood-streaked blade in front of him. "I know there is only one way for your skin to be pierced. You forget that I was there the day you and your brothers made your trade to reclaim your sister's blood. I was also there the day your sister had this blade crafted. Her wedding gift to her lover, created to enable him to do just this to her."

She tilted her head, watching the shimmering red liquid as it made its way over the ledge of his collarbone and followed that ridge to the base of his throat, then flowed down the very center of his chest. She resisted leaning in for a taste—controlling him with her power would be a distraction and burn magic she'd rather save for other things. It would be much easier to simply keep them all trapped for now, and eventually immobilize them completely once her task was finished.

She moved to the golden-haired dragon at his side—the sister who she had only seen once on the fateful day of Nikhil's wedding. "Aurum, is it? So sorry about not letting you breathe. I'm sure you understand why I can't allow it. It is your turn to bleed."

The skin of the woman's delicate throat gave easily under the sharp edge of the knife, and her blood flowed instantly, deep red and fragrant. The others bled even more freely, their skin parting with barely a breath of a stroke of the blade that was designed to cut an immortal dragon.

Standing back, Meri fixed her power on the six flowing streams of red, the keys to her dominion over her world. Hands upraised, she commanded the lifeblood to come to her, and it obeyed, lifting into the air in fluid threads, the six streams coming together and entwining. She cupped her hands and twisted them around each other, pulling the magic fluid into a sphere in the center. One stream glowed with faint green energy. Gaia's power? Curious, she followed it back to its source.

The ursa male who stood closest to Assana had a particular sheen to his skin Meri hadn't noticed before. An ursa male who carried that much power was something she'd never encountered, but this was even better. Gaia's life-creating magic flowed in his veins.

Between her hands, the sphere of blood coalesced, forming into a tiny cell that she had envisioned over the course of centuries while attempting her experiments. For the first time, she had all the power she needed to make it happen without all the mess of forced breedings. The blood of these six merged perfectly. Two dragons, two ursa, and two nymphaea. Three out of four elements would be more than enough with the power of the Source to merge them.

She lowered her hands in front of her belly. The glowing cell flooded with the essence of immortal life, but needing an immortal womb within which to grow. It sank into her on command, easily taking root, that small drop of Gaia's power making it impossible not to grow. She felt the quickening instantly, like an egg cracking open and the life within surging out. Her own blood found it in that moment, subsuming whatever identity it might have had with the one she chose.

Secure in her success, Meri lifted the blade again and with slash after violent slash opened the necks of the first four of her victims and let them bleed. The two ursa and dragons remained frozen, wide-eyed with shock, but still unable to move to stop the flood of their life from leaving them.

She reached Calder and stopped, a building resistant burn in her arm making her wince when she went in for the kill. Agony flooded her hand and she cried out, dropping the blade.

More pain shot through her abdomen, hot wetness flooding down her thighs. She stared down in horror at the rush of blood as the life within her body faded and disappeared.

Nyx.

"No! I will not let you stop me, you bitch!"

She bent down to reach the blade and unbearable pain gripped her from the core, causing her to gasp and double over. She fell to her knees and grabbed the knife, stood, and forced herself to focus the power once more. Holding tight to the blade, she aimed the point at her own breast this time.

"Do not fuck with me, Nyx. I will shove this knife into your chest and force your daughter to do my bidding instead."

The two ursa and dragons had grown pale from blood loss, a lake of red pooling around their feet. Their eyes were glazed, barely holding onto consciousness, but held up by the confining mist. Only Assana and Calder remained unharmed, aside from the cuts she'd first given them, which had all but sealed themselves already.

"You will never succeed, Meri. With my body or any other."

"We'll see about that," she sneered. She summoned more power, commanded more blood into the clawed hand she held out, pushed her magic into it to create that perfect little seed of life once more. This time she infused it with more destructive power before sending it into her womb. "Damage this creature and it will damage you back."

"You would harm your own chance at creation? I have had my children already, I have no use for a womb anymore."

"No!" Meri howled, redirecting all the power of the Source inward at the incessant voice that tormented her. The six frozen figures went slack, four of them falling in limp heaps to the blood-soaked ground. Calder and Assana immediately disappeared in puffs of mist.

Nyx's spirit fought back, holding her ground and refusing to budge. It took all of Meri's command of the Source itself to even maintain a stalemate, to keep the mad Dionarch from sacrificing her own fertile core to spite Meri.

CHAPTER 27

NIKHIL

When the rest of Nikhil's army reached the Source itself, they met the others who had fought their way in from the Sanctuary. Belah exclaimed in joy before rushing into the arms of a brown-haired woman whose coiling green horns identified her as Belah's sister, the dragon responsible for finally finding a way to allow Nikhil and his army to enter.

Five males surrounded Numa, all naked and covered in blood. Numa herself appeared as pristine and put together as her sister. That kind of attention to appearance seemed a uniquely draconic trait, which was verified as he glanced around at the rest of the army, who were on guard but relaxed now that the enemy was subdued. All the dragons looked as fresh as if they had just arrived.

The injured and dead were numerous on both sides, the dragons and ursa spreading out to tend those they could. But despite the relative quiet and subdued mood, there was a sense of unfinished business that Nikhil knew he was not alone in feeling.

Ked approached him first, the black dragon's deep-set,

inky eyes reminding Nikhil of how his power had burrowed into his very soul. He had no secrets from this dragon any more than he had from his own mate. He could have even predicted Ked's words before he spoke.

"Something feels wrong."

Nikhil's blood chilled fully at that observation, so close to his own worry that he could no longer deny his instincts. "What do you sense?"

"Aurum and Gavra should have reported back to us by now. We've heard nothing from them or Assana and Calder. The nymphs who survived are restless, as are the Thiasoi we rescued from Meri's base."

The white-haired Aodh approached,with Neph and Vrishti at his side. The Dionarch looked so grim Nikhil immediately knew something was gravely wrong.

"My sister is compromised," he said.

"And this is different from before somehow? We knew she lost her sanity for a time. Her mate's return was meant to alleviate that problem."

"It isn't her sanity that's in question now. It's her command of her own power."

"She's been possessed by Meri, hasn't she?" Nikhil asked.

"Exactly. She would sooner leave than let the corruption taint her spirit. If she went adrift, it would break her bond to Nereus, prevent him from being manipulated by Meri. Nyx would not risk having the blood meld with her mate used against him."

"This is what she wanted," Nikhil said. "The child she created was taken from her, but that doesn't matter anymore if she has the body of a fucking demigod at her disposal. Can your sister be killed?"

"Enough!" A booming voice cut through the alarmed chatter and the entire area went silent. Nikhil's gaze shot up to the angry horned man who towered above them all, even

Neph who still maintained his primal form. The angry creature who glared at Nikhil wasn't a satyr, though he was close. He had immense horns, but his legs and feet were as human as the rest of his impressive shape.

"Do you have something to add?" Nikhil asked.

"I will not countenance discussion of execution of my own daughter," the man said. "Her death would not serve your cause in the least. Besides, she cannot be killed by normal means, just as any of the immortals cannot."

"Your daughter ..." Nikhil began. "Then who does that make you?"

"Today I am only Numa's mate," the big man answered, turning and bowing his head to display the full effect of the immense glowing dragon mark on his back. "But before she claimed me, you would have heard of me as Dionysus, god of wine and sex. The nymphaea are my creation. Nyx is my daughter, and any creature who makes the ill-reasoned decision to control her is in for a rude awakening. We should wait for Nyx to give us a sign."

Nikhil bristled at the man's confession. "You're a fucking *god*? And you didn't stop this? Did you give up that godhood when Belah's sister marked you? Do you care so little for your creations that you let them be slaughtered?"

Dionysus slowly shook his head. "My hands were tied, I'm afraid. Only humanity is bound by few enough rules to assert free will in every situation. The higher races are more restrictive, due to their origins. The gods are even more tightly bound by law and our power is limited from meddling in the world, thanks to Fate's twisted knots tangled around our lives. We could not intervene without an actual prayer for help, and even if that came, my power can only be channeled in one way."

Spurred by rising anger, Nikhil's voice carried deep and

booming over the rush of the water behind them. "Then I pray to you, oh god of lust, to fucking fix this!"

Dionysus' expression remained impassive until Nikhil had taken a breath, forcing himself to unclench his hands from the hilt of his sword, lest he attempt to shove it through the other man's chest, god or not.

"I will give you a moment to think on your prayer, brother," Dionysus said. "I am not the divine power who can lend the best aid in this situation. If you permit, I will offer my advice on how to proceed, but prepare yourselves to pay a price for the desired outcome."

"Have we not paid enough?" Nikhil spat. "I lost everything and was turned into a monster. All the higher races—including your own—were forced to suffer under the hand of a creature that, by my estimation, is *also* one of yours. If my own children misbehaved so abominably, you can be damn sure I would spank them for it. As it stands, one of my daughters has only just been united with the mate Fate chose for her, and the other ..."

He trailed off, scanning the crowd in search of Neela, realizing for the first time since the battle had stopped that he hadn't yet received any word on how their trip to the Sanctuary had gone. What had happened to the child?

Dionysus dropped his hands to his sides and lowered his head. "Your other daughter is safe," he said in a softer tone. "I have seen to her protection myself. Will you hear me out? When I speak of price, it is not what you think."

Dionysus' tenderness when speaking of Nikhil's lost daughter disarmed him. He wanted to ask more questions, to hear all the details of the child and her welfare, but there was no time.

"Tell me your proposal."

Nikhil's discussion with the god was interrupted by the appearance of a pair of bloody figures popping into existence in the middle of the group.

"Mother needs our help!" Assana yelled, rushing toward him, her wild eyes streaked red with tears and blood. "Meri's slit their throats … my mates are dying. We have to do stop her!"

"Take us now," Nikhil said, and within a split-second, he found himself pulled into the drift by the nymph, hoping the others had heard enough to follow.

He arrived to a tableau of carnage that would not normally have shocked him, except for the sight of Nicholas lying still and pale in a pool of red. Aurum's golden hair was soaked with her mate's blood where she sprawled like she'd collapsed without a fight.

Belah let out a cry and rushed to her sister, calling out for help. More bodies drifted in, brought by the nymphs and satyrs who survived the fight. A dark-haired young ursa woman crouched by Nicholas before Nikhil could reach him.

Green light emanated from her palms as she pressed them to his bleeding throat.

"Don't you dare fucking die, brother," she commanded. "Mama would kill me if I let that happen."

Brother? Nikhil glanced around at the chaos, realizing that the sense of a tight bond among these creatures he had commanded to fight had nothing to do with his skill as a general. They were a family. They were *his* family. And he had to push on to destroy the monster who had dared deny him this for so long.

A trail of bloody footprints led away from the scene along the river bank. He followed them, perplexed by the erratic direction. If Nyx had passed through here, she had done so under duress. There were signs of struggle every few yards, with more blood trailing along the leaves and red handprints left behind on the trunks of trees.

"Calder, you and your sister find your father. If Nyx is compromised, we will need his help," he called back to the others. His mate and her siblings were busy seeing to the wounded that had been left behind. A wash of utter relief flooded through him at the sight of Nicholas rousing from his sister's strong magic.

No more would die today, save one. The crunch of underbrush at his side distracted him from the singular focus on tracking her, and the big horned god fell into step beside him.

He tensed and gritted his teeth. "I have no wish to end your daughter's life, but we can't allow that creature who has her to retain control of this power."

"Nyx is fighting that control," Dionysus said. "But if she fails, let me have a chance to reason with the spirit of the nymph who has her before we take more drastic measures."

Nikhil chuckled. "Meri cannot be reasoned with. I spent three thousand years as her mental puppet. She is finally within reach of the one thing she sought. She will not give it up at this stage."

"What more could she want beyond the power? She could leave this place and still keep the connection she acquired. Not that Nyx would leave her in peace …"

"She has always been obsessed with creating an immortal vessel for herself. To what end, I never knew. The child stole from me and Neela was meant to serve that purpose. Since losing it, I imagine she would try again, if she couldn't hold onto Nyx's body."

The god's brows drew together. "Immortality is over-rated. The true power in life is love and family. Evil is the thing that seeks to tear us apart, to subvert that connection. Are you saying that all this time, she's worked on creating a child? That is odd…"

"Not out of any maternal urge, I promise you," Nikhil said.

"That's the thing about mortals," Dionysus said. "They don't always understand their true desires."

The sounds of mad ranting reached them over the deafening crash of the surf, and Nikhil looked up from the bloody trail. At the water's edge was a majestic nymph more breathtaking than Assana or any of the others he'd seen fight. She also appeared in the throes of utter insanity, a blade held in one hand, jerkily slicing cut after cut into her own torso as she paced up and down the wet sand. The surf at her feet was tinged red, the blood so plentiful it covered her feet with each wave that crashed.

"I will kill them all and leave the Haven as barren as your womb will be, if you don't cease tormenting me!" she snarled. As she turned, her eyes lit on Nikhil and his companion. The wild swirling in those orbs made him dizzy and he stumbled back. A big hand on his arm shook him out of the stupor.

"Christ, she's never done that before."

"She's never had the full power of the Source or the body of an immortal nymph as long as you've known her," Dionysus said.

"Tell her!" Meri yelled. "Tell her I fucking mean it!" The tendons in her arms strained, as though she were trying to shove the blade straight through herself but encountered some unseen barrier.

"I believe you," Dionysus said. "And I believe I have been too long removed from the idea of family. Is my daughter in there, Meri? I would like to speak to her."

Meri's face twisted into a sneer. "Your *daughter* doesn't believe me. I will destroy her and find another way if she doesn't let this baby live."

Nikhil lifted an eyebrow and crossed his arms. "And I see that's going well for you."

Her feral gaze turned to him and her eyes went wide with recognition. The spinning tumult in her irises nearly threw him off balance again.

"You! This is all *your* fault!"

Nikhil jerked his head back in surprise. "My fault? I was your goddamn slave!" His eyes tracked the blade that she no longer aimed at her own flesh. She flipped it in her hand and came at him with the dagger raised high.

"You're the one who turned my Elites against me."

"They were never yours."

"They were the only fucking breeders worth anything," she snarled. "But you were all dragon whores, weren't you? I should gut you for that betrayal!"

Nikhil shot his arm up to grab her wrist as she toppled him over into the sand. Her huge antlers surged down toward his eyes, and her knee came up as they struggled, narrowly missing his groin and grazing off his thigh. She was nearly twice his size in her true form and stronger than him by half, but he managed to focus enough of his own innate power into the hand that held her wrist and seared her skin with fire.

She shrieked and the blade fell from her grip. At the same time, an enormous pair of hands grabbed her shoulders and hauled her back. Nikhil spun in the sand and snatched the blade by the hilt.

The second his hand closed around the grip, memories surged forth like a dam had burst. His hand tightened and he looked down at the dagger in utter disbelief.

The weight and balance were exactly how he remembered from his wedding night, the draconic emblem and inlaid blue stone as perfectly formed, though now they were caked in blood. He had taken better care of this blade when he'd used it, its purpose one of love, not malice.

Rage gripped him in a cold vise. He hefted the blade, and with a swift fling born of ages imagining this moment, he let loose and watched the dagger sail straight toward the heart of the creature who had been his torturer for an eternity.

He had already pictured the knife piercing the target, slamming into the ribcage of the nymph who still taunted him. Instead, a big hand shot out in a blur, snatching the thing out of the air just as the tip grazed her skin.

Dionysus scowled at him. "We had a deal. I protected your daughter. You still owe me."

"She was mine!" Meri howled. "That child was mine, and you stole her! I would have laid waste to this place with the powers she gained once ignited by my soul. She will be *nothing* without me. A soulless shell, worthless and unlovable. This is what you've condemned her to by taking her from me, you fools!"

Dionysus turned her in his arms, gripping her by the shoulders and gazing down into her eyes. His own eyes flashed with power, his horns shimmering as though infused by some light from the heavens and the glow passed down their smooth arcs and continued into his body, leaving him awash in a golden glow. Nikhil found himself admiring the man, resplendent in his naked, blood-soaked glory.

Dionysus gestured behind her back with the blade.

Nikhil stepped forward and took it, frowning up at the big man.

"You will have your moment, I give you my word," Dionysus said, then shifted his attention back to the shell of his daughter and the creature that held her hostage.

"Meri, tell me your desires, your deepest yearning. You wish to create life, don't you?"

She responded with a whining growl. "I ... wish for this crazy *bitch* to leave me in peace!"

"Nyx will never relent as long as you share her body. The power you only just acquired is a power she has owned for her entire life. She's far more practiced at using it than you are. It's a matter of time before she prevails. Why don't you let me help? I can promise you a vessel more powerful than the one you could create yourself."

"A vessel powered by the Source?" she asked, her avid curiosity calming her finally. Nikhil narrowed his eyes, wondering what the god was up to.

"Even better," Dionysus said. "A vessel powered by the gods. I will sacrifice my own blood to create it, just for you."

"Please, yes. Anything to free me of Nyx's torture."

"You will leave my daughter's body and her spirit in peace. You will not return to the Haven, either."

Nikhil sheathed the blade as nonchalantly as possible and moved so he could see her face. He caught sight of the others appearing through the trees and lifted a hand to stall and quiet them.

He met Belah's worried gaze, felt her distress through their bond, as well as the hatred of Iszak and Lukas for the creature Dionysus spoke to. No doubt the pair would as easily have skewered Nyx as Nikhil had nearly done before the god intervened.

More faces appeared, throngs of dragons, ursa, turul, and nymphs all intent on the unfolding promises and warnings Dionysus spoke.

Nikhil returned his attention to Meri, who was nodding in acquiescence to Dionysus' demands. A familiar, telltale twitch of her mouth told Nikhil she was lying. He itched to draw the blade again, but held himself in check. At least half the god's intention was to save his daughter, and Nikhil owed him that chance at the very least.

Finally, Dionysus nodded and stood up straighter. He held his hand out to the side, palm open and fingers spread wide. A deep, bloody cut stretched across the center of his palm—the same hand that had grabbed the dagger by the blade when Nikhil had flung it in his cold rage. His hand went to the pommel of the knife again. Had this blade been able to cut a *god*?

There was no other explanation for it, for the god was bleeding. As his lifeblood spilled onto the sand, he tilted his head back. In a booming voice, he called, "Gaia, it is my prayer to you to take my blood and grant this spirit an eternal body so that she may vacate the one she has possessed."

Nothing happened for a moment, then everything went still. The breezes died, and the crashing surf seemed to freeze. The trees, however, still moved, their leaves rustling in a slow rhythm that mimicked a heartbeat, and then disembodied footprints appeared in the sand leading across the beach, stopping at Meri's side.

Green tendrils like moss appeared out of the air, growing into a female shape until barely a moment later, a divinely beautiful creature stood there with sleek black hair twisting like vines around her head in some nonexistent breeze. She was as naked as Dionysus with abundant, fertile curves, luscious breasts, and a round, pregnant belly. The vine-like tendrils of her hair twisted around her, seeming to clothe her in leaves and flowers.

She cocked her head at the god, then looked at the puddle of blood that had grown in the sand beneath his bleeding hand.

"You would give your blood for this creation? Why not simply seduce me, Dion? You know I would happily share in creation with you again. The binding of our fertile magic makes lovely creatures."

"This is my sacrifice to prove I am in earnest," he said.

Gaia regarded him with her hand sliding in a slow circle over her stomach. "You understand what it means to create a life from your own blood? The creature will be—"

"She'll be immortal, yes, I am aware," he snapped, cutting her off.

Gaia's lips twitched, her eyes narrowing. "Immortal ... of course any creature crafted from the blood of a god will be *immortal*. But there is a cost to any prayer. One *you* must pay."

"I am prepared to pay the price," he said solemnly.

"What love we have for our creations. You surprised me today, Dion. First you submit to a dragon, then you agree to *share* her with four other mates. I knew you craved true love, but had no idea the sacrifices you were willing to make. I do hope this satisfies your need for ... balance ... once and for all."

Nikhil sensed a subtext to their exchange that was beyond his understanding, then Gaia's final words sent a cold chill down his spine.

"Fate preserve you, Dion. Because this will not go unnoticed."

"I never expected it to," he said. "But I will bear whatever consequences Fate sees fit to burden me with."

Gaia lifted her hands, and a sparkling web of greenish vines rose out of the pool of blood at Dion's feet. "It is never as simple as that with Fate, as you are well aware," she said. "I hope you are prepared. All of you." She glanced around at the crowd once more before returning her focus to her task.

Before their eyes, the blood coalesced into a sphere within Gaia's glowing tendrils of power, and within that sphere a shape appeared, then grew. It reminded Nikhil eerily of the tiny embryo that Meri had created in her lab and kept sustained within a tank fed by satyr blood. But this one didn't remain small for long. It grew swiftly, each stage of life passing by until a fully formed woman's shape stood before them.

"Your turn, my dear," Gaia said. Threads of golden power linked her fingers to her new creation and she gently touched Meri's shoulder. The nymph's eager gaze shifted between the goddess and her new body. Then she let out a sharp breath and arched as Gaia's threads linked the new creation with the nymph.

A moment later, Nyx's body went limp, Dionysus bending swiftly to catch her in his arms. The newly created female lurched on her feet, her head snapping up, then shaking slightly. Her eyes brightened as the glow of power gradually faded. Then she closed her eyes and went still for a moment.

Nikhil stood waiting, his hand still gripped around the hilt of the blade. There had been some hidden message in the exchange between the two divine beings, and he wished like hell for some clarity before attacking. He at least wanted to be certain the exchange had happened.

The woman before them still glowed with inner power, and as she opened her eyes, her body transformed, her skin shimmering with subtle textures that finally settled into dark, form-fitting gauzy clothing like the shadows had gravitated toward her and clung to her curves, wrapping around every limb. A sleek black mane fell down her back and rippled like flowing, water and Nikhil realized she'd assumed the appearance of a nymph not unlike Nyx or Assana, though very different in appearance. Shining black antlers rose from her head, razor-tipped and glimmering like they were coated in oil.

The entire crowd gasped and collectively went on guard.

Meri laughed. "You are all fools. I can't fucking *believe* a god actually gave me life again. I think that's a sign, don't you, *sister*?" she sneered at Nyx, who had roused enough in Dionysus' arms to scowl back.

"I told you to leave this place," Dionysus said.

"Let's see you make me," Meri shot back at him, then glared around at the crowd. "All of you, I dare you!"

She straightened her stance, hands spread down at her sides, and turned, surveying the crowd. She raised her arms as she rotated, and with a triumphant yell, launched a blast of power outward. It crashed through the crowd of onlookers in a wave, toppling them all instantly. When they fell, a throng of figures crashed through the trees, blood-soaked men with blank stares who wielded blades. They began to attack the prone figures, who barely had time to stand again to defend themselves. Dragons appeared as Nikhil's army began to shift, and once more bloody conflict broke out, the sounds of combat punctuated by the cries of falcons and the roars of dragons.

They had killed these men already—the ones who fallen before Nikhil and his army had arrived. He should have had their bodies burned.

"No!" Dionysus yelled from behind Meri. Nyx slipped from his arms, barely steadying herself on her feet and still looking weak.

Nikhil snatched the blade from its sheath and drifted to land in front of Meri, ready to stab her. Her head snapped up and she flicked her wrist, sending an invisible bolt of power at him. It hit him hard in the chest and flung him backward into the surf.

Gaia was nowhere to be seen. Everyone who had come to witness, believing the true battle ended, was locked again in a brutal conflict.

As Nikhil lay there, struggling to regain his senses, Meri squared off against Nyx and Dionysus.

"How could you give her this much power?" Nyx snapped.

"It's part of my plan. Patience, daughter," the god gritted out.

"Well, it was a shitty plan," Nyx said. She straightened herself and lifted her head. Her damaged skin healed, the blood disappearing as the thin gauze of her gown reappeared. Letting out a battle cry, she raised her hands. Laughing, Meri tossed her into the water as well with barely a gesture.

Meri fixed her gaze on Dionysus and tilted her head back and forth to loosen her neck. "Let's see if I can beat a god now. Or perhaps you'd like to join me? I plan to birth a race of immortals who will do my bidding and give me ultimate power over *all* the higher races. What would you say to donating that glorious cock of yours to the cause?"

"This cock is already spoken for, I'm afraid," Dionysus said. He stared down at Meri, unperturbed by her behavior. If anything, the god simply looked *weary* and perhaps a little sad.

"Oh, Daddy, are you sure? This body's a virgin. I would love for my first taste of pleasure to be at the hands of one so divinely talented as you. Wouldn't you love a taste?" She slid her hands down over her curves, the shadowy garments fading and revealing her creamy skin beneath before they reappeared, creeping over her like twilight descending.

Dion's face twisted in disgust. "If I were creating a race for my own pleasure, it would not begin with you."

"No? Then perhaps you'll do it to save your lovers …"

Meri cocked her head. Nikhil hoisted himself to his feet and looked beyond her to the edge of the woods. Five of the dead-eyed mercenaries lurched forward, each dragging a struggling shape, which they flung across the sand to lay at Meri's feet. Nikhil recognized Belah's sister Numa and the four men who had fought beside her.

They tried to rise, but with a mere flutter of Meri's fingers, a dense mist gathered around them, freezing them in place.

Numa had made it nearly upright before being immobilized, and Meri darted her gaze between the green dragon and Dionysus.

"I think she is the one whose mark you bear, judging from the matching ones on these four." She gestured at one of the male figures who still crouched on the sand. The green wings that stretched in a glowing tattoo across his back were the same as the ones Dionysus himself sported.

"Should I begin with him, or with her? Tell me, which one are you most willing to sacrifice? Or will you agree to fuck me?"

"I will not. I gave you a body, Meri. It's time for you to leave, or else."

"Give me what I ask! It's one *little* thing. Surely you can spare one dose of that magic juice you so liberally gave these whores of yours. They reek of you."

She reached out and grabbed Numa by the hair, twisting her head back. "I wonder if my power is enough to pierce dragon skin…"

Baring Numa's throat, Meri bent her head and licked,

then lifted a finger and traced a line along the pulsing vein beneath Numa's skin. A long, sharp talon slowly extended from Meri's fingertip, its pointed tip pressing against the other woman's flesh.

When a dark red bead of blood appeared, Dionysus roared.

"No! You will not touch her. You will not taint my lovers with your darkness, Meri. We had a deal." His gaze flicked to Nikhil and a wordless message passed between them. He was only stalling her, waiting until Nikhil was ready. Nikhil gripped the hilt of the blade tighter and nodded at the god.

"You can't hurt me," Meri taunted. "This little link to the Source I have gave me all your godly secrets. You cannot harm your own creations unless Fate allows it. You should have listened to Gaia. Now they will all be under *my* control. If you won't agree to leave the Haven, everyone will submit to my bond or die."

She dug her pointed talon into Numa's neck, then bent her head to lap at the blood.

With a roar, Dionysus flung out his hands. "I cannot *hurt* you, but I can control you."

Meri's body lurched, her hand falling away from Numa's throat. She went rigid and perfectly vertical, a smear of blood striped down her chin. Her eyes flew wide as she struggled against his power. The mindless puppets who had come alive again moved with a twitch of her head, then came to a halt again when Dionysus stretched out a hand.

"How are you doing this?!" she yelled. "I thought your creations had free will!"

"The ones born from fertile unions do. You were not *born* from my seed, Meri. You were *made* from my blood. Was the parallel completely lost on you? My blood runs through your veins now. Anything your blood has tainted is mine, including these abominations."

With a snap of his fingers, the dead things fell to the sand and stayed. Nikhil sensed his time was near and readied himself, awaiting the god's command.

"No, please!" Meri yelled, back to negotiating again, but Dionysus refused to release her.

"You have done enough damage." Power radiated out of him in a wave as strong as the blast she had used to level the crowd of observers. Nikhil felt it this time, his skin tingling and his cock rousing from the potency of the magic. He was perfectly fine with that, especially when his mates dispatched the creatures they fought, and he sensed their heated blood, ready to continue the killing to its bitter end.

"You can't do this!" Meri yelled.

"I can't kill you, that's true." His gaze flicked to Nikhil, who lifted the dagger and strolled toward Meri's immobilized body. "But he can."

"How?!" Meri howled. "Gaia herself said I would be immortal!"

"Yes, but what she didn't say was that you would be bound to me, as a creature crafted out of my own life's blood. What makes you whole is merely an extension of me, and while I cannot directly destroy you, others may, if they possess enough power to do so. Power from the other elements. Now…" He turned to Nikhil and nodded. "Take her down."

Nikhil walked up to stand before her, the dagger tight within his grip. He gazed into her eyes and held the blade up in front of her face. "Remember this? You were there when it was made more than three thousand years ago. It was a gift from Belah to me on our wedding night, the most powerful symbol of her love, because it proved her trust in my *worship* of her as both my goddess and my slave. It was a symbol of her complete surrender."

He paused, his gaze darting to his *'Iilahatan* who stood

clutching the hands of her other mates. Her children were nearby as well, creating a protective circle around their mother.

"Your manipulation took her from me that day. I believed I had killed her with the very tool she'd given me to give her pleasure. I wonder, can you stand the pain my own *Tilahatan* thrives on? Are you as strong as she is? She was bled dry and yet lives. Will you be so lucky when I am finished with you?"

He lifted the blade and made the first slice, just beneath Meri's left eye and across the plump swell of her cheekbone.

"I nearly tossed this blade through your heart earlier. I would have been happy if you'd died then, but this is so much better, I think. Seeing you suffer under *my* hand, for once."

He made another cut, straight down her cheek, grazing the razor-sharp tip of the knife farther until it hit the neck of her shadowy clothing. The dark gauze fell away as though burned by an invisible fire.

The fear in Meri's eyes was unmistakable. Loss of control was probably the source of it, more so than the pain, but the combination was a heady mixture that made Nikhil's blood hot. He sliced the blade through her top, cutting the front of it away. Her breasts spilled free, creamy and perfect and utterly lacking in allure.

"I can endure whatever the fuck you have to throw at me, you weak bastard. I don't believe you can kill me, and when I get free, you will all pay!"

"Quit wasting time," Dionysus said. "That blade drew my blood. It will work to sever a life crafted of my blood too."

Nikhil growled, wishing he had more time to draw this out, but it'd gone on long enough. Letting her have another word to taunt him would be too many. Far, far too many.

He sliced a line into the skin along the inside of one breast, his cock stone-hard from the sight of her blood and the anticipation of the reward. With the tip of the blade, he dug in, found the gap between her ribs, and pushed.

Meri gasped and spasmed, her eyes going wide. The blood seeped out past the blade, then came in a flood when Nikhil penetrated the wall of her heart.

Gritting his teeth, he focused on her face again, smiling wickedly at her terror. This was the best part of victory, feeling the enemy's blood gushing warmly over his skin and the fear in their eyes when they realized they'd been beaten, that their minutes on earth were numbered in the single digits.

Her body slackened, abruptly released from Dionysus' grip as her blood flowed freely. The blade sank deeper as she slumped against Nikhil, a strangled plea escaping her. Her head fell against his shoulder, her hands clawing at his arms. She smelled of the ocean, he abstractly realized, and her blood was scented of a potent spice that he remembered from when he'd first met Numa and her mates. Numa had smelled like this, and so had the god.

He frowned at the correlation, so focused on the slowing tempo of her heart as it pushed the last of its contents out onto his arm over the hilt of the blade, and the last breathy begging words she gasped before going still. When he finally knelt with her limp body in his arms, he became aware of the tumult around him.

Numa cried out, lurching past him and stumbling, then half-crawling across the sand away from the bleeding corpse of their enemy. Her other four mates went after her, surrounding her and another prone shape that Nyx had caught and held in her arms.

The god had fallen. But who had the power to take him down?

CHAPTER 29

NUMA

Numa stumbled in the wet sand, desperate to reach her fallen lover. His chest bloomed with blood as though he too had been stabbed by some invisible blade. She sank to her knees, crying out his name.

"Please stop!" she yelled at Nikhil. "They're linked! Stop. You're killing him!"

Blood gushed between the two figures embracing like lovers. Nikhil's knife was buried in Meri's heart and he murmured dark, vindictive promises in her ear as he bared his teeth and twisted the blade.

Numa yelled his name again and finally caught his attention, but Nikhil stared dumbly at her, his bloody hand still tight around the hilt of the dagger buried in Meri's chest. He glanced back down at his work, hypnotized by the waning arterial spurts, but finally pulled back, leaving the blade jutting from the body that fell to the sand.

It was far too late, though. The bleeding in her lover's chest wouldn't stop, and neither would her healing smoke close the wound.

"Shh, little one. Be still," Dionysus whispered, reaching up to brush his fingers over her jaw.

"No! You are mine, and I won't let you die!"

"Who said anything about dying? I'm a god. Gods can't die."

Beside her, Nyx cursed and Numa blinked, trying to refocus on what had shifted the Dionarch's attention.

"His horns are gone," Nyx said, raking her fingers through the dark hair that fanned across her lap. "He is shrinking, losing his power."

Numa cupped his face, her heart twisting at the realization that he had grown smaller, lighter. "What is happening?"

A worried-looking Zephyrus slipped down to his knees beside her, sliding a hand in a comforting caress over her back. "He paid a price to control her. This was that price. His blood gave her life, and destroying her took some of that life from him."

"But not all of it, right? Please tell me he isn't dying. Don't lie to me!"

A shadow loomed above them, and she looked up into Nikhil's horrified face. "I didn't know," he said. "I would have found another way, had I known."

Dionysus shook his head weakly and coughed. The wound in his chest reopened and another surge of blood spilled from him. "There was no other way, but you can help stop the bleeding."

"Anything. What can I do?" Nikhil asked.

"Burn her. Turn her to ash to sever the link between us, or I will be stuck in this dying state forever."

Nikhil's eyes flashed with sharp desire, incongruous with the moment. "It would be my pleasure."

Nikhil let out a sharp whistle and raised an arm. The army came to attention as he walked toward them, and he stopped before Numa's two nephews and their fire-winged mate. Numa's brothers and sisters also gathered around to hear his command. Nikhil's order passed back through the ranks, and one by one the dragons shifted, rising into the air as their wings spread and caught the currents.

Hundreds upon hundreds of winged creatures twisted on the ocean breeze, the dragons mingling with the turul. They flew up and circled around above the shore. At the lowest point, a few dragons at a time hovered in a circle around the bloody corpse of their enemy, opened their mouths, and let loose torrents of blinding flame.

The turul sang and the wind kicked up, fanning the flames incinerating Meri's body. When the first group of dragons departed, another group circled down and breathed their strongest fire at the sand beneath.

This went on for some time, and with each blast, Dion relaxed in Numa's arms, his breathing growing slower and more even. Eventually the wound in his chest closed on its own and he fell unconscious, but his pulse was strong.

"My father will live," Nyx said, sliding her palm across his forehead, her face a mask of concern. "Let us take him back to the palace to rest."

Numa was only peripherally aware of other figures surrounding them. The familiar stature of an old friend appeared. The fact that Nereus was back at Nyx's side went barely noticed, but lent her comfort nonetheless. Her siblings were alive and whole, their own mates surrounding them. Her sister's long-lost children had survived as well.

Love and hope pervaded the air, but she couldn't shake her own worry, not as long as Dionysus lay unconscious. She held tight to his hand when Nyx and Nereus pulled their group into the drift. Her other mates were near, none of them willing to part with her or Dionysus any more than she was willing to part with them.

They landed in a tower room with a big bed. Cade held

Dionysus in his arms, the god's body as beautiful as ever. Smaller now, he was dwarfed in the ursa's hold. When Cade lay Dion down and covered him, Numa immediately returned to his side.

She stared down at him, troubled by the steady, yet faint aura surrounding him. She knew what it looked like, but was loath to admit what she saw—that he had become mortal.

"Will my breath heal him? Can we bring back his power?" she asked, casting a desperate glance at Nyx.

"I don't know," she replied. "No god in memory has ever made such a sacrifice. Stay with him. Let us know when he wakes."

Numa nodded distractedly, lying down to cradle Dion's head against her chest. When Nyx and Nereus left, her other mates gathered, pulling up chairs or settling on the bed as well.

Zephyrus slipped onto the mattress behind her and wrapped his arms around her middle. "We are alive and whole, and all of us willing to do whatever we must to help him."

"I know," she said, allowing the West Wind's comforting song to lull her to sleep.

CHAPTER 30

*N*othing but a blackened sheet of glass remained on the beach, the only evidence of the fire that had rendered Meri's body to ash. The immense heat of the dragon fire that made it penetrated far into the earth, and the glass extended down for several feet. It possessed a subtle inner glow, retaining some of the magic the dragons had flooded it with to destroy Meri's corpse.

Aodh, Gavra, and Ked worked together in their dragon forms to excavate what remained of their enemy, which was no more than the faint shadow of her ashes suspended in that dense block of glass. While they were certain she was dead, her spirit overtaken by the god's power and cremated with the blood that had bound her, they didn't want to take chances that any remnant of her remained. The glass would be shattered, each shard kept under guard by trusted members of the higher races.

Other piles of ashes littered the beach, the destroyed remains of the other soldiers who had not been freed from Meri's influence. Once they had retrieved the bodies of their fallen, all that remained were the remnants of dried blood scattered across the beach and throughout the Haven. Even those signs faded to nothing with one good rain.

Yet a shadow of the final confrontation still remained, and Nikhil stared at the black patch of sand beneath his feet, wondering if it was merely his own vision playing tricks on him—some remnant of Meri's control lingering like a bruise upon his psyche. The once shining white sand remained darker in this spot, though there had been several rainy days since the battle had ended.

"There is no sign of her," Belah said. "Even my brother who was the first to fall under her spell reports a profound sense of ease, and once we cleared the rubble blocking the Diviner's cave, she confirmed as much. Meri's taint has been burned away from this world. She can no longer haunt us."

"I know. I expect this feeling will fade in time. It's as though a splinter has been removed from my flesh after ages of enduring it. I'd grown used to its constant pressure, and the wound is still so tender I can't help but prod it to remind myself that it's gone."

"We have everything to look forward to now, my love," Belah said, pulling him around to look at her. "Our family is whole again, or will be when your daughter returns."

Nikhil pulled her into his arms, closing his eyes and savoring her warmth and the slight pressure of her round, pregnant stomach against his abdomen. Another child was coming —a son or daughter he ached to meet. Nieces and nephews abounded, more dragon pregnancies being reported each day.

He was not used to such abundant joy, but it was still tempered by worry. The things Meri had said of his and Neela's daughter troubled him. Despite all Meri's lies, he believed those words to be true—that the child would be cursed due to her origins. Her lack of a soul would be a burden no child should have to bear.

He was consoled by Belah's eagerness to be a mother again. Deva would not want for loving parents—not with seven fathers who would claim her as their daughter, and three mothers eager to nurture her. He almost felt sorry for the girl and worried for her independence with such a doting family and collection of overprotective males prepared to watch over her. But the one parent she would *not* lack for was thankfully gone and would never return.

"What of the other ... pregnancy?" he said, hesitating to call the last creature Meri had attempted to create a child.

Belah's expression darkened with pain. "Nyx couldn't counteract the curse Meri put on it, and she refused to let it grow inside her. She destroyed it."

Nikhil's throat constricted. "That means she can't…"

Belah responded with a grim look and a brief shake of her head. "She says she is happy enough to have Nereus back. Assana and Calder are well and happy too. Nyx is more than happy to be a grandmother and leave the honor of having babies to the younger generations."

But he didn't miss the sheen in her eyes when she pressed her hands over her own pregnant belly.

"She's right, I think," Nikhil said. "The one thing I wanted most was to have a child with you. I know this baby you carry is not my blood, but Iszak and Lukas deserve the chance to know that love as well. I have Asha, who is more than I could have hoped for in a daughter. If we could never have another, I would not regret it."

"You have Deva too. She'll come back to us as soon as Dion's able to retrieve her."

There was more to be done, but the rest could wait. As he gazed down into Belah's eyes, that empty ache left behind by the absence of his quest for vengeance slowly eased and filled with his love for her. With it, his old desire surged again and his body heated, his skin tingling beneath the lazy scrape of her nails along the base of his skull.

Her lips spread into a smile and he knew she'd seen inside his mind, felt the need return strong enough to obliterate all his other worries. As though responding to her unspoken desire, Lukas and Iszak appeared, crossing the sand with easy, yet purposeful strides.

The two Princes of the North Wind glanced between Nikhil and Belah. Lukas smirked, and Iszak's eyes sparked with desire, but they both sobered by the time they reached the couple.

"I wish like hell I could tell you two we have time to ourselves for once, but that is sadly not the case," Iszak said. "Dion is awake. We need you to come back to the palace."

*N*uma woke to the warm brush of lips across her own and the familiar scent of ambrosia filling the air. Her eyes flew open with a surge of adrenaline, and she stared up at the god she loved.

"Dion, you're awake!"

"Yes, little one," he said, then frowned. "I imagine I can't call you that anymore, can I?" He gripped her hand in his and twined their fingers, lifting them before his eyes. Holding them up, he spread his fingers again so their hands were pressed flat, fingers tip-to-tip. His hand was still larger than hers, but not by as much as it had once been.

Around her, the other four men roused, Cade and Zephyrus slipping up behind her while Bekim and Theron took up their spots on Dion's side of the bed.

"How do you feel?" Zephyrus asked.

"Alive," Dion said, pushing up to a seated position and pulling Numa back in for a kiss. His lips lingered on hers, savoring and teasing until she was breathless. He pulled back with a soft hum and a lazy smile. "Definitely still alive," he added, tilting his hips up until the sheet slid off his erection.

"I see some parts of you maintained their godly stature," Cade commented. "But do you have the stamina to take on a dragon?"

"I am willing to try," he said, fixing his gaze on Numa and slipping a hand into the bodice of her dress. His palm grazed over her nipple as cupped her breast, heating her core, but she grabbed his wrist and forced him to still. Reluctantly, she tugged the covers back up over his arousal despite her urge to straddle him and ride him to completion.

"Not yet," she said. "I need to make sure you're all right first. This change you've gone through is not insignificant. Will you regain your powers? Your … horns?"

He frowned and raked his fingers through his hair, then grimaced as he discovered what was lacking. "Ah, that's not good. The odd thing is that I still *feel* power, but it's coming from another source. If it isn't a divine link …" He closed his eyes and seemed to concentrate. After a moment, he shook his head and let out a soft chuckle. "This will be interesting."

"What is it?" Numa asked.

"It seems I'm still linked to Meri's bloodline. Which is no longer hers, of course. Not since I took over. But there are several million humans who were linked to her, and it now appears they are linked to me, the poor fools."

"That's a bad thing?" Bekim asked. "Seems like having a divine link would be a blessing."

"At the moment, the link means nothing to them. I can take advantage of the power of the bloodline if I wish, but have no real need to use it as long as I'm satisfied living the life of a mortal. I will eventually regain my divine power— that will happen whether I like it or not."

Numa relaxed and rested her cheek against his chest. "That's a relief."

Dion toyed with her hair and pressed a kiss to the top of her head. "Aye, but I'm in no hurry to reclaim that burden, as much fun as it was to see the five of you drunk on my seed. As the power returns to me, it'll infect those bound by blood to me as well. And while those poor humans might have gone unnoticed by Fate before, with a divine link, that is no longer going to be the case."

Numa bristled at the mention of her father. Though she knew Fate had many aspects that affected the world in different ways, she still viewed the whole eternal entity with little love.

"Why in the world would Fate care about a bunch of humans?"

Dionysus snorted ruefully. "Because they are linked to me now. And because *we* defied the bastard by sharing you instead of making you choose between us."

Numa pushed up off his chest and glared at him. "You would not dare make me choose…"

Dion shook his head and smiled, holding up his hands. "Trust me, this is by far a more ideal arrangement than I could have hoped for." His gaze swept lazily around at Numa's other mates. "And I admit it satisfies me to have defied Fate so well. But there is always a price. It means Fate will have the power to manipulate the lives of those humans that might have otherwise remained at peace. Not to mention the humans themselves won't have a clue what hit them. They will be affected in ways we can't predict, not the least of which will be an ability to recognize others with divine power in their blood."

Numa's skin chilled. "How many humans are affected by your blood?"

Dion shook his head. "Millions. Enough that it will be impossible for the higher races to hide from." He let out a sigh and shrugged. "But perhaps the bigger blessing is that it will distract Fate from meddling in the lives of the higher races for a while."

"Small blessings," Numa agreed. "But this is not good. We'll need to do damage control if we intend to remain integrated with humanity, especially if a large part of the population will recognize what we are. These humans aren't in danger, are they?"

"Only of being the pawns in Fate's little games. Depending on Fate's mood, that usually just means meddling in their love lives. But until I have regained my power there is nothing to worry about. We have plenty of time to enjoy each other, and I get to play the weakling for a bit longer and let the rest of you cater to my needs. But I might need you to go easy on me…"

She gave him a slow smile and pushed the sleeves of her gown up. "Perhaps these will help you last while I make love to you?" She bared her forearms and the pair of matching golden rings that adorned them. Slipping them off, she tugged the covers off his cock again and slipped the rings down his now-flaccid length. By the time she had both rings secured around him, he was fully hard again.

He reached for her, hauling her onto his lap while he pushed her gown off her shoulders, baring her breasts to his hungry gaze. Numa surrendered, arching into his mouth as he descended, capturing one nipple between his lips. She shuddered in pleasure when Bekim's lips found her other nipple and sucked, and then Zephyrus hooked his hand at the back of her head, urging her mouth to his. Theron and Cade slipped in behind her, their hands roaming her bare skin, ridding her of the rest of her clothes and helping Dion's cock gain access to her already soaked channel.

She sank down his thick shaft with a sigh, awash in their desire, the steadily growing power of their auras merging around her like a protective bubble. And even though no crisis depended on the full build of energy and its eventual release, they worked her up to the very limits of her endurance.

"Beg," Dion said, slowing his relentless pace as he fucked her.

"Beg," Cade said, grazing his mouth along her neck and across her ear as she arched back, supported from behind by the big man whose sole purpose seemed to be to drive her mad with the need to come.

"Beg," the West Wind whispered with every light caress of a breeze across her skin and around her nipples.

"Beg," Bekim and Theron rumbled in tandem as their fingers spread her wider, teased her clit, and invaded her slick and tender backside.

"Please!" Numa yelled, finally relenting to her own well of power that had filled with enough energy to create ten portals.

They answered her plea, pushing her to the edge and beyond, and this time all the power and all the love she had to give flooded from her in a joyful cry.

Another portal opened in that moment, but this one was in her heart, a doorway big enough for five men to slip inside and give her all they had in return.

Thank you for reading "Dragon Equinox"! If you loved it, please visit the retailer and leave a review!

This isn't the end...
The Immortal Dragons' quests for mates is complete, but the story is far from over. Read the Epilogue, and revisit all the dragons as they celebrate their victory, and a new member of the family embarks on her own adventure. Pick up "Dragon Avenged" today, or keep reading for a preview.

And don't forget, subscribing to the Dragon Beasties mailing list gets you **two free sexy dragon shifter stories** not available for sale anywhere.

DRAGON AVENGED

A YEAR HAS PASSED since the explosive conclusion of the Dragon Council's quest to find their mates and destroy their mortal enemy. The world of the higher races is on the verge of a dangerous shift. The dragons have one more ritual to undertake to ensure their secrets are kept and the human world remains oblivious to their presence. One woman is the key to their safety.

With powers and a bloodline no other creature in existence possesses, Deva Rainsong is finally on the verge of understanding her purpose. She must cast the spell required to reach all the humans tainted by the enemy, even if it comes at the expense of her innocence. But Deva's nature craves a true awakening, and her rapture might just be the thing that saves them all.

Read on for an excerpt, or buy now.

~

Chapter One

A WARM SPRING breeze roused Numa from an afternoon post-coital doze. She hummed softly under Zephyrus's caress and shifted positions only to realize that the West Wind was no longer lying beside her in bed. The breeze tugged at her tangled hair, flowed down her shoulders, and lifted the silken sheet, tossing it off before nudging her into full alertness.

"Zeph?" She frowned, darting a look around the lush quarters in the Haven's palace that she and her mates had called their own for the past year. She'd made love to Zephyrus and Dionysus earlier that afternoon, opting for a recharge and a nap while her other three mates joined the crew of nymphs preparing for the Equinox festivities just two days away.

The wind swirled around her and she puffed out an irritated cloud of green smoke. Zeph's magic caught it and shaped the cloud into an arrow aimed at the doorway to the room.

"Fine, I'm coming," she muttered, slipping out of the bed and summoning a gown to drape over her as she headed into the corridor. She followed the little ball of green smoke as the breeze toyed with it, pushing it in a haphazard spiral ahead of her.

The palace was a maze of crystalline corridors that gave the illusion of being underwater, with blue light filtering through in eerie ripples. She missed her home in the Glade with its wide open skies, multitudes of high clifftops, and plenty of room to stretch her wings, but the Haven was the better place for Dion to rest while they waited for his powers to regenerate.

Her body still hummed with the remnants of their last coupling, a sure sign that he was nearly at full divine power again. She followed the breeze through a pair of double doors out onto a palatial covered porch where she paused and took him in, the extent of his recovery hitting her for the first time since he'd lost his powers.

He was leaning against a column, gazing down onto the activities below. His huge, muscular body was relaxed and languid, the same light breeze toying with his silken black curls. Zephyrus leaned on the balustrade across from him, lean and silver-haired, the worry lines beside his mouth completely gone as he regarded the god with affection. Laughter drifted up from the courtyard, along with her other mates' voices raised in amused banter. Zephyrus saw her first, his eyes lighting up before darting a meaningful glance at Dionysus.

Her beautiful god practically glowed with health and vigor, and the marked difference in his size was even more apparent now that he was standing next to Zephyrus, rather than lying on his back while she rode his cock to oblivion. He was healed.

Dion said something she couldn't hear over the noises from the courtyard. He glanced at Zeph, then followed the West Wind's gaze to Numa. His lips tilted in a cocky smile and he turned around to face her fully, leaning back against a column.

"You're awake," he said. "I worried I gave you too much at the end. Did I finally find your limit, little one?"

"Impossible. You know better." Her chest warmed and she couldn't resist smiling at his taunt.

"Indeed," he rumbled, his burgundy gaze sliding down her body like a caress, promising that he lived for nothing more than to keep testing her limits.

Numa sauntered toward him, returning the look with a brazen one of her own, but taking the time to thoroughly inspect his aura while she closed the distance. The magic surrounded him in a brilliant golden glow, stronger than she'd seen it in ages, but that wasn't the only signal of his returning strength. He was a full head taller than Zeph, not counting the pair of thick horns that protruded from his head high enough to graze the ceiling. A year earlier he'd barely been taller than Numa, after his power had been sapped in his effort to control their enemy long enough for them to vanquish the evil bitch. Six months ago he'd finally surpassed Cade's size again and was gradually growing, though his horns were only nubs. She'd been aware of the changes, subtle though they were, but until now it hadn't really registered how close he was to his true divine self again.

"Welcome back," she said. "Just in time for the celebration."

She slipped up to the balustrade between Dion and Zeph, her entire being warming at their proximity. Below them, the main courtyard of the palace was alive with activity. Nymphs darted around, draping flowered garlands over everything. Theron and Bekim were at one end with Cade, adding the final pieces to the roof of a pavilion that the nymphs were already swarming over to decorate.

Her three ursa mates hopped down a few moments later and stood back to admire their handiwork. Numa could barely see the artistry due to the throng of nymphs adding the finishing touches. Finally the activity slowed, and they all paused and oohed and ahhed over the finished spectacle.

"What is it for?" she asked.

"Spring fertility rites," Dion said, then bent close and rumbled, "and none too soon." He dropped one big hand to her ass and squeezed. "Now that I'm at full strength, we can put that baby into you that you wished for."

As if attuned to Dion's voice, the three ursa turned and looked up at them. Numa's breath quickened at the expectant looks in their eyes. The baby she wished for had been just a dream for the past year. With five mates, it had been impossible for her to choose which should have the honor of impregnating her, and so she'd resisted allowing it to happen accidentally. Dion had finally urged her to confess her true wish—and so she'd admitted her desire to somehow have a child made from all of them, which she knew was a ridiculous thing to hope for, if not impossible.

"Oh . . . can we really?" she asked, darting a hopeful look up at Dion, then to Zephyrus, and finally down to Cade, Bekim, and Theron below, who looked like they were ready to leap the two-story distance to reach her and take care of business on the spot.

Zephyrus lightly stroked her cheek. "With Dion's power, we can."

"But not today," Dion said.

"Oh," Numa said, deflating.

Dion's laughter boomed through the courtyard, infecting everyone below with mirth. Nymphs dove into the fountain and splashed each other playfully, their games swiftly turning to carnal fun.

"Soon, little one," he said, sliding his hand up her back. "My power has returned, it's true, but there is far more to be had in two days on the Equinox." He turned and tucked a fingertip under her chin, urging her to look up at him. "There is a more dire concern to address first."

The one worry they had all been acutely aware of, yet avoided discussing most days would finally need to be addressed. "The bloodline," Numa said.

Dion nodded down toward the orgy of nymphs that were now tangled half in and half out of the fountain. A pair of the recently returned Thiasoi satyrs dove into the fray to the delighted squeals of the females. "They are already feeling my return to power, but my link to the nymphaea is nothing new. Meri's bloodline is mine now too, and the humans who are part of it may be a danger to the higher races once it fully affects them."

Zephyrus twisted his mouth in amusement at the scene unfolding below. Cade had a pair of nymphs clinging to him, very patiently attempting to peel the two females off on his way into the palace. "No doubt it won't be nearly as fun for the humans as it is for them. My brothers have been monitoring things in the human world. They have begun to see signs of awareness in the humans with the bloodline, but since we warned all the higher races to go to ground before the Equinox, these humans are only noticing each other. They don't understand what it means yet."

Apprehension twisted in Numa's gut and she clenched her teeth. She forced herself to relax when her three ursa mates entered and joined the conversation. "We can't expect all our kind to hide for fear of discovery. The dragons have done enough hiding."

"We're all tired of pretending," Cade said, crossing his arms. "The Ultiori have been dismantled. How much danger are we really in if the humans of the bloodline discover the truth?"

"There are millions scattered around the globe with the

potential to recognize any of the higher races for who we are," Dion said. "How they react remains to be seen, but the larger concern is allowing that knowledge to become widespread. If modern human communication is as powerful as I understand it is, without intervention of some sort, all of humanity might know of our existence within a matter of days. It would be dangerous for it to happen that quickly. We need to control the flow of information, and that begins with the bloodline."

Numa gazed up at Dion, curious. "You already have a plan, don't you? Do you have enough power to control the entire bloodline?"

Dion smiled bitterly. "Potentially, but that would be the wrong approach. Meri's methods of mind control are not what I wish to employ to handle this challenge. There is the added complication of the mutations many of the humans possess. The bloodline is as varied as Deva's, though none of the humans with it possess more than a few drops of divine power, thanks to their link to me. And they all have souls. Attempting to meddle with them unwillingly could corrupt them."

Numa pursed her lips, following the thread of Dion's thoughts. Meri's creation of the Ultiori had involved infusing humans with the blood of the higher races, her own in particular. Once her puppets interbred, that blood, along with Meri's nymphaea blood, was passed down the generations for thousands of years, their numbers increasing to the millions. It had allowed Meri access to immense power at the end, a power that had nearly cost them control of the Source. If Dionysus hadn't intervened, Meri could have beaten them. Now their biggest worry was being discovered by all of humanity, which had its own set of complicated drawbacks. They couldn't treat this issue lightly.

"But you have the power to reach them, right?" she asked.

"Yes. I can sense all the souls attached to the bloodline,

but I can't affect them on my own. I would need power from all five races to do that, and a conduit through which to channel the power—someone with a link to all the races too."

"Not a fucking chance."

Numa's gaze shot to Cade, who had spoken. The big blond ursa shook his head and scowled.

"Cade, you don't even know who would possess that kind of link."

"The hell I don't. You know as well as I do it's Deva he's talking about. The poor girl's been through enough the past year, being shuttled around like precious cargo between all the higher realms, never once allowed to get her feet under her. Now you want her to be the apex of some sex ritual. She isn't ready."

"He never said . . ." Numa objected, but Cade interrupted her with a laugh.

"Sweet pea, you think I don't know how this works? Anything that involves our magic—especially dragon or nymphaea magic—requires someone getting fucked. If it were any one of us, I'd be all over it. The five of us together brought enough power to win a fucking war. But we've got experience under our belts. Eons of it between us. Deva may look old enough—she may be wise beyond her years after living with the gods while we won that war—but she's still a baby, and I guarantee none of her parents are going to sign on, either. Find someone else."

She turned a worried gaze to Dion. "He's right. There has to be someone else who can do it. Meri experimented on thousands. We should at least talk to Neph and Nyx about it, don't you think?"

"You forget I am linked to all the potential options, little one. If they were tainted by Meri's blood, they are now part of *my* bloodline. That includes your brother, who was Meri's first. Yes, I can sense him with Neph and Vrishti and their new daughter in the Sanctuary, though his blood meld to my son is a stronger link. I agree we should open up the conversation to the others when they arrive, but if there was any other option, I would know."

Not prepared to give up the argument, Numa racked her brain for other options. Deva's parents—at least her biological parents, Neela and Nikhil—were the only options that made sense, but Dion would have the final say whether either of them possessed the needed combination of blood.

She accompanied Dion and her other four mates down to the grand hall where Nyx and Nereus were preparing to greet the first wave of guests arriving for the celebration, yet could come up with no other ideas.

The saving grace was that Deva was in the Dragon Glade spending time with her mother, so they would have time yet to discuss the options before she arrived. Neela and her mates had chosen the Glade as their permanent residence owing to Neela's phoenix nature, and Deva spent a few weeks at a time there, learning to harness her own dragon powers under the instruction of her half-sister, Asha. She was a quick study, though the power she exhibited was weak compared to other members of each race.

Numa had received regular messages from Deva over the past year, including the occasional visit, and had never sensed any dissatisfaction in the girl's situation or a struggle to adapt. On the contrary, despite having no soul, Deva's aura carried a patina of hard-earned wisdom belying her true age and she took to her lessons easily. If Numa hadn't been there the day she was born, she'd have believed Deva was as ancient as any of the dragons.

They arrived at the entrance to the grand hall in time to see three figures appear just outside in a cloud of dense fog. When the mist cleared, Numa rushed forward with an exclamation of delight. "Aodh! Brother, you're here!" She embraced him, then Vrishti and Neph in turn, and stood back beaming at them. "Where is the little one? Is she as much of a joy as she was when I last saw her?"

Vrishti's face split into a glowing smile. "She is the loveliest baby, but the kinds of celebrations going on here during the Equinox aren't exactly appropriate for little ones." She shot a coy look at her mates.

Neph chuckled. "As much as we adore her, we are more than ready for a vacation. Sathmika and the other ursa elders have opened up the Rainsong Lodge for anyone who is in similar straits and wants a respite from their offspring. I've lost count of how many babies have been born over the past year. If we aren't careful, they'll have the run of the Sanctuary by the time we return."

"With hope, we will be adding our own soon," Dion said, resting a big hand on Numa's shoulder and squeezing. Her body warmed under his touch and she suppressed a shudder of need. There would be ample time for them to work on that task soon enough.

Neph's broad smile turned serious as he regarded Dionysus. "You're looking well, Father. I assume it's time to have a more serious conversation about the steps we need to take to do damage control with the humans of Meri's bloodline."

"We will," Dion said. "But not until we've gathered all the immortals here to discuss it, and that includes Deva."

Neph tensed and narrowed his eyes. Cade snorted from behind Numa, and she silently willed him to hold his tongue.

After regarding Dionysus for a moment, Neph finally nodded. "We will wait, but I admit I don't like the implications one bit. Deva's too young and inexperienced to be involved in the sort of thing I believe is required. I'd just as soon avoid involving her at all."

Beside him, Vrishti frowned. "She's a grown woman, and perfectly capable of making her own decisions. She's had so little control over her life so far. We owe her the respect due a fellow immortal. She is one of us, regardless of how new she is to the world."

"Agreed," Aodh said, causing the other men to look at him in surprise. "I may consider her a daughter, and have all the protective instincts that go along with that, but Deva is nothing if not strong-willed. It would be more dangerous to force a choice on her. She is in command of her own fate—we should allow her the chance to decide herself. I will support her no matter what."

"Then we shall wait," Neph said, giving his mates a grudging glance. "But I intend to remain cautious. I've assigned one of the Thiasoi to guard her while she's here. And whatever she decides to do, he will accompany her to ensure her safety."

"As long as you're not trying to control her life, I'm okay with that," Vrishti said. "She needs her freedom if she's going to be able to grow." She slipped beneath his arm and embraced him and they headed into the grand hall to greet Nyx and Nereus.

WANT TO READ THE REST? Buy now.

ABOUT OPHELIA BELL

Ophelia Bell loves a good bad-boy and especially strong women in her stories. Women who aren't apologetic about enjoying sex and bad boys who don't mind being with a woman who's in charge, at least on the surface, because pretty much anything goes in the bedroom.

Ophelia grew up on a rural farm in North Carolina and now lives in Los Angeles with her own tattooed bad-boy husband and six attention-whoring cats.

Subscribe to Ophelia's newsletter to get updates directly in your inbox. If newsletters aren't your thing, you can find her on social media.

http://opheliabell.com/subscribe

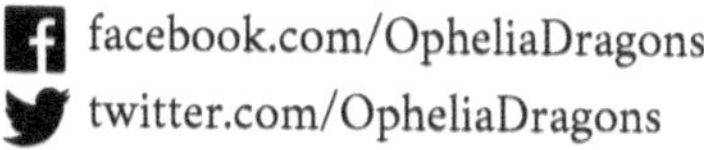

facebook.com/OpheliaDragons
twitter.com/OpheliaDragons

Sleeping Dragons Series

Animus

Tabula Rasa

Gemini

Shadows

Nexus

Ascend

Sleeping Dragons Omnibus

Rising Dragons Series

Night Fire

Breath of Destiny

Breath of Memory

Breath of Innocence

Breath of Desire

Breath of Love

Breath of Flame and Shadow

Breath of Fate

Sisters of Flame

Rising Dragons Omnibus

Dragon's Melody (a standalone dragon novel)

Immortal Dragons Series

Dragon Betrayed

Dragon Blues

Dragon Void

Dragon Splendor

Dragon Rebel

Dragon Guardian

Dragon Blessed

Dragon Equinox

Dragon Avenged

Immortal Dragons Box Sets:

Immortal Dragons: Books 1, 2, & 3 + Prequel

Immortal Dragons: Books 4-6 + Epilogue

Black Mountain Bears

Clawed

Bitten

Nailed

Stonetree Trilogy

Fate's Fools Series

Fate's Fools

Fool's Folly

Fool's Paradise

Fool's Errand

Nobody's Fool

Eye of the Hurricane

Fool's Bargain

April's Fools

Thieves of Fate

Aurora Champions Series

(Set in Milly Taiden's "Paranormal Dating Agency" world)

The Way to a Bear's Heart

Hot Wings

Triple Talons

Midnight Star

Once in a Dragon Moon

Second Skin Series (Romantic Suspense)

Mad Dog

Mile High

Valentine's Day

The Devil's Daughter

Marked Man

Rebel Lust Taboo

Casey's Secrets

Blackmailing Benjamin

Burying His Desires

Doubling Down

Standalone Erotic Tales

After You

Out of the Cold

www.ingramcontent.com/pod-product-compliance
Lightning Source LLC
Chambersburg PA
CBHW030359200726
48286CB00015B/1737